nancy moser
& vonette bright

an
undivided heart

the Sister Circle series book 3

TYNDALE HOUSE PUBLISHERS, INC.
Carol Stream, Illinois

Visit Tyndale's exciting Web site at www.tyndale.com

TYNDALE and Tyndale's quill logo are registered trademarks of Tyndale House Publishers, Inc.

Sister Circle is a registered trademark of Tyndale House Publishers, Inc.

An Undivided Heart

Designed by Jennifer Ghionzoli

Edited by Kathryn S. Olson

Scripture quotations are taken from the *Holy Bible*, New Living Translation, copyright © 1996. Used by permission of Tyndale House Publishers, Inc., Carol Stream, Illinois 60188. All rights reserved.

This novel is a work of fiction. Names, characters, places, and incidents either are the product of the authors' imaginations or are used fictitiously. Any resemblance to actual events, locales, organizations, or persons living or dead is entirely coincidental and beyond the intent of either the authors or the publisher.

The Library of Congress has cataloged the original edition as follows:

Bright, Vonette Z.
    An undivided heart / Vonette Bright & Nancy Moser.
        p. cm. — (The sister circle ; [3])
    ISBN 0-8423-7191-5
    1. Female friendship—Fiction.   2. Boardinghouses—Fiction.   3. Widows—Fiction.   4. Women—Fiction.
I. Moser, Nancy.   II. Title.
PS3602.R5317U53 2004
813'.6—dc22   2004001060

ISBN-13: 978-1-4143-1675-8
ISBN-10: 1-4143-1675-5

Printed in the United States of America

14   13   12   11   10   09   08
 7   6   5   4   3   2   1

Nancy Moser dedicates this book to
Carson, our only son,
who lives life with an undivided heart,
a loyal spirit, and unswerving compassion.

*For the Lord sees every heart and understands
and knows every plan and thought.
If you seek Him, you will find Him.*
1 CHRONICLES 28:9

• • •

Vonette dedicates this book to
my beloved sons, Zac and Brad,
who each desires to serve God faithfully
with an undivided heart.

Why am I discouraged?
Why so sad?
I will put my hope in God!
I will praise Him again—my Savior and my God!

PSALM 43:5

$\mathcal{S}$omething was up.

Evelyn knew it from the moment Herb Evans knocked on the door to pick her up for their date. He usually rang the doorbell, but this time, he announced his presence with a snappy rhythm.

Herb was nice . . . but snappy?

She opened the door and found him grinning at her, holding a bouquet of yellow mums. "Hi-ya, Evelyn."

She drew in a breath. "Hi, Herb."

He shoved the flowers toward her. "These are for you."

"What's the occasion?"

"Oh, nothing."

Just the way he said it told her it was something. And her first inclination was to push the mums back into his arms, keep pushing *him* out the door, shut it, and flip the lock.

How odd.

Herb bounced twice on his toes. "Ready to go?"

I have a headache, a backache. I have to clean the oven. . . .

For the first time, Herb's face clouded. "Evelyn? Is something wrong?"

1

Evelyn was saved from having to answer by the sound of footsteps coming down the stairs. "Hi, Herb. Where you two heading?"

"Hi, Piper." He put a hand on Evelyn's shoulder. "It's a surprise."

She was doomed.

Piper gave her a questioning look, letting Evelyn know she wasn't hiding a thing. If only she didn't have such a transparent face.

"Can I steal her away from you a moment, Herb?" Piper slipped a hand through Evelyn's arm.

"Sure . . . I guess."

"Have a seat in the parlor. I'll get her back to you in just a minute." Piper led her away. Evelyn had rarely felt such relief and would have been content if the minute would be extended tenfold. Or a hundred.

They entered the kitchen. Piper made sure the door was shut before she spoke. "Okay. Spill it. Why the look of total panic?"

It would sound dumb because it was. It didn't make any sense at all.

"Evelyn . . . you're acting like you don't want to go out with him. You've been dating Herb for nearly eight months."

"Has it been that long?"

Piper let out a sigh. "Evelyn . . . what's happening?"

She moved to a chair and sat. Piper joined her. "He brought me flowers."

"How dare he."

"He's smiling."

"A sure sign of a scheming man."

Evelyn's left hand found her right. "He's not a scheming man. He's a nice man."

"I figured as much, or else you wouldn't have dated him so long."

"He's . . . he's serious about me."

"Of course he is. You're both in your late fifties, Evelyn. People your age generally don't date around. They're done playing the games of youth."

Evelyn felt herself being studied. She didn't like it.

"Have you been toying with his affection?"

"No!"

Piper's right eyebrow raised.

"I didn't mean to."

Piper sat back, looking at the kitchen door. "Do you think he's going to propose? Is that what you're afraid of?"

That was it. "I don't know, but when he showed up today, my entire body started vibrating—and it wasn't from anticipation." She leaned toward Piper, whispering. "I wanted to run."

Piper shook her head. "Oh, Evelyn . . ."

"I know. What should I do? I don't want to hurt him."

"I'm afraid there's no way not to."

"Oh dear."

"Surely this isn't a total surprise. Surely the idea of marriage crossed your mind at some point these last eight months."

Evelyn rubbed the space between her eyes, wishing all her thoughts and feelings would become clear. "I suppose it did. But I never let it get past the idea stage."

"Do you love him?"

She opened her mouth to speak, then closed it. "I like him a lot. I like being with him. I like . . . I like having a man tell me I'm pretty. Aaron never did that."

"Herb fills a need."

It sounded so callous. "Well, sure. I guess. But I think I fill a need in him too."

"Obviously. But now he wants more."

So simply said. "He wants more."

They shared a moment of silence. "He's waiting."

"I know."

"What are you going to do?"

Evelyn sat up straight. "Maybe he won't ask. Maybe I've read the situation wrong."

"But maybe you haven't."

She had a thought that contradicted the rest, and yet was very strong. "Maybe I shouldn't fight it."

"What are you saying?"

What was she saying? "What would be wrong with me marrying Herb?"

Piper's hands filled the space between them, fending off the idea. "What just happened here? One minute you're scared he will propose and now you're thinking about saying yes?"

"It might be nice to be married again."

Piper sprang from her chair and began to pace. "If you love someone, Evelyn. *If* you love him."

Love. What was love? "But like you said, Herb and I are in our late fifties. Maybe the type of love we're supposed to experience in order to be married has changed. Maybe there isn't supposed to be . . . passion."

Piper stopped pacing and gawked at her. "Don't you dare say that."

"Companionship is good. It's nice."

"Enough with the 'nice.' If you want nice, be his friend. You're thinking of this all wrong, Evelyn. You don't marry someone as an antidote to eating alone."

"But maybe you do."

Piper shoved her hands on her hips. "Fine. Go marry him. Go settle."

Settle. It was an awful word.

The kitchen door swung open a few inches. It was Herb. "Evelyn? Is everything all right?"

Piper also waited for her answer. Two against one.

Evelyn stood. "Everything's fine, Herb. Let's go."

"Good," he said. "'Cause I have a real nice evening planned."

Evelyn felt Piper's eyes on her back even after the kitchen door swung shut.

●　　●　　●

Piper poured herself a glass of milk, cut herself a brownie—a monster brownie—and sat at the kitchen table. Comfort food was essential to a good pity party.

It's not that she begrudged Evelyn her dates with Herb. She was sincerely thrilled for them.

But what about me?

Ah. That was the bottom line. Herb and Evelyn had been dating eight months, the same amount of time that had elapsed since she'd broken off with Dr. Gregory Baladino. Piper lost a man and Evelyn gained one. Not fair. Not fair at all.

Especially since she'd given up Gregory for God. Not that she'd given up all men for the Almighty, but she'd broken off with Gregory because God was very specific in His instruction not to be "unequally yoked." It was like connecting two different animals to a common yoke. They wouldn't pull the same, or with the same strength and purpose.

So it was with people. A believer in Jesus like herself was not to become romantically involved with someone who didn't believe, because without that common bond, they wouldn't pull the same, with the same strength and purpose. Marriage was about complementing each other, sharing everything. But it wasn't enough to like the same movies and food, want the same number of children, or want to be with each other every moment of the day. It was important to share the spiritual side too, because in the end, in the dark times and the bright, faith would be needed to see them through.

Breaking up with Gregory had been the hardest decision Piper had ever made. And Gregory, who'd grown up not believing much of anything in a house divided between Catholic and Jewish, had actually praised her for standing up for her beliefs, for obeying her God's instructions.

Then why did she feel so empty?

Piper took a bite of brownie and heard the front door open.

"Yoo-hoo? It's me."

Me was Mae. Mae Ames from across the street.

"Back here," Piper said.

Mae appeared holding the handle of a measuring cup with both hands. "I've been sent for macaroni."

"By whom?"

Mae swept one hand through the air, rolled her eyes, and took a seat, seemingly in a single motion. "My dear Collie has decided he wants homemade mac 'n cheese. Can you imagine?"

"What's wrong with the boxed kind?"

"Exactly. And since my kids and I OD'd on the cheapy food after Danny left us, I vowed I'd never eat the stuff again." She placed both hands flat on the table as if bracing herself. "Get this: he even has a recipe for it."

Piper gasped in mock horror.

"I know, I know. He's over the edge."

Piper laughed. "You're getting quite domestic."

"Shh! Don't tell anyone. It will blow my image." She noticed Piper's brownie. "Ooh. Point me to one of those."

Piper pointed to the pan on the counter.

Mae got one the size of a piece of bread and helped herself to a glass of milk. She took a bite as she returned to her seat. "I saw Evelyn leave with Herb. They're a cute couple."

Piper answered with a sigh.

"Uh-oh. What's wrong?"

"Nothing. They are a cute couple."

"Mixed vibes! Mixed vibes. Fess up."

"I'm not sure if I'm distressed or relieved that you can read so much into my sigh."

"Hey, it's a sister's job to read another sister. Sister sighs are almost as telling as sister moans."

Piper suddenly felt tears threaten.

Mae's hand was on hers in a second. "You thinking about your mom?"

Piper was appalled to realize she wasn't. And her mother's death was certainly something to cry about.

"It's only been three months, Pipe. It takes a long time to deal with the death of a parent. How's your dad doing?"

She was glad to talk about someone else. "He's doing okay. He's getting involved in church again. That helps. I'm having dinner with him Thursday."

"Collie wondered if your dad plays golf."

"Not well."

"Perfect. I'll have Collie give him a call."

"That would be nice."

They ate another bite in silence. Piper felt Mae's eyes on her and wished she could deflect some of the sister radar.

It didn't work.

"Have you seen your handsome doctor lately?"

Bingo. "He's not my handsome doctor."

"Which is the real problem before us this evening, isn't it?"

Piper downed her milk so she'd have a reason to get up from the table, pretending to want more. "The book's closed on Gregory and me. You know that, Mae."

"Zounds, sister. I see pages turning, practically flapping in the wind, trying to get to the next chapter."

Piper leaned against the refrigerator. "You're reading way ahead."

"But if he does get with the program . . ."

Piper had to laugh. "I've never heard that phrase used in conjunction with becoming a Christian."

"An oversight, I'm sure." Mae patted Piper's place at the table. "Sit down and tell Auntie Mae all about it."

Piper returned to her seat. "There's nothing to tell."

"Gracious Gobstoppers, Pipe, you still love him. That's plenty to tell."

"I keep praying God will take the feeling away."

"Why? Love's a good thing."

"Not when it can never be fulfilled."

"Never tell God never. Maybe He's working on Gregory's heart this very minute."

Piper shrugged.

"Arghh! I swear I'm going to the legislature to get shrugs banned." Mae grabbed the measuring cup and headed to the pantry. "You are a most frustrating woman."

"Frustrated."

The phone rang. Mae was closest so she picked it up. It must have been Collier because she said, "My, my, you are hungry, aren't you? Hold your tootsies, Mr. Husband; I'm on my way." She hung up, found the macaroni and poured the cup full. "Don't give up on love, sister. Look at me. It was nearly thirty years between Danny and Collie."

"If you think that's encouraging . . ."

"Ah, but it should be. If God can find a strange bird like me a good man, He most certainly can do the same for a nice girl like you."

"I'm not a girl anymore, Mae. I'm thirty-five."

Mae paused at the door. "Yeah, well . . ."

Exactly. What could she say?

Mae backtracked for her brownie, balancing it on top of the cup of macaroni. "If you feel like some company later on, come on over. Collie's starting a new puzzle." She made a finger circle by her ear. "It will be another rip-roaring evening at the Ames residence."

When Mae left, as the silence of Peerbaugh Place tucked around her, Piper cut herself another dose of chocolate.

•   •   •

Evelyn was running out of conversation. Keeping a stream of banter going throughout dinner was exhausting, and yet it was the only way she could think of to prevent Herb from popping the question.

She could tell it was getting to him. His brows were in a holding position, nearly touching. Could she blame him? She was annoying even herself. But what choice did she have?

"Heddy is moving out this weekend because she needs a larger place for her sewing. Catherine's Wedding Creations is a huge success, and she and Audra have weddings booked way into July."

"Speaking of weddings . . ."

She sped ahead. "So you see I'm in the looking-for-tenants mode again. Already have one empty as Gail moved out a couple weeks ago, all nicely reconciled with Terry and little Jacob. Sure, we're sorry to see her go, but we're happy for her too. It's always nice to witness happy endings."

"Or live one."

Evelyn felt herself redden. She dabbed her mouth with her napkin even though it had been ages since she'd eaten a bite. Her mind was suddenly blank.

"Well—" Herb put his fork down—"I finally said something that shut you up."

"Herb!"

"I'm sorry, Evelyn. But you've been going on and on all evening making it impos—"

"I was only sharing my day with you, Herb."

"Your day, Piper's day, Audra's day. . . I didn't take you out to dinner to get an update on the world."

She knew an apology would be appropriate. "Not the world. My world. Peerbaugh Place. If you don't like—"

"If I don't like it, what?"

Did she just pick a fight? "Forget it. Let's move on."

"How nice of you to finally give me a turn."

"I was just trying to make conversation."

"Conversation is two people talking, not one person giving a . . . a . . ." His forehead contorted as he searched for the word. She wasn't about to help him. "A monologue. That's it. Monologue."

It was better than *diatribe*.

"I thought you were interested in my life."

"I am. But I'm more interested in our lives. Us. Together. Plural."

Was this how it was going to play out? A proposal in the middle of an argument? This isn't how she wanted it to happen. Yet she didn't want it to happen at all. So maybe the argument was a way out. Maybe it was a blessing in disguise. Maybe it—

Herb was studying her. Did he see her inner battle? Obviously yes, for he suddenly turned around, looking for the waiter. "Check, please!" He turned back, pointing at her leftover pasta. "You want a doggie bag for that?"

"No thanks."

Oh dear. She doubted she'd ever eat again.

●　　●　　●

A peck on the cheek and away he went. Evelyn stood on the front porch and looked after him until his truck turned the corner. She had the awful feeling her one chance at happiness had just driven away.

She hadn't let him see her in, much less join her for a cup of decaf as was their habit. When she'd seen the light on in Heddy's room, she'd set her feet on the porch, not wanting to venture farther. She didn't want to face her friends. Face Piper. She didn't want to explain her evening—not that it was easily explained even to herself. Exactly what had happened?

She detoured to the porch swing. A few golden mum heads poked their way from the front border through the railing as if peeking at her. The swing's chain was cold in her hand, but she held on anyway. Any feeling was welcome to break through her numbness, to draw her into reality and away from the nightmare she'd just experienced.

The front door opened. Heddy stuck her head out. "I thought I saw Herb's truck, but then you never came in."

"I wanted to sit awhile."

"Uh-oh." She closed the door and took a seat in the wicker rocker. "Piper told me about Herb's intentions. What happened?"

"I think the question is what didn't happen."

"He didn't propose?"

"I didn't let him."

"Why ever not?"

"Because I'm not sure I want to marry him. So I stopped the question before it had a chance to come out."

"How did you do that?"

"I kept talking, not letting him get a word in. Then I made him angry." Her laugh was bitter. "Yes, indeedy, not only did I succeed in boring the poor man, I picked a fight with him."

Heddy wrapped her sweater tight around her torso. "I thought you liked Herb."

"I do. That's the point. I like him but I'm not sure I love him."

"Oh." She sat back. "Love is important . . ."

Evelyn was relieved to hear it—especially from Heddy, whose

main goal in life was to have a husband and children. "I always thought so."

"But is it always possible?"

Heddy had lost her. "You're saying it's okay to marry without love?"

"Maybe . . . maybe . . . sometimes a person doesn't have a choice."

"Then maybe that person shouldn't be married at all."

Heddy's eyes flashed with panic. "But I want to be married! Is that such a bad thing?"

It was an old discussion that had occupied many a summer evening among Evelyn, Heddy, and Piper. Though Evelyn's thirty-one-year marriage to Aaron had been far from perfect, at least she'd had a husband and a son and a home. Piper and Heddy—both in their midthirties—had experienced none of these things.

There was no make-it-all-better answer. God's ways were often unfathomable, yet in hindsight, perfect. For instance, though Aaron's death in a car crash was tragic, it had led to a new, stronger Evelyn opening her home to boarders. Through Peerbaugh Place she had met many wonderful, lifelong sisters she would not have met any other way. But hindsight was the key. Now, coming up on two years after the fact, Evelyn could see the good out of the bad. But that was hard to explain to Heddy or Piper who were planted in the midst of the struggle, their minds ripe with questions.

Heddy stood and moved to the railing, looked out into the yard, and asked the question she'd asked before. "Why does God give marriage to some people who could care less, and withhold it from people like me and Piper who are aching for it?"

"I don't know."

Heddy sighed deeply and turned around to face her. "I'm sorry. I'm a broken record. And this isn't about me; it's about you. Do you think Herb is very hurt?"

"Wouldn't you be? I ruined the evening."

"Do you think he'll ask you out again?"

Evelyn stopped the swing. "I don't know."

"Do you want him to?"

"I don't know that either."

"So what are you going to do?"

She looked out at the black night. Across the street the light in Mae and Collier's bedroom went to black. Mae had found true love in her fifties. Maybe Evelyn . . .

She stood. "I'm going to bed."

"You're avoiding the question."

"As long as possible."

I will turn their mourning into joy.
I will comfort them
and exchange their sorrow for rejoicing.

JEREMIAH 31:13

$\mathscr{T}$he doorbell rang. It was an odd occurrence. So many people felt at home at Peerbaugh Place, so many people did a quick knock then came right in, that to have the doorbell ring . . .

"Coming!" Evelyn wiped her hands on a towel. She was making a dinner for her family. Today her daughter-in-law (and dear friend) Audra turned twenty-five. Evelyn's son, Russell, and their six-year-old daughter, Summer, were coming over. Evelyn was glad she hadn't started making the seven-minute frosting for the cake or she never would have heard the doorbell over the mixer.

The woman at the door was . . . striking. But it took Evelyn a moment to understand if it was a good thing. Or not.

Not won out. The woman's features were pulled too tight, like invisible hands were holding her skin taut from the hairline. From a distance she looked forty, but up close, due to the slightly exaggerated tautness of her skin, she looked to be in her fifties. The entire image reminded Evelyn of what happens when you have a blemish and try desperately to cover it up, often bringing more attention to the problem than if you'd let it be.

"Hello," Evelyn said. "May I help you?"

"Absolutely. I would like to rent a room here."

Evelyn had to smile at the woman's manner. Although her voice had a slight demanding tone, it was also oddly charming, like when a child pretends to be a grown-up. "Come in." As soon as she closed the door she extended a hand. "I'm Evelyn Peerbaugh, the proprietress." Russell had told her that title sounded much better than landlady.

"I'm Lucinda Van Horn, of the Boston Van Horns."

Evelyn felt her left eyebrow raise. She'd never heard of any Van Horns, but assumed she was supposed to be impressed. Actually, Lucinda did have an air of aristocracy about her. Old money?

Then why did she want a room in a boardinghouse?

Evelyn began her tour, moving into the parlor. "This is the main room. All tenants have complete use of the house."

Lucinda picked up a sepia-toned photo from the mantel.

"Those are my late husband's grandparents," Evelyn said. "The Peerbaughs have lived in this home since 1900. I guess we're the Carson Creek Peerbaughs."

Lucinda nodded and set the picture down, making Evelyn regret her words. "I didn't mean for it to sound as if I was making fun."

"Oh, you didn't, Mrs. Peerbaugh. It is the right of every family to be proud of their roots." She gestured to the dining room across the entry. "How lovely. Do we eat in there?"

They moved into the room. "On special occasions. Mostly we eat in the kitchen, which is in . . . here." Evelyn held the swinging door open. "We eat together as often as we can, but the dynamics of how often change with the needs of new boarders."

Lucinda fingered the yellow curtains above the sink. "How many people live here?"

"There are four bedrooms upstairs, including mine. A bathroom is shared between each two. Piper Wellington, a counselor at the high school, is in one and—"

"Didn't her mother die recently?"

"Yes. How did you—?"

"I met her at a flower show this summer, then saw in the paper . . . I'd just started my job at Flora and Funna." Lucinda put a hand to her chest. "It *is* quite a ridiculous name for a shop, but I do like the arrangements they put out. It was her heart, wasn't it?"

It took Evelyn a moment to shift gears from Flora and Funna to Wanda Wellington's death. "A heart attack with some complications. She'd had heart trouble, but they thought they had it under control. It was a horrible shock."

"Yes. Indeed. My condolences. So the daughter lives here?"

"Yes." Evelyn wanted to get back on track. "But there are two other rooms open for rent. One at the—"

"Is the widower still in town?"

It seemed an odd question. "Yes. Wayne's still here."

"I'm sure he's devastated."

"Of course. But he's doing all right."

Lucinda poked her head in the sunroom, then back again. "Can I see the sleeping rooms?"

"Certainly. Right this way."

Goodness.

•   •   •

Evelyn sat on the couch and accepted Lucinda's application. It was neatly filled out, complete with references. "You last lived in Florida. I guess I expected Boston, since you'd mentioned your family there."

"My roots are there, but I lived in the most lovely condo in Cocoa Beach for years. Ocean view. Sixth floor."

"That sounds wonderful. Why did you leave?"

Lucinda shrugged. "My life has drawn me elsewhere—as life often does."

Not so often. Evelyn had lived in Carson Creek her entire life, as had many of her friends. "I don't mean to pry, but were you married?"

"I'm divorced. No children."

"I'm so sorry."

"No need. And to answer your next question, I've come to Carson Creek on the behest of my friend Gwen James—the owner of Flora and Funna. We were roommates in college and have kept in touch all these years. I've been staying with her."

That had been Evelyn's next question. "How nice for you."

"Indeed." She put her pen away. "So. The room. As I said, I'd prefer the front one. I find the balcony quite charming. It will be empty this weekend, correct?"

"I should have it ready Sunday at the earliest. And as soon as I contact your ref—"

Lucinda stood. "Good. I'll be back Sunday. Nice to meet you, Mrs. Peerbaugh." She was out the door.

Evelyn banged a fist against it. "References! As soon as I check your references *I'll* tell you whether you can move in here. Why do people do that to me? I'm the one in charge!"

Kinda. Sorta.

Peppers the cat rubbed against her legs, showing support.

•   •   •

Lucinda Van Horn walked into Flora and Funna. Gwen looked up from an arrangement of carnations she was putting together. She didn't say anything but her face asked, *So?*

Lucinda set her purse behind the counter, checked her reflection in a decorative mirror boasting a price tag that said Sale! $35.99!, then twirled a pink carnation between her fingers. "You will be happy to know I am now a tenant at Peerbaugh Place.

As of Sunday you will no longer have to tolerate my presence in your home."

"Don't be petulant, Lucinda. I've been happy to have you. All I said was that it had been three months and wouldn't you be happier in a place of your own."

"Randy doesn't like me."

"Randy likes you fine." Gwen stuck some baby's breath in the vase. "What surprises me is that you wanted to go to Evelyn's. I'd have thought you'd prefer a nice-size apartment. Peerbaugh Place is a boardinghouse. Those are tiny rooms." She looked up. "Aren't they?"

"They are lovely rooms. Quite adequate. And most importantly, affordable for my situation."

Gwen pointed a flower at her. "You stick to your promise. No more plastic surgery. It's ridiculous to spend tens of thousands of dollars, to get in debt, to—"

"To maintain my beauty?" Lucinda expected the next line to be *But you're beautiful enough already.*

Instead Gwen said, "There are more important things to focus on than looks. Family, friends, career."

"I have no family, my friends are busy with their own lives, and my career is my looks."

"Your career *was* your looks. There is life after modeling, you know. And how long has it been since your last photo shoot anyway? Let it go, Lucy."

The truth was, it had been twelve years since she'd done any modeling. She felt a pout coming on and knew she could do little to stop it. "You know I hate Lucy. It's Lucinda. Lucinda Van Horn, the Silken Tresses girl."

"They don't even make that brand anymore."

"My face was on the back cover of *McCall's.*"

"When LBJ was president."

Lucinda couldn't argue the point; in fact, she didn't want to talk about it at all. "I'll go unload that shipment of candles—unless you have something more important for me to do."

"No. That's about as important as it gets around here. Have at it."

Pitiful. Her life was pitiful.

•　　•　　•

They pulled in front of Peerbaugh Place, and Summer scrambled out of the car to run up to Grandma's. Audra was less enthusiastic. Birthday or no birthday, she didn't have time for this. Heddy was expecting her to cut out three bridesmaids' dresses by tomorrow and the fabric had been delayed and she'd only been able to pick it up this afternoon.

Russell opened her car door. She hadn't meant to make him do that. "Everybody out. And that includes you, birthday girl."

"Sorry. I was thinking."

"About work."

She nodded. "I really shouldn't be taking time out to have dinner with your mom."

"You really should. It's your birthday, hon. You have to eat." He held out his hand, helping her out, then pulled her close. "I'm glad you're a success, but you can't let it take over your life. Our lives."

She knew he was right but that didn't make it easy. To build a business involved hard work. Neither she nor Heddy had expected it to take off so quickly. But brides went gaga over Heddy's unique bridesmaid's-dress designs, and they'd run out of catalogs in two weeks. And their new Web site had even brought in a wedding from Kansas City. Audra's plan to work from home so she could be there for Summer was a mixed bag. Yes, she was there for Summer, but being so busy, was she really there for Summer?

Evelyn appeared on the front porch with her granddaughter. "Happy birthday, Audra!"

"Mommy, come see the cake. It's beautiful."

Audra took Russell's arm. "Coming."

•   •   •

"We have another reason to celebrate," Russell said. He nudged Summer, who sat beside him. "Do you want to tell Grandma the news?"

"Oh! Yeah!" She set her fork down and sat up straight. "I'm 'dopted now. All the way. We got the papers to prove it. I'm . . . he's . . ." She pointed at Russell, obviously not sure how to word it.

Russell leaned over and pulled her toward him. "Summer is officially my daughter."

Evelyn clapped. "Yay! You are now officially a Peerbaugh."

"I'm going to get to move away from the *T*s to the third row of first grade, right between Kevin Pearson and Lindsay Peterson."

Evelyn clapped again. "You can alphabetize? You are such a smart girl."

Summer shrugged. "I know."

Audra laughed. "Summer!"

Summer reddened. "Oops. Sorry. I know I shouldn't say that, but since it's Grandma . . ."

Evelyn just had to hug her and got up to do so. "You bet it's Grandma, and you are a smart girl. And I love you bunches."

"Me too, Grandma."

Evelyn let go, once again amazed that God had brought unwed mother Audra and her little daughter Summer into Peerbaugh Place. What had started as friendship soon evolved into sisterhood, and now into family love. Amazing. God was good.

"Can I get anyone more cake?"

Russell leaned back, patting his stomach. "I better not eat for a week."

"That can be arranged," Audra said. "It would sure make my life easier not to have to worry about dinner."

Evelyn returned to her seat. "I could make a casserole and bring it over if that would help."

"No, no," Audra said. "I can handle it. I don't need—"

"Mom was only trying to help," Russell said.

"I know and I appreciate—"

"Hey, no problem," Evelyn said, backing off. She knew about mother-in-law pressure. Aaron's mother had always pushed too hard to help. She'd vowed not to be that way. "Just let me know if you need me."

They shared a moment of awkward silence. Then Audra said, "How's Herb?"

Oh dear. "He's fine." *I think.*

"Have you heard from him since you didn't let him propose?"

Evelyn was taken aback. "How did you—?"

"Heddy told me." She shoved her plate away. "Have you two broken up?"

"I don't think so. But I don't actually know. He hasn't called."

"Then call him."

Evelyn shook her head. She was from the old school where the men did the calling. Women might have done their share of the pursuing, but there was a certain etiquette to be followed.

"It is allowed now, Evelyn. You can call him. You don't have to wait."

There was more to it than etiquette. "I'm not sure I want to."

"You want to break it off?"

"No. I mean . . . not really." She stood to clear the dishes.

Summer popped up. "I'll do it, Grandma."

"Thank you, sweetie. That's nice." Evelyn sat back down. "I do like spending time with him."

"But if you're on different wavelengths as to where it will lead . . . ?" Audra shook her head. "I'm not sure that's fair."

Exactly. Evelyn decided to get a man's opinion. "What do you think, Russell?"

He squished a cake crumb with a finger and licked it off. "If he wants to get married and you don't, then I'm not sure you should keep going out. You're leading him on."

"But maybe he'll be able to convince me," Evelyn said.

Audra shook her head. "It's not like he's merely convincing you to buy blue paint instead of green. This is the rest of your life you're talking about."

"I know."

"Do you want to be with Herb the rest of your life?"

"He's a nice man." Oops. There was that *nice* word again.

"But do you love him?"

Evelyn fingered the stem of her water goblet. "I think there are different levels of love—levels I've not had to deal with. I've only loved two men in my life. One I would have married if he hadn't died in the war, and the second I did marry. Love made me feel different then than it does now. But I'm older. Maybe it's supposed to be different."

Russell raised a hand. "We can't help you there, Mom. But in a way it makes sense. Love at fifty-eight has got to be different than love at twenty-eight."

Audra shook her head adamantly. "Why? Why does it have to be different?"

"Because it is," Russell said. Evelyn was surprised to see him blush. "It just is. We're talking about my mother here."

His comment bothered her. "I may be your mother, but I'm also a woman, Russell."

He stood, helping Summer clear.

Whatever. She supposed it was hard for a child to think of his parent as a sexual being. Actually, at age fifty-eight she wasn't having that easy a time with the thought herself. But shouldn't she? She wasn't over the hill yet. She still had twenty to thirty good years ahead of her. Why, she could be married to Herb for thirty-one years just like she'd been married to Aaron for that length of time.

Audra looked at her watch. "I'm sorry, but we really do need to go."

Just as well. There was no way Evelyn's love life could be figured out in an evening.

•   •   •

Piper was surprised her father had opted to stay in for dinner. At his place. With him doing the cooking. It's not that Wayne Wellington couldn't cook—he, Piper's mom, and Evelyn had first met at cooking classes—but since her mother's death, he'd lost twenty pounds and getting him to eat anything at all had been an issue. Piper or one of his friends made it a point to bring over casseroles. Last time she'd looked, his freezer was stuffed full. So for him to offer to cook . . .

As soon as he let her in Piper smelled chicken . . . chicken mixed with an unusual aroma. "That smells wonderful, Dad. What's cooking?"

He took her coat. "Cranberry chicken and rice. It's a new recipe." He headed to the kitchen. "Actually, your mother left it for me." He motioned toward a stool. "Have a seat. I have corn to stir."

"Mom left you a recipe?"

He opened a cupboard door and pulled out a blue recipe box that had *Wayne's Recipes* written on the side. "She left this for me. She made sure all our favorites were inside, as well as a bunch of new recipes she'd been wanting to try. This was one of those."

Piper ran her hand over the box as if it were her mother's hand. "She thought of everything, didn't she?"

"Yes she did. I'm still finding notes in odd places. Some are just little love notes and others are instructions."

Piper shivered. "I know she sensed she was going to die—no matter what the doctors told her—but I've never heard of anyone being so organized about it, so practical."

Her father smiled as he stirred. "That's your mother. Always taking care of others. Always thinking ahead, making sure every-thing's covered. Making sure I was covered." His forehead tight-ened and the stirring stopped. Piper was just about to go to him when he raised a hand. "I'm okay. I expect it's going to be a long time before we stop having these crumble moments when it hits us fresh, eh, Piper-girl?"

Her throat was so tight she could only nod.

He handed her a pan of sliced crusty bread, a knife, a tub of margarine, and a bottle of Lawry's garlic salt. "You ever see that movie *Shadowlands* about C. S. Lewis and the love of his life?"

She took up the knife and shook her head.

"He married late in life and soon after, his wife got cancer and died. But before she did they took a trip, and there's a scene where they've taken shelter from a rainstorm in the midst of a beautiful English meadow and he starts crying. She—mind you *she*—comforts *him* and says, 'The pain then is part of the happi-ness now. That's the deal.' I've actually taken great comfort in that line. Because that is the deal. You love knowing there will be pain—then. But you don't live in the then; you live in the now. To love is to care, and even to hurt. That's the deal."

"But is it worth it? To hurt so much . . ."

His smile would have made her mother proud. "It's worth every second. Love's a blessing. No matter how long you have it."

Piper hated herself for immediately thinking of herself again. Her short-lived time with Gregory . . . she needed to change the subject. "How's choir rehear—"

"I saw Gregory yesterday."

Her stomach flipped. "Oh?"

"At the grocery store. He was buying a carton of orange juice. Fresh squeezed."

"I'm happy for him."

"He asked about you."

Really? "That's nice."

"He said to greet you."

"Consider me greeted."

She received a father look. "You could be his friend, Piper."

Her head shook violently. "No! No I couldn't."

He turned off the burner and looked at her. "It's still that strong?"

Stupid throat, tightening again. She nodded and buttered the bread with a concentrated effort more appropriate to a diamond cutter or a brain surgeon.

"Your mother liked him. A lot."

Piper cleared her throat. "I know."

Her father nodded at the cupboards. "I learned to trust your mother's instincts. She was rarely wrong."

"I know."

He suddenly tapped the spoon on the edge of the pan, set it down, and looked at her. "God's got something up His sleeve here."

"He does?"

He spread a hand, ready for counting. "Number one: Your mother started doing her matchmaker thing from the first moment Gregory called you, right?"

"She was embarrassing."

"Merely part of her job description. Two: Your face glowed like a wad of Christmas lights after you were with him."

She had to smile. "A wad of Christmas lights?"

He gave her a level stare. "How soon they forget."

"Actually, Mom had a theory about that. She said you refused to wrap the lights nicely around a piece of cardboard because you'd rather untangle them than fluff the limbs on the tree."

"Yeah, well . . ."

"Ha. She *knew* you."

"You're off the subject." He went back to his fingers. "Three . . ."

She'd forgotten he was making a list. "Three?"

"Dr. Gregory Baladino is a good man, a nice man, who did his best to save your mother." He put a hand to his chest. "He has a good heart. 'A good person produces good deeds from a good heart.'"

"I know. But that wasn't enough. He didn't believe—"

"Hold on. I'm not finished yet. I still have two fingers left."

She waved a hand toward him. "Go for it."

He stood there a moment, his pinky ready to be tapped. "Now you made me lose my thought."

"Sorry."

"Give me that bread and let me get it under the broiler."

"Just a minute." She sprinkled the garlic salt over the top of the slices and handed him the pan.

After turning on the broiler he resumed the pinky-at-the-ready position. "Four . . . yes, four: Your mother thought that maybe you would be the one in Gregory's life to turn him toward Jesus."

"I know. And I wanted to be. But love got in the way. I was falling in love with him. I knew that if I stayed near him love would take over and I'd choose that over any instruction not to be unequally yoked. I would have compromised my faith by staying with him. And it would have put too much pressure on him to do what I wanted him to do, to believe what I wanted him to believe. I pray every day that Gregory will seek Jesus, choose Jesus, and come to know Him, but I can't be the one to get him there. I can't."

"But once he makes that choice you can certainly help him, yes?"

"I'd be there in half a heartbeat."

"Then maybe he's there. Maybe he's ready for you."

"Do you know something I don't?"

He paused, and the electricity in the room was dampened. "No. Unfortunately Jesus did not come into our conversation at the grocery store."

"Gregory hasn't called me," Piper said. "You'd think he'd call if something was happening with his faith."

"If you're expecting a hi-Piper-I-found-Jesus call, you may be waiting a long time."

This comment shocked her because that's exactly what she'd been waiting for. "Why can't it happen that way?"

Her father checked on the garlic bread. "I suppose it's possible. But to go from not talking at all for months to sharing this life-changing moment . . . that's a stretch."

"But I told you, I can't be around him without falling in love with him, and if I fall in love with him I may sacrifice the standard God has set and—"

"And if you don't ever see him, you may lose him and never know about or be a part of this momentous occasion in his life."

Her sigh started at her toes. "It's a catch-22."

He reached across the counter and put his hand on hers. "Pray about it, Piper-girl. Love is a risk. You may get hurt. You may have your heart broken. But that's the deal, right?"

She had a lot to think about.

●　　●　　●

Evelyn put on some socks and got into bed. When Aaron had been alive she'd never needed socks to keep her feet warm. One of the rarely discussed pitfalls of widowhood.

She reached over to turn off the bedside lamp and spotted two pictures there. One of Aaron, smiling from the porch swing, and another recent picture of Herb, eating a slice of baklava at the Heritage Festival in Jackson. The two men in her life. It was so odd to think they had known each other, talked to each other, never once guessing they would share the affection of the same woman. Of course, Herb had been married then too. Samantha had been gone for five years now. Maybe that's why they'd first connected, sharing widowhood.

But it had grown since then and they rarely spoke of their late spouses. They were creating a life in the here and now. And that was good. The present was good. It was fun.

But what about the future?

Evelyn had had a long day and couldn't deal with this now. She turned the pictures toward the wall so she didn't have to see their smiling faces. Then she turned off the light and went to sleep. Alone.

I myself have gained much joy and comfort
from your love, my [sister],
because your kindness
has so often refreshed the hearts of God's people.

PHILEMON 1:7

*E*velyn walked in the door after church to find Heddy coming
down the stairs carrying a box.

"The last one," Heddy said. She set it by the front door, took
a deep breath, and looked over the entry. "I'm going to miss this
place."

"You can come back anytime. Once a sister, always a
sister." But Evelyn knew it wouldn't be the same. Heddy had
moved into Peerbaugh Place as hard to pin down as a will-o'-
the-wisp, a woman whose greatest goal was to be married and
have a family, yet a woman with a secret past: Carlos. A young
man who had stomped on her heart and conned her out of her
savings. A delicate constitution like Heddy's did not recover
easily.

But she did recover. And now she had a new boyfriend—
Steve Mannersmith, an English teacher at the high school—and a
new career with Audra, making bridesmaids' dresses. And a new
home away from Peerbaugh Place.

"When's the new tenant moving in?" Heddy asked.

"Today. I think."

"You think?"

Evelyn didn't want to get into the fact that once again her tenants had taken control of the rental situation. "Today or tomorrow. And I have another possible tenant coming over any minute to see Gail's old room."

"My, my, the rooms don't stay open long, do they?"

Not this time. "That's the plan."

"Have you had many other applications?"

Evelyn thought of the college girl who might have fit in but had horrible references, and the two other lookers who'd thought the place too small, too quiet, or too something or other. "A few. But this next girl sounded really nice on the phone. She teaches second grade. Her name's Margaret."

"I haven't heard that name in a while. How old is she?"

"She sounded twentysomething." Evelyn heard a car drive up and looked out the window. A blue hatchback parked in front. "This may be her now."

"Want me to go?" Heddy asked.

"Of course not. I'd like you to meet her. You can give me a second opinion."

Heddy moved her box against the wall and fluffed her hair. They both waited for the bell to ring. Evelyn opened the door.

The girl was . . . lovely. Not beautiful, because *beautiful* implied being beyond the reach of most women. Not pretty, because *pretty* implied an appearance that stopped at the skin. But *lovely*, indicating a radiance that came from somewhere deep beneath the surface.

"Hello," the young woman said, extending a hand. "I'm Margaret Jensen. I've come to see the room."

Evelyn shook her hand and invited her in. "I'm Evelyn Peerbaugh and this is Heddy Wainsworth."

"Who's moving out today." Heddy shook her hand and let her arm continue in a sweep across the entryway. "I need to make it clear I'm not leaving because I dislike it here, but only because I've started a new business and need more space."

"What kind of business?" Margaret asked.

"Catherine's Wedding Creations. We make bridesmaids' dresses and—" she stopped talking and took hold of Margaret's arm—"are you okay?"

The girl looked decidedly pale. Evelyn took her other arm. "Would you like to sit down?"

Margaret ran a hand over her forehead, then held it up as a stop sign. "I'm fine. I'm so sorry. Please don't make a fuss."

They both let go but continued to study her condition. Momentarily her skin regained some of its original color. She managed a smile. "Silly me. The mention of weddings and I get all emotional. I'm not making a very good impression, am I?"

"You're fine. But what happened?—if you feel like sharing."

Margaret smiled. "I can tell right now this is a caring household. Without even seeing the room I know I'd like it here."

Evelyn felt the same. There was something genuine about this girl—sincere. And though Evelyn wanted to know more about what had made her falter at the mention of weddings, that could come later. She shared a look with Heddy, who gave her endorsement with a subtle nod. "Let me show you around our home, Margaret."

Odd how Evelyn felt the *our* already included Margaret Jensen.

•   •   •

Margaret had come home—at least that's what it felt like. From the first step onto the porch of Peerbaugh Place, from the first glimpse of the carved wood of the foyer, from the first touch of Heddy and Evelyn, Margaret felt she was among friends. Sisters. She knew it was strange and not something she could ever make her parents comprehend, but that didn't mean it wasn't real. Palpable.

After saying good-bye to Heddy and seeing the entire house— including the charming room that was for rent—they headed down the front stairway. Evelyn was telling her how meals were handled, but Margaret mentally excused herself from the conversation so she could engage in one even more important. *Lord, You are so good to me. Too good. I don't deserve this place, but I know it's You who brought me here. Thank You. Help me be a blessing to these women. Use me to accomplish Your purposes at Peerbaugh Place. I am Yours.*

She realized Evelyn had asked her a question. "I'm sorry," she said. "I was kind of overwhelmed with the moment. I know this sounds like a line, but I feel at home here, Mrs. Peerbaugh. I would be very honored if you'd allow me to be one of your tenants. I'll do my part. I'm very organized and I love to clean. I'll help all I can."

Evelyn stood at the bottom of the stairs and stared at her. "You're too good to be true, Margaret. And I'd be very honored . . ."

You're too good to be true. Margaret never, ever, *ever* wanted to hear those words again. For those were the words that had ruined everything and set her on a course away from her parents' house, away from her bright future, to here. With difficulty she kept her distress to herself. She'd already raised enough questions in her landlady's mind.

Evelyn led her into the kitchen. "How'd you like a cup of tea while we handle the paperwork?"

"That would be lovely."

Evelyn smiled as if Margaret had said some secret word.

• • •

Thank You, Jesus! Evelyn put the check from Margaret on the kitchen counter by the phone. Once again, God had provided.

Peerbaugh Place was full. Yes, it was true that once again the propriety of checking references and pondering applications had been set aside, but Evelyn was getting used to choosing her tenants based on instinct. She wasn't a facts kind of woman; she relied on feelings. It had worked so far. . . . She sidestepped to the hot water. "Would you like some more tea?"

Margaret put a hand over her cup. "No, thank you. I've really loved hearing about the past tenants of Peerbaugh Place. I'm looking forward to meeting all of them."

Evelyn laughed. "Oh, Mae will make herself known real soon, I'm sure. We haven't seen much of Gillie since she moved out of town, and Gail lives in Jackson. Tessa won a three-month world cruise and then moved into a garage apartment at her daughter's, so we haven't seen her near enough. Actually, she's off on another extended trip to Italy. Her son-in-law had some business there and took the whole family." She put a hand to her mouth. "Oh, my. I need to find out when she's coming home. We'll need to have a party."

"I make great cheese-wrapped olives."

"Yum. Consider yourself assigned."

Margaret pushed away from the table. "But now, I need to go."

The doorbell rang. Twice, in quick succession. Evelyn got up. She hoped it was Piper or Mae or Audra so she could share her good news, but then she realized they would never have rung the bell. Especially not three, then four times. *Who is so incredibly impatient?*

She opened the door. Lucinda Van Horn stood there with two suitcases. "Evening, Evelyn. I have arrived."

That, she had. Evelyn held the door open and peered into the cloudy late afternoon. She flipped on the porch light. "Can I help you with the rest of your things?"

"You most certainly can. I know the room is furnished, but I have a few accessories that will make the room mine."

Was there an extra emphasis on *mine*, or was Evelyn being overly sensitive?

Margaret came out of the kitchen nuzzling Peppers just as Lucinda came in with her suitcases. Evelyn made the introductions.

"Is that cat yours?" Lucinda asked. She did not look happy.

Evelyn took Peppers out of Margaret's arms. "This is our house cat—in every sense of the word. This is Peppers. She was here the other day when you looked at the house."

"Hmm. Really. I didn't see her."

"Don't you like cats?"

"I'm not a pet person."

Evelyn was not surprised.

"Can I help you with your things?" Margaret asked.

"Of course," Lucinda said.

Evelyn chastised herself for feeling that Lucinda's tone sounded decidedly like "Of course you *should*" rather than "Of course you *could*." Maybe it was because Lucinda had shunned Peppers. Who could *not* like Peppers?

The next fifteen minutes were spent carrying boxes—and boxes—of Lucinda's possessions into the front bedroom. Evelyn was extremely glad that Heddy had insisted on cleaning it herself just this afternoon. Lucinda wasn't giving Evelyn much time to recoup.

Hmm. How interesting that Evelyn felt a need to recoup in regard to Lucinda and a desire to bond with Margaret. Who said first impressions weren't important? or women's intuition valid? For in the short span of time she'd known each woman, Evelyn had already formed strong opinions about her tenants: Margaret was a joy and Lucinda a pain. God certainly liked to make things interesting.

When the last box was deposited in her room, Lucinda escorted the other ladies to the hall outside her door. "If you'll excuse me, I'd like to get settled."

Well. Okay then.

Once the door closed, Margaret and Evelyn stood in the hallway and looked at each other. Then they burst out laughing, covering their mouths so Lucinda wouldn't hear. It was a nice unscripted moment that only reinforced Evelyn's feelings toward the girl. She could hardly wait for her to meet Piper. The three of them would be fast friends.

Whether Lucinda would deem them worthy of her friendship was not known. Sisterhood often took work.

Evelyn moved toward the stairs. "I'll help you get your things now."

"I'm sorry," Margaret said. "I should have made it clear. My things aren't in my car. I didn't know if you'd let me move in. Like I told you earlier, I've been staying with my parents in Jackson. I'll move in tomorrow—if that's all right."

Evelyn found herself disappointed. She'd assumed Margaret's possessions were ready and waiting. They stood at the door. "I'll see you tomorrow then?"

"Absolutely. Right after school—work."

As Margaret drove away, Evelyn waved from the door. A stray leaf blew inside. She retrieved it but instead of tossing it out, she spun it in her fingers.

Dear brothers and sisters,
I love you and long to see you,
for you are my joy and the reward for my work.
So please stay true to the Lord, my dear friends.

PHILIPPIANS 4:1

*L*ucinda awoke to water running and realized it was coming from her—their—bathroom. Margaret Jensen had moved in yesterday, bringing practically nothing with her except a few clothes, a laptop, and some books. She'd said—loud enough for Evelyn to hear, or course—that she found the room perfect and couldn't imagine changing a thing.

Oh, please.

Lucinda switched on the bedside lamp, lay on her back, straightened the covers around her, and listened to the shower run. If Peerbaugh Place were a bed-and-breakfast, this early-Sears-catalog antique look would do, but at best the furniture needed refinishing, and at worst, the pieces could do with a good heave into the city dump. Lucinda had grown up with real antiques. Massive pieces from Europe and genuine Aubusson rugs, not rugs whose only distinction was being called "throw."

Lucinda had attempted to increase the class quotient of her living space by bringing in her beloved collections of Waterford and Lladro statues. She was glad there was a lock on the door.

She looked around her room. Her entire domain in the world. Who was she trying to fool? No matter how many expensive collectibles she owned, she was still staying in a cheap boardinghouse, thousands of miles in distance and prestige from how she grew up. From what she expected. From what she deserved.

The image of her ex, Wallace, invaded. She should have known he was a loser when he'd first told her he preferred to be called Wally. A Van Horn did not marry a Wally. She'd let the fact that he had money sway her when, in truth, his CEO status was nouveau riche, not the old money of her own deep roots. He was way too quick to flash a wad of cash at the golf club, buying a round of beers for his best buds (what a horrible term) then boring her with long renditions of eagles, bogeys, and bunkers. Yes, golf was a game of the wealthy, but they'd joined the club with different agendas. She'd wanted a membership for the lunches, the tennis, and the Tuesday morning massages. Not beer, bogeys, bunkers, and buddies.

Bottom line? Her marriage to Wally Larson was a mistake she walked away from after five years of trying to teach him the finer points of life. Now it had been fifteen years since Lucinda had endured the incredibly ordinary name Lucinda Larson, and she didn't miss him or their life together at all. Why should she? She'd gotten a reasonable settlement that had allowed her to live in an elegant condo at Cocoa Beach. And during that time . . . there had been some incredibly handsome men in Cocoa Beach. Rich men. She had no clue why none of them had proposed. It was a mystery that continued to dog her. Why could she attract the men but not latch on to the men? Maybe if she had collagen treatments in her lips, making them full and pouty again . . .

She crossed her arms in disgust. Unfortunately, it was out of the question. She was out of money. Yes, she should have paid more attention when her stockbroker told her to sell those loser stocks, and yes, she should have curbed her spending through the years. But to one day wake up and realize she had no money to pay the mortgage, much less any social memberships, designer clothes, or beauty treatments, was a disappointment far worse than her failed marriage.

She'd returned home for comfort (and hopefully a hefty check) only to discover that her late father had shared many of the same financial shortcomings as his daughter. The family fortune was gone. It had nearly killed her to sell the family home and all its beautiful furnishings. Plus, she was faced with the task of moving her widowed mother into an extended-care facility that would easily eat up the proceeds. It wasn't fair. The last six months had been a nightmare, forcing Lucinda to reassess everything that had been her life. And change it.

Though she hated to admit it, Gwen and the job she'd offered at Flora and Funna had saved her and given her a place to go. A purpose—such as it was. Actually, she was kind of looking forward to conquering Carson Creek. She was quite positive they had never experienced the likes of a Lucinda Van Horn and looked forward to wowing them out of their comfortable shoes and showing them what true class entailed.

The shower stopped. Lucinda looked at the clock. Eight minutes. Maybe Margaret hadn't been lying when she said she needed only fifteen minutes in the bathroom in the morning. Lucinda hadn't made an issue of it, but knowing she took at least forty-five, fifteen seemed absurd. Why, she couldn't prepare her skin for makeup in fifteen minutes.

Of course, from what Lucinda had seen, the girl didn't wear much makeup. And when you're twentysomething skin care could consist of soap and water. But just wait. Margaret's time would come. Someday she'd be old.

It was a curse.

• • •

"I smell something wonderful," Margaret said, coming into the kitchen.

Evelyn checked the oven and removed the pan. "It's a sausage and grits casserole. There's coffee ready. Or would you like tea?"

Margaret grabbed a mug. "Coffee's fine. You don't have to make a big breakfast, Evelyn. A bowl of cereal is fine."

"I—"

Piper came in the room, taking a big whiff. "I thought I smelled . . . a fancy breakfast? What happened to cereal?"

Evelyn felt herself redden and turned to their newest tenant. "As Piper has so aptly pointed out, cold cereal is the norm. I just thought I'd make something special for your first morning at Peerbaugh Place."

Margaret made herself useful and got out plates. "And I appreciate it. Do you want to serve from the oven?"

"Sure. Hold a plate over here."

Three plates were filled. Evelyn looked toward the front of the house. "I wonder if Lucinda is coming. I know she doesn't have to go to work as early as you two . . ."

"I heard her in the bathroom when I was getting dressed. Should we wait?" Margaret set down her fork.

"No, no," Evelyn said. "You two have to get to work. I'm sure she'll understand. I should have said something last night, told her that I was making a big breakfast. It's my fault."

The ladies began to eat. "No fault possible with this dish, Evelyn," Piper said. "It's delicious."

"Thank you." She heard the front door open.

"Yoo-hoo!" Mae appeared moments later.

"Good morning, birthday girl," Evelyn said.

Mae did a little curtsy. "Thank you very much."

"And how old are you today?" Piper asked.

"Younger than springtime, older than dirt." Mae pointed at their plates. "Yum. I want some of that." She helped herself and took a seat at the table. Only then did she seem to notice Margaret. "And who have we here?"

"Margaret Jensen. I like your necklace and earrings."

Mae flipped her dangly silver earrings as if the act helped her remember which ones she had on. "Oh, thank you muchly."

"Mae made those," Evelyn said. "She's a silversmith. She owns Silver-Wear."

Margaret's face lit up. "I know that place. I bought a bracelet for my mom there. She loved it."

Mae pointed a fork at her. "I thought I recognized you. You lived in Jackson, right?"

"Good memory."

"Yes siree, you'll find I'm good at everything."

"Except humility," Piper said.

"Hey, if you think you're humble you've proven you're not, so why bother?" She took another bite. "And what do you do, Maggie?"

"I teach second grade."

"Oooh, the patient, perky type, eh?"

"On command."

Mae laughed. "You'll have Summer next year."

Margaret turned to Evelyn. "That's your granddaughter, right?" As Evelyn nodded, Mae said, "Good memory."

They all shared a laugh.

•   •   •

Lucinda heard laughter below. She hated not being included. She decided to put on only two coats of mascara, quickly lined her lips, and colored them in with Sunset Orange. There. Done.

She grabbed her gold earrings from the dresser on her way

out, putting them on as she took the stairs. She paused a moment at the kitchen door and straightened her taupe Donna Karan sweater over her hips. Making an entrance was an art she'd mastered. She went in.

Four ladies turned around. Evelyn stood. "Good morning, Lucinda. I was hoping you'd be able to join us."

Then why didn't you wait for me?

A woman she didn't know stood, taking her plate with her. She had amazingly unruly hair and was wearing an awful jacket made of rags tied in knots. "Here, sit here. I can't stay long. Collie will wonder where I am."

"Is Collie your dog?"

The woman laughed. "Playful as a puppy but with a nose blessedly warm. He's my husband. I'm Mae Ames. I live across the street."

Charmed, I'm sure. "I'm Lucinda Van Horn."

"Of the Boston Van Horns," Evelyn said.

Lucinda turned toward Evelyn. *Is she making fun of me?*

Her landlady hurried to the stove. "I'll . . . I'll get you some breakfast."

Lucinda sat in Mae's chair and eyed the mess on everyone's plate. She would have preferred a poached egg or perhaps an egg-white omelet.

From her position near the counter Mae swiped a final bite across her plate before taking it to the sink and putting it in the dishwasher. "Believe it or not, I did not come over here to eat."

"Since when?" Evelyn asked.

"Can I help it if I have finely honed timing?"

"The honiest," Piper said.

"Anyway . . ." Mae's voice rose. "The real reason I came over was to invite you—invite all of you—to a little birthday celebration this evening. Collie's putting it on. I am merely the guest of honor. No gifts. Just gab and grub."

"Sounds wonderful," Margaret said.

"I'm in," Piper said.

"You know I'm there," Evelyn said.

They all looked to Lucinda. Being fairly new to Carson Creek she wasn't sure what she could use as an excuse, but the last place she wanted to be was at this eccentric woman's home. And she did not *gab* or *grub*. Ever.

Mae raised a finger. "Oh, and Piper . . . bring your dad. And Evelyn, you're welcome to ask Herb."

Lucinda perked up.

Mae looked right at her. "Seems the gang is coming. So how 'bout it, Cindy?"

Though she grated at the nickname, she nodded. "Yes, I'll be there."

Men. Single men. She'd be in her element.

•   •   •

Everyone was off to work. Evelyn took her time cleaning the kitchen. This aloneness used to bother her, but she was getting used to it. Funny how it had taken widowhood to get her comfortable with herself. Turned out she wasn't bad company.

As she wiped the counters she found herself repeatedly glancing at the phone, and it took her a few times to realize why. Mae had told her to invite Herb to the birthday party. She should call him.

Yet he hadn't called *her* since the dinner fiasco. Not once. And it had been a week. Sure, she'd been painfully plain regarding the limits of her interest . . . "But I miss him." She hadn't meant to speak aloud. But often truth did that, forced itself out, unannounced.

She put vanilla-scented lotion on her hands and moved to the phone. She dialed the hardware store, her stomach as nervous as a teenager's. What would she say?

He answered, "Handy Hardware, this is Herb speaking."

"Morning, Herb. It's Evelyn."

"Oh. Hi."

"I haven't heard from you."

"I thought you'd be busy."

"Herb . . ."

"Evelyn . . ."

Oh dear. Maybe the best thing to do was come clean. "I'm sorry if I disappointed you the other night. I'm sorry if I talked too much and . . ." she sighed. "Don't be mad at me, Herb."

Silence.

"Herb?"

"Yeah, yeah. I gave it a good shot, didn't I? You don't understand how hard it was not to call you. You obviously know how much I care for you, though the other night you did a good job of deflecting my every chance to tell you."

Her stomach tightened. "I know."

"But don't worry; I got your message."

"You did?"

"I'm not dumb, Evelyn. Rarely have I witnessed such a skilled side step. You should give dance lessons."

"I . . . I didn't want to have to say no."

"I don't want you to say no."

"Then don't ask—" Oh dear. She hadn't meant to be so blunt.

"Don't worry; I won't. Not for a while anyway. Is that all right?"

She tried to curb her relief. "That's great . . . I mean . . . I think that would be best. I don't want to hurt you, Herb. And I don't want to lose you as a friend."

"What we have is more than that."

Maybe . . . we'll see. She couldn't answer aloud.

"I'm at work, Evelyn. Is there a reason you called?"

The party. "No. No reason other than to talk with you again."

"Okay. Glad you did. Gotta go."

Evelyn held the receiver against her chest a few moments after she heard him hang up. She was glad they'd cleared the air, but . . .

Why hadn't she asked him to Mae's party?

It was hard being a complicated woman.

* * *

When the man came in the door of Flora and Funna, Lucinda put on her best smile. He was quite handsome and wore his clothes with an air of dignity. Early sixties, combed back gray hair. Distinguished yet approachable. Most importantly, he returned her smile.

"How may I help you this fine day?" she asked, lifting her chin to show off her best side.

"I need the most colorful flowers you can arrange." He pointed at the cooler of blooms. "Reds, yellows, oranges. Even some purple if you can manage."

It sounded awful. "We'll certainly see what we can do. What's the occasion?"

"My wife's birthday."

Oh. "How nice."

"I'm giving her a party."

The clues connected. "Is your wife Mame?"

He laughed. "Her name's Mae, though she often reminds me of that Mame character. Yes, I'm delighted to say Mae's mine, all mine." He extended a hand. "I'm Collier Ames. And you are?"

"Lucinda Van Horn. I'm—"

He pointed a finger at her. "Our new neighbor. Mae said she'd met you this morning. Welcome to the neighborhood."

"Thank you."

"You'll love it at Peerbaugh Place. Evelyn's a gem."

If not unpolished. "She seems to be a very nice woman."

"You betcha."

You betcha? Lucinda was instantly disappointed. Collier had looked to be a more sophisticated sort. Of course, if he was married to the likes of Mae . . .

Yet it was too soon to rule him out and unwise to *ever* rule out the charms of Lucinda Van Horn.

She grabbed an order pad and leaned on the counter, smiling again. "Now let's see what we can do to give you everything you need."

Double entendre intended.

•   •   •

Mae poked her husband in the ribs. "Tell me!"

He sidled away. "No, ma'am. It's a surprise and will remain a surprise."

She crossed her arms. "You're no fun."

"*Au contraire*, my lovely wifey. Now if you'll put the ice ring in the punch bowl, I'd appreciate it."

She let her jaw drop. "You made an ice ring?"

"Of course."

He continued to amaze her. "How did you learn to do that?"

"I saw it on the Food Channel."

"Since when do you watch—?"

"Wayne told me about it. He and Wanda took cooking lessons, you know."

"With Evelyn." She started for the kitchen. "What else you got going in there? Brochettes, croquettes—?"

He blocked her way. "Come on, Mae. Since you wouldn't let me give you a surprise birthday party, let me at least—"

She flicked the tip of his nose. "You do realize that by asking me if I'd like a surprise party you ruined the surprise?"

His shoulders dropped. "I realized that. Too late."

She adjusted the collar of his plaid shirt. "Which brings me back to this: Since the party isn't a surprise, you might as well let me in on this *big* surprise you mentioned."

He took her busy hands in his and grinned. "No way." He escaped into the kitchen.

"Mr. Husband!"

She heard him laugh. He was the most exasperating, annoying . . .

Wonderful husband there was.

●   ●   ●

The Ames residence was full, and Evelyn had to admit Collier knew how to do things up right. A punch bowl and flowers? The dining room looked gorgeous and the smells coming from the kitchen revealed a menu beyond chips and dip.

Summer ran to her side. "There's an ice circle floating in the punch, Grandma. Come see."

My, my. Collier was going all out. And it had to be Collier. Mae Fitzpatrick Ames was more of a bucket-of-ice-and-Dixie-cup kind of person. An ice ring? And for that matter a punch bowl? He was quite a catch. Evelyn helped Summer ladle some punch into a glass.

"Where's Herb?"

Evelyn turned around to find Wayne Wellington. *He's working; he's out of town; he's . . .* instead of lying, Evelyn tried to sidestep the question. "Hi, Wayne. I hear this ice ring is due to your influence. The Food Channel?"

"A man's got to eat. Wanda and I were really getting into cooking together before . . ."

She didn't need the blank filled in. "I sure enjoyed the classes the three of us took together."

Wayne accepted a glass of punch from Summer. "Why, thank you, sweetie." He turned back to Evelyn. "I did too. In fact, I was thinking of taking some more." His eyes lit up. "You interested?"

"Definitely!" Her enthusiasm came out of nowhere and felt a bit foreign. Yet it could be her good deed to help the poor widower . . .

Lucinda approached and Evelyn stepped away from Wayne, making room for her in their circle. "You'll have to introduce me, Evelyn."

Evelyn did her duty.

"I'm sorry to hear about your wife," Lucinda said. She pointed to the punch bowl. "Would you mind getting me a glass of that punch? I'm parched."

"I'll get it!" Summer said.

Evelyn saw Lucinda's brow dip ever so slightly.

"So where are you from, Lucinda?" Wayne asked.

"Originally Boston," she said.

Evelyn did not offer that she was one of the Boston Van Horns, hoping Lucinda would share the ridiculous phrase on her own. For once, Lucinda restrained herself.

"But most recently I lived in Florida. I had a delicious place in Cocoa Beach."

Evelyn had never heard a condo described as "delicious."

"Uh-oh! Grandma!"

Summer had spilled punch on the table. Evelyn left to help her clean it up. She noticed Lucinda didn't miss a beat and even turned her back on Evelyn, moving shoulder to shoulder with Wayne.

She wanted to burst between the two of them. No way did she want Lucinda—

Just then Collier got their attention by tapping a fork on a glass. "Hear ye, friends! Hear ye."

Everyone gathered close. Evelyn noticed Lucinda take Wayne's arm . . .

"I've been tormenting my dear wife all day, telling her I had a special surprise for her birthday."

"He wouldn't even give me a clue," Mae said.

Russell patted Collier on the back. "Resisting the pressures of Mae? You have got to be the strongest man in all creation."

Collier shook his head and sighed. "It wasn't easy."

Mae swatted his arm. "Oh you. Now out with it. I've waited long enough."

He peered around her to the front windows. Evelyn heard a car door slam. All eyes turned in that direction. Mae ran to the window. "It's . . . oh my." She was at the door in seconds, flinging it open. "Tessie!"

Evelyn moved close to greet her, along with Audra and Piper. They all pulled up short when they saw that Tessa was wearing a costume: a white peasant blouse under a black vest and a full red skirt decorated with embroidered trim. She looked like an Italian folk dancer.

Tessa eyed them all. "Shoo. Back, sisters, back. Let a woman make a proper entrance."

They stepped aside, letting her in. The door closed. There was an awkward moment of silence; then Tessa spread her arms wide. "Oh, come on. Hug me. Hug me."

They all took a turn. Though Tessa was petite, she'd put on a little weight. All that Italian food no doubt.

"My, my. I must say we Americans are the most huggiest people in the world."

"A good thing to be, wouldn't you say?" Piper said.

"That's negotiable. Actually, I prefer the Japanese way of—" Tessa stopped talking when she saw Summer standing close, staring at her outfit.

"That's pretty." Summer's hand came close, but did not touch the fabric.

"Come close, child. *You* I want to hug."

Evelyn knew that everyone felt a special satisfaction in Tessa's affection for Summer. It hadn't always been so.

"Want some punch, Aunt Tessa?"

"I never turn down punch."

"Come in, sit down." Mae said. "I want to hear all about your travels. A world cruise and then a trip to Italy with your family . . ."

Evelyn braced herself for the long haul. Tessa prided herself in her knowledge of history and facts. If she got going telling them about the Doges Palace in Venice or the Edo Castle in Tokyo, they might as well grab a sleeping bag. As for explaining the costume . . .

They all moved into the living room. Tessa took the rocker by the window, adjusting her skirt around her legs.

"When did you get back?" Audra asked.

"Two days ago." Tessa's lined face smoothed a bit with her smile. "But first things first." She nodded toward Lucinda and Margaret. "Two new faces. Introduce me."

Mae did her hostess duty and both women shook hands with Tessa, coming toward her chair as if it were a throne. Lucinda moved back to Wayne's side.

As if she owns him. Evelyn hated herself for thinking such unkind thoughts. She was reading far too much into a little bit of social contact. She wished Herb were here . . .

Was she a fickle woman, or what?

•　　•　　•

"But she's hitting on him."

Collier put a hand on Mae's arm and shushed her. "Lucinda's doing no such thing." He drew his wife toward the kitchen sink, out of earshot of their guests. "But even if she was, Wayne's a single man now. He's probably looking for female companionship."

"But it's only been three months."

"You want him to go Victorian on us and wear black for a year?"

Mae flicked a crumb into the sink. "Of course not. And I'm not blaming *him*."

"So it's all her fault? You think he has no free will? You think he couldn't escape to the other side of the room if he wanted to?"

"You're saying he's attracted to her?" It was incomprehensible. Collier lowered his voice even more. "Lucinda is . . ."

Aha! He seemed uncertain. "Certainly, you can't think she's attractive?"

He shrugged.

Mae waved her hands, nearly toppling the Dawn dish soap. "Her skin's stretched so tight it looks ready to *poing*."

He glanced toward the front of the house where Lucinda's laughter could be heard. "You're exaggerating."

"She's not natural, Collie. It's got to be plastic surgery. She's an aging Hollywood starlet come to Carson Creek. A Frankenstein."

"Ah, yes, I can see the headlines now: Invasion of the Hollywood Frankenstein!"

She tried another tack. "I suppose if you approve, if you want *me* to get some plastic surgery, I could—"

"No!"

Ha.

"You win."

"Of course I do."

He stroked her cheek with the back of his hand, his face suddenly serious. "Don't ever change, Mae. I mean it. I love you just the way you are."

It was impossible to stay mad at this man. She wrapped her arms around his neck and—

Piper's voice rose above the murmur in the next room. "Starr!"

Mae and Collier looked at each other? "My Starr?"

They went into the living room. Mae's daughter, Starr, stood by the front door, suitcase in hand. She was not smiling in spite of the friendly hellos around her.

Mae took her into a hug. "It's so nice to see you." She let go and turned to Collier. "Is this part of your surprise?"

Collier shook his head. "I didn't know a thing. Tessa was your surprise."

Tessa nodded. "I was your surprise."

Starr also shook her head. "No one knew I was coming. It wasn't planned. It—" her face crumpled—"I've left Ted."

That was one way to kill a party.

●   ●   ●

Mae snuggled into Collier's shoulder. He adjusted the quilt around her.

"I wonder what happened," Mae said.

"It's probably only an argument. She just needs some time."

Mae shook her head. She'd had plenty of fights with Danny. She knew the different levels of arguments. Starr coming all the way from New York City signaled more than a tiff. At least a Level C argument. "I wish she'd talk about it."

"She will. The house was full of people tonight. It wasn't the time."

"But when they left . . ."

"She was tired from her trip." He kissed the top of her head. "She'll talk when she's ready. But do me a favor and remember one thing."

Uh-oh. "What's that?"

"Though you *can* listen and commiserate and offer advice, you may not be able to fix it."

Bummer.

•   •   •

Lucinda wrapped herself in a blanket and stepped onto the balcony off her room at Peerbaugh Place. She snuggled onto the chair, tucking her feet into the blanket. The moon peeked through moving clouds. A dog barked in the distance. Carson Creek was quiet.

Unlike Lucinda's heart.

She was in love!

Wayne Wellington had everything she desired in a man: he was nice-looking, witty, attentive. That he was single was certainly a pleasant fact, though not a necessity. But above all this, he was interested. She could tell. The way he looked at her, talked with her, got her punch.

Life in Carson Creek was definitely looking up.

People who despise advice
will find themselves in trouble;
those who respect it will succeed.

PROVERBS 13:13

𝓜ae stirred her tea. And stirred her tea.

Collier looked up from his crossword puzzle. "If you're going to continue to *tink* your mug, at least get a good rhythm going."

She stopped *tink*ing.

He looked over his reading glasses. "You're aching to talk to her. So wake her up. It's after nine. She's had ten hours of sleep."

"If she slept."

He conceded the point with a shrug. Then their discussion was made moot by the sound of feet on the stairs.

"She's up!" Mae whispered.

Collier leaned close and put a hand on hers. "Breathe, wifey. Breathe."

Good advice.

Mae plastered on a smile as Starr came into the kitchen. "Morning, honey."

Her eyes searched the counters. "Is there coffee?"

"Tea. Sorry."

"I forgot. Healthy Mother."

Mae looked to her husband. "Actually, Collier has corrupted me. I made mac 'n cheese the other day."

Starr fell into a chair. "What do you want, an award?"

Collier sucked in a breath. "Watch it, Starr. That's my wife you're talking to."

Mae didn't have time to wallow in his gallantry. Starr headed to the teapot. "Sorry. I'm testy. I know it."

Behind her back, Collier nodded at Mae. *Now.* "Care to talk about it?"

She returned with her tea. "Believe it or not, yes."

"Really?"

Starr laughed. "Why do you think I came home?"

"You needed a place to sleep?"

"I could have found a hotel within a mile of our apartment."

True. "So what happened? Did you have an argument? Are you going back? Are you—?"

"Mae! Don't pounce." Collier put a restraining hand on her arm.

"Sorry." She took a sip of her tea.

Starr did the same. Then she held the mug with two hands as if seeking courage in its warmth. "I walked out, and it wasn't because of an argument, at least not because of *one* argument. We've been arguing a lot lately."

"About what?" Collier asked.

Starr looked up, then down, then up again. "After I got here last night, I realized it was probably dumb coming here because you're going to be on his side."

"Now you've got me even more curious," Mae said. She couldn't imagine . . .

"You see, Ted's become a Christian."

"Yay!"

Starr shook her head. "I knew you'd be on his side."

"But it's a good thing, honey. It's a grand thing."

"He's all into Jesus-this and Jesus-that."

"That's an excellent thing," Collier said.

"Not when I'm not."

"Oh." Mae held her own mug, seeking warmth. It was cool. "I thought . . . after my experience . . . after I turned my life over to Him, I thought you'd—"

"I'm not you, Mother. I don't need . . ." She didn't finish.

Collier's eyebrows raised. "You don't need Jesus?"

"Not Ted's Jesus. He's gone wacko on me. Do you know he wants to move out because he said Jesus doesn't want us to live together before we're married?"

"Wise man to realize your mistake," Collier said.

She slapped a hand on the table. "But it's not a mistake! We love each other. We are getting married."

Mae raised a hand. "I'm in the process right now of helping Ringo and Soon-ja plan their wedding. It would be easy to add another—"

"I'm sure you are. But I'm not Ringo."

Mae chastised herself for bringing it up. "But—"

"But yes, Ted and I were planning to get married. Eventually. So for us to move away from each other now—to not have sex now—it's meaningless."

Mae closed her eyes a moment. *Lord, give me the right words.* She opened them. "I admire Ted, now more than ever."

"For acting stupid?"

"For taking a stand. For doing the right thing no matter how inconvenient."

"Or how illogical?" Starr rolled her eyes. "He's doing it for show. That's all. To show the world he's officially a Jesus freak."

Mae thought about it a moment. "You're right."

"I am?"

"Certainly. Though I could do without the Jesus-freak title, Ted's taking a stand *will* show the world he's chosen Jesus. That's

exactly what we're supposed to do. Christians do more damage
to our cause—His cause—by saying we believe yet living as if
we don't. Ted's a brave man. If you don't want him, I have a few
single sisters who'd love to meet him."

That seemed to get through to her, because Starr didn't
respond and stared into her tea.

Mae softened her voice. "Do you love him?"

"The old him."

"But the change that's happening because of Jesus is a
good—"

"But I don't like change. He knows that."

Mae began to laugh. "I'm sorry. I'm sorry but . . ." Her laughing grew. Collier looked at her as if he was considering throwing a
tablecloth over her head, and Starr looked as if she wanted to bolt.
Mae tried to get herself under control.

"I don't need your insults, Mother."

Lord, help! The laughter dissipated just in time. Mae took a
fresh breath. "I'm not laughing at you, honey. I'm laughing at
the notion that nobody changes, that marriage isn't fraught with
change."

Collier nodded. "Daily."

"Exactly," Mae said. "Gracious gadfly, honey, Collie and
I have been married almost ten months and we've already
changed. We're not the same people we were before."

"And that's a good thing," he said.

"Sure," Starr said. "In your case it might be good, but in
mine . . ."

"Okay, though I agree with Ted's taking a stand about living
together, I do know that one of the pitfalls of a newbie Christian is
being a bit frenzied about their new faith."

Starr snickered. "Tell me about it."

"But that doesn't mean their faith is wrong. Or that they've
made a wrong decision."

"Were you frenzied?" Starr asked.

Mae looked to Collier for guidance. "She was frenzied before, so knowing Jesus was just a new chapter to that story."

Mae made a face. "Is that a compliment?"

Collier hesitated. "I . . . I think so."

"Good save, Mr. Husband." She turned to her daughter. "The point is, finally realizing Jesus is *the* Man, *the* God, and *the* Savior is pretty exciting stuff. You feel like climbing on a roof and telling the world. Your heart feels as if it's going to bust out of its casing. You find yourself grinning like a goofball, vacillating from talking calmly and lovingly to wanting to shout at the world for being as blind as you were. It's all-encompassing. It's quite a trip."

"Your hippieness just slipped out," Starr said.

"Yeah?" She held up the peace sign. "Once a hippie . . . peace; flower power; love, baby."

"Oh, please."

"Hey, it still applies. Especially applies with Jesus in the picture."

"Amen!" Collier said.

Starr pushed her tea away. "I don't like this."

"Like what?"

"You ganging up on me."

"We're not ganging up, we're—"

"I'm going back to bed."

"But, honey . . ."

After she left, Mae turned to her husband. "Did we blow it?"

"We told her the truth."

"'And the truth will set you free.'"

"Hopefully."

"Eventually."

He took her hand. "Prayerfully."

He was such a good, godly man.

• • •

Starr hugged her pillow. What she really wanted to do was punch it. She'd come here for comfort, not condemnation. She was getting enough of that at home.

Don't exaggerate, Starr.

Okay, maybe Ted hadn't condemned her at all. Maybe he'd turned all supersweet and loving and soft-spoken and . . .

Yuck. He wasn't the Ted she'd fallen in love with. That Ted was a pistol, a powerful man who could take it as good as he handed it out. They'd had some fine arguments, awesome arguments that made her blood flow, proving she was alive. Now— since the Jesus thing happened—he argued without even raising his voice, which made her ranting and yelling seem completely foolish and over-the-top. They used to be equally matched, and now his calm façade was taking the upper hand.

Besides, beyond their personal life, this new lovey-dovey Ted was sure to blow his entire career by being so disgustingly nice. He worked for a collection agency. He was paid to skirt the edge of polite, never be nice, and act downright nasty if the need arose.

So you left him because he's too nice?

Starr turned to her other side, taking the pillow with her.

• • •

The question came out of nowhere—as questions often do with second graders. Margaret was giving her students an assignment to write a story about a family gathering when Joanie Mapes said, "You can write about your wedding, Ms. Jensen." That one question started a landslide:

"I want to see your dress; you said you would bring in your dress."

"What colors are the bridesmaids' dresses going to be?"

"Who cares about dresses. You're going to get a lot of presents, aren't you?"

"Is there going to be a big cake with people on top?"

"Is Bobby going to wear a big black hat like a cake person?"

She spread her hands wide, trying to quiet them. "Shh, kids. Shh."

They quieted—like the good kids they were—but waited for her answers, their faces innocent and expectant. What could she tell them? What *should* she tell them? Yet she *had* to tell them. She'd told them all about her wedding during the first week of school, but then, when she and Bobby had broken up . . . she hadn't wanted to burst their true-love bubble.

She leaned against the edge of her desk and tried on a smile. "I really appreciate you being so interested in my wedding."

Linda McMahon's hand shot up. "My aunt got married twice!"

What could she say to that? *Good for her?* "That's interesting, Linda, but I need to tell you children something."

Their eyes lost a little of their flash. Anticipating . . .

"There's not going to be a wedding. I'm not going to get married. Bobby and I have broken up."

An uproar. She might as well have said there wasn't going to be Christmas. A couple of the girls started crying. She moved to comfort them and ended up squatting in an aisle with fifteen little bodies moving in close.

Linda put a hand on her arm. "What happened?"

"Bobby decided he didn't want to be married." *To me. Didn't want to be married to me.*

"But what about the cake?" Joey Baker asked.

Margaret knew Joey wouldn't accept the answer that it was okay, they hadn't baked it yet. She answered with a shrug, and a suggestion. "Why don't we have a party? and a cake? I'll bring one on—" she flipped through her mental lesson plan—"on Friday. We can have our own party."

"A not-a-wedding party," Joanie said.

"Exactly."

"Can I wear a pretty dress?" Breanna asked.

"Sure. Why not?" Actually, she liked the sound of that. She'd done enough crying. It was time to set it behind her. And what better way than by having a celebration with her students.

Margaret stood and made her way back to the front, touching heads as she passed. "Now, let's get back to your stories. Besides a wedding, what other family gatherings might you write about?"

"Christmas!"

"Easter!"

"Football games!"

She let the enthusiasm of her children wrap around her like a cozy blanket. Keeping her warm. Keeping her safe. Keeping her sane.

•   •   •

"Tessa!"

"Well? Are you going to ask me in, or what?" she said.

Evelyn stepped back, making room. "Of course, come in."

Tessa came inside, holding up her Indian sari as she crossed the threshold. She handed Evelyn her fringed shawl, which looked decidedly Spanish. Evelyn draped it over the coat tree.

"How do you like it?" Tessa asked, doing a three-sixty.

"It's beautiful. Almost as beautiful as your Italian costume last night."

"Actually, I like this one better." She went into the parlor and sat down on the rocking chair, smoothing the flowing orange fabric around her.

Evelyn sat on the couch. "Did you get that on your cruise?"

"I didn't order it on sari-dot-com." She put a quick hand to her brow. "Oh dear. There I am getting all defensive again."

"Again?"

She stroked the silky fabric. "My family thinks I'm acting totally eccentric suddenly wearing these ethnic clothes out of the house."

And your point is . . . ? "They're very pretty. Uh . . . how many of them do you have?"

Tessa looked to the ceiling and counted on her fingers. "A Japanese kimono, an Indian sari, a Scottish kilt, a Greek Amalia, Swiss lederhosen—"

"Oh my." Evelyn had to stop her there, the mental picture of tiny, seventy-six-year-old Tessa in leather shorts . . .

"Do you agree with Naomi? Do you think I shouldn't wear them?"

A loaded question. "Do you like wearing them?"

Tessa rearranged the folds of the sari. "Yes, I do. I had such an amazing time on my trips seeing all the different cultures. Meeting all the different people. I really felt compelled to buy these outfits, but I haven't worn them before now because I wasn't ready."

"Ready for what?"

Tessa rocked up and back. "I haven't seen much of you—or anyone—these past seven months, Evelyn. I'm sorry for that."

"You've been traveling."

Tessa shook her head. "I've been home plenty."

"Settling into your daughter's garage apartment. You like living there, don't you?"

"Yes, yes. It's wonderful. But I'm afraid I've been a bit holed up there. On purpose. I've had a lot to think about."

Evelyn felt a tinge of worry. "Tessa . . . what's going on?"

The older woman traced the arm of the rocker. "I saw so much, Evelyn. Met so many amazing women. These clothes help me remember them. They need to be remembered." She leaned toward Evelyn. "Our world here in Carson Creek is so small."

"It's a small town."

Tessa sat back. "It has nothing to do with size. We're small in what we know. What we think about. We're too . . . too safe here."

"It's good to be safe, Tessa."

"Not that kind of safe. Too controlled. Too caught up in ourselves. Too content."

"I've never thought of contentment as a bad thing."

"It is when it prevents us from thinking globally. There are a lot of people out there, Evelyn."

She had to smile. "So I've heard."

Tessa flicked a hand at her. "Oh you. You know what I mean. You, the woman with the big heart, know what I mean."

Evelyn nodded and took a moment to look around the parlor. Her lovely, safe, inviting parlor. With all the amenities and comforts of home. She had so much. When was the last time she'd really thought about people across the world who had little?

"I want to help," Tessa proclaimed. "Need to help. I need to help the world!"

Evelyn had never seen such fire in Tessa's eyes. Not even when she was angry about something—which used to be often. "What kind of help are you talking about?"

Tessa stood and began to pace, her sari floating behind her as if it were trying to catch up. "I am starting a movement. A Sister Circle Network for women all around the world, helping them find what we found right here at Peerbaugh Place. I'm going to help them form their own Sister Circles. You can't imagine the freedom we have compared to the women in some countries."

"I've heard. Some are treated like property."

"Cheap property," Tessa said. "Some of them don't receive decent medical care; they don't know how to read; they can even be killed for the slightest thing like laughing in public. They have no rights." She stopped pacing. "Most of the time their opinions don't even count. No one listens."

Now *this* fact would stir the opinionated Tessa. And rightfully so. Though Evelyn had spent most of her married life being complacent, holding in her thoughts for the sake of keeping the peace, she was learning to speak out, take a stand, and be counted. Her previous silence was a choice she'd made—a wrong choice, but her own. She couldn't imagine being told not to speak out, not to think, not to share.

Tessa pointed at Evelyn. "I said no one listens, and I have the feeling no one's listening now. Did you hear me, Evelyn?"

"I heard you completely. And I'm very impressed by your passion. But do you really think getting the women to form Sister Circles will help them with their huge problems and issues?"

"It will help them cope, survive, and hopefully thrive, and if I get it set up right, we'll also address some of their physical needs." She leveled Evelyn with a look. "And what about prayer? Are you discounting the power and impact of women praying together?"

Evelyn laughed softly. "No, no. I wouldn't dare."

"You bet you wouldn't."

"I think the Sister Circle Network is a great idea, Tessa. But how are you going to do it?"

Tessa clasped her hands. "When I went back to Italy with my family, I made a few contacts. There's a woman in Rome who's helping me. I don't know all the details about how everything will work. Yet. But I will. I will."

"How?"

She put her hands on her hips. "Why God's going to tell me, Evelyn. He's the one who started all this, giving me the trips, opening my heart to these women . . . that's His doing, plain and simple. That's what I've been working out in my apartment. Taking time to think and pray and get guidance from Him. And I've got it. Now, it's time to move to the next step." She'd formed a fist in an I-will-do-it mode.

Evelyn clapped. "Bravo!"

Tessa lowered her arm and curtsied. Then she went over to

Evelyn and touched her hand. Her voice was soft. "That's why I came over this morning, Evelyn. To ask you to pray for me, pray that I continue to get God's guidance and do this thing right. He'll listen to you."

Evelyn's throat tightened. She was a fairly new Christian. For Tessa to trust her, to ask her . . . "I'd be honored to pray for you, Tessa. Thanks for trusting me."

"You're my sister, aren't you?"

Evelyn stood and pulled the little woman into a hug.

When Tessa pulled back, she flipped away a tear. "Now. I think it's time for some tea."

"Tea? You only drink coffee."

Tessa retrieved her purse. "Yes, well . . . that was before I discovered the wonders of tea." She pulled out some tea bags. "Straight to you from Japan."

Evelyn laughed. "Our Tessa, drinking tea. What *will* Mae think?"

Tessa marched toward the kitchen. "Mae will think nothing because Mae will never know."

"But you should really—"

Tessa winked over her shoulder. "I should. But I'm not going to. Now let's get that water going."

●　　●　　●

Mae had had a long day at work. A long day—for good reasons. In the past two weeks she'd gotten four commissions, and more were certain to come. People liked to give jewelry as Christmas presents. At any rate, right now she longed for Collie to order a pizza. Then she'd take a nap before choir.

But when she walked in the door and smelled pot roast, all thoughts of pizza vanished. She headed to the Crock-Pot to take a good whiff when she noticed the orange ceramic canisters were in a different place. She stepped back and scanned the kitchen.

Everything was in a different place. Gone was the stack of coupons, gone were the empty canning jars that needed to be taken to the basement, gone was the potpourri of this and that which marked Mae's world.

The counters were clean.

"Collie!"

He sauntered in from the living room, his reading glasses perched on his nose. "You screeched, my dear?"

"I scream and you *stroll* in? What if I was hurt?"

"That was not your I'm-hurt screech; it was your I'm-really-peeved yelp."

She wasn't sure she liked that he knew her so well.

"Am I right?" he asked.

She avoided answering. "What happened to my kitchen?"

He looked around the room as if seeing it for the first time. "It's clean."

"I see that!"

"There's no clutter."

"It was never cluttered. I knew exactly where everything—"

"There's room to cook."

"There was always room to cook." *If you used the stove top as a counter.*

"Starr did a really good job," he said.

"Starr did this? Starr, the princess of the messy room, did this?"

"All kids have messy rooms. They grow out of it."

"Apparently so."

Mae noticed the blender was missing. "Where's the blender?"

"I think she put it in the appliance garage."

"The what?"

He went over to the cupboard in the corner that sat directly on top of the counter. Sure enough, inside were the toaster, the blender, the mixer, and the food processor. "It's a much better use for it than a place to stash plastic bags," he said.

"But where are my plastic bags?"

He opened the cupboard under the sink. Attached to the door was a plastic bag dispenser. "She bought it for you. And she also bought this rack for the pantry."

Collier showed her the rest of the new-and-improved kitchen. "Starr worked on it all day. And she made the dinner too."

"Where is she?"

"She went to the hardware store for a few holders for the broom closet."

"She's invading that space too?"

Collier took off his glasses. "*Tsk, tsk*, mighty Mae. You're being quite the ungrateful mother, aren't you?"

"But it's *my* kitchen."

"She's only trying to help as a thank-you for letting her stay here."

"I don't want her help!"

"Mae . . ."

She hated when his voice took on that tone. The let's-placate-the-childish-Mae tone. She headed for the door. "I'm going over to Evelyn's."

"Why?"

She slammed the door.

*   *   *

Mae withheld her usual "Yoo-hoo, it's me" and stormed into Peerbaugh Place—a woman scorned, a woman on a mission. She slammed into the kitchen and saw Evelyn, Piper, Lucinda, and Margaret working on dinner.

"Whoa!" Piper said from the opened refrigerator. "I think we've just been invaded."

Evelyn stopped stirring at the stove. "Mae, what's wrong?"

"It's Starr!"

Evelyn hurried to Mae's side. "Is she all right? What happened? Did she hurt herself?"

Lucinda was setting the table. "It must be bad. Looks like you've been through a tornado."

Mae ran a hand through her hair. It felt the same as it had this morning. "Starr's not hurt."

Margaret joined Evelyn at her side. "Maybe not physically. But emotionally? She was in quite a state last night when she showed up at your party. How can we help?" She looked at the bag of Doritos in her hand. "Breaking up with her fiancé . . . I felt for her."

Evelyn pulled a chair out. "Sit. Has she been crying all day?"

They didn't get it. They just didn't get it. "This has nothing to do with Starr's breakup with Ted."

Piper joined them at the table, holding a bottle a Catalina dressing. "Then what is it?"

Before she said a word Mae knew it was going to sound ridiculous. *Then don't say it. Leave now!*

"Mae? Why are you so upset?"

Oh well. Humiliation was an old friend. "Starr . . . she cleaned my kitchen." Mae tried to put the proper drama into the words, making them sound with the same intensity as "She wrecked my car" or "She threw away my autographed Judy Collins program."

It didn't work.

Eight eyes stared at her. A laugh escaped from Piper in short puffs.

Margaret looked at Piper, then at Mae. "I'm sorry. I don't understand."

Evelyn sat nearby, her eyes also moving from the chuckling Piper to the confused Margaret, landing on Mae. "I'm afraid I don't either."

Lucinda pulled out a chair and sat.

How had everything gone awry? She'd stormed across the street for some sisterly commiseration because her daughter had invaded her domain, changed things without her consent, having the audacity to make things better.

Retreat, Mae! There's still time!

For once she decided her inner voice of common sense *made* sense. She stood and headed for the door, making a twirling motion on either side of her head. "Rewind! Rewind!"

Piper cut her off at the door, extending the Catalina bottle as if it were a stop sign. "Hold it right there, sister!"

Mae tried to juke to the right. Then the left, but Piper countered—probably a move she learned as a high school counselor. "Piper, get out of my way."

"Not until you explain yourself."

Mae sighed deeply. "If that's your criteria we'll be here till the moon turns blue."

Behind her, Lucinda burst out laughing. It spread around the room, reaching Mae last. She was only partially successful in stifling it.

Piper lowered her arms. "So. Are you going to tell us what this is about?"

"I'd love to hear," Lucinda said. "What can be so earth-shattering about a cleaned kitchen?"

"You haven't seen Mae's kitchen."

"Evelyn!"

Evelyn slapped a hand over her mouth. "Oh, Mae. I'm so sorry. I didn't mean to imply—"

Sheesh. The whole thing was getting out of hand. Mae turned back to the table. "Fine. I know when I'm railroaded and need to hold up the train. You want to hear why I'm mad?"

"I do," Margaret said.

"Me too," Evelyn said.

"You bet," Lucinda said.

"This I gotta hear." Piper set the dressing on the table. It sounded like a period to their words.

Mae waited until everyone was settled into a listening mode. "When I came home from work my entire kitchen was clean, but not just clean—reorganized. My counters were cleared off except for a plant and my orange canisters."

"How wonderful," Evelyn said. "Now you have room to cook."

Mae lowered her chin. "Surely you jest?"

"Anyway . . ." Lucinda said.

"Anyway, it was horrible. Starr had even emptied out that corner cupboard and put—"

"That appliance garage?" Piper asked.

"And put what in it?" Margaret asked.

Mae knew she was doomed. "Appliances."

Piper slapped her hands to her chest. "Oh . . . my . . . goodness." Then she slapped her hands on the table like an outraged defense attorney. "I cannot believe your daughter had the absolute gall to do such a thing. I mean putting appliances in an appliance garage . . . the nerve!"

"What *did* you have in there?" Lucinda asked.

There was no way to make it sound right. "Plastic grocery bags."

A moment of silence was followed by gales of laughter. All except Mae. "Stop it! You're not being nice. Don't you realize the bigger principle at stake here? A woman's kitchen is her castle. Her haven. Her—"

Evelyn and Piper looked at each other and renewed their laughing. Piper recovered first. "Mae, you're a good enough cook. Mae's manicotti is right up there with the have-to-tries in a person's life, but face it, you set your egg timer to see if you can get out of there in three minutes or less."

Mae crossed her arms. "I only did that a few times."

Margaret giggled. "You race your egg timer?"

"And I win too." She had to face it. She was toast. Burnt. Best to brush off the crumbs and leave. She raised her hands to make an announcement. "Fine. In the interest of my own sanity I'll tell you what you want to hear: I, Mae Fitzpatrick Ames, do readily admit that I overreacted and—"

"Luckily, it's her first time," Piper said.

"*Ahem.*" Mae cleared her throat. "It's rude to interrupt a confession."

Piper bowed, extending an opened hand. "Forgive me. The stage is yours, Ms. Ames."

"Rightly so. Anyway, as I was saying . . ." She raised her arms higher, trying to collect her thoughts. They were scattered. Oh well. She lowered her arms and let different words come out in a rush. "Mae Ames is a foolish, ungrateful mother who should be thrilled somebody stepped in to organize her messy, discombobulated—"

"But charming," Evelyn added.

"But charming household." Mae sighed and added the benediction. "Even if it is her own daughter, proving that the girl has far surpassed said mother in organizational skills—and can use a screwdriver too. There. I'm done."

They all clapped. Mae offered a deep curtsy, did a perfect pivot, and left the way she came. On the way out she overheard Margaret ask, "Does this happen often?"

And Piper answer, "Often enough to make life interesting."

Well then. At least she was good for something.

There are three things that will endure—
faith, hope, and love—and the greatest of these is love.

1 CORINTHIANS 13:13

$\mathcal{E}$velyn waited outside a hospital room and listened to the sound of joy inside. A few days a month she volunteered at the hospital, usually with her elderly friend Accosta Rand. They took turns delivering flowers.

When Accosta came out she was beaming. "She really, really liked them," the old woman said. She pointed to a stunning vase of pink roses on the cart. "Who gets that one?"

Evelyn read the card: "Linda Willis. West wing. New baby girl."

Accosta set her hand under one of the buds and took in the aroma. "My, how she's blessed."

Indeed she is. Pink roses for a baby girl . . . it made Evelyn think of her own little girl, put up for adoption so many years ago. *Bless her, Lord, wherever she is.*

"Every new mama deserves flowers as thanks for getting through labor." Accosta giggled, making her look even more childlike in her five-foot, eighty-pound frame. "Little does she know the real labor's just beginning."

Evelyn smiled, once again filled up by the company and the job. She'd been volunteering since January, when Accosta had been a patient and Evelyn had happened into her room. They'd chatted and Evelyn had discovered that Accosta was lonely and alone—her son lived far away. Since that time she'd taken it upon herself to volunteer at the hospital and to be a part of Accosta's life. Now every Sunday, Evelyn picked her up and they went to church together.

Only recently had Accosta joined in the flower rounds. She was a natural. The patients loved her. After all, who wasn't comforted by the attention of a grandmotherly woman bearing flowers, a soft pat on the hand, and the words "I'll pray for you"?

They were nearing the room where the roses were to be delivered when Evelyn spotted Dr. Baladino—Piper's Gregory. Carson Creek's hospital was small so she often saw him, and they'd exchanged awkward pleasantries since Piper had broken it off with him. But today when he saw her he waved, grinned, and came toward her.

Something was up.

"Evelyn, Mrs. Rand. How nice to see both of you." He spotted the roses. "Um-um. Gorgeous. Who gets these?"

Accosta answered. "Linda Willis. She just had a—"

"Baby girl. I've seen her. A sweet little thing with a shock of black hair."

"I love babies," Accosta cooed.

"Who doesn't?"

As Accosta chatted with Gregory about babies and the flowers in her garden, Evelyn felt as if she were separate from the scene, as if it were being played out for her on a screen. She had a chance to study this handsome Italian man. He was always groomed to perfection but there was something different about him today. A sparkle in his eyes? A special strength in the way he held himself? When the flower discussion wound down, Evelyn knew her time to study him was fading fast. Soon she would be brought into the conversation and—

"So, Evelyn," he said, "how's Piper doing?"

"All right."

"Does she have some interesting kids at school this year?"

This was more than he'd ever asked before. Evelyn smiled. "Why don't you ask her?"

He blushed. "Maybe . . ."

She eyed him and felt a surge of boldness. "You seem different today, Dr. Baladino. More . . . something."

Accosta cocked her head, looking at him. "I noticed it too. You seem more . . . more . . ." Her eyes widened, and she put a hand to her mouth.

He reddened, looked to the floor, and turned to leave. "I'll leave you two ladies to analyze this new aura of mine. Nice talking to you. Tell Piper I may give her a call." He walked away.

"You do that," Evelyn called after him.

When he was out of earshot, Accosta clapped her hands. "Oooh. I can hardly wait!"

"For what?"

"For Dr. Baladino and Piper to get back together."

Evelyn looked down the corridor where he'd gone. "He did seem more interested than usual." She shook her head, remembering. "But Piper is adamant. She's being very obedient to God's direction. She will not get involved with him until he gives his heart to Jesus."

Accosta took her arm. "But didn't you see it? The change in him?"

"He did look more alive, more . . ." It was hard to pinpoint.

"It was Jesus!"

Accosta's voice had gotten loud. Evelyn smiled at a nurse passing by before asking quietly, "Why do you say that?"

"You can see it in his eyes. The doctor's been introduced to Jesus."

"How—?"

"Maybe he hasn't made a commitment to Him, and he may

not even know there's a special light shining from his eyes, but *I know. We* know." She shook a finger and leaned close, whispering. "It's Jesus!"

Accosta took over the cart, pushing it down the hall, leaving Evelyn standing alone. Could it be true? *Lord, Jesus, make it be true!*

Accosta stopped. "You coming?"

Evelyn hurried after her, an extra spring in her step.

• • •

"Evelyn on line two."

Piper picked up the phone in her office. "Hey, Evelyn. What's up?"

"I saw Gregory!"

Piper was taken aback with the intensity of Evelyn's voice. "You often do. You volunteer at the hospital."

"No, no . . . I mean . . . yes, yes, but this time was different."

"How so?"

Piper heard the whole story—including more details than she needed about Accosta and the pink roses. Her mind zeroed in on Gregory. "Accosta thinks the change . . . it's Jesus?"

"That's what she said. And I, for one, trust her instincts. She's a very insightful woman. Her faith's leapfrogged over mine since she started coming to church with me. Sometimes I feel like she's leaving me in the dust."

"A dusty faith . . ." Piper let the comment out, but it was said as an afterthought. Her mind was busy with the idea that Gregory—her Gregory—could have had an encounter with their dear Savior.

"Piper? You there?"

She found a stronger voice. "I'm here." She got practical. "Accosta sensed this, but how about you?"

"I . . . I think she may be right. There *was* something different about him, and it came from the inside. Plus, he said he might be calling you. He knows the guidelines for your involvement with him, so he wouldn't—"

"I don't like the word *guidelines*. It sounds so clinical."

"But it's true, isn't it? You've set a standard—"

Piper snickered. "God set the standard in the Bible. I'm merely trying to follow it. And believe you me, if I had my way, I would have rationalized my way out of Gregory's lack of faith and been snuggled safe in his arms months ago."

Evelyn's voice was soft. "You loved him."

Love him. Present tense. Piper fingered a little plaque on her desk: *Characters live to be noticed. People with character notice how they live.* How much easier life would be if she could reconcile herself to being a character, doing what she wanted when she wanted, making a scene, proclaiming to the world, "This is just the way I am. I'm living life my way, so don't try to stop me!" Having character took hard work.

"Maybe you should call him?" Evelyn suggested.

Piper perked up. "Do you think I should?"

"Sure. You've waited long enough. Take matters into your own hands and—"

"No." Evelyn didn't know it, but she'd just made the key point for the other argument that always held Piper's romantic side in check.

"But you just said—"

"I've changed my mind. You said I should take matters into my own hands. But that's exactly what I *shouldn't* do. My own hands would muck things up. I know it. I've gone through this entire experience at God's direction and if I stop letting Him handle things, if I barge in and take control now, then it'll be ruined."

"Wow."

Piper laughed. "There's no wow about it."

"Sure there is. You're so strong, so determined to do things His way."

"Occasionally, only occasionally. But on this? Yes. I guess I am. It's too important to do otherwise. If Gregory *has* found Jesus, if he does want to tell me about it—"

"And get back together . . ."

"Then it will happen. It will play out perfectly. I will be stunned by the perfection of it."

"Double wow."

Piper tapped a finger on top of the plaque. "Yes indeed. I know it will be worthy of a double wow. If I wait."

Please, Lord. Please . . .

●　　●　　●

Piper brushed aside a cache of leaves that had settled too close to the headstone and set a golden potted mum at her mother's grave. There. That was better. She backtracked to a bench nearby and sat, adjusting her coat to protect her from the cold stone and the cold air. She looked around the cemetery to make sure she was alone. She was.

"Hi, Mom. I have to fill you in on the newest development. Evelyn talked to Gregory and it sounds like he's come closer to Jesus. And he might be calling me. I don't know the details, I don't know what's in his heart, but it's got me hoping . . ."

What *did* she hope?

She leaned forward, slipping her gloved hands beneath her thighs. "I've tried not to love him, Mom. I really have. For eight months I've kept myself busy, tried to push all thoughts and memories of him aside, and even dated a few other men. But it doesn't work. When I'm busy, I get tired, and then I think of the relaxing times I had with him. And when thoughts of him come flooding in, I virtually have to force my mind away from it."

She touched a stray leaf with her toe. "Remember when you used to take me to the Theatre in the Park? We saw *My Fair Lady* and *Brigadoon* and *Fiddler on the Roof*. Remember at the end of the night, even after the curtain call, I didn't want to leave, didn't want to go home and break the magic of the experience? That's how I feel about my thoughts of Gregory. When they start coming I don't want to walk away from them. I want to linger in the magic of the experience. If I'm not careful, an hour will go by. It's very unproductive and I've prayed that God would take these thoughts away. But He hasn't."

Piper heard a noise to her left and saw Oscar, the cemetery maintenance man raking leaves a distance away. She waved at him. He waved back. It was okay. He wouldn't disturb her.

"As for my other dates?" She wrapped her arms around herself. "I actually *want* to fall in love with someone else so I'm probably more tolerant, more forgiving of faults and annoying idiosyncrasies than I should be. But no one seems right. No one captures my heart. No one erases Gregory from my mind."

She sat quietly a few moments. Her mother had liked Gregory and had grieved with her when they'd discovered his absence of faith. And even after Piper had broken it off, her mother still saw him—as her doctor. An awkward situation, but Piper was not about to tell her mom she had to change physicians. Especially since she trusted Gregory so much.

It wasn't Gregory's fault her mom died. It wasn't. A blood clot from her leg had zoomed to her lungs. Odd that she hadn't died of heart disease, but something fluky. It wasn't Gregory's fault.

And in a way, it had been expected. Wanda Wellington had sensed she wasn't going to live long. Way back in January when she'd first come back from their RVing life so she could have heart surgery, Piper had found some letters—to her and to her dad and written by her mother—about her feelings, hopes, and fears about her illness. Piper had felt guilty reading them, because they appeared to be letters she should read after her mother was gone, but it had turned out Wanda *wanted* Piper to read them then. She could say things in the letters she had trouble saying in person. Piper cherished those letters as well as the discussions that had come about because of them. Her mother's faith during her ordeal had been an inspiration, nearly a guidebook, on how to face adversity and death.

Such an attitude had eased the pain from her mother's parting. Somewhat. Piper and her father still mourned, but it was a pain that came from feeling sorry for *themselves* for being without Wanda rather than any mourning about her side of the process. For they knew Wanda Wellington was in heaven, sitting at Jesus' feet, listening to every word He said. Learning, laughing, glorying in His presence. She was eternally happy and content. And that made Piper's *un*happiness and *dis*content much easier to tolerate.

A bird landed on the gravestone and cocked its head, eyeing her, almost as if asking, "Are you okay?"

She smiled. "I'll be fine."

Satisfied, it flew away.

•   •   •

Piper carried the groceries up the stairs to her father's apartment. She knocked with a spare knuckle. She heard footsteps. Good. Her father was home. She didn't want all this food to go to waste.

He opened the door, a book in his hand. "Piper! What? Let me take some of those."

They took the groceries into the kitchen. "I've come to cook you a grand feast," she said.

"More than one grand feast from the amount of food you brought." He picked out a can of artichokes. "And what will you be making with this?"

She grabbed it away from him. "Something wonderful. Don't be picky."

"Hmm. I defer to the chef." He helped her unpack. "What's the occasion?"

"No occasion."

"Piper . . ."

She wasn't going to give in. "You cooked last time. My turn. I felt . . . domestic."

He stopped all movement, holding a bag of pasta. "Did you talk to Gregory today?"

"No!" She felt herself redden. "Why would you think that?"

He shrugged and she was actually glad it was her father standing before her and *not* her mother. Her mother would delve deeper and not accept her answer. But her father?

The phone rang, saving her from finding out the extent of his interest. "Oh, hi, Lucinda," he said.

A mental warning bell chimed. Piper had witnessed Lucinda's blatant flirting with her father at Mae's party the previous week. She'd been wary then and had actually spent the days since studying her fellow boarder, fending off Lucinda's probing questions about her father.

She listened. "Hmm," he said. "That does sound kind of interesting."

Piper tapped him on the shoulder, making her eyes ask the question *What's interesting?*

He angled away from her and continued talking. That one subtle movement changed her radar from a single chime to the mighty clanging of an entire bell tower.

Her father leaned against the counter, getting comfortable as the conversation continued. And then he laughed.

Uh-uh. No way. Her father wasn't supposed to laugh at a strange woman's jokes. He wasn't supposed to lean against the counter and look like he was enjoying the conversation.

Especially not with Lucinda Van Horn.

"Sure," he said. "I think that would be nice. . . . Friday at seven would be fine. I'll pick you up."

Piper found herself seeking the counter for support. This couldn't be happening.

Her father hung up. He glanced at her, then away, busying himself with the groceries. "You were going to tell me about Gregory?"

She put a hand on his shoulder, whipping him around. "Oh no you don't! Did I hear correctly? Are you going out with Lucinda?"

He stacked a can of corn on top of the can of artichokes. "There's a jazz concert in Jackson Friday."

"You hate jazz."

He met her eyes. "Your mother hated jazz. I like it."

Somehow this fact made it worse. "But Lucinda . . ."

"What do you have against her? She's a nice lady—" he hesitated—"isn't she?"

Piper suddenly had to pinpoint her reservations. Yes, she was nice enough. Yes, she was a good conversationalist—if not a bit of a complainer. What could she say? "She's . . . she's been around, Dad."

"So have I. We're both over fifty. I'm over sixty."

"I'm not talking about age." She changed her weight to the other foot. In truth she didn't know many details of Lucinda's life. So far their conversations had skirted around her past, but there was something in what was *not* being said that was telling. "She's been married before."

"So have I."

"There was a divorce."

"Unfortunate, but not a crime."

How could Piper say what she only sensed? "I think there have been a lot of men."

He pointed a finger at her. "Don't gossip, Piper-girl."

He was right of course. But that didn't take away the bad feeling she had. She tried another tack. "Do you think she's attractive?"

He adjusted his can tower, making it perfectly straight. "In her own way."

"Don't her looks seem a little . . . contrived? Doesn't it bother you that she's trying to look thirty? Doesn't it bother you that she tries too hard?"

"Looks aren't everything. And I'm not proposing to her. We're just going to a concert. There's nothing wrong in that, is there?"

"No, but—"

He put a hand on her arm. "Your mother was the love of my life. You know that. And I will always love her. But the fact is, I don't want to be alone."

"Evelyn's alone. I'm alone. We don't seem to mind." *Much. At least at this moment.*

"You are women. You're better at being alone. In many ways you're stronger than we men. Men need women—and not for the reason you think."

"You're not a needy man."

His face turned serious. "Of course I am. Everybody is. People need people. Companionship. Love."

But not you, Dad. Not with Lucinda.

He put an arm around her shoulder and pulled her close. "Don't you worry. What if I promise you something?"

"What's that?"

"If Lucinda and I decide to elope, you'll be the first to know."

It wasn't funny. Not funny at all.

I, the Lord, search all hearts
and examine secret motives.
I give all people their due rewards,
according to what their actions deserve.

JEREMIAH 17:10

*P*iper hesitated at the front door of Carson Creek Hospital, the Get Well Soon balloon gyrating at her sudden stop. The last time she'd been in the hospital was the day her mother died. The last time she'd gone through these doors was arm in arm with her father, he supporting her, and she supporting him.

"Miss?"

She was standing in the way. She stepped to the side. Another visitor opened the door, then looked back at her. "You okay?"

"I'm fine. Thanks."

He looked unconvinced but went inside.

This is ridiculous. Open the door and go inside.

She reached toward the door, then withdrew her hand as the other reason she was hesitant stepped front and center. She was going into the hospital on the auspices of seeing a sick student, Becky Sands, but the real motivation was her hope that she'd run into Gregory. All week she'd been waiting for his call.

Pitiful. Absolutely pitiful.

The balloon bonked her on the back of the head as if spurring her in. She might as well. She'd come this far.

Inside, Piper tried not be too obvious as she scanned each hallway, nor look too nervous as the elevator opened. But Dr. Baladino was nowhere around. And what would she say to him if she did see him?

A proverb invaded her thoughts: *"People may be pure in their own eyes, but the Lord examines their motives."*

The door opened to her floor. A woman exited, holding the door for her. "You getting off?"

Piper shook her head. "I'm sorry. I forgot something." She pushed One. She'd forgotten her senses—that's what she'd forgotten. Did she actually think she could come here pretending to do a good deed and sneak her real motives by God? As if He didn't know her heart . . .

She thought of the rest of the proverb: *"Commit your work to the Lord, and then your plans will succeed."* That's where she'd gone wrong. She'd gotten on the wrong track by thinking only of herself.

The elevator opened on One and people waited for her to get out. "I'm going up," she said. Up. Down. Up again. The elevator—and her emotions. Only God could be the great leveler. On the way up this time, while other passengers watched the lights of the floor indicator change from One to Two to Three, Piper looked down, bowing her head in prayer.

By the time she got off the elevator on Becky's floor she'd scrapped her plan to look for Gregory and was determined to focus on her student. The girl had suffered through an emergency appendectomy. She needed support. Piper promised herself *not* to ask Becky the name of her doctor.

•   •   •

Piper got in her car and let out the breath she'd been saving. No Gregory.

She had to admit she was disappointed. After all, she'd admitted her impure motives and had given the situation over to God in prayer, but by doing so, she'd half expected Him to reward her by making Gregory come into the room, his smile at seeing her making her world complete.

But he hadn't come. And she hadn't seen him. Anywhere.

She turned the ignition, shaking her head. "Sorry I tried to tell You how to do Your business, Lord. You didn't want me to see Gregory, so I accept not seeing Gregory." She backed out of the parking stall and emptied the rest of her heart. "But I have to say one thing—and I ask Your forgiveness before I say it. Pooh, God. Pooh."

●   ●   ●

Evelyn was dusting the parlor to the accompaniment of Johnny Mathis when Mae came in. "Yoo-hoo, it's me."

"In here."

Mae turned to the left and waved a stack of letters. "I caught Maury at the curb. Mail call."

A few ads, a *Good Housekeeping,* a letter for Lucinda, and a letter for her. No bills. It was a good day.

Mae moved to the stereo and picked up the record's dust jacket. She swayed to "Chances Are." "I love this song. Johnny Mathis is dreamy."

"'Chances are 'cause I wear a silly grin . . .'" Evelyn sang absently. The letter was the sign-up form for cooking classes that she'd requested.

Mae looked over her shoulder "Oooh. More cooking classes. I'm inviting myself to your graduation dinner."

"Wayne and I were thinking of taking a class."

"Wayne?"

"We took classes before. He, Wanda, and I."

"I know, I know. I need to add a trailer on my question: Wayne? Not Herb?"

Evelyn put the letter back in the envelope. "Herb's a good dicer and chopper but he's not interested in *cooking*."

"So he was dicing and chopping . . . grass clippings? Wood chips?"

"Of course not." Evelyn took up her dust cloth. "But he's not interested in cooking; he's just interested in eating."

"Funny how that works."

Surely Mae understood . . .

Lucinda came into the room. "Hello, ladies. Is that the mail?"

"There's a letter for you."

As Lucinda opened it, Mae transferred Peppers from the rocker into her lap, getting the rocker up to speed. "Hey, Cindy, I hear you're going to a jazz concert with Wayne tonight."

Evelyn flashed her a look. "What?" *Why didn't I know this?*

Lucinda practically glowed as she opened her mail. "I know we'll have a marvelous time." She looked down at the letter. "Oh my, this is interesting. Very interesting."

"Let me guess. It's a letter from Sean Connery asking you out."

Lucinda got a glint in her eye. "I'd go. Wouldn't you?"

"You bet. Collie could drive the limo." Mae looked at Evelyn, mischief in her eyes. "How about you, Evie? If a certain handsome, sixtyish man asked you out, would you go?"

"Sean Connery?"

"Whoever."

Lucinda interrupted and shook the letter in her hand. "This is an announcement for my class reunion."

"Which one?"

Lucinda pulled the pages close to her chest. "I don't believe that's any of your business, Mae."

"That never stopped her before," Evelyn said.

"And never will again," Mae said. "I repeat my question: which one?"

Lucinda ignored them and studied the envelope. "This was forwarded. It was mailed six weeks ago but I'm only getting it now. It nearly came too late."

"When's the reunion?"

"Ten days."

"Zounds," Mae said. "You'd best forget mailing your registration and call."

Lucinda's head started shaking. "No. I'm not going. I can't go."

"Why ever not?" Mae asked. "Big doin's at the flower shop? A visit from the Queen? Oprah coming to town that weekend?"

Lucinda's head kept shaking but she didn't explain.

"Go," Evelyn said. "Aaron and I always had fun at our reunions. It's nice seeing old friends."

Lucinda held the letter against her lips. "*Some* old friends, maybe."

Mae stood, leaving the rocker to rock without her. "I go to see how everyone's changed. The potbellies on the class presidents, the cheerleaders who've been divorced six times."

"You go to see how people have messed up their lives?" Evelyn asked.

"Hey, I'm due a few moments of satisfaction. Surviving high school ranks right up there with surviving a world war." She raised a fist. "Remember the Alamo!"

"They all died at the Alamo."

"Oh. Then strike that. The point is that I go to those reunion thingys to make myself feel good about *my* life. The years are a good equalizer. Suddenly it doesn't matter if you were a nerd or a BCOC."

"Huh?" Evelyn asked.

"Big chick on campus."

Lucinda folded the pages in half and tossed them in a waste-basket near the stereo. "I'm not going." She fled from the room as if distance could keep her from changing her mind.

Evelyn and Mae looked at each other. "Well then," Mae said. "I think she wanted to go at first."

"I wonder what made her change her mind." She looked down at the wastebasket. "And I wonder which reunion it was. Thirty-fifth? Eightieth? Shall we peek?"

Before Evelyn could answer, Lucinda came back in the room, made a beeline for the wastebasket, and retrieved her mail. All without saying a word.

They waited until they heard the door to her room click shut upstairs.

"Well then again," Mae said, "I guess we'll never know."

"It *is* none of our business, Mae. A woman can keep her age secret if she chooses."

Mae turned over the Johnny Mathis record. "The Twelfth of Never" filled the room. "Any woman who has spent as much money disguising her true age as Cindy has is hiding some mighty big numbers. And don't tell me you weren't thinking the same thing."

Evelyn shrugged. "How old do you think she is?"

Mae closed her eyes and moved to the music, holding her hands as if she had a partner. "Sixty-two."

"Really?"

She stopped dancing. "In spite of Cindy's plastic surgery, there's some hefty decades showing in her face. In her eyes."

Evelyn had never pinned it down. "I'd have guessed fifty."

"She tries to look forty."

Evelyn shook her head. "She'd never pass for forty."

"But she obviously thinks it's worth a try." Mae ran a finger along the ridge of the stereo. "Give me that dust cloth." She finished the piece of furniture, then handed the cloth back. "Unfortunately, she's not the only woman at Peerbaugh Place who's trying to disguise the truth."

Evelyn started dusting the mantel. She handed Mae a porcelain figurine of a woman in nineteenth-century dress. "What are you talking about?"

Mae passed the woman from one hand to the other like a hot potato. "Oh, I know a certain widow who is pretending she isn't interested in a certain widower . . ."

Evelyn felt her cheeks redden and dusted the far end of the mantel. "It's just a cooking class, Mae."

"It's not the cooking class that gave you away, sister."

"I don't know what—"

"It was the look you had when I asked Lucinda about her upcoming date with Mr. Eligible."

Evelyn dusted a set of candlesticks. "It was just a shock, that's all. Nothing more. She didn't offer any details and I don't need any details."

"Since when do the women of Peerbaugh Place *not* share the details of their dates? of every event in their lives?"

"Why shouldn't Lucinda go out with Wayne? You're reading far too much into one look."

"Not so, sister. You'd be surprised what words, what sentences, what reams of pages can be expressed with one little look."

Evelyn took the figurine away from her, setting it in place.

Mae leaned against the mantel. "How's Herb?"

"Fine."

"When was the last time you saw him?"

She wasn't sure. "Recently."

"This week?"

"Sure." She wasn't sure.

"Then you must have been in Chicago because Herb's been out of town visiting his son since Monday. I know. I went to

Handy Hardware and they told me. He was getting back last night. Of course you knew that . . ."

Herb left town without telling her? "Of course I knew that." She moved on to the bookshelves.

Mae followed her like a plague in search of a victim. "Sure you did."

"Mae . . ."

Mae took the dust cloth and spray away. "Look at me."

Evelyn had no choice.

"Now tell me the truth, sister to sister. Tell *yourself* the truth."

Evelyn shrugged.

"I'll take that shrug as an adamant yes. Admit it hurts to see the man you're interested in go out on a date with someone else. Hurts bad."

"Don't be ridiculous."

Mae flicked a finger at the tip of her nose. "I promise not to be ridiculous if you promise not to be blind." She dropped the dusting equipment on a chair, took Evelyn's right hand, and raised it into the pledge position. "Promise?"

"Mae . . ."

"Promise?"

"Fine. Anything to get rid of you so I can finish my dusting."

Mae let go of Evelyn's hand and headed for the door. "Works for me. Ta-ta."

Evelyn stood in the parlor and watched her friend skip across the street. She hated when Mae was right.

And she was. She was.

•　　•　　•

The last person Evelyn expected—or wanted—to visit with today was Herb Evans. "What a nice surprise," she said, opening the door. "Are you on a lunch break?"

"Just have a few minutes."

"How about a tuna sandwich?"

"That would be super."

They moved into the kitchen. Evelyn spotted the cooking-class application on the table. She'd been on the verge of calling Wayne to discuss which class to take when Herb showed up. She quickly stuck the paper in a cookbook.

"Have a seat. I hear you've been in Chicago?" She got a can of tuna from the cupboard.

"That's one reason I wanted to come over. I feel bad for leaving without telling you. But I've been confused. Suddenly we're not as close as we were and I don't know what happened. I was wondering if you could tell me."

Do it. Break it off completely. Quit tormenting this man. "I've been a little busy lately, Herb. What with Heddy and Gail moving out, renting the rooms, getting to know new tenants."

"So that's all it is?"

"Well, I . . ."

"Because if that's it, I was wondering if you would like to go to a jazz concert in Jackson tonight."

Wayne's jazz concert. Before Evelyn's conscience could get a word in she heard herself saying, "Sure. That would be nice."

Oh dear. What was she doing?

•   •   •

Starr moved a planter full of mums to the space in front of the porch swing. She got comfortable on the swing with her laptop, feet on the planter, ready to work. It was a gorgeous fall day and she could think of no finer place to edit a book. Who needed a stuffy office in New York City?

She was just starting the second page of the file when her mother came outside. "Phone, honey." She lowered her voice. "It's Ted."

"I don't want to talk—"

Her mother left the phone on the porch then slipped inside. Sneaky.

She heard a muffled "Hello? Hello?"

She picked up the phone. "Hi, Ted."

"Hey, Starlight. I've been thinking about you."

"That's nice."

"Are you having a nice visit with your mom and Collier?"

"I'm not here on a social visit, Ted."

"Then come home."

"Which home? Yours or mine?"

"I haven't moved out yet." A pause. "We need to talk."

"We have talked. If you love me you'd stop this ridiculous notion that we have to live apart and—"

"It's because I love you that I suggested it."

"That makes no sense whatsoever."

She heard him take a breath in, then let it out. "What does your mom think of our situation?"

Should she tell the truth or a lie? She couldn't think of a viable lie so . . . "She wants to farm you out to all her single friends. You have brownie points enough for a . . . for a . . ."

"A set of steak knives?"

In spite of everything she loved his humor. It was a good counter to her serious nature. "I'm not coming back." She hadn't meant to be so blunt.

His voice took on a panicked tone. "But, Starr, we can work it out. I know we can. Jesus is supposed to bring us together not tear us apart."

"Tell Him that." She hung up and threw the phone over the railing into a cushion of maroon mums. She was shaking.

"I feel like doing that quite often." Piper Wellington was walking toward her from Peerbaugh Place. Had she overheard the conversation or just seen the aftermath?

Starr stood, going to retrieve the phone.

"No, no. Allow me," Piper said. She brought the phone up to the porch, setting it—and herself—on the railing. "Care to share? I'll keep the secret of your phone throwing."

"I prefer to demure. Today at least."

"A woman of keen words." Piper pointed to the laptop. "What are you working on?"

"I'm editing a book."

"Ooh. What's the title?"

"*How to Get More out of Your Man.*"

Piper's dangling legs stopped moving. "You're kidding."

"It's predicted to be a best seller."

"I don't doubt it."

The tone of her voice was telling. "You don't approve?"

Piper shrugged. "Does the world really need a book that promotes dissension between the sexes?"

"It will sell."

"Should that be the only consideration?"

Sounds good to me.

Piper continued. "I'm sorry for coming on so strong. We barely know each other and all, but you've pushed a button."

"Hey, I'm used to outspoken women." Starr cocked a head toward the house. "Let it out."

"Well, since you asked . . . I think books should entertain, instruct—"

"Yes and yes . . ."

"Let me finish. They should entertain, instruct, and lift up. If a book doesn't do all three, then maybe it shouldn't be published."

Forget being gracious. Starr wished Piper would leave. She had work to do. "Not every book has to inspire."

"I think it does. If nothing else, inspire toward change. A humor book should inspire us to laugh more; a how-to book should inspire us to learn a new skill. A biography inspires us to persevere and learn from others' mistakes."

Starr closed her laptop. "What about a murder mystery? Where's the inspiration in a book about a serial killer?"

"A murder mystery should inspire us to pray harder for mankind. There is such evil in the world. But evil doesn't have to win—and it won't win in the end. Jesus will be the final victor."

Great. Another Jesus freak. "You sound like my mom and Collier. Like Ted."

"Somehow I get the feeling the comparison is not a compliment?"

"My fiancé and I broke up because of Jesus."

Piper's face lit up. "Same here. Actually he wasn't my fiancé, but he was my boyfriend and things *were* getting serious. I broke it off with him because of Jesus."

"You're kidding."

Piper jumped off the railing and took a seat beside Starr on the swing. "We have a lot in common, you and I."

Starr didn't see it. "You're the religion nut in your twosome and Ted has that position in our duo. You broke your relationship up, but in my case, I'm the one who left. Not much in common at all. We're on opposite sides."

"But the situation's similar. Your Ted and I just want to share the joy we have with the ones we love most."

"By blowing our world apart?"

"How so?"

Starr told her about Ted's stand on living together.

"Would it be so bad to live apart?" Piper finally asked.

"Absolutely! We've created a wonderful life. There's no reason to change it because of some ancient, out-of-touch rule—"

"It's more than a rule; it's a commandment. They aren't called the Ten Suggestions, you know."

"Cute." And she *did* laugh. Starr didn't want to like Piper, but she couldn't help it. There was something genuine about her. "So is your man coming around? Is he doing the Jesus jive?"

Piper looked to the floor of the porch and moved a leaf with her toe. "I don't know. I haven't talked to him in months."

"So he could be doing the whole hallelujah thing and you wouldn't even know it."

"If that were true I'd hope he'd tell me." She looked up. "Actually, Evelyn saw him the other day and he *did* tell her he would be calling."

"When was that?"

"Monday."

"Five days ago. That can't be it."

Piper's face was pathetic. "You think so?"

Starr felt bad. "Hey, don't listen to me. What do I know about how a person reacts to Jesus?"

"You know how Ted handled it."

True.

They both looked across the street as a car drove up and parked in front of Peerbaugh Place. Piper started to stand, then sat down, angling her body away from the street like she was hiding. She whispered, "That's my dad."

"Don't you want to say hi?"

She shook her head. "He's going out with another woman."

"He's cheating on your mom?"

"No, no. Mom died three months ago."

"Then isn't it okay for him to date?"

Piper didn't answer. But as soon as her dad went up the porch steps of Peerbaugh Place, she stood. "I gotta get out of here. Want to take a walk with me?"

"Can't. I have work to do." She smiled. "I have to get this book ready for women like you who need to get a little more out of their man."

Piper's eyebrows dipped; then she got up and headed down the street. She didn't say good-bye.

Starr looked after her and felt a twinge of regret at her rudeness. So much for making friends.

Oh well. She turned back to her work.

Dwelling on one's faults never did anyone any good.

•   •   •

Evelyn spotted Wayne as he drove up. Suddenly, she didn't want to see him, or rather, she didn't want to see him pick Lucinda up for a date. Knowing Lucinda was upstairs, she raced toward the back of the house and out the back door. She'd pinch a few dead mum blooms. Something. Anything.

As the door closed behind her she thought, *This is childish.*

Yeah? Well. So be it.

•   •   •

Lucinda liked that Wayne came to the door to pick her up, but was disappointed that none of the other ladies were around to see it. She'd just seen Evelyn dusting in the dining room. Where had she gone? Part of the fun of dating was having an audience. Especially if that audience was a fellow single woman.

They were on their way to Jackson, a half hour away. Lucinda hated jazz, but had pretended to like it in order to be in the company of a handsome, eligible man. All part of the game.

Lucinda angled her body toward Wayne. He glanced over at her. "You need to put on your seat belt."

"I dislike seat belts."

"Sorry, it's the law. Mine and the state's."

So much for angling toward him. Plus, seat belts wrinkled her clothes. She tried another tack and crossed her legs. She had great legs and wore skirts to show them off.

At her movement, Wayne did a double take. He'd noticed— even though he was now pretending *not* to have noticed. Victory was hers!

"Tell me about yourself, Lucinda," he suggested.

I thought you'd never ask. She settled into her routine. "My family is the Boston Van Horns."

"I'm sorry to be out of the loop. Exactly what does that mean?"

Whatever I want it to mean. "My father worked for a Rockefeller." *Once. He was fired by a Rockefeller too.*

"Oh. So you're one of that crowd."

"Exactly." Lucinda beamed. Mission accomplished. Over the years she'd been amazed at how the mention of that one famous name enticed people to fill in the blanks, far beyond any lies she could tell. So what if she didn't dispute their assumptions? Where was the harm in that?

"Actually," Wayne said. "I think my family has some distant connection to the Duke of Wellington. The story is that when my family immigrated to the United States they assumed that title as their last name and—"

"My family has a summer home in the Grand Caymans, and often wintered in a chalet in Interlaken, Austria."

He looked at her. "I thought Interlaken was in Switzerland."

"I'm sorry. Switzerland. I was a child. I guess I didn't pay much attention to the country I was in." Lucinda wondered why no one had called her on this fact before. Had they known her mistake and laughed at her behind her back? The idea was horrifying.

Best to change the subject. "So, Wayne. Tell me when you first started to like jazz."

Lucinda allowed herself to daydream, nodding at all the right places.

• • •

She isn't listening.

Wayne wanted to go home and they hadn't even gotten to Jackson yet. Although Lucinda said all the right things at all the right times, there was something *off* about her. Something contrived and put-on. And it went far beyond her obvious obsession with her looks. Though Wayne admired beauty as much as the next man, he much preferred genuine beauty to Lucinda's pasted-on, surgically enhanced version. His Wanda had been a genuine beauty.

Sorrow grabbed with fresh teeth. To see Wanda's face one more time, run a hand along her cheek . . .

But he *would* see her again. Heaven held the comfort of the Father, and also of seeing his dear Wanda. But for now, his place was here. Not understanding the whys of the arrangement was something he was coming to accept. God knew best. Period.

When Wayne stopped talking, Lucinda jumped right in and rambled on about tennis matches, shopping trips to Palm Beach, and who sat next to whom at a fancy dinner. Maybe he was just as guilty as she for not listening, for there was no reason for him to tune into her boasts. They were not part of his world, nor did they add to his opinion of her. They were the frosting rose on a cake. Pretty and enticing to eat, but almost too much to savor. One taste was plenty.

Worst of all, Wayne suspected she was lying, or at least gilding the dozen calla lilies (flown in from Italy, of course) that were the centerpiece at some banquet. But maybe he was spoiled in that regard. He was used to spending time with Piper, Mae, Audra, and of course, Evelyn. These women shunned pretense as if it were a four-letter word. What you saw was what you got, and what they said, they meant. These women of Peerbaugh Place had been his comfort during his loss, his balm of Gilead.

And now, Lucinda was a burr. Maybe if he pretended to fall ill? He'd go home, make himself some microwave popcorn, and settle in to read a novel. Maybe something by James Scott Bell or Jefferson Scott . . .

It sounded good. Too good.

And impossible.

For above everything, Wayne was a gentleman, and he would not lie to get out of a date. He would endure it. And learn from it. What was it Paul had said in the book of Romans? Something about trials being good for us, helping us learn to endure and developing our character?

So be it. He'd endure it for Jesus.

●　　●　　●

"Looking for someone?" Herb asked.

Evelyn turned toward him. She'd tried not to be too obvious while scanning the jazz festival for Wayne. "Just looking around."

His eyebrows dipped. Was he unconvinced?

She put her arm through his. "I'm ready for that bratwurst now."

●　　●　　●

Lucinda's face was the epitome of disgust. She held the brat as if it were a writhing squid. "Are you sure this tastes good?"

"I could get you some nachos instead . . ."

She shuddered. "No. This is fine." She took the tiniest of bites at one end, only getting bun.

Wayne checked his watch. The first set was starting in five minutes. As soon as the performance was over, they'd head home. He led Lucinda to their seats. It was already filling up, and they slipped into the back row.

"Wayne!"

He looked up to see Evelyn, then Herb, sitting in the same row. "What a pleasant surprise!" Wayne meant every word and took a seat next to Evelyn.

She waved past him at Lucinda. "Aren't their brats wonderful?"

Lucinda made a face and wiped a streak of mustard from her thumb. "It's certainly a unique dining experience."

Herb looked over the row. "If you don't want that, I'll eat it."

She handed it down the line. Wayne caught Evelyn's look and returned it. *Yeah, yeah. I know.*

"Have you heard this group before?" Evelyn asked.

Wayne hadn't, but Herb had and launched into a story about how he and his wife had first heard them on a vacation in Oklahoma. Evelyn joined in, but Lucinda looked totally bored. Though Wayne tried to engage her in the conversation, it was apparent she was not interested.

Eventually he stopped caring. Was that awful of him?

So be it. Even gentlemen had their limits.

•   •   •

Evelyn came into Peerbaugh Place, searching for Lucinda. Was she already home? Or were she and Wayne still out . . . ? She looked upstairs and saw light coming out of both Piper's and Margaret's rooms, but couldn't see Lucinda's. Then she heard clattering in the kitchen. She hung her jacket on the coat tree and went in that direction.

Lucinda was setting a pan on the stove.

"I didn't know if you'd be back yet," Evelyn said.

"None too soon. I'm starving. I'm making myself an omelet. Would you like one?"

"No thanks. I'm still full of bratwurst. And Herb and I stopped for ice cream."

"How could you eat those hot-dog concoctions? Disgusting."

Evelyn let the comment go and looked around the kitchen for a chore that would allow her to hang around. Yet ever since Margaret moved in there was little left to clean. "Want some coffee?"

"Sure." Lucinda broke two eggs into a bowl.

Evelyn started her coffee-making duties. "So. Did you have a good time?"

Lucinda turned toward her, a hand to her chest. "Ignoring the awful food, the evening was marvelous. Wayne and I really hit it off."

Evelyn was confused. "You did?"

"He's very attracted to me. I know he'll ask me out again."

This did not compute. Not at all. From what she'd seen Lucinda had been a royal pain, complaining about the volume, making fun of the people who stood up and moved to the music, complaining about the temperature (first too hot, then too cold). Plus the general feeling that Lucinda thought the entire thing was beneath her. Evelyn couldn't imagine Wayne being attracted to that.

But Lucinda is an available, interested woman.

Suddenly Evelyn needed to be alone. She couldn't stand to hear one more word about how Wayne had complimented Lucinda on this, or how Lucinda could tell his love intentions by the way he did something else.

She flipped on the coffeepot, then said, "Coffee's coming up. But I've changed my mind. I'm feeling weary. I'll see you in the morning."

Coward.

𝓛ucinda waited until her boss, Gwen, was busy with a customer out front. Then, using the Flora and Funna computer, she
went to the Web site listed on her reunion invitation. Within seconds she found the page she'd been looking for: a listing of all
those who'd signed up to attend the reunion.

She scanned the list, looking for one particular name.

Eureka! *Sid Ricardo.*

He was coming!

She was disappointed there wasn't a photo but very heart-
ened to see that his reservation was for one. Divorced, widowed,
or still single, it didn't matter. Ever since she'd seen the article in
Newsweek touting his business acumen during some merger, she'd
placed him in the back of her mind as a contender for the position
of the male in her life. She hadn't thought about him again until
last night when she'd had a dream about him, remembering their
one evening together in the backseat of his Mustang. She'd awakened early this morning with his name vivid in her mind.

Perhaps he was the reason she should go to the reunion.

Perhaps he was ripe for her picking. She could sure use his money and his status. And it would be nice to once again be on the arm of such a man. It had been too long. Way too long.

Lucinda saw Gwen coming her way. She exited the page.

"So," said Gwen, "you were going to tell me about your date with Wayne last night? How did it go?"

"Fine. Nice." For an interim date.

"Will you go out with him again?"

"Probably." Actually, *absolutely*. Sid or no Sid. It never hurt to have a spare man kept in reserve.

• • •

"Need some help?" Piper asked.

Evelyn swiped an arm across her forehead then pointed to the bucket of wilted chrysanthemum heads in front of the porch. "Pinch away. I'm on a mission."

Piper positioned herself over a row of flowers and began to help. "What did the poor mums do to make you so mad?"

"That bad, huh?"

"I get the impression the flowers are only your symbolic victim." Piper illustrated with a violent pinching motion. "Whose head are you pinching off?"

Evelyn didn't want to sound petty. And she certainly didn't want to talk about this with Wayne's daughter. . . .

Piper straightened and nodded. "Ah. I get it. Would her name begin with an *L* and rhyme with a kind of xylophone?"

"Huh?"

"Marimba?"

Evelyn laughed. "Sorry. That's not a word oft used in my everyday conversation."

"I expect you to use it twice today to make it stick."

"I'll work on it."

"So? Is it our dear Lucinda's head you're pinching?"

Evelyn shrugged.

"Are you being protective of my father?"

That was one way to put it. . . . "I think she's a man killer. I don't want him to get hurt."

"Me either. Especially not by Lucinda."

"You're concerned too?"

"Of course I am." Her head shook back and forth with her words. "She's nothing like Mom."

That didn't seem to be the point. "She doesn't need to be, does she?"

"I suppose not. But she is a spitting sparkler compared to my mother's warm ember. I don't want Dad to get burned."

This brought to mind something Evelyn had thought of numerous times since becoming a widow. "I've often wondered if God gives us different types of mates for different seasons of our lives."

"Or gives us no mate."

Oops.

"I never knew your husband. Is Herb that much different than Aaron?"

"Definitely. Herb laughs more. He's balding."

"You're not delving very deep here, Evelyn."

She looked across the yard, trying to capture her thoughts. "Forget Herb a moment. Let's just talk in general."

"Fine. Shoot."

The air was crisp and felt good going down. Evelyn moved to the porch steps and Piper joined her. "Though I loved my husband, if there ever is another husband in my future, I want him to be different than Aaron. In big and small ways."

"For instance . . ."

"I want him to know God and be able to talk about Him easily."

"Sounds good."

"I want him to not hold grudges. I want to be able to discuss problems without him blowing up."

"You've mentioned Aaron's temper before. That must have been awful."

Evelyn plucked a leaf off a step and twirled it between her fingers. "I used to escape to this porch. I can't tell you the number of times that swing swayed with my anger. What I couldn't say to Aaron, I said out here. Alone."

"Nonconfrontational Evelyn."

"That was me. I'd do anything to make peace, keep the peace. I hated to argue."

"But sometimes arguing is a necessity. Sometimes it can even be productive."

"I realize that now, but then . . . so much of my life was spent avoiding arguments. Mostly because nothing ever came of them. Since Aaron never talked—only yelled—we never discussed anything, and nothing was ever resolved. Our arguments were like a broken record. Over and over. Round and round."

"And where they stop nobody knows?"

Evelyn was surprised to feel a tear threaten. "I'm sorry. This is dumb. It's been a long time. I shouldn't still have these feelings."

"Thirty years of marriage is not forgotten in a few months. The bad—or the good, right?"

Evelyn immediately felt guilty. "I'm afraid I think of Aaron's faults far more than his good points. That's not right."

"Have you forgiven him?"

Evelyn pulled back. "It's a little late now."

"No, it's not. Besides, the forgiveness isn't for him; it's for you."

"I don't know . . ." She'd never thought of this. What was past was past. There was nothing she could do to change it, so she'd never thought of working through it.

Piper put a hand on Evelyn's knee. "Just think about it, okay?"

She'd do that. She really would.

•   •   •

Margaret loved sleeping late on Saturday mornings. But she hadn't planned to sleep until 10:30. She sprang out of bed. The other ladies would think she was lazy. That would never do.

She rushed into the bathroom to take a quick shower. She was assailed by a scene that had become way too familiar: Lucinda's used towels were lumped on the edge of the tub, the countertop was wet with her splashes, and her makeup was tossed every which way. How could one woman cause so much mess *every* morning?

The first time it happened, Margaret had decided to say nothing. She'd cleaned it up hoping Lucinda got the message. Besides, serving others was a God thing. If Jesus had lowered Himself to wash the feet of His disciples, the least Margaret could do was clean up after her bathroom mate.

Margaret's resolve to be a humble servant had been tested from day one. Lucinda never said thank you. She never even acknowledged the fact that her mess was gone. Did the woman truly think there was a maid lurking around Peerbaugh Place, cleaning up after the ladies? *A maid named Margaret.*

It was inevitable that Margaret's desire to be a servant to this ungrateful woman waned. But that made her feel even more guilty. For she knew God wanted her to do it without thought of reward. Just because she should.

It was exhausting being good all the time.

Margaret's thoughts took a sudden detour. Was Lucinda's bedroom in the same level of disarray?

She took a step toward the bathroom door leading to Lucinda's room. She knew Lucinda was gone. Margaret had heard her leave for work during one of her half-awake moments. Her hand hovered above the doorknob. *Just one peek . . .*

It was locked. That fact upset Margaret much more than it should have. A locked door meant secrets, and secrets weren't polite. Evelyn and Piper didn't lock their doors. In fact, most of the time, even if the women were in their rooms, their doors were open. Such a policy promoted budding friendships. Sisterhood.

It bothered her that Lucinda's door was always shut. But in truth, she hadn't had much time to think about it, or cause to want to bond with the woman sharing her bathroom. But now . . . the locked door and the mess combined . . .

She stormed out of the bathroom, leaving Lucinda's mess intact. It was the hardest thing she'd ever done.

●   ●   ●

Margaret's resolve did not last. By the time she got dressed and made her bed, the offense of Lucinda's mess in the bathroom had waned, overcome by her own guilt for being a conditional servant of Christ. God didn't want her to do the right thing only when it was easy. He wanted her to be a shining example of His ways *all* the time—without grumbling.

In truth, it was often exhausting. But the inner battle that raged when she didn't do it His way was even more tiring. So, within minutes of deciding Lucinda's mess would remain Lucinda's mess, the damp towel was folded in thirds and hung on the towel rack, the makeup was neatly arranged, the sink and counter shining, and the water-spotted mirror Windex-ed. There. Perfect. *Are you happy now, God?*

Margaret started to head downstairs to join the other women. From the landing she heard the voices of Audra and little Summer added. It sounded like they were making cookies. Evelyn was such a good grandmother.

But that one thought—a grandmother making cookies with a granddaughter—brought about a sorrow so intense Margaret retreated to her window seat, drawing her knees to her chin.

For there would be no grandchildren for her own mother. Because there would be no children for Margaret. Because there would be no wedding to Bobby. All because Margaret insisted on being perfect. Perfect for God.

She looked toward the spotless bathroom. If Bobby were here, he'd make fun of her cleaning. When they'd first started going together, she'd laughed at his taunts about Margaret the Magnificent. She'd even been proud of that title. But over time his tone changed from one of admiration to mocking.

In fact, they'd broken off their wedding because of this title— and a basket of clean laundry. It had all happened a month ago. They'd stopped by his apartment and she'd seen a basket of clean clothes on the couch. She'd started folding them, trying to help. Trying to be a servant for Christ.

Bobby had gone ballistic, ripping the clothes out of her hands, overturning the basket all over the floor. Yelling at her! She'd stepped back, dumbfounded at his outburst. All she'd been trying to do was help and be the kind of woman she thought God wanted her to be. Didn't he understand that?

His words were forever embedded in her mind: *"But I don't want your help! Not all the time. I don't want a perfect woman who is obsessed with doing all the time. Sometimes I just want a woman who's here, with me, doing nothing, who's not thinking of what chore she should do to earn her brownie points to heaven. Sometimes I just want a woman who's content with being human."*

That had led to a long discussion about God and faith, and a person's responsibility to try to be like Jesus.

"But I'm not marrying Jesus. I'm marrying you."

Margaret had quoted the verse she'd taken as her banner, 2 Corinthians 3:18: "'As the Spirit of the Lord works within us, we become more and more like Him and reflect His glory even more.'"

Bobby had laughed at her, and had even bowed down in a mock kowtow. "Oh, holy Margaret, I am not worthy to bask in the reflection of your glory."

Not my glory—Christ's glory. She'd tried to explain but her words only riled Bobby more. He listed every act of kindness, holding it up as if it were an offense against him, like she was making him less of a man.

It didn't make sense. As a believer, he should have been striving for the same thing. That was her hope, that their marriage would unite them in their quest to live lives dedicated to Christ. They'd met in church—in a college youth group. God had been a part of their conversations since the beginning. So why was His constant presence in Margaret's life the reason for their breakup?

It didn't make sense.

Margaret hugged her knees even tighter, letting her tears soak into the denim of her jeans. *Father, help me understand. Show me what I did wrong. Or are You trying to show me?*

She heard a child's footsteps on the stairs. "Aunt Margaret! Aunt Margaret!"

She wiped her tears and found a smile for Summer by the time the little girl appeared in the doorway. "Hey, little one."

"We're making cookies and Piper says to quit being a lazy bum and come down and help or else you don't get any."

She swung her legs over the side of the window seat. "Well then, I guess I'd better come down."

●　　●　　●

Audra opened the door to the garage that served as the office for Catherine's Wedding Creations. "I'm so glad you wanted to see my business."

Margaret had not *wanted* to see Audra's business, but after they'd finished the cookies, when Audra had offered to show it to her, there was no polite way for Margaret to say no. *No, I don't want to see your wedding business since I've just called off my wedding.*

Evelyn had piped up in Margaret's defense, saying that it might be hard for her to see such a thing considering . . . and Audra had immediately withdrawn the offer. But by then, it had become a personal challenge—or a test?—for Margaret to go. *And who knows? Maybe it would help. What does not kill us makes us stronger.* At least Margaret hoped so.

The garage also served as a showroom and a sewing workroom. Audra explained how brides came to see the designs. Then she and Heddy Wainsworth—whom Margaret had met that first trip to Peerbaugh Place—did the actual sewing. The gowns were lovely. Margaret ran her hand along the satins and chiffons. She could easily have picked from one of these for her own bridesmaids. The emerald green color was exactly what she'd been thinking about . . .

She suddenly realized Audra was quiet. She turned around and found her watching. "Sorry, Audra. I wasn't listening."

"You okay? Maybe this wasn't such a good idea."

Margaret forced a smile. "I'm fine." She took a fresh breath and motioned to the entire space. "You've done a wonderful job here. Everything is so perfect, so organized. There's not a spool of thread out of place."

Audra laughed and straightened a bolt of fabric so the raw edge didn't show. "Russell laughs at me. Calls me a perfectionist. He teases that if he ever wants to get my goat, all he has to do is come in here and mix up my thread rack, putting the blues amongst the pinks and placing a yellow smack-dab in the middle of the purples."

Margaret smiled. "He wouldn't dare."

"He threatens." Audra ran a hand over the rack of dresses, stopping to adjust a sleeve. "I can't help it if I like things orderly. I don't see it as a fault at all."

"It's not a fault. It's a gift."

Audra's eyebrows rose.

Margaret felt a surge of hope. Maybe Audra would understand her own predicament, her own battle. It would be so nice to have a confidante. "My engagement broke up because of my own need for . . . order. My need to make things—and myself—as perfect as they can be. For God."

Audra's head tilted to the side. "I never thought of doing it for that reason."

Margaret's hope withdrew. "Don't you do all this for God? As a way to serve Him? To show your gratitude to Him? To make things orderly and clean and fresh and—"

Audra shook her head. "I'm afraid my motives are a mile away from yours. I do all this for me. Because it feeds my own need, not God's."

Margaret had a sudden thought. "Do you believe in God?"

"Sure. Thanks to Piper. When I got pregnant with Summer, Piper was my high school counselor. She helped me through all that and helped me find comfort in Him."

From comments she'd heard around Peerbaugh Place, Margaret had known there was more to Audra's story. "Was . . . I mean, is Russell . . . ?"

"Summer's father? No. Her father was just a guy I used to date. Our relationship was a mistake. But our daughter was not. She's the joy of my life. I lived at home until I got my degree; then I moved into Peerbaugh Place and met the son of the landlady. . ." She laughed. "A nice perk, don't you think?"

"The best."

"But back to God . . . Piper invited me to go with her to church. I found Jesus there, waiting for me. Waiting to forgive me and help me and love me. So, yes, to answer your question, I believe in God. Big time." She pulled out a chair for Margaret and took one herself. "I'd love to hear more about your philosophy of order."

Margaret laughed. "Philosophy of order. I wish I'd had that line when Bobby dumped me. Maybe it would have made my case stronger."

"Case?"

She told her about the breakup. It felt good to share it with a sister in Christ—who just happened to be a neat freak like herself. "So that's it. That's why I came to Peerbaugh Place."

"You're too good to be true, Margaret."

She sucked in a breath. "Don't say that."

After a moment's shocked look, Audra leaned her arms on the table. "I've never met anyone with an attitude like yours. Someone so in tune with God during the regular minutes of the day. It's a wonderful thing. I admire you. You've even got me thinking about my own motives. You make me want to be a better person, stronger in my faith." She shook a finger at Margaret, but she was smiling. "Don't dumb down for the rest of us. You have a servant's heart. If Bobby couldn't see that, it's his loss."

Margaret's throat tightened. "Really?"

"Really." Audra laughed and nodded toward a pile of brown boxes stacked near the door. "Want to help me organize a new shipment of trims?"

"I'd love to."

• • •

"Silver-Wear. How may I help you?"

"Mae?"

Mae put down the necklace she was working on. "Ted?"

"I'm sorry to bother you at work. But I didn't want to risk calling the house and having Starr pick up."

Mae was glad there were no customers in the shop. She settled into her workbench. "Why don't you want to talk to her?"

"I've tried. We're at an impasse. I don't know what to do." His voice was pitiful. "Is she miserable?" he asked. "Not that I want her to be in pain, but . . ."

"Does she miss you?" Mae finished the question for him.

"Yeah."

"She's confused."

"That's all?"

"You want me to short-sheet her bed? cut off her coffee supply?"

"If it would help my cause . . ."

Which led to what Mae really wanted to know. "How did this come about, Ted? I've heard Starr's side. But how did Jesus finally get your attention?"

"I ran out of excuses."

Mae got up, locked the front door, and put the "Out to lunch, back in a bunch" card in the door. She didn't want to risk an interruption. Not about this. "How so?"

"Working in a collection agency I hear excuses every day. You wouldn't believe the excuses I hear."

"Creative?"

"Plots, sub-, and sub-subplots as to why people can't pay their bills."

"Lies?"

"It's assumed."

"That's got to get old."

"You get used to it. It's part of the job."

But he'd just said . . . "Then what—?"

"It's not the variety of excuses that got to me; it was the underlying theme of 'it's not my fault.' One out of a hundred people I talk to are honest and admit they messed up and *that's* the reason they can't pay on time. The rest? Someone else is always to blame."

"There's no accountability."

"Exactly. I don't like the trend. Which made me look at what society thinks is important, the kind of behavior it encourages. Which made me think about my own accountability. Which made me think about my own standards and how I'd let myself be sucked into the everyone's-doing-it way of life. Nothing seemed stable anymore. Where are the standards? Where are ethics and morals?"

"They've moved to Poughkeepsie."

"They've moved somewhere because I certainly can't find them. It really got me down. I took a look around and didn't like what I saw."

"God opened your eyes."

"'I was blind, and now I can see.'"

Mae recognized the verse. "The book of Luke, right?"

"John. John 9:25."

She felt like a proud teacher, even though she'd had nothing to do with this particular pupil.

"And then there was your example."

"My—?"

"When you told us about your experience at the May Madness potluck, when you heard that hymn and were moved to choose Him . . ."

"I didn't think you were listening."

"I was. It moved *me*. Moved me a step closer myself."

Tears popped up unannounced. To think that her saying yes to Jesus had helped someone else make that commitment.

"Are you crying?"

She sniffed loudly and found a tissue. "You made my day, Ted."

"I'm glad."

She took a cleansing breath. "Tell me the rest. Was it gradual or a big moment or—"

"God chipped away at me. I've got to say I didn't like it much at first. He was blowing apart my world, everything I was comfortable with."

"He can be quite persistent."

"And stubborn."

"And you weren't?"

"Touché, Mae."

"He does whatever it takes. I'm beginning to think we're the ones who can choose to do it the hard way or the easy way."

"I'm just thankful He wanted me enough to not give up. I didn't make it easy on Him. I had plenty of excuses of my own."

"But He finally broke through?"

"Like I said, I ran out of excuses."

"What happened?" Mae got comfortable.

"I'd been after this one guy, Joe, for months, trying to collect on a car loan. Every time we talked he had a bigger, better excuse as to why he couldn't pay. At first, it was almost funny, but then one day I was not in the mood. When Joe started in on his newest saga of his-dog-ate-it, his-mother-was-sick, his-wallet-was-stolen, I lost it. I got mad and yelled at him, telling him to can it. I mean I blew it big time, telling him that I'd had enough of his baloney, I didn't want to hear more, and I wasn't calling him back. If he wanted to be a welshing creep he was welcome to the title, but I wasn't going to be a part of it. I was done with him. Finis."

"Lost your cool a bit, eh Ted?"

"Any cool I had melted in the heat of my words. I was brutal. Totally unprofessional."

"What did he do?"

"He got quiet and I thought he'd hung up. I was just about to hang up myself—and was bracing myself for the reprimand I'd surely get from my boss—when he said something."

"What did he say?"

"He said, 'I know I'm a welshing creep, but I don't want to be. Don't give up on me. Help me get out of this.'"

"Oh my."

"I know. He blew me away. So I talked to him, man to man this time. And we had a nice talk—about all sorts of things. And you know what? At the end he thanked me. And since then he's made a real effort to get paid up."

"Very cool, Ted, very, very cool."

"I know. But the best part of it is that I saw myself and God playing the same roles. Except God played my part, and I played the part of Joe, the welshing creep. I'd been giving God every excuse in the book as to why I couldn't come clean on my commitments, and He had every right to call me on it, just like I'd called Joe on it. And just like Joe, I didn't want Him giving up on me. I *wanted* to be held accountable. I wanted to become something beyond who I was. I wanted someone to believe in me."

"Oh, Ted . . ."

His voice quivered. "So right there in my cubicle I took off my headset, bowed my head, and stopped making excuses. I owned up to who I was and how I was living. And Jesus was right there, comforting me, calling me close, telling me He forgave me." His voice broke. "He took me just as I was. I didn't have to be perfect or even good. Just willing."

Mae let the tears fall. "I'm so happy for you, Ted. He changes everything, doesn't He?"

"It's astounding. There's no part of my life He hasn't touched. But it also makes me mad."

"How so?"

"Why didn't I realize what I was missing? Why did I go on, year after year, thinking I had a good life, thinking it was as good as it gets? There is no way to describe the *after* when you're absorbed in the *before*."

"It's like there's no way for us to comprehend what life will be like in heaven. It's going to be even better than it is for believers here. And it can be pretty good here."

"We have a lot to look forward to."

"An eternity to look forward to," she said.

Ted's voice suddenly changed to one of determination. "But I want Starr there!"

His passion made Mae suck in a breath. "I do too, Ted. I do too."

"But how do we reach her? She doesn't want to listen. She wants things to go back to the way they were, and I won't do that. I can't. I've made a commitment to Christ that can't be compromised."

"She loves you. She'd come home in a minute, you know."

"The home we had is gone. We can't live together anymore. We can't."

Mae understood but wished there was a loophole that would make it possible. It would be so much easier. *Shame on you, Mae! Wanting easy over right.*

"I don't know what to do, Mae. I ache for her to know what I know. I've tried to share, but she thinks I've gone over the top."

"*Jesus freak* was the term she used."

"Being persecuted by my own fiancée . . . that hurts."

Fiancée. "How about you commit to the marriage thing. Set a date. Soon. After that she *can* come home and your living situation will be legal in all ways."

"Actually, I was thinking of postponing the wedding."

"What?"

"The Bible says we shouldn't be unequally yoked."

Shades of Piper and Gregory . . .

Ted continued. "I want to get the faith issue resolved before we get married. I want to go into marriage as true partners in every way. I want to share my faith with my wife, not be afraid I'll offend her with it."

Mae remembered Starr as a child, vehemently refusing to try peas. It had taken two years of prompting for her to take her first bite. And then she loved them. Getting her to try God . . . "That might be a long delay, Ted."

"I want to do this right."

"But she may not agree to the delay. Especially if you insist on living apart."

"My terms are nonnegotiable."

"She won't like that."

"I know. But I love her too much to settle for less. Our eternal future is at stake."

"But God doesn't work on our timetable. He chooses the time. He chooses the way. He does the revealing."

Ted was silent a moment. "I've already pushed too much. It's hard accepting the fact that I'm not Starr's Holy Spirit. It's hard backing off and trusting God to handle it."

Mae's heart ached with Ted's. "We just want them to know what we know. To have what we have."

"Sometimes I want to shake her and yell in her face, 'Wake up! Don't you understand what's at stake here? what's waiting for you? how incredibly cool life can be when you commit to Christ?'"

Mae laughed. "I don't think that will work with Starr."

"Don't I know it."

"We have to take comfort in the fact that God wants her to be His even more than we do."

She heard him take a breath. "Wow. He does, doesn't He? I never thought of that."

Mae thought of the kernel of a verse and got her pocket Bible out of the drawer by the cash register. "Just a minute. Let me find a verse here—" she found it in John—"listen to this: 'Those who obey My commandments are the ones who love Me. And because they love Me, My Father will love them, and I will love them. And I will reveal Myself to each one of them.'"

"But what if Starr doesn't love Him first?"

"I know that one by heart: 'We love each other as a result of His loving us first.' He loves us first. He cares even if we don't. He forgives even if we don't deserve it."

"I'm glad."

"Me too."

She heard his sigh. "So what do we do, Mae? How do we make Starr see the light—His light?"

"We don't *make* her do anything. We live right and hope she wants what we have. We don't hide the fact God is working in our lives, but we don't throw it in her face either. But most importantly, we pray."

"I've been doing that a lot."

"Me too. But do it more. Prayer changes things, Ted. God hears and He answers."

"But when?"

"When the time is right and perfect. He won't mess up. He can't."

"But we can."

Ah yes, Mae knew that for a fact. "Sometimes I wish we didn't have free will. God can't mess up but we most certainly can."

"Then let's also pray that Starr doesn't miss a chance to know Him, to choose Him. We both know He'll jump in at the slightest opening."

Mae laughed. "It may take a pry bar on our Starr."

"He can handle it. He'll just get a couple hundred angels, flexing their wings . . ."

"Calling all reinforcements! We have a tough one here!"

Ted's voice grew soft. "It'll happen. I know it will."

"Me too. How about we pray together right now?"

They did. And God and His angels heard every word.

Get the truth and don't ever sell it;
also get wisdom, discipline, and discernment.

PROVERBS 23:23

*I*t was now or never.

Lucinda sat at the desk in the parlor with the sign-up for her high school reunion spread before her. Ever since finding out her old flame Sid Ricardo was going to be there, she'd made the decision to go. But that had been three days ago.

The holdup had come about when she'd really looked at the form they wanted her to fill out. Such innocuous blanks for *Address, Occupation, Spouse,* and *Children* left her hand shaking. *Boardinghouse, clerk, none,* and *none* sounded pitiful. But worse than that, they *were* pitiful. Her life was pitiful.

And then there was the little bio paragraph she was supposed to fill out: *Tell us what you've been doing since we last saw you.* She could almost hear the chirpiness in the question. Or the condemnation. Everything she'd ever accomplished was in the past. She *used to be* a successful model. She *used to be* married. She *used to be* living in an oceanside condo in Cocoa Beach. She *used to be* a socialite debutante, in demand for parties and the spare arms of handsome men with noteworthy names.

She was a has-been. A desperate has-been in search of a man who could make her feel worthy again. Pretty again. Useful again.

She bit the end of the pen and made a decision. Then she began to write.

• • •

After calling Lucinda into the kitchen to get the phone, Evelyn went to the desk in the parlor to retrieve an envelope. She spotted Lucinda's reunion sign-up sheet on the desktop.

She looked away. It wasn't her business.

She looked back. She wasn't doing anything wrong by wanting to know more about her tenant, was she? She wanted to know Lucinda better, that's all.

That wasn't all, but Evelyn didn't belabor the motive. She didn't have time. She could hear that Lucinda's phone call was winding down. She only had a few seconds . . .

Evelyn ignored the top half of the sheet that contained the normal name-address information and let her eyes zoom to the bottom paragraph where the attendees were to write a bit about themselves.

I've enjoyed a varied life. My modeling has taken me around the world, landing me on numerous covers of magazines such as McCall's *and* Cosmopolitan. *I have had the pleasure of residing in Boston, Cocoa Beach, and Palm Springs. Currently, I am using my expertise as a consultant handling decorating and floral arrangements for large events.*

Evelyn was thoroughly impressed—and was even thinking there was good reason for Wayne to be interested in Lucinda—until the last line about being a consultant. She was a clerk. And the most consulting she was asked to do—for a *large* event—was probably helping Evelyn pick out which carnations she'd like at the church's upcoming luncheon. One carnation in a bud vase. Per table. If Lucinda lied about the latter, was all her talk about being an international model a lie too?

When she heard Lucinda hang up, she grabbed her envelope

and returned to the kitchen just as Lucinda came out. "You heading to work?" Evelyn asked.

"In a couple minutes. I have something I need to finish."

I bet you do.

•   •   •

After Lucinda left for work, Evelyn got herself quite worked up thinking about the woman's lies. If only she'd noticed the name of the school, she'd call them up right now and expose Lucinda for the liar she was.

Or might be. Other than exaggerating about her job, you don't really know.

And suddenly she *had* to know. She was heading to the church for a Bible study in a half hour. If she left now she'd have time to swing by Flora and Funna . . .

•   •   •

Evelyn was disappointed when Gwen told her Lucinda was out on a delivery.

"Can I help you?"

Actually, this might be better. "You've known Lucinda a long time, haven't you?"

"We were roommates in college. We were out of touch for years—until recently, when everything fell apart and Lucy needed a bit of help."

Oh? "That was nice of you. In her time of need . . ."

Gwen pulled the outer layer of petals off a rose. "I'm glad she found a home at Peerbaugh Place. It's not that Randy and I minded having her stay with us, but three months is approaching the hospitality limit."

Evelyn had no idea Lucinda had stayed with Gwen that long.

She chose her next words carefully. "It's kind of exciting having a celebrity like Lucinda as a tenant. An international model who's had her picture on the cover of *McCall's* and *Cosmo*."

Gwen stopped plucking. "Not the cover."

"I'm sorry. I must have misunderstood."

"Lucinda did a lot of ad work for Silken Tresses. She calls herself the Silken Tresses girl, but it wasn't like being one of the Breck girls like Cheryl Ladd or Jacqueline Smith or anything. I'm sure the ad was *in* those magazines many times, and it did appear on the back cover of *McCall's* once back in the late sixties but—"

Strike one. *The sixties? Forty years ago?* Lucinda's bio made it sound as if her modeling success was more recent. "Being a model sounds so glamorous. What countries did she get to visit?"

"I think she's been to Mexico once, and I think her family took her to the Alps when she was little."

Strike two.

There was one other point to clarify. "I know Lucinda is from Boston and lived in Cocoa Beach but—"

"Her parents were quite wealthy. And then her husband . . . she thought he was rich, and he *did* have money enough, but he was low class in every other way. Not what Lucy had in mind at all. It was one of those cases when both parties married for the wrong reason. She bought the Cocoa Beach condo out of the divorce settlement, wanting to set herself up right so she could find herself a *real* rich man. A classy man."

"Did she ever live in Palm Springs?"

"Live? No. I think she and Wally won a weekend there once in a raffle or something." She leaned toward Evelyn confidentially. "We both know that Lucy's never let *not* having money affect her image of *having* money. Right?"

"Oh. Right."

Gwen went back to plucking her petals. "But we love her anyway. She's a character, that she is."

That she is.

"Can I interest you in some roses? We have a special going on."

No, thank you.

* * *

Evelyn met Piper at the door after school. "Piper!"

"Goodness, Evelyn. Let me get both feet in the door!"

She backed up a step, giving her friend room to hang up her coat. Piper turned around. "Now. What's got you in a frazzle this afternoon?"

She found herself whispering. "Lucinda."

Piper whispered back. "Is she here?"

Evelyn realized how ridiculous she was acting. She spoke in a normal tone. "She works until six."

Piper headed toward the kitchen. "Join me for an apple?"

Evelyn fell in behind her. "No thanks. But I do need your advice."

Piper chose an apple from the basket on the kitchen table. She took a seat, as did Evelyn. "It must be serious. You're in a tizzy."

Evelyn found a breath. "Lucinda's been lying to us, and worse, she just lied on the sign-up she sent to her high school reunion."

"The first bothers me; the second doesn't surprise me."

"Why not?"

"Reunions are a place to see old friends and brag. If you don't have anything to brag about, it's only natural to embellish."

"Did you go to your reunion?"

"My tenth. I have the twentieth in three years." She stopped chewing. "Out of high school twenty years. It makes me feel old."

"Don't complain. My fortieth is next year."

"Where did the time go, Evelyn?"

"I don't know." They'd gotten off the subject. "Back to lying
. . . did you lie on your reunion bio?"

"No, but we moved to Carson Creek when I was ten. I went
to high school in Carson Creek. I still live here. I still see many
of my classmates. I'm beginning to counsel some of their kids.
It would be pretty pointless for me to pretend I was something
I wasn't."

"I would guess Lucinda's high school is back in Boston.
Unless she's lied about that."

"The miles leave plenty of space hanging between reality
and fantasy." Piper turned the apple around, taking another bite.
"What kind of lies did she tell?"

Evelyn filled her in. "Embellishing to a reunion committee
to save face is bad enough, but I hate that she lied to me. To us.
There's no reason for it."

"I don't know about that."

"Are you on her side?"

"Being a counselor I'm faced with all sorts of motives and reasons people do things. They'll go to great lengths to maintain their
public persona, and who they are in public versus who they are in
private can be very different. Occasionally the facade drops—or is
broken—and it can be unsettling for the person involved *and* for
those who witness it."

"But she doesn't have to pretend around us. Peerbaugh Place
is not a judgmental place. We're not judgmental people."

Piper hesitated a moment. "Aren't we? Isn't everybody?
Don't we judge each other every time we meet? First impressions, fourth, tenth . . . we are constantly making assessments
about who the other person is, whether we agree with them,
and especially, whether we like them. And right or wrong,
Lucinda believes we will like her more if she's an international,
rich model who's merely in transition between one caviar
moment and the next."

"But that's silly."

"Not to her."

Evelyn looked around the cozy kitchen. Its warmth epitomized the residents of Peerbaugh Place. Until now. "Maybe I'm most bothered because we're heart-on-our-sleeves kind of women. We don't pretend to be something we're not."

"Wanna bet?"

"I don't—"

"We are not without secrets, Evelyn. What about Gail pretending she worked for a big corporation when she'd gotten fired and was working at Burger Madness? We didn't even know she was married with a child for ages. Or Heddy who didn't let on that she'd lost her savings to a con man?"

Evelyn had handily forgotten those facts. "But they're friends now. Sisters."

"Because we hung in there and got to know them. Because they learned to trust us enough to let us see their true selves— flaws and all."

Evelyn felt a twinge of regret. She'd wasted an entire day pouncing on Lucinda's secrets as if by catching her in a lie she'd win a prize. "Do you think Lucinda will ever trust us enough to tell us the whole truth?"

"That's probably up to us," Piper said.

Oh dear. "What's that thing Mae did the other day?" Evelyn made a twirling motion by her head.

Piper laughed. "Rewind! Rewind!"

"And erase!"

Piper winked at her. "Consider it done, sister."

∙ ∙ ∙

In spite of her words to Evelyn about how they should be nice to Lucinda and earn her trust, after hearing about this latest slice of her character Piper was even more adamant that Lucinda *not* get involved with her father. Was she being unfairly judgmental? or merely discerning?

And maybe none of it was necessary. Piper had been a very good girl and had not asked her dad about his Friday night date. Maybe he'd decided on his own not to go out with Lucinda again.

It was time to find out. After changing clothes, she headed for her father's apartment.

After she knocked she heard a muffled, emotional "Come in."

She quickly opened the door and found him on the couch in the living room, clutching a pillow. He was crying.

"Dad?"

He blew his nose, talking behind the tissue. "Hey, don't mind me. I'm just having a little visit with your mother and she got me crying."

Piper didn't understand at first—until she saw her mother's letters littering the coffee table and the couch beside him. One balanced on his lap. She moved a few of them and sat nearby. "We really should have these bound. They are her legacy."

"They are my lifeline." He stuffed the tissue in his shirt pocket and sighed deeply. "She left a hole in me. I know good can come from bad. But I can't see the good in this."

Piper scooted close and hugged him. She took the letter from his lap. "This is her last one, isn't it?"

"It's the one I always go back to, the one that gives me the most hope. It reveals such an eloquence of the soul." He slumped into the couch, closing his eyes. "Read it aloud."

Piper hoped she could do this without bawling, but took comfort in the fact that if she did, it was acceptable. She and her father had shared many a tear. . . .

She cleared her throat and read:

"I've been thinking of heaven a lot lately. Don't worry. I haven't given up. The doctors say I'll be fine. And who am I to argue with them? I feel fine. And what does it hurt to think about heaven even when we're healthy. Especially if we're healthy. Too many people wait too long. Heaven and eternity are too important to handle in a crash course. Besides, it's fun."

Piper's father chuckled. "Only your mother . . ."
Piper continued.

"Sometimes I look at you and our daughter, and my breath leaves me (in a good way!). Why did God give me such blessings? To be single and find a soul mate. To be childless and be given the gift of this child—now a lovely, godly woman . . . I have everything I need—and more. The good thing about this illness is that I'm beginning to see God in every moment. In the way you chop green peppers with the intensity of a surgeon, to the way Piper bops in and out, forever young and full of life. And hope.

"Having just given you much credit for my happiness, I now must take a bit of it away to tell you that the one I rest my hope in is not you. And not our daughter. It's Jesus. My hope lies in Him and in His promises. To think of spending eternity in His presence, in a place He's told us is even better than here.

"I often look at the pictures we took on our RV trips. Mountains, brooks, wheat fields, layers and layers of fall trees going on forever. The tug of the ocean on my legs as we waded, the coolness of the boulder we sat on during our picnic. The smell of mown hay, salt air, pine, burning leaves. And that's just nature. That doesn't even take into account the people we met.

"How many times did we comment on the delightful accents we heard during our travels? Maine, Georgia, Texas, Minnesota. Uff-da, y'all, and a-yup. Everywhere we went people made us smile, made us love them just because they were different. And yet so much the same.

"And the food! Crab cakes, barbecue ribs, lefse, dumplings, kolaches. No wonder we gained weight!

"All this to say, dear husband, that God has promised us even more in heaven. More natural beauty, more lovely voices, more fabulous food. Why, it will take eternity just to drink it all in!

"But most of all, He'll be there, delighting in our delight. How I ache to sit at His feet and listen and absorb and love . . . and one day you'll be there too. And Piper. All those I love who believe in Him. I take such comfort in that. Though I might go first, just know that with every sunset here there is a sunrise there. When the time comes I'll save you a place, dear one. What a reunion we'll have! Lord, Jesus! What a day!"

Piper set the letter down. She hadn't noticed when the tears had started, but was not surprised to find them present.

"It's like a prayer," her father said.

Piper leaned against his shoulder. He opened his arm and let her in.

Amen.

•   •   •

Piper looked up from the pan of browning meat. "Mom was right. You *do* dice like a surgeon. Quite the intense brow line going on."

Her father scrunched his forehead, making deeper rows. "Really?"

"Absolutely."

She thought of her mother's letter. "Do I bop?"

"What?"

"Mom said I bopped in and out. Do I?"

"Absolutely." He slid the green pepper into the burrito meat. "I'm thinking of taking cooking classes again."

Piper perked up. "Evelyn mentioned that. I think it's great.

You need to get out." As soon as she said it . . . "I mean, with Evelyn. Cooking. Something like that."

He nodded a few times, then said. "But not with Lucinda. Not something like that?"

"You can do whatever you want. You're a big boy."

"Yes I am and yes I can."

She checked his face. He was smiling.

"Oh pooh."

He laughed. "You want to know about my date with Lucinda, don't you?"

"Only if you want to tell."

"In that case . . ."

"Dad!"

He started chopping onion. "Lucinda is a very interesting woman."

"And?"

"I won't be going out with her again."

Piper looked to the ceiling. "Thank You, Jesus!"

"Piper!"

"Sorry."

"You dislike her that much?"

"Not dislike." She hunted for the right words. "I don't think you're a good match, that's all. Two people can be nice in their own right but simply not a match, can't they?"

"Of course."

She stirred the meat twice around the pan. "So why *aren't* you going out with Lucinda again?"

"You want me to gossip?"

"I want you to share. There's a difference."

"Hmm." He seemed unconvinced so she was surprised when he said more. "She's very insecure, isn't she?"

Audacious was the word Piper would have chosen. "Why do you say that?"

"On our date I think she embellished a few things. About her life."

Piper let out a laugh. "I'm afraid she's the queen of embellishment, the empress of exaggeration, the princess of stretching the truth."

"Now who's exaggerating?"

Piper felt her face redden. To elaborate on Lucinda's faults would be fun, but she'd gone far enough. "I'm glad you're not going out with her again."

He poured the onions in the pan. "I'm glad we agree, but you have to know, Piper-girl, someday there might be a woman I *do* like. Even love."

She could handle that.

•   •   •

The phone rang as Piper and her dad were clearing the table. "Oh, hi, Evelyn." Wayne leaned against the counter as he listened. "The garbage disposal? . . . Oh, that's too bad. . . . Sure. No problem. I'll be right over."

He hung up. "Evelyn's garbage disposal stopped working. I'm going over to fix it."

"She probably just needs to push the red reset button on the bottom of it," Piper said.

He put his dishes on the counter. "Maybe. Just leave the dishes. I'll do them when I get back." He headed for the coatrack.

"Why don't you call and tell her to try—" She stopped herself and a memory came flooding back. One of a previous clogged disposal, of Evelyn pushing the red button.

"What?" he asked.

"Nothing."

Her father dangled his keys. "I'll be right back. Like I said, leave the dishes. Relax awhile."

He left. Piper laughed as her father's words came back to her: *"Someday there might be a woman I do like. Even love."*

She washed the dishes and thought of the possibilities.

•　•　•

I can't believe I did that!

Sure it was true Evelyn hadn't remembered about the red reset button until she had the phone in her hand, ready to call Wayne. But she hadn't dialed *yet*. She could have hung up and taken care of the problem herself.

But what was the fun in that?

The buzzer on the oven went off. She checked the cinnamon-apple bundt cake. Perfect. The smell created the perfect ambiance. Nothing like the taste of warm cake—did she have any ice cream in the freezer?—to soften a man's heart.

Soften a man's heart? Evelyn, what are you up to?

Plenty. Hopefully. God forgive her. And help her.

•　•　•

Lucinda walked in the kitchen to find Wayne and Evelyn sitting at the table eating cake. "Well, well. What do we have here?"

Wayne wiped a crumb from his lip. "I came over to fix the garbage disposal."

Evelyn popped out of her chair. "Want a piece of cake, Lucinda? It's probably still warm."

There was a hint of guilt in Evelyn's words. Interesting. "No, I'm fine. Just passing through. I left my copy of *Vogue* in the sunroom." The doorbell pulled her attention in the other direction. "I'll get it."

It was Tessa Klein. Lucinda had met her at Mae's party. She was wearing a kilt. She looked ridiculous.

"Hello, Lucinda. Is Evelyn at home?"

"Back in the kitchen. Go on in."

Lucinda was ready to head upstairs—forget the magazine—but Tessa stopped her. "Come with me. I have news about my costume party."

Costume party? Now *that* sounded interesting . . .

•   •   •

Evelyn tried not to giggle when she saw Tessa in her kilt. But there was something disconcerting about a kilt worn with Hush Puppies.

"Well, hello, Wayne," Tessa said. Her attention was immediately distracted. "Is that cinnamon-apple cake?"

"Want a piece?"

"Of course. Coffee too if you have it."

Evelyn stood. "I thought you'd converted to tea?"

"I'm wearing a kilt. I feel like coffee."

Evelyn laughed. "Coffee coming up."

Tessa took a seat across from Wayne and patted the remaining place. "Sit, Lucinda. Sit and listen to my idea."

As usual, Tessa took over the room. "As Evelyn may have told you, I am starting a Sister Circle Network for women around the world. Getting them into the loving support of a Sister Circle, helping them get medical care, an education, books. The Bible, of course."

"That sounds wonderful, Tessa," Wayne said. "Evelyn did mention it. We've been praying about it in my men's group."

Lucinda laughed. "Men praying about women? Now that's a miracle."

Tessa scathed her with a look. "Mine is an equal-opportunity prayer request. I'll take any prayers I can get." She lowered her chin. "Even yours, Lucinda."

"Don't hold your breath."

Tessa's right eyebrow rose and Evelyn waited for the ax to fall. Tessa may have been tiny, but her passion for the Lord was mighty. Too mighty sometimes.

Tessa's chest went up and down. Twice. Then she turned away from Lucinda. "Anyway . . . I have an idea about how to kick it off. I want to have a costume party with an international theme."

"That sounds fun," Evelyn said.

"You can wear your kilt," Lucinda said. Her voice was sarcastic.

"I could, but my best ensemble is yet to come. I've been saving it for a special occasion."

"This would be the time," Evelyn said. She gave Tessa a piece of cake and her coffee.

"This would be a fund-raiser?" Wayne asked.

"Thank you, and yes. I need to raise money to hire staff, cover printing and distribution costs, travel, plus all the necessities we hope to offer the women to make their lives better. Which is where you all come in."

"Here it comes," Lucinda said.

Tessa ignored her completely. "I need your help in coming up with unique ways to open people's pocketbooks. An auction perhaps? Or a raffle?"

"Those are hardly unique," Lucinda said.

Tessa's head turned slowly in her direction. "Then come up with something better."

•   •   •

Lucinda had *not* had any better fund-raising ideas, and the tension between her and Tessa did not lessen. Evelyn kept wishing Lucinda would remember her magazine, get it, and go away. Rude thoughts she couldn't seem to shake.

The tension was somewhat lessened when Piper showed up—kidding her father about abandoning her in his apartment as he'd run off to help Evelyn. Soon after that, Wayne said his good-byes, and finally—finally—Lucinda went upstairs. Piper said her good nights and followed.

Leaving Evelyn alone with Tessa.

"More coffee?" Evelyn asked.

Tessa covered her cup. "No thanks. But what I do want is information."

"About what?"

"About when this romance started between you and Wayne."

"What?"

"And how is that Lucinda woman involved? It's not fair for you to have a love triangle at Peerbaugh Place and not keep me informed."

"It's not a love triangle. Lucinda *did* go out with Wayne once, but I haven't. He was merely over here fixing the garbage—"

"Garbage. Exactly. That's what you're telling me. Garbage."

Evelyn poured herself more coffee even though she didn't want it. "There's nothing between us." *Yet.*

"I may be old but I'm not blind."

"Really. I mean it." She returned the coffeepot to its place.

Tessa pushed her chair back and stood. "Whatever you say."

"Tessa . . ."

She headed for the door. "If you don't want to share with me . . ."

"There's nothing to—"

Tessa moved to face her. She reached up, took her chin, and squeezed. "I approve, Evelyn. Just thought you ought to know that."

Well, then.

Dear children, let us stop just saying we love each other;

let us really show it by our actions.

1 JOHN 3:18

*E*velyn headed down to the kitchen, determined to do better. It had been five days since she'd found out the truth about Lucinda's lies and vowed to earn her trust.

Easier said than done.

No matter what Evelyn did, no matter what she'd said since then, Lucinda had been polite but standoffish. Was her behavior tied to catching—finding—Wayne eating cake in the kitchen with Evelyn? And why did Evelyn feel a sort of smugness, wanting the answer to that question to be yes?

Some Christian sister you are, Evelyn Peerbaugh.

That's why today, Sunday morning, Evelyn was going to pull out all the stops. Christ's love would ooze out of her, Lucinda would open up and share, they'd have a true sister chat, and everything would be better. Why, maybe Evelyn would even have a chance to tell Lucinda about Jesus. Wouldn't that be perfect?

Dream on.

●   ●   ●

The breakfast casserole was in the oven. Evelyn stood before Lucinda's bedroom door, ready to knock. Wake her up. On a Sunday morning when she usually slept late.

Oh dear.

Margaret came into the hall dressed for church. She headed to Piper's open door. "Piper, do you have a pair of hose I could borrow; mine have a—"

She saw Evelyn, hand poised to knock. She took a few steps toward her, whispering. "Evelyn, what are you doing?"

Piper appeared in her doorway. Her face also registered shock.

Goodness. They were acting like they'd caught her setting a bomb outside Lucinda's door.

Not exactly. But if you knock, there may be another kind of explosion.

Evelyn tiptoed away from the door to speak to them. "I'm going to invite Lucinda to join us at church. I've made a French toast casserole to make it special."

"We've invited her before," Piper said. "She's made it clear she's not interested."

"So we should stop asking?" Evelyn said. She leaned closer to whisper. "Remember when we talked about gaining her trust?"

Suddenly, Lucinda's door flew open. "*What* is going on out here? Can't a woman sleep late one day of the week?"

Though it took a moment for Evelyn's heart to return to its proper rhythm, the seriousness of the moment was broken because of Lucinda's appearance. Her hair was in a zebra turban, her pajamas were yellow flannel with orange duckies on them, there were odd pieces of paper stuck around the outer corners of her eyes, and a fuchsia sleep mask—complete with black lace— was pushed onto her forehead.

Evelyn looked at Margaret and Piper, whose mouths were agape. Then Piper started laughing. It was contagious.

Except for Lucinda. "What?" she asked.

All they could do was point at her. She looked down, and Evelyn could tell that a decision was being made whether to be huffy or go along. Evelyn only had time for the quickest of prayers: *Please, God . . .*

Lucinda looked up and straightened her shoulders. "The ensemble is nothing without my fuzzy slippers."

Piper covered her eyes. "Please no! I don't think we can take any more."

"You're just jealous of my duckies," Lucinda said.

Evelyn headed for the stairs. "Come join us for breakfast. I've made a French toast casserole."

She hesitated. "Is coffee ready?"

"Hazelnut creme."

Lucinda touched her turban. "It will be a while. I need to put my face on."

Evelyn checked her watch. "There's twenty minutes until the timer rings . . ."

"I'll see what I can do."

Her door closed, and the three other tenants of Peerbaugh Place exchanged a thumbs-up.

•   •   •

Lucinda came to breakfast wearing jeans and a red sweater. Evelyn wished she'd thought to ask her to join them for church while they were up in the hall. Not being dressed properly would be too easy of an excuse. Yet, if they gave her time to change . . . ?

The breakfast was delightful, the mood light. Margaret entertained them with talk about the cute things her second graders had done lately, Piper added the antics of high schoolers, and Lucinda joined in with some floral horror stories. It was a good start—a very good start.

When Margaret excused herself to finish getting ready, Piper was the one who slipped the invitation in. "Why don't you join us at church this morning, Lucinda? We'd love to have you and since you're up and—"

Lucinda shook her head and swept a hand to encompass both of them. "You're ready. I'm not dressed."

"Just exchange the jeans for khakis and you're set. People wear most anything."

"But not jeans."

Red flag. Piper continued. "Some people do wear jeans, but usually women of your age—"

Lucinda crossed her arms. "My age?"

"Mature women."

"Mature—?"

"Grown women?" Piper's face pulled in an odd expression.

Evelyn was no help. She had no idea how they could get out of this one.

Just then Margaret came back. "You'll be happy to know I cleaned the bathroom for you, Lucinda. All spick-and-span."

Lucinda glared at her. "So I'm a slob now, am I?"

Margaret scanned their faces, totally confused. "I didn't mean . . . I just meant . . ."

Lucinda pushed her chair back. "I've had just about enough of your Pollyanna act, Margaret. I've seen your room. I've witnessed your obsession to have everything in excruciating order."

"Lucinda!" Piper said. "That's not nice."

Margaret sat down, straightened the salt and pepper shakers into a neat line, then, realizing what she was doing, withdrew her hand. "I don't know what to say."

"Don't say anything. Or do anything. I'm sorry that my mess

has offended you, but be assured you won't need to pick up after me anymore."

"I was just trying to help."

"Just trying to impose your standards on me."

"Come on, ladies," Evelyn said. "There's always a time of adjustment, but there's no need to get nasty—"

"Why didn't you just say something to me?" Lucinda asked Margaret. "Why did you choose to show me up by cleaning *for* me?"

"I wasn't showing—"

"You were. You say you're a Christian, but where's your Christian tolerance? love? You're always making yourself out to be better than everyone else."

Margaret put a hand to her mouth. "Oh . . . my. I didn't realize."

Lucinda walked toward the door. "I'd clean up my plates, but why should I when we have Miss Perfect living here?" She left the room.

Evelyn could hear Margaret's breathing. Her hands were flat on the table. "What just happened?" the girl asked.

Evelyn patted her hand. "Obviously there are issues here beyond a clean bathroom."

"And it started before you came back in the room," Piper said. "We asked Lucinda to come with us to church; then suddenly she's taking offense to comments about her age." She looked at Evelyn. "What's a better term than 'mature woman'?"

"You called her that?" Margaret said.

Piper tossed her hands in the air. "I can't win. You'd better lock my lips and set me in a corner."

"Now you sound like Mae," Evelyn said.

Piper took her dishes to the sink. "I wish Mae *had* been here. She would have known exactly what to call someone Lucinda's age."

Evelyn thought a moment. "A hot mama?"

Piper laughed.

Margaret did not. Her forehead was furrowed. Evelyn shook a finger at her. "It's inevitable we're going to bug each other around here once in a while. Don't let Lucinda get to you."

Margaret let out a sarcastic laugh. "But she should. And she did. When the bathroom first bothered me, I should have said something. I *did* act 'better than.' I'm chasing her off just like I chased Bobby away."

Evelyn didn't know what to say. Margaret *was* a little obsessive in her ways.

Suddenly, Margaret knocked a hand into the salt and pepper shakers, making one go left, the other go right. She yanked a few napkins askew in their holder and pulled a handful of toothpicks out of their cup, scattering them on the lazy Susan. Then she sat back, folding her arms across her chest. "There," she said.

Piper and Evelyn looked at each other. "What are you doing?"

Margaret pushed back from the table and stood with a determined strength in her posture. "I have just proved that I can embrace imperfection." With that, she pivoted and left the kitchen.

Piper and Evelyn held in their laughter as long as they could. Yes, indeed, life was never dull at Peerbaugh Place.

●　　●　　●

After her wonderful phone conversation with Ted, Mae had been praying all week for Starr to see the light, come to the Lord, and snap out of it—in no particular order.

And today being Sunday was the perfect time for her daughter to join them at church. If Starr would only sit herself down in a pew, surely some God stuff would rub off. And hopefully stick.

At least that was Mae's plan.

Mae went to knock on Starr's bedroom door, but stopped because she heard sounds inside. A keyboard. "Starr? You up?"

"I'm working, Mother."

"But it's Sunday."

"So it is. What do you want?"

Mae hated having conversations through a closed door.
"Come down for breakfast."

"I'm not hungry."

Arghhh! "But we'd love to have your gracious presence, honey
bunny."

"Stop clenching your teeth, Mother."

Mae hit a fist on the door. Once. "Then open this thing!"

Starr appeared at the door. "You thumped?"

"I'm making mountain mash. Your favorite."

"And you're doing this because you want me to . . . ?"

Mae did a quick turn, flipping her hair. "Fine. More for me."

Starr groaned. "Coming, Mother."

•   •   •

Collier opened the Sunday paper and glanced at the stove.
"Mmm. Mountain mash? What are you up to, wifey?"

She heard Starr's feet on the stairs. She answered him with
a whisper. "Bribery!"

"It won't work," he whispered back.

Starr entered the room. "What won't work?"

Collier was the epitome of nonchalance. He lifted the paper.
"Your mother helping me with the crossword puzzle. She's
hopeless."

Mae licked cinnamon off her finger. "What's the seven-
letter name of a man who's going to get chili powder in his
oatmeal?"

Starr poured herself a cup of tea. "Ted was a fanatic about
crossword puzzles. On Sundays he used to do two of them."

"Used to?" Mae asked.

"Used to," Starr said, taking a seat. "Ever since Jesus took over his Sunday mornings he's had no time for fun. Not when church is calling."

"Church can be fun, honey," Mae said.

"Oh yeah. A laugh a minute."

Collier looked over his glasses. "I think you're confusing church with a comedy club. You don't go to church to be entertained; you go to worship."

Starr made a Shirley Temple–pouty face. "Oh. Right. We must be serious."

"We must be joyous," Mae said as she cut up an apple. "And Pastor Parsons—"

"Your pastor is named *parson*?"

Mae pointed the paring knife at her. "See? Isn't that funny?"

"Ha-ha."

"Anyway, as I was saying . . . Pastor Parsons can be very funny." She looked at Collier. "Remember when he told the story about seminary when his professor got a case of the giggles while he was trying to teach Leviticus?"

Collier chuckled. "Something about washing goats' legs and cubits?"

"Something like that." Mae glanced at Starr. They were losing her. "It *was* funny."

"Sorry I missed it."

Sarcastic or not, it was an opening Mae was glad to take. "You don't have to miss it, honey. Come with us today. We'll have a nice breakfast, do church together, and even go out to lunch afterward if you want."

"I have work to do."

"Forget lunch then."

Starr found the funny papers. "I need to be here."

Somehow seeing Starr choose the comics section—meaning she had time for fun here but not at church—Mae slammed the knife on the counter. "What you need, young lady, is church!

And God! And Jesus! You need to snap out of this selfish pity party you're having and see that your dear fiancé is right on and you're way off. He's got his life on the right track and you're hurling toward a cliff. And only Jesus can save you from yourself!"

Collier's mouth was open. Starr's mouth was closed. Tight. Mae watched as her daughter calmly folded the comic section into fourths, stood, put it under her arm, and took up her tea.

"If you'll excuse me. I believe I'll read my paper on the porch."

She grabbed her jacket and left the room. The next thing Mae heard was the front door clicking shut.

"Oops."

Collier shook his head. "Mae, Mae, Mae . . ."

She covered her face with her hands. "What did I just do? Where did that come from?"

"Your heart."

"I think you're mistaken."

"No, I'm not. It definitely came from your heart. Unfortunately, your mind and your common sense were disengaged at the time. Hence, the absence of tact?"

Mae peeked through her fingers. "I blew it, didn't I?"

Collier came to her side and hugged her. "Fortunately for you—fortunately for all of us—God can't be stopped by our less than stellar methods of sharing our faith. You tried. Your intentions were sincere. God appreciates that."

"I hope so." She looked toward the porch. "It's got to be chilly out there."

He snickered. "You got that right."

"Do you think she'll come with us if I go apologize?"

Collier snapped the paper, back to front. "Not a chance."

• • •

Starr fumed. It took a full minute of sitting on the porch swing before she realized the comic section was becoming imbedded in her rib cage. She set it on the swing and let the breeze take it away.

Good riddance.

How dare her mother talk to her that way, as if she were some heathen in need of saving? She was a good person. Just because she didn't feel the need to be all mushy-gushy about God didn't mean she didn't believe He existed. He was out there. Somewhere. When—if—she needed Him. She just didn't so happen to need Him now. And she certainly didn't need to go to any building to *commune* with His higher power. How hippie-ish could you get?

She hated getting bombarded from all sides. Ted had called three times this week. And with the constant pressure from her mother . . .

It was nearly intolerable.

Starr looked up when the door to Peerbaugh Place opened. Margaret, Evelyn, and Piper came out. They saw her and waved. Piper came across the street while the other two women chatted and went to Evelyn's car.

"Morning, Piper."

Piper retrieved the comic section that had landed on the bottom step. "Hey, you. Isn't it a little nippy to be reading the paper outside?"

Starr shrugged and accepted the paper back. "It's not bad."

Piper eyed her a moment. "Care to join us? We're heading to church." She grinned. "It's the fourth Sunday of the month—sprinkled donut day."

Was it the grin that clinched it? Or the thought of donuts with sprinkles? Starr stood. "Sure. Why not? Give me two minutes." She hurried inside and ran up the stairs.

Her mother came out of the kitchen. "Where you going so fast, honey?"

Starr leaned over the railing and called down to her. "I'm going to church, Mother."

Her mother's face registered shock. "Well . . . that's wonderful!"

Now, to twist the knife . . . "I'm going with Piper."

So there.

• • •

"There, there."

Mae stood in the kitchen and nuzzled into Collier's shoulder, rubbing her tears against his chest. "Why'd she have to be so mean?"

"You two have always had a tit-for-tat relationship, haven't you?"

She pulled back to look at him. "But that doesn't mean I like the tats."

"They *can* be mighty sharp. Maybe that's something you should remember. At least she's going to church. That *is* the goal, isn't it?"

She pushed him away. "Oh you. Making sense and all that." She buttoned his top shirt button. "You can be quite annoying, Mr. Husband."

He unbuttoned it, giving himself air. "Only as needed, wifey. Only as needed."

• • •

If Starr's going . . .

From her bedroom window, Lucinda had seen Piper cross the street to talk to Starr, and had heard her come back and say that Starr would be out in a minute. She was coming with them.

Go! Get ready. You've complained about being left out.

She ran to the closet, pulling the sweater over her head as she went. They'd said she could wear the sweater if only she changed out of her jeans, but no way did she want to present herself in church wearing something so mediocre. She ran her fingers along the hangers then pulled out a navy coatdress. When she sat, it had a tendency to slip open a bit, giving her the chance to show off her beautiful legs.

Maybe Wayne will be there . . .

She just finished putting it on when she heard voices. She hurried to the window and saw Starr running across the street. One, two, three, four car doors.

But wait!

The engine roared to life.

I wanted to come!

The car pulled out of the driveway.

And away.

They left without me!

She slumped onto the bed. The coatdress flung to either side, completely open.

But there was no one there to see.

●   ●   ●

Starr sat in the pew between Piper and Evelyn, knowing she had a chip on her shoulder. She didn't care. If God wanted the chip to be gone, He'd have to be the one to knock it off. If He wasn't up to the challenge, so be it.

She was tired of hearing reports of a loving God who wanted to change her life. He'd already changed it. He'd made her move away from the man she loved and was preventing her from being happy. Ted questioning their living arrangement. Piper questioning the subject matter of the books she edited. They were threatening her very life, wanting her to change everything she knew to follow some unseen God who only wanted to brainwash those ignorant enough to follow Him.

It was pitiful. And more than a little annoying.

Piper nudged her. "You can unfold your arms, Starr. Relax. Enjoy yourself."

She thought of her mother's insistence that church could be fun. "I'll keep them where they are, thank you. Got to be on the defensive, you know."

Piper rolled her eyes. "Fine. Be that way. But you do realize you're putting God on the offensive. And who's going to win that battle, eh?"

Starr did not unclench her arms. She wasn't afraid of God.

She suffered a shiver.

The prelude started. The next time she noticed, her arms were at her sides. She let them lie.

•　　•　　•

Lucinda was back in her sweater and jeans. She added a jacket and afghan and went out on the balcony off her bedroom. To pout.

A boat of a car came down the street, so slow a jogger could have passed it. Suddenly it swerved and pulled up front. Tessa got out and looked up in Lucinda's direction. "My, my, a sentry at the gate. I thought I saw you up there."

"Hi, Tessa." *Bye, Tessa.*

The woman came around the car and headed up the walk. She was wearing a German dirndl skirt and a white peasant blouse, the majority of which was blessedly covered by a trench coat. She positioned herself directly below Lucinda. "Why aren't you in church with the rest of them?"

"Why aren't you?"

"I go early. I'm done for the day."

"Got it out of the way, huh?"

"Don't be flip."

Don't be nosy. "Is there something I can help you with, Tessa?"

"Actually, I think you've done *your* duty. I *was* coming by, but then saw the flash of your red sweater through the trees. Thought it was a big bird at first."

"Just me. What duty are you talking about?"

Tessa pinched her lower lip. She shook her head. "You're looking mighty lonely up there."

"Alone. Not lonely."

"So you say. Which leads me back to my first question. Why aren't you in church with the others?"

"I'm not into church."

"Why ever not?"

Somehow Lucinda had expected a "you should be." Not the question of why. "I like my Sunday mornings free."

"And lonely."

"Alone."

"So you say."

This wasn't getting anywhere.

"When the ladies get home for lunch, I'll tell them you stopped by."

Tessa put a hand to her mouth. "Goodness gracious, what's gotten into my brain? They won't be home for quite a while. They like to go out to eat. I knew that." She laughed and raised her hands to the sky. "Lord above, You're going to stop me one way or another, aren't You?"

"Stop you from what?"

"From sharing something that shouldn't be shared." She shook her head quickly as if ridding herself of the thought. Tessa moved on. "Since they're not around, you're going to be alone for lunch, aren't you?"

She didn't like the sound of that. "Like I said, I like being alone."

"You want to come eat with me and my family? I left them heading toward Ruby's for brunch. I'm sure they haven't even been seated yet."

Lucinda did not allow herself to be touched. "No thank you. I'm fine. Really."

Tessa's dark eyes gave Lucinda a good stare. "I'll leave you then. But I'll leave you with a secret."

Lucinda braced herself. "What's that?"

"I know a way to never be lonely. Not even when we're alone. Does that interest you?"

"Sure . . ."

Tessa put on a smug smile and turned. "Have a nice morning."

"Tessa! Aren't you going to tell me what it is?"

"'Seek and ye shall find,' Lucinda." She waved good-bye, got in her car, and drove away.

Exasperating woman. Absolutely exasperating.

•   •   •

As soon as Tessa turned the corner heading away from Peerbaugh Place, she shouted to the Lord, filling the car with her voice. "Thank You for saving me from the pits of temptation, Father God. Thank You for placing Lucinda as a guard to the door, preventing me from going inside to wait for Evelyn and Piper. Thank You for *not* letting me spill the beans. Forgive my weakness and help me keep my mouth shut."

There. She felt better.

She'd come distressingly close to blowing everything. After spotting a certain someone at church this morning, she'd found herself in a frenzy and had begged off brunch with her family. She'd asked to be taken home so she could get in her own car and drive to Peerbaugh Place to ring out the news.

She'd started to doubt it was the right thing to do in the last few blocks, causing her rush to slow to a crawl as she prayed for direction. And she'd gotten it. In the unlikely form of Lucinda sitting on her balcony.

Obviously, God didn't want her blabbing about what she'd seen. So—though it was harder than drinking one cup of coffee instead of two—she would keep quiet. For once in Tessa Klein's seventy-six years she'd lock her lips and let God handle the telling. Or not telling.

She hoped He appreciated her sacrifice.

* * *

Okay. This isn't fair at all. Who called the pastor and told him I was coming?

Evelyn touched Starr's arm. "You okay?"

"I'm fine." *Fine* came out in two syllables. But she wasn't fine. Every verse was directed at her. Even the pastor's eyes seemed to be locked on hers. It was a conspiracy.

"'Blessed are those who have a tender conscience, but the stubborn are headed for serious trouble.'"

Is that a threat?

"'You stubborn, faithless people! How long must I be with you until you believe? How long must I put up with you?'"

I don't know. How about forever?

"'For these people are stubborn rebels who refuse to pay any attention to the Lord's instructions. They tell the prophets, "Shut up! We don't want any more of your reports." They say, "Don't tell us the truth. Tell us nice things. Tell us lies. Forget all this gloom. We have heard more than enough about your 'Holy One of Israel.' We are tired of listening to what He has to say."'"

Ditto. Ditto. Ditto.

She was just getting her dander up and was ready to pop to

her feet and proclaim, "I object!" when the pastor hit her with another verse.

"'Fear of the Lord is the beginning of knowledge. Only fools despise wisdom and discipline.'"

Fool? She was not a fool. And she already valued knowledge and wisdom and discipline. Therefore . . .

Did she need to fear the Lord?

But I'm not afraid of anything.

As soon as the thought materialized, the pastor had a counter. As if he'd heard . . . "The word *fear* doesn't mean being afraid," he said to her. "For repeatedly God tells us to 'fear not.' This kind of fear means we need to respect the Lord. Acknowledge who He is, what He's offering us, and what He expects of us."

Expects of us. Starr nodded. *Oh yes, here's the catch.*

"He expects—He *wants* our love—because He loved us first. And if we trust Him and surrender our stubbornness to Him He'll change our lives. He'll do amazing things we can't even imagine." He leaned toward Starr. "This isn't what I say; it's what He says. Listen to His promises!" He recited from memory. "'Look at the nations and be amazed! Watch and be astounded at what I will do! For I am doing something in your own day, something you wouldn't believe even if someone told you about it.' And this! 'By His mighty power at work within us, He is able to accomplish infinitely more than we would ever dare to ask or hope.' Isn't that exciting?"

Starr's throat tightened. It *was* exciting.

But then another voice beckoned. *Don't let them get to you! It's a trap to do things their way. Ted's way. Your mother's way. They're not right. They can't be. You want wisdom? Look around. Watch the world; then make your own choices. But don't get dragged into this emotional mumbo jumbo. Don't—*

Everyone was standing for the final hymn. She was glad for the distraction and used the time to regain her bearings.

Whew. That was close. Too close.

●   ●   ●

Margaret was pleased when Audra, Russell, and Summer invited her along for lunch in Jackson after church. What a delightful family. Audra was very blessed.

However, as was the case lately, whenever Margaret started feeling warm and fuzzy about a family, she was immediately assailed with thoughts of her breakup with Bobby and their family that would never be. Would she ever get over it?

They were just leaving the restaurant—Russell was in line at the cashier, waiting to pay—when Margaret spotted Bobby sitting in a corner booth with a friend from church.

He saw her.

After gathering her senses, she waved and managed a smile. He scowled and hid behind a menu.

Audra spotted the exchange. "That was rude. Who's that?"

Margaret bolted for the door.

Audra rushed after her, Summer in tow. Once outside, Audra asked, "Was that Bobby?"

Margaret reached the car first. She tried the door. It was locked. Russell had the keys.

Audra turned to Summer. "Go get the keys from Daddy, baby." Summer ran back inside. "Bobby could at least have waved at you."

Suddenly, Margaret feared Bobby could see her from inside. She tried the door again and again. *Open up! Let me hide!*

Summer came running back, the keys jangling.

Audra opened the door and Margaret slid inside. Before shutting the door Audra said, "He doesn't deserve you, Margaret."

True or not, that didn't change the fact that she still loved him.

11

God has not given us a spirit of fear and timidity,

but of power, love, and self-discipline.

So you must never be ashamed

to tell others about our Lord.

2 TIMOTHY 1:7-8

Two days were two days too many.

Mae couldn't take it anymore. She *had* to know what had happened to Starr at church on Sunday, but her dear daughter wouldn't tell her a thing. Something *had* to have happened, didn't it?

Mae kissed Collier on the top of his head. "Bye."

"Aren't you leaving for work a little early?"

"I'm making a pit stop across the street."

He smiled. "Evelyn always is good at gassing you up and checking you out for leaking air."

She slipped a fringed poncho over her head. "You know it's the only way I'll ever get to the winner's circle."

"I know." He slapped her on the behind. "Now git."

She headed out, but paused at the door. "But do remember, Mr. Husband, you're the only one who truly revs my engine."

It was fun leaving 'em with something to think about.

•   •   •

"Yoo-hoo? It's me."

Evelyn peered over the stair railing from the upstairs hall. She had a towel around her neck, her hair full of dye with the dry ends sticking out. "Come on up, I'm dying my hair. Just a few minutes to go."

"Oooh, some funky color, I hope." Mae took the stairs two at a time.

"Sorry to disappoint you. Same old boring brown." Evelyn returned to the sink in her bathroom. "I think it says that on the box."

Mae put the lid down on the commode and took a seat. "Maybe you should try something fun? Go red. Or blonde." She fluffed her own hair. "Blondes do have more fun, you know."

"Is that *your* real color?"

Mae pulled a hunk into her sight line. "I'm not sure. I've forgotten."

"How long have you been dying it?"

Mae thought a moment. "Remember doing the hustle?"

"I remember watching other people do the hustle."

"Around then."

"That's the seventies."

"Give or take. How about you?"

"Only since I started turning gray. About ten years I guess." She held the bottle out to Mae. "Since you're here . . . it's time to put the rest in, over all my hair. Can you do the back?"

"Sure. I'll squirt it on, but you mush it around—since you have the gloves."

"It's a deal."

Mae wasn't sure how she could segue from dying hair to God but she aimed to give it a shot. She saw in the mirror that Evelyn was studying her as she worked. "What's that look supposed to mean?"

"Shouldn't you be at the store?" Evelyn asked.

"The perks of being self-employed include being late—if need be."

"So what's the need that be?"

Their eyes locked in the mirror. "Starr. Church. I need to know what happened when she went with you Sunday."

"Why don't you ask her?"

"You think I haven't? She's the poster child for the World War II ad 'Loose Lips Sink Ships.' She isn't talking."

"I'm not sure I can be much help."

Mae sighed. She needed *something*. "Can you tell me if the earth moved for her? Was the sermon totally inspired? Did the music make her tear up?"

"Did I see an angel chorus gathering above her pew?"

"I'd settle for kazoos. Something. Anything to get her blood moving about God."

Evelyn's face showed she was trying to remember. "At one point during the sermon she *did* seem agitated. She kept squirming, and her breathing got loud enough for me to hear it."

"Oooh. A good sign."

"I asked if she was okay and she said, 'I'm fine-nah.' Just like that. 'Fine-nah.' Like she was peeved at me for asking."

"What had the pastor been talking about?"

Evelyn rolled her eyes. "If I'd known there was going to be a quiz I would have taken notes."

"Try to remember. It's important." Mae tossed the squeeze bottle in the trash. "There. Mush it around." She looked at her watch. "Five minutes?"

"Right," Evelyn said. She worked the dye onto every strand. The rubbing motion seemed to help her thought process because she soon brightened. "The sermon was about being stubborn and having to let go and have a proper fear of God."

"Stubbornness? Gracious gadfly. No wonder Starr seemed agitated. She is the most stubborn female I know."

"Are you sure about that?"

She mimicked Starr. "Fine-nah. She's the *second* most stubborn female."

"Just want to keep the facts straight." Evelyn looked at her watch again. "Hate to have you dye and run, but I have to be in the shower in three minutes or else I will have funky hair."

Mae headed for the stairs. "Thanks for your help, sister."

"What are you going to do? You're not going to confront her, are you?"

It *was* her first impulse but she didn't want to alarm Evelyn. Mae tapped her lip and pretended to consider something. "I think I'll let God handle the confronting."

Evelyn let out a breath. "Good. I think that's—"

"This time. Ta-ta."

● ● ●

Starr adjusted the telephone's hands-free headset on her ear. "What did you say, Carl?"

Carl, the other nonfiction editor at her publishing house repeated his words. "I said, 'Fear not. You'll get this manuscript whipped into shape in no time.'"

Fear not.

"I'm not afraid. I'm not!" She heard the frenzy in her voice.

"Hey, where'd that come from?"

Starr realized she'd gotten off track. "Sorry. I'm having a hard day."

A pause. "How are things with you and Ted?"

"Same ol', same ol'."

"Same ol', same ol' *good*? or bad?"

"Same ol', same ol' I'm in limbo land."

"Oh."

"You don't approve of what I'm doing?"

"Hey, I'm no one to give advice about anybody's personal life, but I do know that being stubborn is—"

"What did you call me?"

"*Sheesh.* You *are* having a hard day, aren't you?"

"I am not stubborn."

"Whatever you say."

"I'm not!"

"I bet you a hundred dollars your arms are crossed."

Starr looked down and uncrossed them. "They are not."

"Whatever you say."

"Stop saying that!"

"I'll call you later."

"But we aren't done."

"Bye, Starr." He hung up.

●　　●　　●

Mae didn't feel like going to lunch at Ruby's with her friends. Not today. She was too agitated about Starr. So she headed home for lunch. Where she'd see Starr. And probably get even more agitated.

Oh, well. Since when did Mae's actions make sense?

She came through the kitchen door to the sound of Collier saying, "Give it a rest, Starr. Stubborn is as stubborn does."

Stubborn? How odd. "Hello, you two. What's—?"

Starr set her feet, her cheeks red. "Stubborn? Where did you get that word? Who told you to say that word to me?"

Collier stood at the stove, next to a griddle of grilled-cheese sandwiches. His eyebrows dipped. "But I didn't say—"

"You did!" Starr tossed her hands in the air. "What's with everybody? Is it pounce-on-Starr week?"

Mae hung her poncho on the hook by the door. "What's got you so upset?"

"Life!" She fled to the front stairs. "Count me out for lunch. I'm not hungry."

Stomp, stomp, stomp, stomp . . . slam.

"Gracious grapevine, Collie. What did you do?"

"Told the truth—that's what I did." He checked the sandwiches. "I didn't expect you home for lunch."

"I didn't expect to be home. I just didn't feel up to small talk at Ruby's today."

"It appears we have an extra sandwich. You want Starr's?"

"Gladly. Want an apple or a banana?"

"Banana." He flipped the sandwiches. "Your daughter was acting extremely stupid. So I told her so."

"You told her she was stubborn."

"No, I didn't. I said, 'stupid is as stupid does.' Then she gets off on this 'stubborn' tangent . . ."

"You said that phrase but you put in *stubborn* for *stupid.* I heard you when I came in."

He looked into the air, as if trying to replay the last few minutes. "She *is* stubborn."

Mae had to laugh. God worked in mysterious ways. "At this rate, not for long."

•　　•　　•

The whole thing was absurd. She was not stub—

Starr looked down to see her arms crossed. "I give up!"

No, you don't! Stop that. Don't let them get to you. They're trying to take your power away by taking what makes you you away. Don't give in to them.

She leaned back against the chair in her bedroom and let a few breaths in, then out, bringing with them a new determination.

Everyone was wrong and she was right. What they called *stubborn-ness* she called *purpose* and *focus*. She knew what was what. That knowledge was an indication of intelligence and strength.

She picked up her laptop. Enough of this nonsense. It was time to get back to work. The world was waiting to learn about *How to Get More out of Your Man*.

Weren't they?

•   •   •

At the sound of Wayne's voice on the phone, Evelyn felt a tug in her midsection.

"Want a ride to cooking class tonight?"

She remembered back to the first cooking class she'd taken. Wayne and Wanda had picked her up. And so began their friend-ship. Now, Wanda was gone. . . .

"That would be great," she said. "Six thirty?"

"You got it. See you then."

Evelyn hung up and went back to her bill paying, but her mind detoured into the realms of what she should wear. Her green cable-knit sweater and her tweed skirt, or her brown pants with the leather vest?

Her decision was delayed when the phone rang a second time. Did Wayne . . . "Forget something?" she answered.

"Not that I know of. Fill me in." It was Herb.

Evelyn felt a different kind of tug in her midsection. "Oh. Sorry, Herb. I thought you were someone else."

"Happens all the time. Mel Gibson, right?"

"What?"

"You thought I was Mel Gibson. People are always confusing the two of us."

She laughed. "*Not* Mel Gibson." Dick Van Patten was a closer match.

"Don't tell Mel that. He'll be disappointed." He cleared his throat. "Would you like to go out tonight? Catch a movie?"

Her mind rushed with excuses, real and contrived. "I can't tonight, Herb. I have another commitment."

He didn't say anything for a moment. "Maybe later in the week?"

"Sure."

"Don't sound so enthused, Evelyn."

She tried to perk up her voice. "Sorry. I'm just tired. Later in the week would be fine."

Another pause. "I'll call you tomorrow then?"

"That would be great."

She hung up, her entire body heavy. She raked her fingers through her hair. "Ahhhhhh!"

"Tough phone call?"

Margaret stood in the entryway, home from teaching. She took off her jacket and hung it on the hall tree. Evelyn wasn't sure how to answer her. "That was Herb."

She came into the room and sat in the rocker across from the desk. "You two having an argument?"

"No, no. He was just asking me out on a date for tonight."

"Which normally makes you pull your hair and groan?"

It was an interesting observation. "It shouldn't, should it?"

Margaret rocked forward, then back. "Why do you want to break up with him?"

Evelyn was taken aback. "I don't."

Two more rocks.

"Do I?"

Margaret planted her feet, stopping the movement. "Why didn't you want to go out with him tonight?"

That, she could answer. "I couldn't. I'm going to a cooking class with Wayne."

Margaret started rocking again, eyeing her in a most disconcerting fashion. "Is it the class that made you say no, or the company?"

"I'm busy. Truly."

"Does Herb know you're taking a class with Wayne?"

"No . . ."

"Why not?"

"There's no reason for him to know. He doesn't know my entire sched—" She cut herself off. Actually, Herb *did* know her entire schedule. And she knew his.

"Could Herb join you?"

"No!" Why had her answer exploded so? "I mean, I suppose he could, but—"

"You don't want him to."

Evelyn felt her shoulders drop in defeat. "I don't want him to."

"Why? And be honest about your answer."

Evelyn straightened the pile of bills with her thumb and forefinger. "Would you like some tea?"

"No, thank you."

Evelyn started to get up. "Because I could really use a cup of chamomile right now and—"

"Just say it, Evelyn."

She sat back down. "Say what?"

Margaret could garner quite a look for a second-grade teacher.

"Fine!" Evelyn stood, but held onto the desk for support. "I don't want Herb to take cooking classes because I'm taking them with Wayne, whom I'm beginning to like way more than I should."

"More than you should? What do you mean by that?"

"You know . . ."

"I don't know. He's not married."

"Of course not, but—"

"Or otherwise engaged?"

"He did go out with Lucinda . . ."

Margaret waved a hand as if that didn't count. "Does he have a police record?"

"Margaret!"

"Are his teeth falling out or is he obsessed with reruns of *Hee Haw*?"

"Now you're being silly."

"Who's being silly?"

Evelyn landed on the couch. "This whole discussion is silly. Wayne isn't interested in me as a woman. We're just friends."

"But you'd like it to be more."

"Maybe."

"Evelyn . . ."

"Okay. Yes, I'd like it to be more. When he went out with Lucinda I was jealous."

"Gracious green-eyed monster!"

She smiled. "You're catching on to Mae's lingo mighty fast here, young lady."

Margaret shrugged. "So what are you going to do?"

"Do?"

"About Herb."

"Do I have to do anything? I told him I can't go out tonight."

"And had a conniption afterwards. That's not the sign of a healthy relationship."

Evelyn put a hand to her chest. "You want me to break up with him?"

"I want you to be fair to him. Treat him as you want to be treated. 'Do for others what you would like them to do for you.'"

"But . . ."

"Is there a problem with that?"

Actually . . . The truth came out in a rush. "I don't want to break up with Herb before I know if Wayne is interested in me—in me as a woman, not just a friend."

"You want to cover your bases."

"Well . . . yes."

"So it would be all right for Herb to date another woman at the same time he's dating you?"

"He could. We've never really had any agreement between the two of us that we couldn't."

"Didn't he come to the edge of proposing to you a few weeks ago?"

Oh dear.

Margaret moved next to her on the couch. "You can't hedge your bets when it comes to love, Evelyn. And you can't protect yourself from getting hurt—especially when your actions might hurt someone else. You have to let it all out in the open." She put a hand on Evelyn's back. "But even falling out of love must be done with love."

"How did you get to be so wise?"

Margaret's voice broke. "I loved—and was hurt."

It was Evelyn's turn to comfort. "I have got to be the most selfish woman in the world. Making you talk about love and relationships when you're suffering—"

"No," Margaret said. "I want to help. God never wastes a hurt. We're supposed to share our life lessons."

Evelyn looked on this woman seated beside her with new eyes. Up until now she'd only seen Margaret as a sweet girl, a tenant who was no trouble at all. A naive child who didn't know much about the ways of the world. How wrong she'd been. In many ways Margaret knew more about love at age twenty-two than Evelyn knew at fifty-eight.

And yet . . .

A slice of the past slid before her. A young man's face smiled at her, a dimple in his right cheek. Frank Albert Halvorson. The lovely boy she'd loved. And lost. *Remember me?* Frank seemed to say. *I was the love of your life. You were just about Margaret's age . . .*

Evelyn suddenly realized she had something to share,

something that might help this young woman know that Evelyn understood her pain. "I have loved twice in my life. And been hurt."

Margaret looked up. "Twice?"

Evelyn had only spoken of Frank to one other person—and it wasn't her husband, Aaron. About a year and a half ago, after she'd first opened her home to boarders, Piper had discovered the picture of the baby girl Evelyn had hidden in the drawer of an old dressing table in the attic. Only then, after over thirty years, had Evelyn shared her past. . . . Now it was time to do it again.

"Frank Halvorson and I were in college. And very much in love. We were planning to be married."

"What stopped you?"

"Frank was sent to Vietnam. I found out I was pregnant a month after he left. And then he was killed."

"Oh, Evelyn."

Evelyn had not expected tears, but she let them come. "Frank died within weeks of getting to Vietnam. I'd sent a letter telling him the news of the baby but the letter was returned. The news of my pregnancy and the news of his death crossed in the mail."

Margaret let out a puff of breath. "Oh. I'm so sorry." She got up and returned with a tissue.

Evelyn dabbed her eyes and laughed softly. "This is silly."

"No, it's not. It's a part of your life and you're not supposed to forget it; you're not supposed to look on it without feeling."

"Good. Because I *do* feel it deeply."

Margaret patted her back. "Do you know where your child is?"

"No. It was a closed adoption."

"You could find out."

Evelyn shook her head. "I don't want to do that. I won't do that to *her*. Intrude on her life to please myself. It wouldn't be right."

Margaret didn't argue.

Evelyn remembered the issue that had started all this. "I need to break up with Herb, don't I?"

"If you have feelings for Wayne, yes."

"But I don't know if Wayne has feelings for me."

"Which means you run the risk of having no man in your life."

"Bummer."

Margaret laughed. "Seems we've both been influenced by Mae's vocabulary."

"It *does* say it all, doesn't it?"

"Right on, sister."

•   •   •

Herb looked up from the paint he was mixing. "Oh, hi, Evelyn."

"Hi, Herb."

His eyes lingered a bit longer than necessary. "You ready to pick out the new color for your dining room? This one's pretty: Ocean Breezes."

She focused on the can of paint and shook her head.

He put the can down. "You didn't come here for paint, did you?"

She shook her head again but forced herself to look at him. "I'm sorry, Herb. I haven't been fair to you."

His eyes hardened the slightest bit . . . "In what way?"

"I . . ." *Just say it!* "I've been leading you on. I've been using you as a companion, as someone to go out with, as—"

"We have fun together."

She touched his hand, then withdrew hers. "We've had wonderful times together."

"Had."

"Yes. Had." She found a fresh breath. "You've said you want more from our relationship."

He snickered. "I want to marry you."

"But since I don't feel the same way, I don't think it's fair to keep you on a string."

Herb looked around the paint section. Even though they were alone, he lowered his voice. "Couldn't you learn to love me, Evelyn? Given time? More time?"

Yeah, Evelyn . . . couldn't you learn to love him? She was about to give in when the image of Wayne came to mind. And she found herself smiling inside . . . while on the outside she was frowning, on the edge of tears, as she gave up on a relationship that had sustained her for eight months. They'd had good times. They'd laughed. Yet had Herb ever made her smile in the same way the image of Wayne had just made her smile? Had Herb ever made her smile *inside*?

"I'm sorry, Herb. I do love you—as a dear, dear friend. I will always love you as—"

He picked up the opened can, sloshing blue paint over the side onto his hand. He flipped it back, spraying paint over the entire counter. "Don't do me any favors." He grabbed a towel. "If you'll excuse me, I have work to do."

●　　●　　●

Evelyn didn't come to the cemetery often. She knew Piper found comfort in visiting her mother's grave, but she'd never felt the need to visit Aaron's more than a couple times a year to bring new flower arrangements.

And she didn't visit Aaron now.

She sat on the bench in front of the grave of Wanda Wellington and immediately wanted to leave. Though the pain of losing Aaron would always be present, the pain of losing her dear friend was still fresh. Yet she didn't feel a need to talk to Aaron about her love life—not that he would have been patient enough to listen. But Wanda . . . Evelyn felt the need to let Wanda in on her plans. Woman to woman. Sister to sister.

Evelyn brushed some leaves off the bench and began her monologue. It came out in a rush of words. "Hi, Wanda. I just broke up with Herb, which you probably don't find very surprising because you always made comments about us being an odd pair, but you need to know why I did it." She took a breath and looked heavenward. The sky was an amazing blue. Set against the gold and rust of the trees, the day was striking. Clear.

As were Evelyn's thoughts.

She forced herself to slow down. The rest of what she had to say deserved time. "I think I'm falling in love with your husband." She paused, then realized she was waiting for an answer. She continued. "You have to know I didn't plan it, but you, of all people, know what a wonderful man he is." She hastened to add, "You also must know that he's made no designs on me. He's not encouraged me at all. He's still totally in love with you and has merely been a good friend. And I think I've been a good friend to him."

Evelyn sighed deeply. "But you know Wayne. He's charming, kind, funny, handsome, bright. What's not to love?" The memory of blue paint on Herb's hand returned. "Though I hated to hurt Herb, I know it was the right thing to do. And in a way, a burden has been lifted. But I'm also scared, Wanda. Except for the year between Aaron's death and me starting to date Herb, I've always had a man in my life. There's security in that. Always someone to go to dinner with. Always someone *there*. But now . . . if your husband *doesn't* reciprocate my feelings, I'm going to be left out in the cold and that's scary."

Speaking of . . . she was getting chilled. It was time to go. "So what do I want from you, Wanda?" She thought a moment. "If it's possible for you to pray for me up in heaven, will you do that? Your faith was always such an inspiration; I know you have the Father's ear. So if you have time, ask Him to guide me to do the right thing. If He wants me alone, I'll be alone. But if He wants me to be with Wayne . . . if that's the right thing. I ask for His blessing."

She got up to leave. There. She felt better now. She really did. There was nothing like getting the first wife's blessing.

* * *

Knowing how she spent her day, knowing her new attitude about Wayne . . . once Wayne picked her up for the cooking class, Evelyn found herself tongue-tied.

"You're quiet," he said. "Is there anything wrong?"

"Not a thing." *Everything's wrong! I've started looking at you in a new way. In a man-woman way. And it's messing up everything. I can't concentrate. All I'm doing is trying to think of ways to flirt with you. If only I was more like Lucinda . . .*

She heard him talking but had trouble concentrating on his words. *Focus, Evelyn, focus.* Finally, she zeroed in on what he was saying, only to find herself totally confused.

"And then Wanda went up to the man and said, 'Excuse me, sir, but do you have that in magenta?'" Wayne hit his hand against the steering wheel and laughed.

Evelyn tried to laugh too, but it was hard when all she'd heard was the punch line.

Wayne's laugh died a natural death. "You realize you have the advantage here," he said.

Seems like a disadvantage to me . . . "Why do you say that?"

"When I tell stories . . . you knew Wanda. I never met Aaron."

The late wife and the late husband. Considering the direction of her thoughts, it was appropriate to have their images brought front and center.

"Tell me about him," Wayne said.

Evelyn's mind swam with stories of their arguments, their money troubles, the weak, nonconfrontational person she used to be. And yet, maybe, since they were heading to a cooking class she could tell one story . . . "One time, I saw a recipe on TV for

Fontina Chicken. It looked like a glorious dish with sautéed mush-rooms and a special cheese spread over chicken breasts."

"Sounds wonderful."

"I thought so. So I copied it down, made a special trip to the store for the ingredients, and made it for dinner. It took a lot of time."

"I bet Aaron loved it."

She snickered. "Hardly. When I served it—I even had a sprig of parsley on the plate for garnish—he stared at it a few seconds, then shoved it away." She changed her voice to mimic Aaron. "'If I want to eat restaurant food, I'll go out. I want real food.'"

Wayne glanced in her direction. His eyebrows were raised. "Excuse me, but that was horribly rude of him. Did he eat it?"

"Wouldn't touch it. I threw it out and made him a burger."

"I'm so sorry, Evelyn."

She found her jaw clenched. She didn't want to talk about Aaron anymore.

They made the final turn toward the community center where the cooking class was held. Just as well.

"It's good we can share like this, Evelyn—share memories of our spouses. I wouldn't feel comfortable doing that with just anyone."

She was glad for the compliment, but the negative aspect of *her* memories clung to her like scum on clean water.

Suddenly romance was the furthest thing from her mind.

$\mathcal{L}$ucinda burst into the sunroom where Evelyn was reading a book. "Has FedEx come?"

"No."

Lucinda checked her watch. "I have to get to work. Could you go read your book in the parlor so you won't miss the doorbell?"

Evelyn marked her page with a fringed bookmark. "I suppose I could. What are you expecting?"

"A package. Something I need desperately for the reunion tomorrow."

"Doesn't your plane leave early? Isn't this cutting it pretty close?"

Lucinda gave her a *duh* look. "Why do you think I paid for the overnight shipping?" She took a step into the kitchen and made a gesture toward the front of the house. "Please? For me?"

Goodness. "I'm moving. I'm moving."

•　　•　　•

Evelyn had a hard time concentrating on her book. What could Lucinda want so desperately for a reunion? Her imagination ran a wide gamut: a new pair of shoes? A private investigator's report on some long-lost chum? A check from some obscure source needed to pay her way? Nothing made sense.

Every time she heard the sound of a bigger vehicle, Evelyn ran to the curtains. She'd probably seen the van of every appliance-repair service, landscaper, and building subcontractor in Carson Creek. She was about to call FedEx and demand to know the exact location of Lucinda's package, when the white truck pulled up.

She was at the door to meet him. "Boy, am I glad to see you!"

The man chuckled. "That's what we like to hear."

Evelyn signed for the package and closed the door. Only when she had it in her hand did she realize she still couldn't find out what it was until Lucinda came home from work.

Then she thought of the return address: Precious Beauty Ltd. She'd heard of them. She'd seen their infomercials on TV. They sold face cream and stuff like that.

Peppers rubbed against her legs, giving Evelyn someone to talk to. "I've wasted my entire morning waiting for face cream?"

She tossed the box on the table in the entry and went on with her day.

• • •

After work Lucinda burst in the door. "Evelyn? Did it—?"

She saw the FedEx box on the table and grabbed it. She was pulling the tear strip when Evelyn came out from the kitchen.

"It came right before lunch."

"You should have called me. I would have come home."

"It's just face cream, Lucinda."

"How—?"

Evelyn pointed at the box. "I saw the return address."

Lucinda moved into the parlor. She sat on the couch and

pulled out the lavender box. "It's not just face cream. It's their Miracle Magic serum. It takes years off your face instantly."

"That stuff doesn't work."

"Yes it does. Haven't you seen the ladies on TV? The before and after pictures?"

"That's fake."

How could she say such a thing? "It is not. It's real. They couldn't say it was true if it wasn't."

"Actually, they can. At least for a while. Until the government proves they're lying. And by then they've made millions."

Lucinda ran her hand over the beautiful box. They couldn't be lying. They couldn't. Her future depended on this working. By tomorrow. By the time she saw Sid Ricardo again.

"It certainly is a pretty box," Evelyn said. "I've heard that cosmetic companies spend more on the packaging than they do on the product itself. We women like pretty packages."

Lucinda clutched the box. "I didn't buy it for the package. I bought it for the promise."

Evelyn opened her mouth to speak, then closed it. "I hope you're not disappointed."

●   ●   ●

Lucinda spread the contents of the package across her bed. Creamy Cleanser, Face Freshener, Magic Moisturizer, and the coveted Miracle Magic serum. She'd already read the entire booklet, studying every page. She knew the only way for the product to work was to use it exactly as directed.

And it had to work. It had to. She didn't have money for more face-lifts, skin peels, or Botox injections. This was her final chance.

She took the products into the bathroom, locked the doors, and prepared to be beautiful.

• • •

"She's grasping at air," Piper said as she cut apples into a bowl.

Margaret got out the jar of peanut butter and placed it in the middle of the kitchen table. "My mom's ordered a lot of that stuff. It's not bad. Some of it's even pretty good, but it doesn't do miracles."

"And that's what she's depending on." Evelyn poured three glasses of milk. "You should have heard her. Seen her. She's desperate."

They sat at the table and each took a section of apple and swiped it through the peanut butter. "I wonder how many face-lifts she's had," Piper said.

"I've never seen any scars," Evelyn said. "And I've searched for them—when she's not looking, of course."

Piper pulled her own hair back. "They hide them up here. Where it doesn't show."

"Her face looks too tight," Margaret said. "Sometimes when she smiles I'm afraid something's going to pop."

"*Poing!*" Piper said, with hand motions.

They laughed and Evelyn felt the odd combination of pleasure and guilt. "We really shouldn't be talking about her like this," she said, trying to make the guilt part go away.

Piper and Margaret nodded, but shrugged. "I'm just concerned for her," Margaret said. "It's normal for a woman to cling to youth, but not so obsessively."

"That does seem to be the focus of her life," Piper said. "That, and chasing after men. I'm sure glad Dad wasn't impressed with her."

"He wasn't?" Evelyn asked. She tried not to sound pleased.

"Not a bit. He's not asking her out again, that's for sure."

• • •

He's not?

Lucinda put a hand on the frame of the kitchen door, steadying herself. Her mind swam with all she had just heard. How could these women be so mean? Just because they were content looking less than their best didn't mean they should attack her for wanting more. Why, Evelyn looked every bit of her fifty-some years, and Piper? Lucinda didn't see any men beating down her door. And at twenty-two Margaret had no right to talk about age at all.

Her heart pumped, making her ears ring. Before she knew it, she found herself in the kitchen, standing before them.

"Lucinda!" Evelyn said. "Where did you come—?"

She must have realized what a stupid question it was because she never finished it.

"You three are the most rude, horrible, mean women I have ever known!"

Piper pushed her chair back. "Oh, Lucinda, I'm sorry. We didn't mean for you to hear—"

"I'm sure you didn't. But I did hear. And now I know what goes on behind my back. You hate me! You've always hated me." She turned to leave, then turned back. "You're just jealous."

She banged through the kitchen door and headed upstairs. The ladies ran after her.

"Lucinda, come back!"

"We're really, really sorry."

"Don't be mad."

Lucinda stopped at the landing and looked down at them, stopped dead in their tracks on the stairs. "I'm heading out early to my reunion tomorrow. I plan to have a marvelous time. And I don't want to see any of you until I get back. If I come back."

"But we need to talk—"

"There's been enough talk."

She went into her room and slammed the door.

• • •

The three women sat at the kitchen table. The edges of the apples were brown; the milk lukewarm.

"What can we do?" Margaret asked.

"I feel absolutely wretched," Evelyn said.

Piper kept shaking her head. "Me and my big mouth."

"Our big mouths. We need to make it right."

Piper looked upward. "She won't listen."

It was then Margaret knew what had to be done. She held out her hands. "Lucinda won't listen to us right now, but someone else will. Ladies?"

They all nodded, took each other's hands, and shared their contrite hearts with the one who would forgive them. The only one who could ever make things right.

• • •

"Who wants some of Tessa's Japanese tea?" Evelyn asked. She carried a tray with a pot and cups into the dining room, where the ladies were working on Tessa's costume fund-raiser idea. She hoped the aroma of the tea would bring Lucinda out of her room to join them.

"I would, please," Margaret said.

"Smells heavenly," Piper said.

Audra raised her hand too, but Mae stood up from her chair, her hand doing a side to side, overhead wave. "Excuse me? Excuse me? Tessa's *tea*?" She put a hand to her chest and shuddered. "I'm sorry, but this does not compute. Ms. Coffee Bean would never be caught drinking lowly tea."

Tessa pulled at her sleeve. "Sit down! Quit making such a commotion." She pointed a finger at Evelyn. "I told you we shouldn't let her know."

Mae looked down at Tessa, her hands finding her hips. "You were purposely keeping this from me? You were denying me the pleasure of making fun of you? Of telling you, 'I told you so'?"

Tessa thought a moment, then nodded once. "Absolutely."

They all laughed. Mae pinched the fake red hibiscus that was wedged above Tessa's ear, the one that matched her muumuu. "Watch it, or I'll change this flower to the other ear and then you'll have all sorts of trouble."

"Trouble how?" Audra asked.

"I don't know," Mae admitted, "but I'm sure wearing it over the right or left ear sends out some sort of symbolic signal to the world."

They all looked at her.

"Well? Shouldn't it?"

Piper pointed to Mae's wrist. "Maybe you can tell us the symbolic signal behind wearing a Mickey Mouse watch on your left wrist and a leopard-skin scrunchy on your right?"

Mae didn't miss a beat. "Mickey's here to remind me not to be too serious."

"Was this ever a problem?" Audra asked.

Mae spoke above their giggles. "And the leopard scrunchy represents my desire to be prepared."

"Like a Boy Scout."

"Exactly."

"Funny," Margaret said. "I don't remember seeing scrunchies mentioned in the Scout handbook."

"It's an addendum. One must be prepared to tackle unruly hair at all times."

Tessa leaned back to look up at Mae's hair. "I'd say it's time. Past time."

Evelyn thought this was a great time to say, "Who wants that tea?"

• • •

"I could take flyers around to all the businesses downtown," Mae said. "And I'm sure I could get some of them to donate something for the charity auction."

"I could make cookies," Evelyn said.

Margaret was writing everything down. She was so glad they included her in the planning. It helped keep her mind off the wedding she *wasn't* planning.

They stopped talking when they heard footsteps on the porch. The doorbell rang. Evelyn went to open the door.

"Hi. Is Margaret Jensen here?"

Margaret's head jerked toward the voice. *Bobby?*

Evelyn looked at her questioningly, then back at the man. "Who may I say is calling?"

"Bobby Cullins. Her fiancé."

Fiancé? Margaret pushed her chair back. "I'll see him, Evelyn. Let him in."

Audra put a hand on her arm and whispered. "Are you sure?"

She nodded but she wasn't sure.

Bobby came inside, looking adorable in his bulky turtleneck. He shoved his hands in his jeans pockets and smiled. "Hi."

Margaret had a million questions. "How did you find me?"

Bobby's eyes scanned the ladies, and Margaret knew she should make introductions. But she needed to hear his answer first.

"I called your parents."

"They *told* you?" She hadn't told them *not* to tell, but had assumed . . . yet they'd always liked Bobby. Even after he'd dumped her, they'd hoped everything could work out.

"It's okay I'm here, isn't it?"

Mae stood at her chair. "That depends on your intentions, bucko. You've hurt our sister here and we don't take that lightly."

Bobby reddened. "I just want to talk." He looked at Margaret. "Can we talk?"

"You don't have to, honey," Tessa said. "Not after what he's done."

"It's okay," Margaret said. "I'll talk." She looked to the parlor. It was too close. "Let's go out to the porch."

She was glad the porch furniture was in front of the parlor end of the house, not the dining room where the ladies were working. If she and Bobby kept their voices down . . .

Though she preferred the swing, she sat on the rocker. She didn't want him sitting beside her. Actually, she *did* want him sitting beside her—*that* was the problem.

He sat on the swing. He looked everywhere but at her.

She wished he would say something. She wrapped her sweater close. "Why have you come?"

"I miss you. I needed to see you."

She felt her jaw drop. "You didn't seem to need me on Sunday when I saw you at the restaurant. You hid behind your menu."

"I was flustered."

There was more to it than that. She hadn't read *flustered* on his face. She'd read *dislike*. Yet she'd only seen him for a few seconds. Maybe . . .

"Do you miss me?" he asked.

Should she play a strong-woman number and make him suffer? or play the sympathy card and make him feel as bad as he should feel? Or should she be honest and say her heart ached for him? If only Mae or Tessa could speak for her. They'd know what to say. They'd get him good.

But was that the point?

"Meg?"

He was the only one who called her that name. And in the

saying, he melted any resolve she had to be anything other than who she was. She covered her eyes with a hand. "I miss you terribly."

She felt him touch her free hand. Take it. And pull her out of the rocker into the swing beside him. He wrapped an arm around her, and her head leaned against his. "I want you back, Meg. I made a mistake. I want us to be engaged again."

Life was good. And God was great.

•   •   •

"I'm telling you, she really should have a jacket," Tessa said for the third time.

The woman was a broken record. "Will you forget the jacket!" Mae said from the entryway. She turned to Audra, who was at the parlor window trying to eavesdrop.

"Oh my!" Audra said. "She won't be needing that jacket!"

"What happened?" Piper asked from her seat on the stairs. Beside her, Evelyn nodded.

Audra peeked through the edge of the curtains, then tiptoed back to the group. "She's sitting beside him on the swing and he has his arm around her. Their heads are touching."

"He wants her back!" Piper said. "How romantic."

Audra stood in the entry but looked toward the window. "Maybe, but . . . I don't know . . . this doesn't seem logical."

"What's logical about love?" Evelyn said.

Audra took a step closer to the group. "You don't understand. On Sunday we saw Bobby at lunch and he was extremely rude to her. She waved and he made a face and hid behind the menu."

"And now he's here, making up?" Evelyn asked. "You're right. That doesn't make sense."

"What happened between then and now?" Piper asked.

Enough of this. Mae grabbed Margaret's jacket. "Like Tessa said, it's cold out there."

She didn't wait for them to argue with her.

• • •

Margaret popped off the swing, pulling Bobby with her. "Mae! Come hear the happy news."

Uh-oh. She handed Maggie the jacket. "Put this on. It's cold."

Bobby pulled her close. "I'll keep her warm."

Instead of being impressed by the affection between two young lovers, Mae was totally turned off. Her warning bells clanged a dissonant tone.

"The wedding is on again!" Maggie said. She looked up at Bobby adoringly.

Mae's feelings were so strong, so opposite of what they should have been, she had to get a second opinion. And third. Fourth. Fifth. "Come inside and tell the others."

Mae vowed she wouldn't say a thing, wouldn't make a face. Nothing that would influence popular opinion. She held the door and followed them inside to the waiting swell of ladies.

"What's going on?" Tessa asked.

"Bobby and I are getting married again!" Maggie said. She held out her left hand. "Look! He brought my ring back."

They oohed and aahed over the ring and let Maggie chatter on about her news.

Mae did a check of the body language being played out in the foyer of Peerbaugh Place:

Evelyn hung out on the edge of the dining room, biting her thumb.

Piper stood on the second step, one hand on the railing, her eyes constantly moving between Margaret and Bobby.

Audra stood on the parlor side, her eyes never leaving Bobby's face. She played with her own wedding ring.

And Tessa blocked the way to the kitchen, her arms gripping each other across the red-and-orange muumuu. The addition of her narrowed eyes and red hibiscus gave the effect of a living and breathing stop sign.

So. Mae's instincts hadn't been wrong. Unless they were *all* wrong.

Maggie seemed oblivious to any emotion other than her own joy. She barely stopped to take a breath. Her hand was linked in the crook of Bobby's arm, and she kept pulling herself closer and closer. Yet he seemed to resist, tighten at each of her efforts. Interesting.

"We're going to go out and celebrate," she finally said. Bobby helped her on with the jacket she'd been holding.

"But it's late," Tessa said.

Bobby looked at his watch. "It's only eight thirty."

Mae knew it could have been midnight and Margaret would have gone.

They headed out the door. "Don't wait up!"

The door was shut. The hall clock ticked. Then tocked.

"Well?" Mae asked.

The women exchanged glances as if no one wanted to be the first to say something negative.

"Tessie . . . don't let me down here. Speak your mind, hula sister."

"Something's not right."

Five breaths were let out, then taken again as the women started talking at once.

"Why would he suddenly come back after being so mean?"

"Did you see him tense up?"

"His eyes were shifty. He's up to something."

Mae applauded softly. "Now we're talking. I feel exactly the same but wanted to be sure."

They returned to the dining room, all plans for the costume party forgotten. A sister in trouble always took precedence.

"Perhaps we're not being fair," Evelyn said, warming everyone's tea. "We've never met the boy before."

"We *are* going on first impressions," Piper said.

"This is my second impression," Audra pointed out. "My first impression—before I even knew who he was at the restaurant—was that he was terribly rude. I saw none of this charm Sunday. None. He hurt her badly. She was a wreck on the way home."

"I don't want that girl hurt again," Tessa said. "What's the saying? 'Hurt me once it's your fault; hurt me twice, it's my fault.'"

"She's so in love, so happy," Evelyn said.

"Wish we could bottle that," Mae said. "We'd make a fortune."

Piper took a sip of tea. "Her parents felt good enough about him to give him this address. That must mean something."

"It means her father is trying to justify the money he's already spent on the wedding," Mae said.

"I'm sure that's not it," Evelyn said. "They must trust him. They wouldn't want their daughter hurt again. They love her even more than we do."

It was a piece of logic they couldn't ignore. "I still don't trust him," Mae said. "It's something around the eyes."

"I second that," Tessa said. "God didn't give us women's intuition for nothing. We need to be wary."

"And wise," Piper said.

Audra nodded her agreement. "We also need to be careful not to judge him. Yet."

"She's *so* happy," Evelyn said. "I don't want to ruin that for her."

Mae hated to agree, but she had to. "Me neither, but let's be wise, okay? Her common sense is clouded by visions of wedding cake and flowers. We need to be wise *for* her."

"That Bobby better watch out," Tessa said. "He's got five pairs of eyes on him."

"Sister sleuths, unite!"

• • •

Margaret tiptoed up the stairs of Peerbaugh Place. It was late. Nearly midnight. She didn't want to wake—

Piper opened her door. "How did it go?"

"It was wonderful."

Piper studied her a moment. "Want to talk?"

She shook her head. "Tomorrow. Night."

Margaret flipped the light on in her room. Then flipped it off. By moonlight she made her way to the window seat and settled in. What would she tell Piper and the other ladies? Yes, the wedding was on. Yes, she was happy to be back with Bobby. Feeling his arms around her, and his kisses . . . it was like coming home.

And yet . . . Bobby had not been able to fully explain to her why he was back. After all, she was still the same woman she'd always been. And as far as she could tell, he was the same man.

So what made him change his mind? And what made him change from the rude Bobby on Sunday to the fawning Bobby today?

"Stop it, Margaret," she whispered to herself. "Be happy. Quit trying to dissect everything." This was an answer to prayer.

Wasn't it?

When she let her mind rest a moment, she remembered her prayers. She'd prayed that God would show her what she'd done wrong with Bobby. He was back. But she still didn't have an answer to that question.

So was God behind this reunion or not?

Lord, please show me the truth. I know I should be happy—I am happy. But there's something here that doesn't feel right. Reveal it to me.

Then she added three words that were harder to pray than any of the rest: *whatever it is. . . .*

O Lord, You are my rock of safety.
Please help me; don't refuse to answer me.
For if You are silent,
I might as well give up and die.

PSALM 28:1

𝓛ucinda set her suitcases in the entryway and checked to make sure she had her airline ticket and photo ID. She hoped she hadn't forgotten anything.

Evelyn came out from the kitchen. "You heading out?"

"All set."

"You'll be home tomorrow evening?"

"That's the plan." *Unless I decide to run away with Sid and move out of this hateful house.* She stooped to pick up a suitcase, then stood without it as curiosity overrode anger. "Did I hear correctly last night? Did Margaret's fiancé come back? Is the wedding on?"

"Yes. On both accounts. Why didn't you come down—for that, and to help with Tessa's costume fund-raiser?"

Lucinda ignored the question. "You don't sound very enthused about Billy being back."

"Bobby. And no . . ." She looked upstairs where Piper and Margaret were still sleeping and lowered her voice. "We don't understand his sudden turnaround. We're wary, that's all."

"People *can* change, you know."

Evelyn fingered the collar of her robe. "Are you excited about the reunion?"

Petrified. Lucinda shrugged and picked up her luggage. "I hope it's not a waste of time and money."

"Don't expect too much," Evelyn said, getting the door. "Do you need help?"

"No. I can handle it."

Hopefully.

•   •   •

Once settled into the Grand Hotel, Lucinda treated herself to a bubble bath, a facial mask, a manicure, and her new Miracle Magic serum. She studied her face in the magnifying mirror, then turned it to the regular mirror. Better.

She wished she'd had money enough for a new dress, but with the airfare, hotel, cab . . . no one would know she was wearing an old ensemble. After all, they hadn't seen her in twenty years. She'd been at the ten-year reunion, alone, but on the edge of famous. She'd attended her twentieth on the arm of her ex, Wally, their upcoming divorce making her feel infamous. She had skipped her thirtieth due to some nasty bruising after a face-lift. How ironic that she'd had the surgery to look her best . . .

Once her primping was complete she took the elevator down to the lobby and sashayed her way into the ballroom where the dinner and dance were being held. She walked with feigned confidence. The butterflies in her stomach were doing the tango—big dips included. She felt conspicuous entering the room alone. She should have brought a man. Wayne even. And yet, if Wayne were here she would not be able to properly flirt with the man of the moment—

There he was. Sid Ricardo. He stood by the bar with a group of his old buddies, a mixed drink in his hand. He'd filled out, but not in a bad way. She'd known the boy. This was a man. His hair had thinned and receded, but his smile was the same. Full of invitations.

Okay, Lucinda. Go RSVP.

As she strode toward him, she nodded at someone who called her name, but did not even turn to see who it was. She ignored all but her target. She felt like she was walking in slow motion and half expected his sea of friends to part. The entire room would fall silent as they faced each other, as Sid looked at her and she looked at Sid . . .

She found herself faced with the backs of those who had his audience, and were his audience. It was a wall, as their football-player bulk had only gotten bulkier over forty years. The few wives present gave her a full body scan, then went back to their conversations.

She looked between shoulders, hoping for Sid's attention. Once his eyes met hers there would be electricity, chemistry, alchemy . . .

Finally, he looked her way. She smiled and raised a hand to—

He did not miss a beat in his conversation and looked away as if she'd been no more important to his evening than a waitress offering hors d'oeuvres.

Two wives put their heads together, smiling. Whispering.

This was not how it was supposed to work. She didn't come all this way to be dismissed!

"Excuse me." She pushed between two bulky shoulders until she was directly in front of Sid.

"Well, what have we here?" he said, eyeing her like she was a chocolate in a heart-shaped box.

All eyes were on her. "Hello, Sid." She tried to sound confident. "It's nice to see you again."

He glanced down at her name tag then up again. Then he nodded and Lucinda waited for a hug.

He grinned. "I remember you."

Yes! I knew he'd remem—

"You're the girl who threw up in biology class when we dissected the cow's eye."

Laughter surrounded her.

A woman twenty years younger than the rest of them, wearing a to-die-for necklace, slipped her hand around his arm. "Don't embarrass her, Sid. I'm sure she did no such thing, did you, sweetheart?"

Being called sweetheart by this . . . this trophy . . .

"Sure she did," said one of the guys behind her.

Yes, I did, but that's beside the point.

One of the ladies socked him in the arm. Lucinda thought she recognized her . . . "You men haven't changed." She sidled up to Lucinda, putting her hand on her shoulder, as if presenting her to the others. "Don't you know this is Lucinda Van Horn?"

"Oh, of course!" said one of the beefeaters, making a limp wrist. "Of the Boston Van Horns."

Their laughter was acid. Lucinda ran through the crowd.

●　　●　　●

Lucinda regretted her decision to find solace in the women's room. The constant stream of party goers made escape impossible without running into someone she knew. Or who knew her. Surely word of her humiliation had made the rounds through the entire event.

And so she sat on the toilet lid, hugging her purse to her chest, not even able to cry properly lest someone hear.

Finally silence. She perked her ears, listening. She peeked through the crack in the stall. The coast was—

The restroom door opened. " . . . always one at every reunion. I think it's a rule."

"She's pitiful."

The two women took their places at the mirror, fluffing and primping. Lucinda didn't recognize their voices.

"Like I said," the first woman said. "There's one at every reunion. The one who holds youth in a death grip."

The second woman laughed. "That was quite eloquent."

"Why thank you."

The sound of compacts clicking shut. Water running. "Don't get me wrong, I'm all for looking good. But there comes a time. We're fifty-eight years old."

"You don't look a day over forty-five."

"Thank you. You too. And that's doable. That's acceptable. I'm not even against a nip and tuck when appropriate. But Lucinda . . . she reminds me of a certain rock icon who went under the knife a few too many times . . ."

No! That's not true!

"I mean, who does she think she is?"

"I think the better question is *how old* does she think she is? Trying to look thirty when you're nearly sixty is sick. Plus, it doesn't work. It's too . . . too . . ."

"Desperate?"

"Exactly."

"There," said number two, clicking a purse shut. "You ready?"

"As I'll ever be."

●   ●   ●

Lucinda didn't remember leaving the stall in the restroom, nor leaving the building. The first cognizant moment she had, she found herself walking the streets of downtown Boston. She wasn't near the hotel anymore. She wasn't near the stores or the restaurants. The buildings were dark. Some boarded up. There was trash in the street.

She sidestepped a broken beer bottle and stopped walking.

Suddenly wary, she wrapped her coat tighter, clutching her purse beneath her crossed arms.

She had to go back. This was not a good place to be, especially dressed in fancy heels and a short dress. Suddenly, looking her best was not a good thing.

"Uahgggh."

She jerked toward the curb, startled by the sound in the doorway to her right. A man lay in the shadows in a heap. He pushed himself to sitting and squinted up at her. "Money, lady?"

She ran the way she'd come, looking back to see if he was after her.

"Hey!"

The word was said too late. She ran into someone, falling onto the sidewalk.

"Uff-da!" the man said. "That's gotta hurt." He extended a hand to help her up.

Lucinda pulled her skirt down, trying to be modest in her sprawl. She drew her knees beneath her to stand. "I'm fine. I'll be—"

"Come now. Don't be stubborn. Let me help you up."

She allowed herself to really look at him. He looked normal. Sixtyish. Wearing khakis and an oxford shirt under a navy poplin jacket. She let him help her up.

"Any broken bones?" he asked, retrieving her purse from the curb.

"No. I'm fine."

"So you said. Your knee's bleeding."

She looked down. "My hose are ruined."

He seemed to notice her clothes for the first time. "Why are you dressed like that?"

She didn't want to answer any more questions. "I need to get back. If you'll excuse—"

He pointed in the direction of the bum. "What were you running from in such a frenzy?"

She rebuttoned her coat. "I wasn't in a frenzy. I just got fright-
ened. There was a man in the doorway and—"

"Really?" He started walking toward the man.

"Don't go up there! He wants money. He's drunk. He's—"

She watched as Oxford Man stopped right in front of the
doorway and started talking to the bum. *What is he doing?* Then
she had the horrible thought that he might be chastising the der-
elict for scaring her. She took a step toward him. "Hey, mister. You
don't have to—"

Her savior helped the bum to stand and actually patted him
on the back. She hoped he wasn't arranging a face-to-face apology.
Oxford started walking the other man toward her, talking softly to
him, gesturing and pointing to the right.

Enough. Lucinda turned her back on them and walked away.
Her knee hurt. Bad. She'd find the hotel, get a bandage from the
concierge, and hide in her room until morning.

"Miss?"

She turned enough to see him, but continued walking. "I'm
heading out. Thanks for your help. Sorry for bumping into you
like that."

"Your knee needs attention," Oxford said.

"Hey, lady, you're bleeding."

"I'm fine."

"No, you're not. You hold up there. Wait a minute." Oxford,
along with the bum—who had one arm slung over the man's
shoulder for support—caught up with her. He extended his
hand toward her. "I'm Pastor Enoch. The Save-You-Mission is
just around the corner. I'm bringing my friend there for a meal
and a bed. Come with us and I'll get your knee patched up. I
may even find you a ride back to wherever it was you came
from."

The ride sounded good. And her knee *did* hurt.

He took her silence as a yes. "Come on then. Come with us."

•   •   •

Pastor Enoch pointed to a coffeepot in the corner. "Help yourself and have a seat. I'll get my friend something to eat then come join you."

Lucinda didn't feel much like coffee—especially coffee that was probably hours old, but she filled a Styrofoam cup anyway and took a seat at a nearby table. Across the room a couple of men were playing cards, and in the other corner an older woman spoke with a mother holding a young child. The child was coloring, but the mother looked like a damp dishrag. Wadded up, used, and dirty. When the woman looked at Lucinda, she looked away.

Pastor Enoch came out of the kitchen accompanied by a man wearing an apron. He introduced him to the bum, pointed in Lucinda's direction, and they parted. He came toward her carrying a first-aid kit and a wet washcloth.

"Now, let's get you fixed up here." Pastor Enoch knelt at her feet, his eyes on her knee. Her hose had pulled away from the wound, providing access. After assessing it for a few seconds, he glanced up at her. "This might hurt, but I need to get it clean."

She nodded and he gently dabbed at the scrape. "That coffee good?"

She set the cup on the table. "I've had better."

He laughed. "Not surprising. But it's hot. And free." His eyes slid over her black cocktail dress. "If you don't mind me asking, why are you all dressed up?"

Lucinda pulled her coat over the dress as much as possible. "I was at my class reunion at the Grand."

Pastor Enoch sat back on his haunches. "That's six blocks away. What brought you over here?" He smiled. "Not that I mind, but . . ."

"I was upset. I had to leave. I just started walking."

"Ah," he said as if he understood completely. "Walking is a

good antidote to *upset*, but it's best not to do it alone. At night. In an iffy part of town."

"I know. I need to get back."

"Is your husband waiting for you?"

"I don't have a husband."

"Ah." He dabbed ointment on the wound and applied a bandage.

Just the way he said it. "What's that supposed to mean?" she asked.

He seemed surprised by her reaction. "Oh, nothing. Really. It's just the reality of a single woman going to a reunion . . . some people go to those things with less than honorable intentions. Trying to rekindle past love."

"Or showcase past humiliation."

The pastor's eyes were kind. "I'm so sorry. Not what you had in mind, was it?"

She shook her head and was appalled to feel tears threaten.

He groaned as he got to his feet. "I know what you need. Sit right there."

He went into the kitchen and returned with two pieces of chocolate cake on paper plates. "Here we go." He sat across from her. "Chocolate is a gift from God, and chocolate frosting is manna from heaven."

She couldn't remember the last time she'd eaten with a flimsy plastic fork.

He took a bite. "Eat. Enjoy."

She cut off a corner. It was delicious.

"Good, huh? Better than any stuffed mushrooms or cheese on a cracker that they serve at those fancy functions." He took another bite, savoring it. "You can't beat chocolate cake."

He was right. She ate every crumb. He took their plates and threw them away. "Well then . . . I never got your name."

Where were her manners? She stood and shook his hand.

"Lucinda Van Horn." She did *not* add, *of the Boston Van Horns*.
"And you are Pastor E . . . E . . . ?"

"Enoch."

"I've never heard that name before."

"Enoch was a godly man mentioned in the Bible. He didn't
die. God just took him up to heaven."

"Huh?"

He laughed. "Wish I could tell you the details, but God chose
not to divulge much more." He spread his arms and recited:
"'Enoch lived 365 years in all. He enjoyed a close relationship with
God throughout his life. Then suddenly, he disappeared because
God took him.'"

"That's impressive. A little weird, but impressive."

He shrugged. He reminded her of the father character on
Everybody Loves Raymond—minus the attitude. "I'm working on
the close relationship, am curious about the disappearing part,
and would certainly like the 365 years." As he looked around the
shelter, a veil of sorrow fell over his face. "There's not enough
time . . ."

It was the exact opposite of Lucinda's thoughts. She'd spent
too much time in this place. "I really need to go . . . you mentioned
a car?"

He pulled keys from his pocket. "A van actually." He
extended a hand toward the door. "After you, mademoiselle."

●　　●　　●

Lucinda could hear the beat of the music coming from the ballroom. The party was still in full swing. Without her. She was not
missed.

She punched the button for the elevator. While she was waiting, one of Sid's jocks staggered into view.

"Hey! I know you!"

She pushed the button again. Twice. *Come on!*

Suddenly, his arm was draped around her shoulders, his hand too close . . . his whisper slithered from his lips to her ear, bringing with it the smell of booze. "Sid told us all about making it with you back in high school." His lips touched her ear. "So? Wanna head up together?"

With a strength she didn't know she possessed she shoved him back. He fell to the marble floor. "Get away from me, you creep!"

The elevator door opened and she went inside. He got to his feet and stumbled toward her. "Come on, baby. Don't be difficult."

She pushed the button for her floor with one hand while extending the other arm toward him. Her stop-sign hand turned into a pointing finger, which she shook at him with each word. "Don't. You. Dare."

The door closed. The tears started. The trembling. When she reached her floor, she ran down the hall, fumbling her key card. A porter was coming her way.

He hurried to her side. "Are you all right, ma'am? Your knee . . . ?"

She couldn't even manage a no or a yes. Her knee was fine. Her knee had nothing to do with the cretin who'd made her cry. So many tears tonight. For so many reasons . . .

"Let me help." He took the key from her and opened the door. With a last look toward the elevators, she rushed inside.

"Is someone after you?"

She nodded.

"Do you want me to call security?"

She shook her head, mouthed her thanks, and closed the door. She locked every lock, then looked out the peephole. The porter had not left, but stood in front of her door, looking up and down the hallway. Her own personal guard.

She backed up when she saw him come toward her door.

He tapped a knuckle on it and spoke softly. "I don't see anyone, ma'am, but I'll stay outside awhile to make sure no one bothers you. And I'll say a prayer for you, ma'am. Everything will be okay. I promise."

New tears came. Tears of relief.

She moved to the bed and fell upon it. She drew a pillow to her chest. Sleep eventually came and saved her, replacing her living nightmare with oblivion.

●   ●   ●

Lucinda awoke in the middle of the night to find herself still in her coat. Still in her dress. One shoe off, one shoe on. She looked at the clock. It was 3:16. She was safe. Just like the porter said, everything would be all right.

At least for now.

She got up, peeled off her clothes, put on her pajamas, and used the bathroom. As she was heading back to bed she saw a piece of paper slipped under the door.

> *Dear lady in distress,*
>
> *I'm so sorry you were afraid. I stayed a long time outside your door and no one came. I prayed for you. You're safe now. But I can't make you feel safe forever. No one can. Only God can do that. With Him you'll never be alone or lonely. And He's available to you any time of day. Anywhere.*
>
> *I share these verses with you on this night when you've been so afraid. I hope they help.*
>
> *The Lord is my rock, my fortress, and my Savior;*
> *my God is my rock, in whom I find protection.*
> *He is my shield, the strength of my salvation,*
> *and my stronghold.*

I will call on the Lord, who is worthy of praise,
for He saves me from my enemies.
Psalm 18:2-3

But as for me, I will sing about Your power.
I will shout with joy each morning
    because of Your unfailing love.
For You have been my refuge,
a place of safety in the day of distress.
O my Strength, to You I sing praises,
for You, O God, are my refuge,
the God who shows me unfailing love.
Psalm 59:16-17

Let me know if I can help.

LeJames Wallace

Lucinda read the verses through twice. There was such comfort there. A note from a man she didn't even know . . . to think that tonight she'd found pain among those she knew and comfort through two strangers. Pastor Enoch and LeJames Wallace. Strange names. But names she would never forget.

She set the note on the bedside table, got under the covers, turned out the light, and went back to sleep.

Safe. Safe at last.

[God] is a shield for all who look to Him for protection.
For who is God except the Lord?
Who but our God is a solid rock?
God arms me with strength;
He has made my way safe.

PSALM 18:30-32

$\mathcal{L}$ucinda slept in, all safe and cozy in her bed. She awoke to find the sun streaming in the crack of the curtains like a beacon beckoning, *Come here. Come toward the light of a new day.*

She did just that. She pulled the curtains aside and looked out over Boston. It was quiet. A Sunday. Almost peaceful. But above all, safe.

She put her fingers on the glass, a thin wall keeping her from harm, holding her back where she belonged. Ridiculous really. That something you could see through, something you could break, could have that power.

She thought of LeJames's note and retrieved it to read again: *But I can't make you feel safe forever. No one can. Only God can do that. With Him you'll never be alone or lonely. And He's available to you any time of day. Anywhere.*

Lucinda sat on the bed, looking at the note, reading the first set of verses again. One stuck with her: *"He is my shield, the strength of my salvation, and my stronghold. I will call on the Lord, who is worthy of praise, for He saves me from my enemies."*

Was that what had happened last night? Had God—through Pastor Enoch and LeJames—saved her from enemies?

She shook her head against the thought. Why would God help her? She certainly hadn't paid any attention to Him. In fact, she'd gone out of her way to avoid Him, refusing to go to church with the ladies, putting down any talk about faith.

Suddenly, Tessa's voice came to mind. Tessa's words: "'Seek and ye shall find,' Lucinda. I know a way to never be lonely. Not even when we're alone."

Lucinda looked back to the note: *With Him you'll never be alone or lonely.* She looked to the ceiling. "Is that true, God?"

She clapped a hand over her mouth. Had she just prayed?

The thought made her smile. How odd to smile about prayer. Wasn't it supposed to be a serious transaction? And yet wasn't there something about joy . . . ?

She read the second set of verses LeJames had given her, read them aloud: "'But as for me, I will sing about Your power. I will shout with joy each morning because of Your unfailing love. For You have been my refuge, a place of safety in the day of distress. O my Strength, to You I sing praises, for You, O God, are my refuge, the God who shows me unfailing love.'"

She found her hand at her mouth a second time, this time stifling a sob. A sob of joy. Then she bowed her head. "Thank You, God. Thank You."

·　·　·

Lucinda stopped at the hotel desk to check out. She held an envelope containing a thank-you note and a twenty-dollar bill. "Is LeJames Wallace on duty?"

"I'm afraid not. He works the night shift."

"I know."

The woman lowered her head, wary. "Do you have some concern?" It sounded like she expected a complaint.

"No, no concern," Lucinda said. "In fact, I wanted to thank him."

The clerk's smile was full of relief. "That's very nice of you."

"Not at all. LeJames is the one who's nice. Beyond nice. In fact, he deserves a raise."

"Goodness. That's wonderful to hear. I've always thought LeJames was a good man. But can you tell me . . . what did he do for you?"

How could she word this? "He saved me."

Lucinda handed her the envelope and was assured that LeJames would get it. Then she headed for the airport . . . and home.

●   ●   ●

Evelyn loved Sundays. Church with dear friends, eating out. Lounging around in the sunroom, reading *Taste of Home* magazine. *God sure thought of everything when He declared this a day of rest.*

The only flaw in the day was her concern for her two newest tenants. Lucinda would be home from her reunion any minute. Evelyn hoped it had been a success, but was doubtful. There was something about Lucinda that seemed to ask for confrontation, seemed to set herself up for failure.

Then there was Margaret. Happy, happy Margaret, thrilled to be back with Bobby. The young couple had spent all yesterday together. Two lovebirds in love. And this morning Margaret hadn't come to church with the ladies but had driven all the way to Jackson to go to church with Bobby—in their old church. Nothing wrong with that. They *should* attend together.

Evelyn threw her magazine on the table. Oh, fiddle. She wished she could figure out why she distrusted Bobby so much. Or if she couldn't pin it down, she wished she could embrace him as Margaret's intended. Be happy for them. Put up or shut up.

She heard the front door open. "Hello? I'm home."

Lucinda? It was Lucinda's voice, but hardly Lucinda's style.

Evelyn got up to see and nearly had a collision at the swinging kitchen door.

"Here you are." Lucinda took Evelyn into a bear hug.

That was definitely not Lucinda's style. They separated and Lucinda made a beeline for the fridge. "What's to eat? The airlines don't feed people anymore."

"There's meat loaf and Jell-O salad," Evelyn said.

"Perfect."

Since when? Evelyn had purposely made meat loaf last night because Lucinda had previously informed her it was *not* one of her favorites. "How was the reunion?" she asked.

"Awful. Horrible. Humiliating."

Evelyn grabbed the back of a chair, needing to hold on to something that was real, that made sense. "You don't act like it was awful."

Lucinda stopped midway to the microwave. "That's because it was also amazing, astonishing, and enlightening."

"Oh my," Evelyn said. "All that in twenty-four hours?"

Lucinda pushed the buttons on the microwave. "Hey, lives have been changed in less time than that."

"Your life was changed?"

"It certainly got a good nudge."

Evelyn couldn't take her constant motion a moment longer. She intercepted Lucinda at the dish cupboard, putting her hands on her arms. "Stop. Please. Stand still. Tell me what happened."

Lucinda told her about Sid Ricardo, hiding in the restroom, the bum and Pastor Enoch, the sleaze at the elevator, and the note from LeJames Wallace. "I prayed, Evelyn. I actually prayed." She grabbed Evelyn into another hug.

Evelyn was stunned. If anyone had asked her the odds of Lucinda Van Horn's saying yes to God in *any* way, she would have rather bet the sky would turn lime green. "From what you say . . . those two men certainly seemed God-sent, Lucinda."

"You really think so?" She returned to the microwave, which had dinged during her recitation. She checked the meat loaf, turned the dish, then zapped it some more.

"I most certainly do. That's the way God works."

"Really?"

"Absolutely," Evelyn said. "Sending the right people at the right time. How do you think I ever opened this place? It was His timing. And He sent me Mae and Tessa and Audra and—"

"And me?"

Actually, she was going to say "Summer." Evelyn felt bad for not thinking Lucinda had been sent by God. Had she?

Lucinda set the plate of meat loaf on the table and added a scoop of Jell-O. "Want some?" she asked.

"No thanks." But Evelyn sat at the table with her. "So what happens now?"

Lucinda stopped with the fork halfway to her mouth. "What do you mean?"

What *did* she mean? "You've had a mountaintop moment."

Lucinda smiled. "*Mmm-mmm.* I like that term."

Oh dear. Maybe Evelyn should keep her mouth shut. Who was she to bring Lucinda down to earth? And yet, she knew it was inevitable. No one could stay on the mountain.

"To answer your question about what happens now?" Lucinda said. "I haven't a clue. But for the moment I'm going to enjoy the feeling." She took a deep breath. "You know what? Life is good."

Evelyn wasn't about to argue.

•   •   •

Mae purposely put the catering and floral brochures for Ringo and Soon-ja's wedding on the dining room table so Starr would see them. Maybe if Starr would get interested in the planning of her brother's wedding, she'd start wanting to have one of her own and stop this foolishness of staying away from Ted. When Ringo had first announced his engagement, the idea of a double wedding had been mentioned. Nothing had come of it, and now it seemed impossible.

Mae heard Starr's footsteps on the stairs and tried to look busy by flipping pages and jotting down random numbers. She waited for *"What are you working on, Mother?"*

It didn't happen. The front door opened and Mae panicked. She ran after Starr, out to the porch. "Where are you going?"

"Piper and I are going to a movie in Jackson."

"I didn't hear the phone."

"I called her."

"But I could really use your help with your brother's wedding . . ."

Starr was already heading across the street with a backward wave.

Mae stomped her foot. That girl! Why couldn't she do what Mae wanted her to do?

She heard the screen door behind her. Collier came outside. "Where's Starr going?"

"To a movie. With Piper."

"That bad, huh?"

Mae realized her voice had been full of contempt and let out a puff of exasperated air.

"Come here, wifey." Collier took her hand and led her to the porch swing. "Come here under my protective wing."

They sat and she glanced at his favorite flannel shirt. "Your wing has a hole in the elbow."

"Battle scars," he said. "Now shush."

"Don't I get to say anything?"

"Nope. We're just going to swing."

"But that doesn't accomplish anything."

He put a finger to his lips. "Shhh."

Up, back, up, back. They watched Piper's car drive away. Starr didn't even wave.

"But—"

"Shhh."

Up, back, up, back. The swing found its rhythm. Mae adjusted herself to the softness of Collie's chest. She heard his heart beating and willed her breathing to be its complement. He patted her side, a silent congratulations.

She hated when he was right.

•   •   •

"Mommy, I'm beautiful!" Summer twirled before the full-length mirror in her princess costume for Halloween.

Audra put the needle back in the pincushion with extra force. She'd better like it. The dress had been a bear to make, the lamé fabric raveling like crazy and mucking up her sewing machine.

Summer swished back and forth in the mirror, playing with the voile overskirt. "Mary Beth's costume isn't near as nice. Her mom bought hers and it just has funny ties in the back. It's not a real princess dress like mine."

Ah, to buy a costume . . . what a relief that would be. But there was no way Audra could do such a thing. The reputation of Catherine's Wedding Creations was at stake.

She stood and arched her back. Just a few more hours and she could sleep. "Go get Daddy. We need to stop by Grandma's and Mae's then get to the party at church."

Just a few more hours.

•   •   •

"Meg!"

When Margaret's head fell off her hand she heard laughter. It took her a moment to remember where she was. Oh yes. They were at their—Bobby's—apartment. Bobby and one of his buddies from work were playing some stupid Nintendo football game. Would he ever grow up?

Bobby patted the couch beside him. "Come on, Meg. Come sit by me and help."

Help? She looked at her watch. "It's nearly midnight. I really need to get home." This was the third time she'd asked.

"Yeah, yeah. Just a few minutes more."

Margaret got out of the chair and decided to clean up the mess from their pizza and pop. Next time she'd drive herself to Jackson and not let Bobby pick her up. She'd thought he'd been quite the gentleman offering to come get her for church. With the forty-minute drive each way, it showed effort.

The trouble was, it also left her stranded and at the whim of Bobby's timetable—which had always been a bit different than her own.

Suddenly, Bobby shouted. "Touchdown!"

Dale tossed the controller on the couch and stood. "That was no fair."

"Totally fair. How about another game?"

Dale glanced at Margaret. "She wants to go home. She has to teach school tomorrow."

Bobby laughed. "She won't need that job much longer."

At the dishwasher, Margaret turned toward him. "What's that supposed to mean?"

He switched off the set. "Oh, nothing. Where are my keys?"

•   •   •

Piper's eyes shot open. What had awakened her? She held her breath and listened. She heard some paper shuffling and something slide to the floor.

The clock said 2:30. Who was up?

She got out of bed and went into the hall. There was a light under the door of Margaret's room. She'd heard her get in shortly before one, but why was she still up?

She tiptoed close and put her ear to the door. More rustling. She tapped on the door with a fingernail. It opened. Margaret was in her robe. Papers littered her bed.

"What are you doing up?" Piper whispered.

"I have papers to grade that I should have done last week, and lesson plans due." She looked to the floor, the unspoken speaking volumes.

"I know you're happy to be back with Bobby but don't let him run you ragged."

She shrugged. "He just wants to be with me."

"As he should. But . . ." *He needs to be considerate too.* "Doesn't he have to work in the morning like the rest of us?"

"He works at a computer store. They don't open until ten."

Piper could have said more but didn't. "Do you want help?" Surely grading second-grade papers couldn't be that difficult.

"I'm fine. I can handle it."

"This time."

"Yeah, yeah, I hear you."

Piper pointed a finger at her. "You'd better. Don't be long. Good night."

Piper got back in bed. Something wasn't right here. Not at all.

Truly, O God of Israel, our Savior,
You work in strange and mysterious ways.

ISAIAH 45:15

𝒢or the first time ever, Lucinda was excited about going to work at Flora and Funna. She had so much to tell Gwen about her weekend. She was actually humming when she came in the door.

Gwen looked up from stocking the cash register. "My, my. Is that a spring I see in your step?"

Lucinda accentuated her bounce. "The springiest." She put her purse under the counter.

Gwen shut the cash drawer, giving Lucinda her full attention. "Juicy details, please."

"*Juicy* isn't quite the right term."

"You and the great—single—Sid Ricardo didn't . . . ?" She raised and lowered her eyebrows.

"No." The negative aspects of her trip rushed toward her, threatening her mood. "I don't want to talk about him."

"So some other eligible man came into your life?"

She thought of Pastor Enoch and LeJames. "Eligible? Hardly. But men. Yes."

"Men. Plural?"

Lucinda told Gwen the entire story, just like she'd told Evelyn.

When she was finished she felt the need for a deep, cleansing breath. "There. That's about it."

During the telling Gwen had leaned against the counter and crossed her arms. Her face was hard to read.

Lucinda waited. "Aren't you going to say something? Isn't it amazing how it all fits together?"

Gwen shook her head and turned away, straightening the stack of order forms. "It's amazing all right."

Lucinda pulled her around to face her. "I thought you'd be happy for me."

Gwen snickered. "I don't see much to be happy about." She counted on her hands. "Sid turns out to be a jerk, and his friends bring up one of the most humiliating moments in your high school career; you overhear other so-called friends making fun of your looks; you nearly get mugged by a bum in a dark alley—"

"It wasn't an alley. I was walking on the street."

"Whatever." She continued her list. "You get to visit a home-less shelter and hobnob with the poor and grungy."

"Gwen. That's not fair."

"Sid's buddy makes a disgusting pass at you so that you're afraid and run and need saving by the porter. Then you are so scared you fall into bed wearing your clothes."

"But LeJames protected me. He prayed for me. He gave me verses that were perfect and meant a lot to me."

Gwen dismissed her comments with a flip of her hand. "Pasted-on, feel-good platitudes."

Lucinda's breath left her. All she could manage was a weak, "But I prayed."

"Yeah? Well so do I when I need something." She pointed a finger at Lucinda's nose. "But if you're smart, you won't count on an answer. I never do." She picked up the stack of order forms, banged them against the counter, then set them down again. "The gift shelves need dusting and I've got a shipment to unload." She walked toward the back room.

Lucinda couldn't move. She felt drained and deflated.

Gwen glanced back at her, then returned to her side, putting a hand on her arm. "I'm not saying it didn't happen, Lucinda. I'm sure it did. But you can't go around living in la-la land, thinking God spoke to you from on high. He doesn't do that. It just doesn't happen. I'm glad you got through a horrible weekend. But now it's time to come down to earth with the rest of us. Okay?"

Lucinda could only nod.

So much for the mountaintop.

• • •

Tessa entered the back door of her daughter's home. Ever since they'd converted the detached garage into an apartment for her, she'd made a point of having her evening meals with the family as often as possible. Breakfast was a different story. It took an act of will to get Tessa to walk across the yard to the kitchen. With Naomi and Calvin hurrying off to work, and thirteen-year-old Leonard getting ready for school, it was chaos. When Naomi was growing up, Tessa had always set a nice breakfast. Even if it was only a bowl of cereal, they'd sat together. Now, it was Pop-Tarts, granola bars, yogurt to go, or—if they did sit down—frozen waffles in the toaster.

In her daughter's defense, Tessa had been a stay-at-home mom. And she actually admired Naomi's professional abilities. She was a lawyer. Imagine. Her daughter the lawyer. Such options weren't even a blink on life's radar screen when Tessa was young.

It wasn't that she had regrets about being *just* a mother, *just* a wife. It wasn't that she'd wasted a moment. Though she didn't have a degree, she'd received her own education by reading. History was her passion. That's why the world cruise and the trip to Italy had been such a blessing. In all her reading about Casablanca, Amsterdam, Istanbul, Rome, and Singapore, she never thought she'd actually go there. And to have that experience lead to God giving her the idea for the Sister Circle Network . . .

It had all happened so effortlessly. On a long cruise making friends was inevitable. Ann Fleming from Neenah, Wisconsin; Sally Whitmore from Lincoln, Nebraska; and Laney Newsome from Big Canoe, Georgia, were dear women with varied backgrounds. Ann had worked in the auto industry, Sally worked in publishing, and Laney was quite the artist and musician. All very different from Tessa. Yet despite their differences, they found they had much in common. Or at least enough. They were women, they wanted to be all they could be, and they were seeking direction and inspiration from God.

The four women had been in their second week of meeting on the Lido deck for morning exercise when Tessa realized they'd moved beyond mere acquaintances sharing small talk about diets and recipes, and were becoming friends. Sisters. Discussing their families, their own shortcomings and dreams, their frustrations, victories, and their faith became as natural and refreshing as taking in a breath of Mediterranean air.

So the Lido Queens Sister Circle was born.

But it went further. When the ship had docked at port so they could visit the historic sites, Tessa was struck by the bond she felt with all the women she met, no matter what nationality. Whether it was talking in broken English with a shopkeeper selling tacky scarves and teacups with *Pompeii* on them, or a waitress bringing them tiramisu and espresso, or the darling little tour guide in Istanbul who shared the photos of her new baby, Tessa came away from her cruise changed. Sure, she'd gained a deeper knowledge of history, but more importantly she'd gained a deeper knowledge of women. The fact was, women were more the same than different. And one big need they shared was the compassion and love of sisterhood.

Women need women. Women bond with women. It's natural. It's right and good.

It's a God thing.

And suddenly a new idea just was, as if it had always been there, waiting for her to discover it. Why not take the Sister Circle Network to the world? Why not get women to support each other, help each other, pray for—and with—each other? Tessa came home with a keen knowing of a profound truth: the fastest way to change the world is to mobilize women. And God willing, she was going to do her part. She had to. It was her duty. As a woman. Starting right here, where she'd been planted seventy-six years ago. . . .

But she'd had no idea how to do it, and frankly, the scope of it had been so huge it scared her. That's why she'd laid low all summer, waiting for God's direction, gaining courage, making sure it wasn't *her* idea, but His.

The fact that the idea had not gone away, had grown, and made her stomach pull with anticipation more than fear, was proof the Sister Circle Network had to be pursued. And then when Calvin was offered the opportunity to go to Rome on business and decided to take the family . . .

It was perfect. Because while on her cruise, on a day she'd taken a side trip in Rome and was standing at the spot on the square in front of St. Peter's where the apostle Peter had been martyred, Tessa had met a very special woman, Rini Fudecio. They'd ended up at a sidewalk café, talking about life, women in general, and the needs of so many. Rini had a zest for life, a heart for the Lord—and international connections. And so when Tessa had a chance to see her again, she'd known it was the Lord at work. Since then, under Rini's direction, she'd plowed through the paperwork for a nonprofit, opened a special account to handle the funds, and found three people they could trust in three third-world countries.

God continued to amaze Tessa daily. For this *was* His doing. There was no doubt. And yet there was still much to do . . .

This morning she had a meeting at the community center in Jackson. Jackson, because she and the ladies had decided if they were going to do this fund-raiser, Jackson's greater population should be tapped. In preparation for the meeting she'd put on her Turkish robe and turban and headed for the kitchen for breakfast. "Morning, family," she said.

Naomi looked up from the coffeepot. "And what are you supposed to be?"

"I got this in Istanbul."

She gave Tessa the once-over while sipping her coffee. "I still don't understand why you suddenly insist on wearing these ridiculous outfits in public."

"Because you don't appreciate them in private." *Because the women who wear these clothes are me. And I am them.*

Leonard popped in, on the run. "Where's my math book?"

"Say good morning to your grandmother, Leonard."

"Hi, Grandma."

"Hello—"

"I really need my math book. I'm late."

"It's on the TV."

Leonard darted out of the room, narrowly missing his father coming in. "Oh, morning, Tessa." He winked at her. "I like the turban."

"Calvin, don't encourage her."

He bussed Tessa's cheek. His aftershave was woodsy. "Why not? She's not hurting anyone."

"She's making a fool of herself."

Tessa recoiled at the slap of the words.

Calvin eyed the two women while pouring himself a cup of coffee. "That was rude, Naomi. You need to apologize."

Tessa's jaw hardened. "I'm merely trying to increase awareness, trying to get people to think globally. If my Sister Circle Network is ever going to have a worldwide impact—"

Naomi opened a granola bar and took a bite. "That's another thing, Mom. I think you're taking on way too much. You want to raise money for an established charity, go for it. But to think that you can start a movement, that you can impact the lives of women around the world . . ."

Tessa felt the blood pump in her chest. "Why can't I do this?"

Naomi looked at her husband.

He raised a hand, "Don't look at me. This is your opinion."

Naomi turned on him. "So you think there's nothing wrong with her attempting the impossible?"

"Maybe it's not impossible," he said.

Tessa smiled. "I knew there was a good reason I liked you, Calvin."

He gave her a wink.

Naomi stepped between them, waving her arms. "Hold on, now. This is a pipe dream we're talking about here—"

"No, it's not," Tessa said. "I'm working hard to make it happen—with God's help, of course."

"Come on, Naomi." Calvin said. "The costume party sounds like a good idea. And what can it hurt?"

"What can it help?" Naomi threw half her granola bar away with the wrapper. "It can get Mom believing she can actually . . ." She suddenly looked at Tessa.

"Believing I can actually contribute to society? Do something worthwhile? Be used by God?"

Naomi let out a breath and took a new one. She came close, putting her hand on Tessa's arm. "I just think you deserve calm in your life. Quiet. Peace."

Tessa crossed her arms. "You want me to sit in a rocker on the porch and watch the world go by, is that it?"

"Of course not. But why take on something so ambitious at your—" She didn't finish the sentence. She didn't need to.

"At my age? Is that it? You don't think a seventy-six-year-old person has any worth, has any business starting something new? You think I don't have enough time? Jesus' ministry only lasted three years. Are you implying that wasn't enough time?"

"She's gotcha, hon," Calvin said.

Naomi emptied her coffee in the sink and put the mug in the dishwasher. Only then did she turn and face her mother. "I only know that I look forward to retirement, to a time when I don't have to do any more."

"Then I feel sorry for you," Tessa said. "Because I don't ever want to come to a point in my life when I don't want to do something, when I don't want to contribute to the world. If I ever do get to that point, then I hope God in His mercy will take me home."

With that, she tapped her turban in a salute, and strode from the house.

Kids.

•　•　•

It took half the distance to Jackson before Tessa's breathing slowed and her heart was not pounding in her ears. But when the anger left her, doubt entered.

Maybe the points Naomi made were valid. Whatever made her think she could start a worldwide movement at her age? From little Carson Creek no less, which was as far removed from the women of Iraq, India, and China as it could be. Then there was the language barrier. Different cultures, rules, bureaucracy. Persecution. How could she ever hope to reach one woman, much less many?

Suddenly, the doubt became so oppressive Tessa pulled to the side of the road. The car leaned to the right on the narrow shoulder. Other cars whizzed by her ear, some honking.

Let them honk. She had to stop. With all the negative thoughts trying to purge her dream, she was more a danger on the road than parked beside it.

She put the car in park and leaned over the steering wheel, placing her forehead on her hands. "Lord God, I know doubt is the work of the devil, but I also remember something my mother taught me, an old George Müller quote: 'The stops of a good man, as well as his steps, are ordered by the Lord.' I know I've been going full speed ahead with this thing. So if this doubt—if Naomi's words—are meant to stop me, then let me pull up now. But if this is something You want me to do . . ."

She stopped talking, hoping God would fill in the silence.

She heard tires on gravel and looked in her rearview mirror. A sheriff's car pulled behind her. Her first thought was that her tires weren't completely off the highway. She always did have trouble gauging things with this huge boat of a car. She rolled down her window, letting in a rush of autumn air. "Morning, Officer."

He approached her warily, but said the same. "You having some trouble with your—?" His words broke off as he noted her outfit.

She put a hand to her turban. "You like it? It's from Turkey."

"Can't say as I've seen one. If I might ask, where are you going dressed like—" He stopped himself, then looked at her again. "Are you Mrs. Klein?"

She smiled. "Why, yes, I am." She glanced at his name badge: *Orcowsky.* "Do I know—?"

He moved in front of her side mirror so she didn't have to turn in the seat awkwardly. "My sister goes to your church—Dana Bowers? She told us about you—how you've taken to wearing international outfits and how you're starting some women's movement around the world."

"It's called the Sister Circle Network."

He pointed at her. "Yeah. That's it. Sounds like a good idea."

Tessa nearly laughed with the joy of it. "Yes, it does, doesn't it?"

He seemed to remember why he'd stopped. "So why are you sitting here, on the side of the road?"

What could she tell him? She decided on the truth. "I was having a little trouble driving and praying at the same time, so I decided to stop to get things done properly."

He didn't look too shocked. "Did it work?"

"It most certainly did."

"I'll be moving on then. Good-bye, Mrs. Klein."

"Oh, Officer Orcowsky? I'm having a costume party fundraiser on November twelfth in Jackson. I'd sure like it if you and your family came."

"We wear costumes?"

"If you'd like. It's optional, but it does make it more fun."

"I do have a magician's cape . . ."

"Perfect. We'll see you then."

Tessa pulled onto the highway and gained speed. With each revolution of her tires she seemed to hear the voice of Jesus saying, *Why did you doubt Me?*

"I should know better!" Tessa laughed all the way to Jackson.

●   ●   ●

Deadlines drove Audra, and commitments were taking the fun out of even the most enjoyable part of her job. So much so that she wasn't looking forward to Mae's appointment to plan Ringo's wedding. Mae, who could make her laugh. Mae, who was always up and upbeat.

Exactly. She didn't want to laugh, and she didn't want to

be around someone who was up. Audra liked being down and depressed. She'd grown comfortable with the feeling. Besides, it took too much effort to be otherwise.

Audra arranged the table in her workroom-showroom with the catalog, the samples of fabric, a pad of paper, and a pen.

"Yoo-hoo!" Mae tapped on the door and came in.

They hugged, then took seats at the table. "I'm so glad you brought Summer by last night. She's a pretty little princess. That costume was gorgeous."

"Thanks. I'm just glad it's over with—until next year."

"She said with joy in her heart . . ."

"Sorry." Audra pulled the catalog close. "Do you know what kind of bridesmaids' dresses Soon-ja wants?"

Mae flipped the pages. "I sent her your catalog and she likes this one." She pointed at a simple sheath with a detachable chiffon train.

"I only met her the one time but this does seem to suit her style."

"Simple Soon-ja—I say that in the nicest way. Now as far as fabrics . . ."

A thought passed through her mind, and before she could stop it Audra found herself saying, "You're doing so much planning for their wedding. Doesn't Soon-ja want to do it?"

Mae flipped the pages of the notebook of fabric swatches. "They trust me. Besides, I have time and they don't. They're still on the road with that rock tour."

"Somehow they don't seem the big-wedding type."

"Soon-ja's family is in Korea. I'm helping her get the wedding of her dreams."

Or yours. "They're coming back here to get married?"

"Collie and I belong to a church. They don't. At least not yet."

"Starr and Ringo never lived in Carson Creek, did they?"

"Oh, no. This was the end of my odyssey, not theirs."

"But Starr is here now . . ."

"Not for long. She and Ted will get this worked out. I know they will. Then she'll be back in New York."

"But it's been . . . hasn't it been nearly a month?"

Mae shrugged and seemed to avoid Audra's eyes. "Oooh. I like this one." She'd pegged a pale yellow organza.

"That's too lightweight for the dress." Audra turned the pages to the crepes. "Here. You could use this yellow crepe for the dress and the organza for the train."

Mae sat back. "I like it."

"You're easy to please."

"I know what I like."

"But it's for Soon-ja."

"Same thing. Can you give me samples to send her?"

Audra got up to snip samples from their stock.

Mae followed her. "You sure sigh a lot."

"I do?"

Mae took the scissors away from her. She set them down then put her hands on Audra's shoulders. "Out with it."

"What?" Audra knew it was a dumb response.

Mae backed away. "Fine. If you want to be a prideful, arrogant—"

"I am not prideful!"

"Not accepting the help of a sister makes you both those things."

"I'm perfectly fine!"

Mae scathed her with a look. "My, my, you are a moody mama, aren't you?"

Audra knew she should cover up but couldn't. And didn't have to. This was Mae. She fell into a chair, a lump without form. "I'm just so incredibly tired."

Mae moved behind her and began kneading her shoulders. "Poor baby. You're succumbing to SMS."

Audra closed her eyes and let Mae's fingers move her. "What's SMS?"

"Super Mom Syndrome."

She snickered under her breath. "Hardly. I'm not super at anything."

"Because you're trying to do everything. Something's got to give, sister."

Audra turned around to face Mae. "But what? I quit my regular job at the bank and started this business at home to be near Summer."

"One sparkle star."

"We moved into a new home. I've tried to make it nice for my family. There are actual blinds and curtains on every window."

Mae applauded. "Two sparkle stars."

"Give me an extra star for that one. You don't know how I hate making valances."

"A third is duly noted. Continue."

Audra got up to pace. "I've started a Web site for the wedding business, put together a catalog; I pay bills, I order fabric, I meet with customers, I cut out dresses, I—"

"What does Heddy do?"

"Heddy does plenty. She sews 90 percent of the dresses."

"But you need help."

She and Heddy had talked about this. They were both hesitant about relinquishing control. There was the quality issue too. Working with satins and sheers was difficult. That's why Audra let Heddy handle most of the sewing.

"Don't shake your head at me," Mae said.

Audra hadn't realized she'd been shaking it. "It'll be okay."

Mae made herself a human roadblock, stopping Audra's pacing. "Not as is. That's the problem. Hire someone part time to do the bookwork, the ordering."

"But I'm good at the administrative part. That's my strength, my main contribution."

"Then let someone else meet with customers."

Meeting with the customers was fun. Sometimes. But that *was* the great unknown timewise. "It usually takes at least an hour for the first visit and sometimes it takes three or four visits before customers make up their minds."

Mae clapped her hands once. "Exactly. But look at me. *Bing. Bang.* I'm done."

Audra smiled. "I think you set a world's record."

She leaned close. "You'll have to call me if anyone else gets close and I'll zip over and muddle their minds."

"To hold on to your record?"

"I want to be known for something."

Audra laughed. "Believe me, you are." She looked across the room, her mind reeling. Admitting she needed help made her feel like a failure. And yet . . . "Maybe we *could* hire a saleswoman." She started thinking of people she knew who had a flair for fashion.

"There you go. I think you're up to a dozen in the sparkle-star department, but there're two items you've neglected to mention."

"Two?"

"One has beautiful brown eyes . . ."

Audra was appalled that she'd gone through her entire list without mentioning her husband of ten months. "Russell!"

"Yeah. I think that's his name."

She found the chair a second time. "Our time together *has* been kind of sparse."

"I'm sure he feels the same way."

Audra looked up. "You said there were two items? Russell is one . . ."

"The old JC, Audra. The worst part of busyness is that it takes us away from Him. When was the last time you had a little one-on-One with the Big Guy?"

"I pray." *While I work. While I drive. While I cook. While I . . .*

"I'm not talking about sending off a snippet of prayer while you're busy doing other things. I'm talking about concentrated, affectionate attention to the Almighty, full of gratitude, praise, confession, and good conversation."

Audra looked at her lap. "It's been ages."

Mae strode to the door of the workroom to leave. But before she left she turned over the Open sign, showing Closed to the world. "There. Go on."

"Now?"

"You bet. God likes now."

• • •

Audra cozied into the oversize chair, resting her slippered feet on the ottoman. She took a sip of hot chocolate and set it on the end table. She was ready to open her Bible when she stopped. And listened.

Silence.

The absence of sound was overwhelming. When was the last time she'd allowed silence into her life?

She thought about all the tasks she did in this house—this house that was her world. Cooking, cleaning, eating, sleeping, playing, talking, working. But what accompanied each task?

Noise.

Sure, some of it was music and quite lovely. She often liked to play CDs while she did chores. She also liked to watch TV while she cooked. Russell had even gotten her a counter-size set so she could be entertained while she mixed and stirred. She even wore headphones when she went for a walk or mowed the lawn. And in her car? The radio was always on as she flipped from one station to another. With horror she realized they even had a water-proof radio in their shower so as not to miss a lick of the morning news.

In fact, there were usually layers of noise present. Music or

TV mixed with the *clatter-bump-bang* of their activity, layered with their voices. Why, there were even times when she had the kitchen TV on, Russell had the family room TV on, while Summer played music in her room. A cacophony of sounds.

Did you hear Me? Did you hear Me talking to you?

Audra covered her face in shame, answering with a violent shake of her head. "No! I didn't hear You! I couldn't!" *I wouldn't?*

Then hear Me now. Listen! I've been wanting to talk with you. . . .

Audra nodded. "I'm here, Lord. And I'm all Yours."

It was exactly what He wanted to hear.

● ● ●

Returning home from work, Lucinda was not thrilled to see Tessa's car in front of Peerbaugh Place. Tessa was not one you could merely chat with. In the few times they'd talked, they had argued, or gotten to the edge of arguing. After her less-than-stellar day with Gwen, she didn't feel up to the challenge. Hopefully, the ladies were in the kitchen. Maybe if Lucinda slipped in the front door and up the stairs . . .

She took hold of the front door gingerly, turning it slowly so it didn't rattle and alert—

"Lucinda!" Evelyn pulled the door into the entryway—and Lucinda along with it.

"Hi, Evelyn." She looked up. Tessa was seated in the parlor. So was Piper. "Hello, ladies."

Evelyn led her into the room. "I was just telling everyone about your amazing experiences at the reunion. How God turned what could have been a negative into a positive. How He led Pastor Enoch to you, and that porter . . . what was his name?"

"LeJames," Lucinda said. She pulled away. "I'm sorry, but I've had a really hard day and I don't feel up to talking—"

"Come on, Lucinda," Piper said. "Evelyn told us you were

practically skimming the ceiling you were so high on your experience. Share, sister, share."

She thought of Gwen. Been there. Done that. "I'm tired. I'm tired of talking about it."

She saw Tessa glance at the other two ladies. "Uh-oh. Who else did you tell? Somebody obviously didn't listen well, did they?"

Evelyn put a hand on Lucinda's shoulder. "Who pulled you down off your mountaintop?"

Lucinda didn't have the energy to take the stairs, so she slumped on the couch beside Tessa. "I told Gwen at work. She made me see that things weren't as . . . weren't as . . ." She couldn't think of a way to word it.

"Weren't as God inspired as you thought?" Piper asked.

"Something like that."

Tessa moved close until her tiny arm reached around Lucinda's shoulder. "You hear me, Lucinda Van Horn. You don't let anyone tell you God hasn't worked in your life when you know He has. From what Evelyn's told us, you had yourself a God-given, God-driven weekend and no one—friend or otherwise—has a right to tell you different."

Piper moved to the edge of the coffee table, facing them. "The world is eager to explain away every miracle, Lucinda. And some people just can't stand it when amazing things happen to others and not to them."

"They're just jealous," Evelyn said with a nod.

"Exactly," Piper said. "Why Tessa just shared with us about her daughter doing the same type of thing. Naomi told her she was too old to start an undertaking like Sister Circles."

"Made me doubt too. Until God sent me a handsome sheriff named Officer Orcowsky to set me straight."

Lucinda had to smile. "Officer Orcowsky?"

"See? If God can use a man with a name like that, He certainly can use two men named Enoch and LeJames," Tessa said.

"I wonder what happened to all the Toms and Bobs of the world," Evelyn mused.

"They were obviously busy." Tessa patted Lucinda's knee. "You should feel very honored about all this."

"Why?"

Tessa lowered her voice as if sharing a secret. "Because it's God who does the revealing. He chooses the time and place to show Himself and His ways to us. And He chose you, Lucinda. He chose you."

Lucinda pulled in a long breath. The idea was too preposterous. Too disconcerting. Too wonderful. She looked to Evelyn and Piper. They nodded their agreement.

Piper went to the desk where Evelyn's Bible lay open. She brought it back, flipping the pages, and sat down, her knee nearly touching Lucinda's. "Listen to this: 'But I will reveal my name to my people, and they will come to know its power. Then at last they will recognize that it is I who speaks to them.'"

"See?" Tessa said, spreading her hands to the truth. "Plain as day. God does speak to us—in many ways. It's up to us to recognize Him." She put her hands in her lap and gave Lucinda a pointed look. "So do you? Do you recognize that it was God who did all this for you last weekend?"

Lucinda couldn't speak. But she did nod.

It was time for a group hug.

Just as I have loved you, you should love each other.
Your love for one another
will prove to the world that you are My disciples.

JOHN 13:34-35

*M*ae sat at the kitchen table and took one last look at the catalog for Catherine's Wedding Creations before sending it to Soon-ja.

Collier looked up from his crossword puzzle. "You're drooling."

Close. She turned the page so he could see it. Again. "The dresses are going to be so pretty. I hope Soon-ja likes them."

"She's liked everything else you've picked out."

She slipped the catalog and fabric swatches into the brown envelope. "I happen to have good taste."

"And she happens to be a very sweet, compliant girl who wants you to like her."

"I'd like her even if she disagreed with me."

He peered at her over his reading glasses.

She sealed the envelope shut. "I just wish Ringo would give me the go-ahead. He's the holdup."

"Like most men, he probably doesn't really care."

"How can he not care about his own wedding?"

"Let me amend my statement. He probably doesn't have a strong opinion one way or the other."

"Good save, Mr. Husband."

"I thought so."

Mae added stamps. "Then why doesn't he say so? Things are hanging here. Decisions need to be made. The wedding's in four months."

"It could be postponed."

"You do not postpone a wedding as easily as a golf date."

"Ted and Starr did. Have. Are."

"They never had a date set."

He erased a word on his puzzle and filled in another one. "And it appears they never will." He glanced up at her. "You need to come to terms with that, wifey. It'll be a month on Friday. Maybe it's time for Starr to find her own place."

"You don't like having her here?"

"I'm fine with it, though being surrounded by two opinionated women twenty-four hours a day was never one of my life goals."

Mae put her hands on his. "We make your life interesting. Admit it."

"What's a five-letter word for temperamental?"

She shoved his hand away and moved on. "Actually, toward that end . . . I have an idea."

Collie put his pencil down and gave her his full attention. "Mae . . . what are you up to?"

"It's a great idea really . . ."

"Don't go meddling where it's not wanted."

"There's nothing wrong with a mother meddling with love."

"Most meddling is done in the name of love. But that doesn't make it right."

"You haven't even heard my idea."

He folded the newspaper neatly into fourths and set it aside.

He moved his mug of tea out of harm's way. Then he placed his hands flat on the table and took a deep breath. "Okay. I'm ready."

"You're not funny."

"Very funny."

She rolled her eyes. "My idea is to invite Ted for a visit."

"On what pretense?"

"On the pretense of reconciliation. That's what we're after, isn't it?"

"That's what *you're* after. I'm not sure Starr would agree."

"Oh, her. She doesn't know what she wants."

"I think she's made it very clear what she wants. She wants to be away from Ted. Obviously she doesn't miss him that much or she would have gone back to New York weeks ago."

Mae folded over the corner of his newspaper. "Have you noticed how restless she's gotten?"

"Understandably. Living with her mother and stepfather was probably not on her list of life goals either."

"There's more to it than that. It's like she's going through an inner battle. She's grumpier than usual—toward both of us." She sighed. "I think I'm losing her."

He retrieved his tea and took a sip. "Maybe. Or maybe your loss is God's gain. Would you want her to be sweetness and light and still not know Him, or are you willing to deal with her being difficult if it means He's drawing her close?"

"You really think that's it?"

"I started seeing a change in her after she went to church with Piper, ten days ago."

Mae slapped the table. "Me too!"

He shrugged.

Mae jumped on the idea. "She's never been an easy person to have around, and her cleaning and rearranging my house has taken some getting used to, and yet—"

"Personally, I like being able to find the peanut butter."

"Oh you . . ." She put a hand to her mouth, thinking hard. "It's a fact: some people go down without a whimper and others fight it."

"Somehow I don't think the act of surrendering to God should be described as 'going down.'"

"You know what I mean. Her old nature is not giving in without a fight. That's what we're seeing. The battle. She's a stubborn girl."

He grinned. "Takes after her mother."

"But I did give in. I did let God in."

He reached across the table and took her hand. "And so will she, wifey. So will she."

"I hope so."

"Let's pray so."

She gave him a huge smile. "But isn't that meddling?"

He leaned over and gave her a kiss. "Meddling with love, wifey. Meddling with love."

•   •   •

Although Mae was usually the one who visited Peerbaugh Place, that day, while she was home for lunch, she was the recipient of a visit from Evelyn.

They went to the kitchen. "Collie's making egg-salad sandwiches. Want one?"

"Sure," Evelyn said.

Mae could tell food was the last thing on her mind. Collier looked up from the counter where he was cutting the sandwiches—on the diagonal, just the way Mae liked. "Make us another one, Mr. Husband."

"Sorry to interrupt your lunch like this, Collier."

"Not a problem. We have plenty."

While Evelyn was settling in at the table, Mae slid to his side and whispered in his ear. He nodded.

"Here you go, ladies." He set down two plates. "If you don't mind, I'm going to eat mine in the family room. I want to check the stock market."

Mae took a seat. "So. What's up?"

"He didn't need to leave the room, Mae."

"Sure he did." She put a finger on the crease between Evelyn's brows. "This crevasse means you came over here for some serious sister talk. Am I correct?"

"Well . . ."

She took a bite. "Shoot."

Evelyn toyed with her sandwich, but didn't eat any. "This morning I got a phone call from Wayne."

"Good, good. . ."

"He said the words I've longed to hear."

"He adores you, thinks you're one hot tomato, and wants to snatch you up before some other single man beats him to it."

She raised an eyebrow. "Not exactly. He said, 'Hi, Evelyn. It's Wayne. I need you.'"

"Hey. I like my version better, but it's close enough."

"No, it isn't. He needed me to help him pick out a new suit because he has a blind date with the cousin of someone at church who has asked him to go to *Annie Get Your Gun* in Jackson on Friday." She took a fresh breath.

"You've got to be kidding."

"I'm not."

"You didn't go, did you?"

Evelyn hesitated.

Mae gasped. "You did! Why would you encourage a man who is so completely clueless?"

"I wanted to be with him." She pinched the corner off her sandwich. "He bought a really nice gray pinstripe."

Mae shoved her plate toward the center of the table, knocking it into the saltshaker. "Gracious gabardine, Evie, you don't help a man pick out a suit so he can date someone else."

"He says I'm a good, good friend."

"So is a cocker spaniel."

When Evelyn looked up, her eyes were full of tears. "Oh dear . . . he doesn't see me as a woman at all, Mae. When I started having feelings for him, I thought . . . but he doesn't . . . and . . ." The last came out in a rush. "I gave up Herb for him!"

Mae made a T with her hands. "Time out. You're making squeaking noises as if—if it weren't for Wayne—you'd still be with Herb, yet you gave up Herb, which means you didn't really care for Herb . . ."

"I know, I know. I'm fickle."

"Actually, you're brave."

Evelyn shook her head.

"Sure you are. You gave up Herb because you were beginning to have feelings for Wayne. You gave him up without any guarantee that Wayne would reciprocate."

"But he's dating someone else!"

True. Mae tried to think of something positive but she wasn't well versed in courting games. She much preferred the direct approach. Yet Evelyn . . . going up to Wayne to say, "I'm interested in you as a man, Wayne Wellington, and I want you to be interested in me as a woman" was not Evelyn's style.

Finally, Mae lassoed a ray of hope. "You're taking cooking classes together, aren't you?"

"Yes."

"You see him in church, don't you?"

"We usually sit in the same pew—with Piper, Russell . . . whoever's around."

"That still counts."

Evelyn nodded as if she'd take what she could get.

Mae clapped her hands once. "He came over and fixed your garbage disposal. If that's not interest, what is?"

Evelyn laughed. "You're grasping, Mae."

"All in the sisterhood pledge, Evie dear."

Evelyn finally took a bite of sandwich and dabbed her mouth with a napkin. "So what do I do?"

Mae hated the desperate look in her friend's eyes. "You continue doing what you have been doing. You take any opportunity you can to be with him. You make yourself available." She thought of something. "Does he know you broke up with Herb?"

Evelyn's eyes grew wide. "No. I don't think he does!"

"Well then. That's part of it. Wayne is not the kind of man who would date a woman who was unavailable."

"No. No, he's not." She pushed away from the table. "I've got to go."

"But your sandwich . . ."

She was already out the door. Mae looked at Evelyn's sandwich that had one bite taken out of it. She exchanged the bitten section for her own untouched half. "Collie! I hope you're hungry . . ."

●　　●　　●

Evelyn didn't remember her stomach feeling like this since she was a teenager. It reminded her of the extensive maneuverings she and her girlfriends used to implement regarding boys. *Tell him that I like him—no! Don't tell him I like him; tell him that I think he's cute or that I could think he's cute if he thinks I'm cute. . . .*

She dialed the phone. Maybe he wasn't home.

"Hello?"

"Wayne!" She fairly yelled the word. *Calm down, Evelyn!*

"Goodness, Evelyn. What's wrong?"

She took a breath. "Nothing. Sorry. I . . . I just wanted to tell you something . . . I mean I think it's important you know something."

"Sounds ominous. What is it?"

What was she doing? It was going to sound way too blatant

and forward. For there was no reason Evelyn would share this with him unless she *did* have romantic intentions—

"Evelyn. Tell me."

"I broke up with Herb."

A moment of silence. "I'm so sorry. Why?"

"I feel as though I've been leading him on. He was more interested in me than I was in him and, at our age . . . I don't think it's fair to keep going out with him."

"That's very commendable, Evelyn. I admire you for that."

He admires me for that! "You do?"

"Of course. It's far too easy to hang on to what's easy and comfortable even when it's not good for the other person."

"That's what I thought."

"How's he taking it?"

"He's disappointed."

"I can imagine."

He can imagine!

She suddenly realized she hadn't thought about how to end the conversation. "Well . . . I guess that's it. I just thought you should know."

"I'm glad you told me."

"If I don't see you . . . have a good time on your date."

"Thanks. And thanks for helping me with the suit."

"Anytime."

Anytime.

Evelyn wondered if it was unchristian for her to hope the date would be a total bust.

•　　•　　•

The phone rang. Mae answered. "Ringo! Just the man I need to talk to. I've been working on the wedding and you have some decisions to make and—"

"I have something to tell you, Mom."

Mae's heart did a nosedive. "Are you okay? Is Soon-ja—?"

"We're pregnant."

Mae found a chair and sat in it. Old adages sprang to mind: *Putting the cart before the horse. Having a bun in the oven. Shotgun wedding . . .*

Being a grandmother.

But before she could voice any of these feelings, Ringo said, "We're also married."

She was glad she was sitting down. The table was still covered with wedding books. Maybe she'd heard wrong. "You're *going* to get—"

"No, Mom. We got married. We eloped."

She pulled in a breath. "You can't do that. I'm planning a wedding here. I picked out dresses and invitations and flowers and—"

"You'll have to use your ideas for Starr's wedding. Whenever. If ever . . ."

Fat chance. "Why didn't you wait? We could have moved the date up. You could have had a beautiful ceremony."

"Once Soon-ja found out, she was devastated. Her family back in Korea is very strict. She felt shame."

Having come from a hippie, free-love lifestyle, Mae had trouble taking a strong stand on premarital anything.

"Soon-ja insisted on being married immediately. For their sake. I couldn't argue with her. I want her to be happy."

Mae was moved by the devotion in her son's voice. She wished she could be assured that her own voice wouldn't be whiny with disappointment. This was an important moment in her son's life. She needed to respond correctly. *Lord, help me . . .*

"Mom?"

She cleared her throat. "I'm here. I was just thinking . . ."

"What?" His guard was up.

"You're not going to make the child call me Nana Mae, are you? Because that sounds like a goat's name."

He laughed. "What would you like to be called?"

Grandmother was too sophisticated for her taste, *Grammy* too country. "How about Grandma?"

"You got it."

It felt good to have moved into the middle of the situation instead of standing nervously on the edges. "How is Soon-ja feeling?"

"Nauseous in the morning. But not bad."

"When are you coming to visit? I want to hear all the details."

"Soon, Mom. Soon." Some mumbling in the background. "I have to go. I just wanted to tell you the news. I hope you're not too disappointed."

"That I don't get to make a fuss over a wedding? I'll save my fuss for the baby. You can bet on that. Congratulations, Ringo."

"Thanks, Mom. Thanks . . ." His voice cracked. "You're the greatest."

Not really. But she'd work on it.

She hung up and stood to fill her lungs with air. "Collie! Starr! Come quick! I have news!"

•　　•　　•

Her brother a father. And a husband.

He beat you to it, Starr. On both counts.

She pushed the thought away and got back to work. From her favorite place on the porch, Starr saw Piper drive up after school and waved.

Piper came over. "Always working," Piper said. "Is it quitting time soon?"

"Soon." She moved over so Piper could sit on the swing.

Piper looked at the computer screen. "I see you're still working on your anti-man book."

"It's not anti-man. It's about relationships."

"*How to Get More out of Your Man* definitely sounds more about taking than giving."

"Hey, women give much more than they take. Surely you can't disagree with that one."

"Perhaps. But maybe we're supposed to."

"Says who?" As soon as she said it, Starr knew what the answer was going to be.

To her credit, Piper just smiled. "Women are made with a deeper capacity to love, to empathize, to feel."

Starr shook her head. "You're perpetuating the stereotype of emotional, weak beings. I think women are incredibly strong."

"Oh, me too," Piper said. "I think showing love, empathy, and emotions make us strong, and in regard to relationships, perhaps strong*er*."

Starr snickered. "You'll have to explain that one."

Piper turned toward her on the swing, bringing one leg onto the seat. "Men tend to be factual beings. They see things in black and white."

"You got that right."

"Women see the grays, the nuances, the bigger picture—the effect on the future. Men are more concerned with the moment."

Starr nodded, her fingers flying on the keyboard. "I like that. Keep going."

"Oh, no . . . I don't mean for you to use this."

"Sure you do," Starr said. "You don't like the premise of this book; then convince me otherwise."

Piper moved the swing forward and back with her toe before speaking. "It's like when I broke up with Gregory because he wasn't a Christian, because God tells us not to be unequally yoked."

Starr laughed. "Sounds painful."

"It would be. That's why He warns us against it."

"But according to you, Ted and I are unequally yoked. Should he leave me?"

Piper hesitated. "It sounds like he's trying to get you to see the light."

Starr splayed her hands above her head. "Oh, holy Jesus, help this poor sinner see the Light!"

"You kid about it, but you just uttered a valid prayer."

"Don't hold your breath."

Piper looked across the yard. "It was the hardest thing I ever did to let Gregory go. But since he was unwilling to seek God, I had no choice."

"It seems dumb to me."

Piper looked at the floor. "Dumb to the world."

"Then why do it? 'Fifty million Frenchmen can't be wrong,' right?"

That got a smile out of her. "Actually, they can. And it wouldn't matter if 50 billion people thought it was okay for me to stay with him. If God doesn't approve . . ."

"If you don't mind my saying so, you sound a bit fanatic."

"A fanatic for Christ. I take that as a compliment."

Starr shook her head. "You *are* far gone."

Piper put both feet on the ground, sending the swing into a sudden gyration. "I am not!"

Starr closed her computer, keeping it safe. "'The lady doth protest too much, methinks.'"

Piper stood and faced her. "Actually, I probably don't protest enough."

"You could have fooled me."

Piper pointed at the laptop. "You're working on a book that will create dissension between men and women—more dissention than there already is."

"I'm helping women learn to cope."

"By giving them ways to *get*? to *take*?"

"I'm helping them learn to deal, to survive."

Piper tossed her hands in the air. "It's not a war. It's a partnership. Men and women are different in both physical, mental, and emotional ways in order for them to complement one another, so all the bases are covered in every situation. When the world deals with situations from a purely factual standpoint, it fails. Same if only feelings are utilized." She intertwined her fingers. "Only when all aspects of a situation are accounted for and melded together does it turn out right."

Balancing her computer on her lap, Starr applauded. "Bravo! Encore! Encore!"

Piper frowned, her eyebrows dipped, and Starr feared she might cry. She didn't mean to make her cry.

Piper moved to the top of the porch steps. "If only you'd let yourself think for yourself, Starr, you'd find you agree with me. And you'd agree with God. You may not be writing the book, but you're still responsible for it."

"It's not my decision to publish or not publish it."

"But you do have input. You could say no."

"I could. But if I don't do it, someone else will. So why fight it?"

Piper stared at her, her face no longer showing a hint of wanting to cry. Actually, Piper looked as if she wanted to strangle her. "You are the most stubborn—"

No! Not that word! "Don't call me that!" Starr said.

"Then I'll leave you with a parting thought: 'For they loved human praise more than the praise of God.' Pick your partner, Starr. But choose wisely."

• • •

Joyful. Be joyful.

"*Shout with joy to the Lord, O earth! Worship the Lord with gladness. . . .*"

Audra dropped an egg on the floor. She looked in the carton. Good. There was another one.

She grabbed a paper towel and cleaned it up. She tried to regain the verse where she left off. *"Come before Him, singing with joy. Acknowledge that the Lord is God! He made us, and we are His. We are His people, the sheep of His pasture."*

Sheep. She could relate. She felt a lot like a sheep right now, following blindly, going where she was told to go, doing what she was told to do. Russell was having two of the bank's clients over for dinner. She did not have time to do it today, and yet she had to. And she wanted to do it with the right attitude. Thinking about doing it for Jesus, to please Him, helped, but it was still a struggle. . . .

"Enter His gates with thanksgiving; go into His courts with praise. . . ."

She turned on the mixer. The beaters clanked loudly. She shut it off. She hadn't got them in all the way and now one of them was bent. She bent it back, but it would never be the same.

"Give thanks to Him and bless His name."

Oh yeah. She really felt like thanking God right now. She had the pot roast in, and would slip the potatoes in the Crock-Pot next. But this cheesecake was *not* cooperating. And the dining room table was still covered with the remains of the bridesmaid dress she'd just cut out. The bathroom needed cleaning, the living room vacuuming . . .

While the mixer did its duty, she closed her eyes and tried to concentrate. *"For the Lord is good. His—"*

The phone rang. It was Russell. "You working hard on the dinner, hon?"

She held in a snide comment. "I'm getting there."

"Well, I'm calling to tell you to stop. Mr. Geddys has the flu so we're going to reschedule."

While part of her was doing handstands, another part said, "But I already have the roast in."

"We can eat it—tomorrow."

That didn't make sense. "Tomorrow?"

"When they canceled, it gave me an idea. You've been work-ing so hard, and I know this dinner party is the last thing you needed."

At least her martyrdom was duly noted. "Yeah, well . . ."

"I'd like to take you out to dinner tonight. To our place."

"Chez Garsaud?"

"I'll make reservations immediately. I already called Mom. She'll take Summer. And maybe we can take a stroll through the park afterward and look at the stars."

"The nights are pretty chilly . . ."

"I'll keep you warm."

Suddenly overcome, Audra clapped a hand over her mouth.

"Audra? Does that sound okay?"

She nodded as if he could see, then said aloud. "It's wonderful."

"I was hoping you'd say that. I'll be home at six. Wear your blue dress. You look so pretty in that dress."

"I love you, Russell."

"I love you too, hon. See you soon."

Audra turned off the mixer and let the room wash with silence. Then she finished the verse, calling it out to the heavens to make sure God heard. "'For the Lord is good! His unfailing love continues forever, and His faithfulness continues to each generation.'"

•   •   •

Margaret stood in the middle of her bedroom at Peerbaugh Place. The lack of motion, emotion, and commotion was a bit disconcert-ing. She'd been spending so much time with Bobby, cramming so much into every day, that to have an evening free caught her off guard. She didn't know what she wanted to do first: give her room a good cleaning, go downstairs and spend the evening chatting with the ladies, or sink into a deep tub of bubbly water . . .

"Margaret?"

She looked toward her door, which she'd left ajar. A little hand appeared, sliding up and down the doorjamb. "Come in, little one." Summer appeared, dressed in a green sweater with a Scottie dog appliquéd on the front. "I used to have a sweater with a Scottie on it," she said.

Summer pushed her belly forward, making her torso a smoother canvas. "Grandma gave this to me."

"It must be a grandma thing because my grandma was the one who gave me my sweater too."

Summer patted the dog's head, but looked at Margaret. "You're here."

"Yup, I'm here. And so are you. Any special reason for the visit?"

"Daddy took Mommy on a date. I wasn't invited." She pointed to the bookshelf near the window. "Can I . . . ?"

"Help yourself." Margaret had brought home a stack of second-grade readers just for times like this.

Summer chose three and made herself at home on the window seat.

Lucinda appeared at the opened door. "You're here," she said.

It wasn't that much of an oddity, was it? "Bobby got invited to some sports something or other with one of his friends. I'm a free agent."

Lucinda leaned on the doorjamb, studying her.

"What?"

"You look in need of rejuvenation."

Margaret ran a hand through her hair. "That bad, huh?"

Lucinda didn't answer. "Have you ever considered using a bit more makeup?"

"I've never been very good at putting it on."

"Want some tips?"

"I—"

Lucinda's face lit up. "How about a makeover?"

From Lucinda? "Oh, I don't know. I'm not sure that would be a good—"

"Sure, you're sure. I could make you into a knockout that would knock Bobby's socks off."

"He's never mentioned not liking the way I look."

Summer jumped off the window seat. "Can I get made up too?"

"Sure you can," Lucinda said. "Come on. Lucinda's House of Beauty is now open for business."

Uh-oh.

•   •   •

They moved to their shared bathroom, where Margaret sat on the toilet lid, her face raised to receive the magic machinations of Lucinda's skills.

Once she began, Lucinda did not let her look in the mirror. A surprise would be best. Even when Evelyn knocked on the door wanting to know what was going on, Lucinda barred her access.

Only Summer was allowed inside, and only on the condition she not peek. Summer sat behind Margaret in the dry bathtub, playing with Lucinda's old makeup, talking to herself and making faces in a little hand mirror.

"Are we about finished?" Margaret asked. "I've never spent this much time on my looks."

"Natural beauty takes a lot of work," Lucinda said. She dabbed the end of Margaret's chin with a powder puff, then tilted it upward for a final look. "Lovely. Now we'll take your hair out of the curlers and you'll be finished."

"I wish you'd let me see," Margaret said.

"Soon, impatient one, soon." Lucinda removed the cooled rollers and combed through Margaret's thick mane. *Oh, to have hair like this* . . . she grabbed the can of hairspray. "Close your eyes." She blanketed the hair with a veil of spray, fluffed a bit around the face, then called it complete. "Perfecto!"

"Is she done?" Summer asked from the tub.

"Indeed she is," Lucinda said. "Come see for yourself."

"But I want to see it first," Margaret said.

Before Lucinda could hand her a mirror Summer scrambled out of the tub and stood before them. Lucinda waited for the *ooh*s and *aah*s, the exclamation "You're beautiful!"

Instead all Summer said was "Uh . . . wow."

Margaret's eyebrows dipped. "Do you like it?"

Summer was staring at her hair. "Is that a wig?"

"No, silly," Lucinda said, adjusting a stray curl. "All this is Margaret's hair."

"Wow."

Lucinda grew impatient with the child. "Don't you like it?"

Summer bit the inside of her cheek. "She looks like you."

Lucinda smiled. It was the greatest compliment.

"Can I see now?" Margaret asked.

Lucinda stepped aside giving Margaret access to the mirror above the sink.

Margaret's hand flew to her hair. "Oh!"

"I know," Lucinda said. "Isn't it amazing what a little extra effort and a few more products will do?"

Summer pulled open the door leading to Margaret's room. "I'm going to go get Grandma!"

Margaret swung toward the door. "No! Summer . . ."

"Too late. She's off," laughed Lucinda. "Maybe Evelyn will want me to give her a makeover next." She put the caps back on the various liners. "It's a shame you aren't seeing Bobby tonight. Can you imagine his reaction if you'd waltz into the room looking like this?"

Margaret's head shook no. She was in awe. It was understandable. Lucinda had turned her from mousy to magnificent.

"Come on, Grandma! Hurry up! You'll never believe what Margaret looks like."

Margaret bolted for the bathroom door, shutting it. "No!"

A few seconds later Evelyn knocked. "Why did you close the door? Let me see the new you."

Lucinda had trouble reading Margaret's face, whose eyes were flitting around the bathroom. "Where's a washcloth?" Margaret asked.

"What do you need with a—"

Margaret found one, wet it, and to Lucinda's horror, swiped it across her carefully lined Carnival Red lipstick.

"What are you doing?"

"I can't let people see me like this!"

"What—?"

The bathroom door opened and Evelyn peeked in. Her smile faded immediately. "Whoa!"

Margaret set to work double time with the washcloth, rinsing it in the sink. The water swirled with red, tan, and blue.

Evelyn started to laugh. "Your hair reminds me of Miss America contestants twenty years ago."

Lucinda looked from Evelyn to Margaret's hair, then back again. "What are you—?"

Summer squeezed in beside Evelyn. "Do you like my makeup, Grandma?"

"You and Margaret could be sisters."

Lucinda took a step back, toward the door leading to her room. What were they talking about? Summer's self-applied makeup looked clownish. Margaret's had been beautiful—until she'd started wiping it off.

Margaret must have seen Lucinda's face in the mirror because she turned around, washcloth tight against her cheek. "Lucinda. I'm . . . I'm so sorry."

Evelyn looked confused.

"I thought you looked pretty," Summer said.

"Oh dear," Evelyn said.

Margaret set the washcloth in the sink and came to Lucinda's side, putting a hand on her arm. "I really appreciate the effort; it was just a bit too much for me. Too glamorous. I'm not a glamorous kind of gal. Not like you. You were a model. I guess I just have to be me. I have to let me shine through—whatever that is."

Evelyn tried to make amends too, but Lucinda stopped listening. "If you'll excuse me."

She went into her bedroom.

She locked the door.

●　　●　　●

Margaret herded Evelyn and Summer into her bedroom, softly closing the door to the empty bathroom.

"I'm so sorry," Evelyn said. "When I saw you, I just assumed it was a joke. My girlfriends and I used to make each other up and it was always too much. That was the fun of it."

Margaret looked toward Lucinda's room. She could only imagine the pain she was feeling. "Her intentions were good."

Summer looked up at both of them, her face a rainbow of misdirected makeup. "I told Aunt Lucinda that you looked just like her and—"

Evelyn gasped. "You didn't!"

"Wasn't that okay?"

Evelyn put her hands on Summer's shoulders. "Let's go in my bathroom and get you cleaned up."

"But I like the way I look." Summer said.

"Shh, sweetie. Not now."

Margaret ran into the hallway after them. "What should I do?" she whispered.

Evelyn kept her voice low. "Fix your face, then go knock on her door. Apologize."

"What if she won't see me?"

Evelyn shrugged. "She has to come out sometime."

•   •   •

Lucinda lifted her head from the pillow and listened. The bathroom was quiet. She heard voices below. Maybe she could pack her things and slip out without them seeing her.

And go where?

She'd go someplace where they wouldn't make fun of her. Where she'd be appreciated. Where people wouldn't laugh—

They laughed at the reunion too . . .

She sat up, taking her pillow with her. She tossed it across the room. "What's with people, anyway? Are they blind? I'm a beautiful woman."

She marched into the bathroom, braced her arms on the sink, and looked into the mirror. *I'm beautiful. I'm—*

Lucinda had heard the phrase "the veil was lifted," but she'd never experienced it. Until now. It was like she was looking at a stranger.

And she didn't like what she saw.

Starting at her collarbone, she ran her hands up her neck, across her cheeks, along the corners of her eyes, ending across her forehead. The fingers ran over wrinkles and touched upon areas that seemed pulled too tight. Her makeup was like paint layered upon a peeling chair, covering up, not enhancing.

She looked like the aging star in *Sunset Boulevard*, her face a contorted mask of her youth. "All right, Mr. DeMille, I'm ready for my close-up."

She couldn't look any longer. She covered her face with her hands and let herself slip to the cold bathroom floor.

•   •   •

"Gin!" Margaret laid down the winning cards just as Piper came in from choir practice. "Hey, Piper. Want to join us? I'm on a roll."

Evelyn groaned as she counted up her points. "Don't do it, Piper. She's too hot to handle."

Summer ran in from the sunroom and attached herself to Piper's waist. "Aunt Piper, come see what I drew."

Piper looked down at the little girl and wiped her thumb against her hairline. "Why do you have blue in your hair?"

"Uh-oh," Evelyn said. "Did we miss a spot?"

"I put on makeup. Lots of it."

"Not mine, I hope."

Summer shook her head. "Aunt Lucinda's. She gave Aunt Margaret a makeover."

Piper looked at Margaret. She didn't look any different.

Margaret got up from the table, her voice lowered. "Lucinda did the makeover, but I cleaned it off."

"That bad?"

Evelyn nodded. "When I saw her I laughed. I thought it was a joke."

Piper started to see the picture. "Lucinda was serious."

All three females nodded.

"She's been up in her room for over an hour," Margaret said. "I tried knocking. I even tried going in, but she doesn't answer and the door is locked."

"I don't like the sound of that," Piper said. "Looks are everything to Lucinda. They are her identity."

Evelyn's eyes grew wide. "Oh dear. And we just insulted her

identity." She headed for the stairs. "We need to get in there. See if she's all right."

The four of them hurried upstairs and down the hall to Lucinda's door. Piper put a finger to her lips and took the lead. It was probably best she be the one to knock. "Lucinda? You in there? I just got home from choir, and I wondered if you wanted to watch an old Jimmy Stewart DVD with me."

There was no answer. She put her ear to the door. Nothing.

Piper tried the knob. It was locked. She turned to Evelyn. "Do you have a key?"

"Yes, but I hate to use it."

"We might not have a choice."

"I'll go get it." She headed downstairs. "Summer? You come with me."

"In the meantime, we'll try through the bathroom." The other two ladies slipped into Margaret's room. Margaret's door to the bathroom was closed. Margaret tried it. "It's open!" She swung the door open, but could only go halfway. She stuck her head in. "Lucinda!"

Both of them slipped into the small space of the open door to find Lucinda lying on the bathroom floor. *She's dead. Oh, Lord God, no . . .*

But Lucinda sat up and pulled her legs out of the way toward her chest. Streaks of mascara bisected her cheeks.

"Are you okay?" Margaret asked.

Lucinda nodded and held out her hand. The two women helped her up and led her to the window seat in Margaret's room.

Evelyn and Summer ran in, but stopped short. "Oh dear." She turned to Summer. "Get Aunt Lucinda a damp washcloth, sweetie."

Margaret sat beside Lucinda. "I'm so sorry. I didn't mean to hurt you."

Summer returned, and Piper knelt beside Lucinda and gently

wiped the awful streaks away. She had no idea what to say. What was Lucinda thinking right now?

Lucinda seemed to come back from the daze she'd been in. She took the washcloth away. "I'm fine. Really. Please don't make a fuss."

"But you were on the floor—"

"Life-changing revelations tend to make a person a bit weak in the knees."

"What revelation?" Piper asked.

●　　●　　●

Lucinda folded the stained washcloth into a neat bundle. "I'm not a beauty anymore."

"You're a nice-looking woman," Evelyn said.

Lucinda smiled. "I used to be beautiful."

The women looked uncomfortable. What could they say? You still are? Although a couple hours ago she would have accepted the lie, things were different now. It was time to wake up to reality. Grow up. "I'm old."

Evelyn raised a hand. "Excuse me; I think we're about the same age so if you're old then I'm old and I'm not old."

There was soft laughter. Piper took the place on Lucinda's other side. She put a hand on hers. "You're far from old, but you certainly are older than you were when your beauty paid the bills."

"I have wrinkles."

Piper laughed. "So do I. And I'm only thirty-five."

Summer extended her arm and pointed at the crook in her elbow. "See? I have a wrinkle too."

Lucinda smiled at the little girl then looked at the women around her. "I . . . I feel so foolish. It's quite a shock to suddenly see yourself the way others see you. The money I've wasted on plastic surgery. And my makeup . . . I'm a painted ghoul."

Margaret popped up. "We can fix that."

Piper was next to stand, taking Lucinda with her. "Makeover time!"

Lucinda pulled back. "I think we've had enough makeovers for today."

It was four against one.

·   ·   ·

Lucinda stared at herself in the mirror. The tight look due to her surgeries was still present, and the wrinkles had not disappeared, but she did look better with only a thin layer of foundation, just a little taupe eye shadow, a smudged line above her eyelid, and some mascara. And the Tawny Copper on her lips was nice.

"Well?" Evelyn asked.

Lucinda put the mirror down. "I love it."

"Yay!" Summer clapped.

Piper picked up the wastebasket and held the Carnival Red lipstick above it. "Shall we banish this and a few other gems from your collection?"

"Remove the temptation?" Lucinda said.

"Remove the crutch of covering up," Margaret said. "It's time the real Lucinda showed through."

Lucinda cringed at the thought of throwing away makeup. Was this how an alcoholic felt, emptying bottles of booze down the drain? "Go for it."

Piper did her duty and the counter was soon clear.

Summer peered into the wastebasket. "Wow. Can I have that stuff? For dress-up?"

The ladies looked at each other; then Evelyn spoke. "We'll ask your mom when she picks you up." She looked at her watch. "She should be here any minute."

Summer skipped off, carrying the wastebasket like it was a treasure chest.

The room turned silent. It was up to Lucinda to wrap things up. How odd that the ones who'd hurt her were also the ones who'd helped her. She gave each woman a hug. "Thank you. All of you."

"Anytime," Margaret said. "It was kind of fun."

Lucinda sighed. "But now what? I'm all dolled up and no where to go."

Piper extended her arm. "The offer of a Jimmy Stewart movie is still on . . ."

"Oooh," Margaret said. "I'll make the popcorn."

Lucinda could think of no better way to spend the rest of the evening. How odd. Not a man in sight.

•   •   •

Audra listened as Russell's heartbeat eased into the gentle rhythm of sleep. It was warm and safe in the crook of his arm and she was content. They'd had a fabulous evening together at Chez Garsaud. Good food, good conversation, and laughter—lots of laughter. When was the last time they'd enjoyed each other so thoroughly?

It had been too long. Way too long.

And she was to blame. How easy it would have been for Russell to find fault, accuse her, point out the ways she'd caused her own distress.

But he hadn't.

She snuggled her cheek against his chest, remembering the words he *had* said. *"You don't have to do everything, Audra. You are everything. Everything to me."*

Yes, indeed. She was very blessed. And she wasn't about to waste it. Not again.

In relationships among the Lord's people,
women are not independent of men,
and men are not independent of women.

1 CORINTHIANS 11:11

*L*ucinda tied a royal blue ribbon around a philodendron. She hummed as she worked.

Gwen came out of the back room. "You can put ribbon on all those potted plants near the window," she said. "Mrs. Klein doesn't care what color. And she shouldn't. Not when we're letting her borrow the plants for free."

Lucinda fluffed the bow, not breaking a beat in her song.

Gwen jutted a hip and placed a fist on it. "What *has* gotten into you the past few days? You are positively cheery."

Lucinda looked up. "I feel cheery."

Gwen gave her a wicked smile. "Okay, spill it. What aren't you telling me? What man's made you grin like a lovesick goomba."

Lucinda stopped working. "*What* is a goomba?"

"Make up your own definition and don't change the subject."

Lucinda shrugged. She didn't know what to say. Gwen would never understand. *She* didn't understand.

Gwen studied her. "It has to do with your new look, doesn't

it? Ever since you came into work on Thursday, looking like . . .
looking like . . ."

This, Lucinda had to hear. "Looking like what?"

"Like a normal person instead of a . . . a . . ."

"Are you having trouble finishing sentences today, Gwen?"

Gwen pulled a plant between them. "You know what I mean.
You look good now. Natural."

"Thank you. I feel good."

A moment of silence passed between them. "Speaking of
Mrs. Klein's do-da, what costume are you going to wear?" Gwen
asked.

"I'm going as a Dutch girl. Van Horn is Dutch."

"Wooden shoes? All that?"

"If I can find some. How about you?"

She smiled smugly. "Randy and I will represent the Egyptian
locale. We're going as Anthony and Cleopatra."

Lucinda immediately thought of the part Elizabeth Taylor
played in the movie: the gold gown, the black hair, the thickly
lined eyes . . . she smiled. "I volunteer to do your makeup."

Ha-ha. Very funny.

●　　●　　●

Tessa taped an announcement for the Sister Circle Costume Fund-
raiser on the walls of the hospital cafeteria. But in negotiating the
tape and the pile in her arms while wearing a kimono . . .

The papers fluttered to the floor.

"Here. Let me help you, Mrs. Klein."

She looked up to see Dr. Gregory Baladino. *Thank You, God.
I've been wanting to chat with him.* She let him do most of the work
picking up. He straightened the stack on a table, then handed
them to her. "I've seen a couple ads in the papers about this. Nice-
size ads."

"The newspapers have been wonderful about donating space. And in case you're wondering, I do have permission to put these up in the lobby and in here."

"I wasn't questioning you," he said. "I think it sounds like a great cause."

Aha . . . "So, you're coming?"

"I don't know. I'm not into costumes much."

"You don't have to wear one. But it's a lot more fun if you do." He looked unconvinced. She needed to pull out all the stops. "Piper's going."

His eyes brightened. "Is she, now?"

Tessa nodded and finished taping the flyer. "She's going to be an English milkmaid. The name *Wellington* is English, you know."

"I have Italian roots."

She pretended to be surprised. "No. You don't say."

He blushed. "But I have no idea what my ancestors wore."

"Then think of a famous Italian for your inspiration."

He looked to the ceiling. "I wouldn't make a very good Sophia Loren."

She swatted his arm. "I was thinking along the lines of Caesar or da Vinci or—"

"Oh, those guys."

"Oh, you."

His pager went off and he checked it. "I'm sorry. I have to go. It's been nice talking with you, Mrs. Klein."

"Tessa. I hope to see you at the party."

"We'll see."

He'd started to walk away when she remembered the most important question. She called after him. "Doctor?"

He paused.

"Will I be seeing you in church tomorrow?"

He returned to her side, his face full of concern. "You haven't told Piper about me going to your church, have you?"

She didn't mention the struggle she'd had *not* to. "Haven't said a word. I didn't think it was my place to hint at what *might* be happening." She looked at him intently. "Is it happening for you, Gregory? Is *He* happening?"

His smile was glorious, yet full of mischief. "You'll be the second to know."

Second to know. She could deal with that.

Now, to keep her mouth shut . . .

●   ●   ●

Evelyn decided to take advantage of the warm day and took an old chair out to the backyard to paint. She was stirring a can of yellow when Piper came outside.

"Hey, I'm heading to the grocery store. You need anything?"

"We're nearly out of coffee."

Piper added it to a list. "Whatcha doing?"

"I'm painting a chair for Summer. She's been using that step stool as a chair far too long."

"I like that yellow."

"The rungs are going to be blue and the legs green. I was thinking of painting her name on the seat."

Piper sat in a lawn chair. "Grandma Evelyn, spoiling her grandchild. I bet you can't wait to have more."

"Passels. I'd love passels."

Piper laughed. "I'm not sure Audra could handle passels."

Evelyn looked up from her stirring. "Do you know if they're thinking about it?"

"They are. In fact, I think they're trying."

Evelyn felt a glow of excitement. "It would be so wonderful to hold a baby."

"Maybe you'd better leave room on that chair for other kids' names."

Good idea. Evelyn dipped her brush in the paint. She loved yellow. Such a happy color. But the color she really should be using right now was green. Because she was feeling green with envy about a certain subject . . . "How's your dad?" *Start out slow . . .*

"I talked with him last night." Piper hesitated. "You want to know about his date with Amanda, don't you?"

"No! I was just—"

Piper leaned her arms on her legs. "It's okay, Evelyn. I've been a little slow on the uptake. I should have encouraged you a long time ago."

Evelyn felt herself blush. "I don't want to intrude, and I certainly don't want you to think because your mother died that I . . ." She had no clue how to word it.

"Did you break up with Herb because of my dad?"

She couldn't lie. She nodded, then quickly said, "But that doesn't mean I expect him to return the feelings. It's all so new; I don't know if it will even lead anywhere but—" she wiped a drip off her hand—"I thought things could happen with Herb, but when they didn't, and when . . ." She shrugged.

"When you recognized the feelings you had for Dad, you broke it off."

"I did."

Piper sat back. "It must be horrible for you to see him go on dates with other women."

Evelyn snickered. "How about helping him buy a suit for one of those dates."

Piper stood and walked to the edge of the patio and back. "Being blind must run in the family. How dare he ask you to do that."

"It's okay, Piper. I like helping, and I'll take his company any way I can get it."

She took a step toward the back door. "I need to go talk to him right now and make him—"

Evelyn pushed herself to standing, nearly swiping the brush across her jeans. "You will do no such thing!"

"But my dad . . . I mean, he's a man. Sometimes they need a little nudge in the right direction."

"I don't want a man who's been nudged. I want one who turns toward me of his own free will."

"But—"

"No."

"Are you sure?"

Not really. "I'm fine. Actually, I'm feeling very patient about the whole thing."

"Yeah?"

"Absolutely." *Liar, liar, pants on fire.*

Piper headed to the grocery store, leaving Evelyn to her painting—and her thoughts. She was *not* feeling patient about her relationship with Wayne, but the thought of Wayne being goaded into it was unacceptable.

She balanced the chair on two legs so she could paint the underside and found her thoughts turning into prayer. *Father, I've left Herb because I'm interested in Wayne. But he doesn't think of me that way—and Herb did—and here I sit, alone. Maybe I should have held on to Herb until—*

No. That would have been wrong. I was right to break it off, but whether or not Wayne will ever look at me romantically, as a woman he could love, is unknown.

I hate the unknown, Lord! But at least I know You've got my best interests in mind.

She paused and shut her eyes tight. *So do what You want, Lord. Hook me up with Wayne or not. You choose. Just help me through it.*

Amen. There. She felt better.

She resumed painting. Yellow was such a happy color.

• • •

Margaret sat on the couch beside Bobby, watching college football. At least Bobby was watching. Her mind wandered and she ended up scanning the living room of his apartment, thinking of ways to make it prettier when it became *their* apartment.

"I'd like to make a valance," she said.

He scooped a chip through the French onion dip. "Valance? What's that?"

She moved to the sliding door leading to the small balcony. "It would extend across all this glass, coming down about eight or ten inches. Maybe a rust floral."

"Flowers?"

"It's going to be my home too."

He set the bowl of chips on the coffee table. "I've been think-ing about that. I think we should look into buying a house."

It was laughable—and one escaped. "Buy a house with what money?"

He shrugged and took the chips back into his lap. "Never mind. It was just a thought."

"But what made you even consider such a thing? You have a rich uncle I don't know about?"

"Like I said. Never mind. Could you get me another Dr Pepper?"

"What about the valance?"

"Whatever. But watch the flowers, okay?"

• • •

Audra entered Handy Hardware, her list ready. The agreement with Russell in regard to weekend honey-dos was that she acted as gopher. That's why she made him write everything down—in detail. What did she know of wood screws and drywall nails? She turned to the left, heading toward the tool section to get a socket-wrench set—whatever that was.

She was intent, looking at the tool display, when she heard her name.

"Audra!"

She turned around to find Luke standing there. Luke Ottington, Summer's biological father. Though right after her marriage to Russell, Luke had magnanimously backed off from inserting himself into Summer's life—acknowledging the difference between fathering a child and loving one—just the sight of him made her nerves stand and salute.

"What are you doing here?" she asked. Surely he hadn't moved to Carson Creek from Jackson. *Please let him not have moved—*

"I'm helping a buddy fix up a house. Joe Ambrose?"

She shook her head. "Don't know him."

He looked down at a list and Audra had to contain a laugh. He knew less about tools and nails than she did. "I'm looking for some clamps."

She pointed to her left. "I saw some over there, eye level."

He took a step in that direction, then back again. "How's married life?"

She noticed he didn't ask about Summer first. "I'm very happy."

He looked at her intently. "You look tired."

She didn't want to go into it. The less Luke knew about the details of her life the better. "I've been busy."

He nodded. "How's the girl?"

Her name's Summer. "She's great." She decided to change the subject to one Luke was more comfortable with. "What are you doing now—besides shopping for clamps?"

He looked down the aisle as if wanting to escape. "Mother's cut me off."

Audra had known that was a possibility. When they'd last

spoken Luke had stood up to his mother, which was not something Dorthea Ottington took well. "I'm sorry."

He shrugged. "I'm getting by. Doing construction work now. Actually, Joe's teaching me. I work for him."

Wealthy, spoiled Luke, working with his hands. Sweating. Getting dirty. "Do you like it?"

"It pays the bills."

Audra felt a sudden need to be nice. "I'm proud of you, Luke. I hope everything goes well."

He looked shocked at her good tidings, yet pleased. He raised his list. "I'd better go. Work to do."

"Bye, Luke. Take care of yourself."

"You too."

He grabbed some clamps—almost, but not quite stopping in front of the shelf—and was gone.

Why did she feel wistful? Maybe history was history. Good or bad, Luke would always be a part of her life.

She found the socket set and headed toward the nails. Another male voice called out to her. "Audra!"

This man she'd expected to see. "Hi, Herb." She braced herself for his questions about Evelyn.

"How's that little girl of yours?"

"Summer's thriving. She's a whiz at math."

"Takes after her mother, eh?"

"How have you been, Herb?" *Are you suffering much without Evelyn?*

His smile was wide. "I'm doing super. I've been going out with a great gal who works at Ruby's diner. Agnes Gault?"

Agnes was a mousy thing, but had a laugh that tore through any sorrow of your day. "I'm happy for you, Herb."

"Thanks." He pointed to her list. "Can I help you find anything?"

Besides the items on her list, Audra wished Herb could help

her decide whether she should tell Evelyn that he'd already found someone else.

By the time she was ready to check out, she'd decided. Until she figured out otherwise, she'd keep it to herself. If possible, sisters should protect one another from unnecessary pain—as long as they could.

*　　*　　*

Margaret looked at her watch. It was ten thirty, she was beat, and her stomach didn't feel right. She felt achy. She needed to get to bed.

She got up from the couch, picking up their glasses.

"Where you going?" Bobby asked.

"I need to get home. We both have church in the morning."

He took her hand, trying to pull her back beside him. "The movie is almost over. Stay for the end."

Her aches and pains made the decision for her. "I really have to get home." She put the glasses in the dishwasher and tried to lighten the tone. "You're running me ragged, Bobby-boy."

For some reason that got him off the couch. He came to her side. "I've been meaning to talk with you about something. Something that will make both our lives easier."

Her head ached. She didn't feel like talking about anything. "Can't this wait?"

He turned away, his arms raised. "Fine. If you don't want to hear—"

She sighed inwardly and turned him back around. She found a spare smile. "Tell me your idea. I'm listening."

He put his hands on her shoulders as if holding her in place so she didn't flee. What could he have to say that would—

"I think you should move in here. With me."

"That's the plan," she said. But she was wary.

"Now. I think you should move in now."

It was not what she wanted to hear, and she removed his hands from her shoulders, letting them fall into the space between them. "I can't believe you'd even think such a thing."

He put on his wicked grin and slipped a hand behind her waist, pulling her close. "You know you want to stay . . ."

She pushed him away. "*Want* and *right* are not necessarily the same thing."

"The God thing." His voice mocked.

She looked at him incredulously. "Yeah, the God thing. The Ten Commandment thing to not commit adultery."

"That applies to people who are already married, not sleeping around."

"It's about any sex outside of marriage. You can't change the rules just to suit you, Bobby."

He leaned against the counter, his arms crossed, his jaw tight. "Priscilla and George go to our church and they're living together."

Really? "You're wanting to start a trend?"

"It's more than a trend, Meg. It's the way of the world."

She stared at him, uncertain she even knew him anymore. "We're told to 'fight the good fight for what we believe.'"

He gave her the grin again. "I don't want to fight. I want to love. Love you."

It was too much. "I gotta go."

"So what's your decision?"

She grabbed her jacket and purse. "I gotta go."

• • •

Between Jackson and Carson Creek Margaret's anger and confusion sapped what was left of her energy. She nearly drove off the road.

When she stumbled into Peerbaugh Place, Evelyn was coming down the stairs. "Margaret! What happened to you?"

She took hold of the railing and headed upstairs. "I don't feel so hot."

Evelyn put a hand on her forehead. "Actually, you feel very hot. You have a fever."

Margaret wasn't surprised. "I'm so tired." It was the understatement of the year.

Evelyn helped her up the steps. "You get to bed. I'll get you some medicine."

"I'll be fine."

Piper and Lucinda appeared in their doorways. "What's wrong?"

"She has a fever," Evelyn said.

"I'll get some Tylenol," Lucinda said, disappearing into her room.

Margaret hated the fuss, but also welcomed it. Piper was already gathering her nightgown. Lucinda came through the bathroom with two pills and a glass of water.

Margaret took the medicine. Then—since her room was Grand Central Station—she went into the bathroom to change. When she came out her bed was turned down and the bedside lamp cast a mellow glow. Her three nurses stood ready.

She climbed in and Evelyn adjusted the covers. "Can I get you anything?"

An uncomplicated life would be nice. She couldn't trust her voice but merely shook her head.

Piper sat on the other side of the bed. "What's wrong? Did you and Bobby argue?"

Margaret laughed. "I don't say a word and you guess—"

Lucinda was nodding. "So it *was* an argument."

Evelyn touched her hand. "You might as well tell us."

"We aren't leaving until you do," Piper said. "You'll sleep better if you let it out."

They were probably right. With a deep breath as fuel, Margaret told them about Bobby's proposition.

"It *would* be easier if you lived together," Lucinda said.

"No!" Piper said. "We're not talking *easy* here; we're talking *right*. Two unmarried people should not have sex nor live together."

Lucinda laughed. "And what century do you live in?"

Evelyn ignored their argument and looked at Margaret intently. "Has he ever considered moving to Carson Creek? You're the one with the teaching position here."

"What does Bobby do?" Lucinda asked.

"He sells computers and electronics at a huge store."

"Carnahan's down on the square might be able to use him," Piper said.

"I suggested that." Margaret decided to let it all out. "Actually, he also talked about us buying a house."

"Can you afford that?"

She smiled, and scootched deeper into her pillows. "See that dresser over there? It's full of money."

"Very funny," Piper said. "Margaret . . . this doesn't make sense. Why is he saying these things, pressuring you like this?"

Lucinda nodded. "Forget his latest suggestion. Bobby's demanding too much of you. You're a wreck. It can't continue."

"The wedding's in six months."

"You won't last that long."

"I'm just trying to be a good woman. Submit and—"

Piper held up a stop sign. "Whoa there, sister. The Bible says wives are to submit to their husbands 'as is fitting for those who belong to the Lord.' But husbands are to submit to Jesus, and love their wives and never treat them harshly."

"Sounds to me like Bobby's being *very* harsh," Lucinda said.

"He's not loving you; he's using you." Evelyn looked to the floor. "I know about these things."

Piper adjusted the top of the sheet. "Submission is a good thing, a God thing, when the circumstances honor God. But if Bobby is acting mean or abusing you in any way—"

"He's not abusing—"

"Not taking care of you, only thinking of himself, trying to get you to live with him when he knows it's against your beliefs, is abuse. Abuse is about control. He's controlling you emotionally and psychologically. A lot of times that is just as destructive as physical abuse. And if you go along with his actions, you are allowing him to do wrong. Your submission enables Bobby to sin and doesn't help him change for the better. And isn't that what true love is? Helping each other become the best man or woman each of us can be?"

Margaret felt an inkling of hope, yet was too weary to let it settle.

Evelyn must have seen it because she stood. "Enough, sisters. Let's let her rest. Our Margaret has a lot to think about."

Indeed she—

She fell asleep.

When the sun goes down, they will be clean again.

LEVITICUS 22:7

*E*velyn came out of her bedroom just as Piper came out of hers. They were both dressed for church. They looked toward Margaret's door; then Piper motioned Evelyn into her room.

"Her light's not on," Piper whispered. "Should we wake her?"

Evelyn shook her head. "Let her be. She needs her rest. Before we leave I'll check on her and see if she wants anything."

In agreement, they moved to the top of the stairs and both looked up as Lucinda's door opened.

Evelyn immediately put a finger to her lips and pointed to Margaret's door. Lucinda nodded and came into the hallway with extra care. It was then Evelyn noticed she was wearing a dress. Could she be going to—? No. Not Lucinda.

As they headed downstairs, Evelyn sought Piper's eyes. When she had them she pointed at Lucinda. Piper shrugged but it was obvious she was thinking the same thing. Evelyn decided to hold her question until they entered the kitchen. And then . . . how to word it . . . ? She was afraid if she was too direct Lucinda might shy away like a spooked colt.

While Evelyn was trying to figure out how to ask, Piper made the first move as she filled the teapot with water. "I like that color on you, Lucinda."

Lucinda smoothed the hunter green coatdress over her hips. "You do?"

Piper switched on a burner. "It brings out the color of your eyes."

Good one, Piper. Evelyn moved to the pantry. "Applesauce pancakes okay? That might be something Margaret will feel up to eating later."

"Sure," Piper said.

Lucinda set the table. "She's not going to church with us?"

Evelyn nearly dropped the jar of applesauce. "No."

Lucinda placed forks all around the table. "She shouldn't. She needs her rest." The table complete she asked, "You want me to make coffee this morning, Evelyn? Or are you having tea with Piper?"

Will wonders never cease?

• • •

So far, so good. Lucinda had been nervous with her decision to go to church with the ladies. Yet in the kitchen, everything had slipped in so smoothly. Not a single comment like "It's about time!" or questions about why she'd changed her mind.

She knew if she'd received either reaction she would have run to her room, slipped back in bed, and declared the subject forever closed. It didn't make sense to be so skittish, but that's how she felt.

For one thing, she didn't know why she'd decided to go to church this morning. She'd awakened with an odd feeling of total refreshment, and had even sat up in bed and stretched with a grin reminiscent of Scarlett O'Hara the morning after.

Why was she so happy?

She had no idea.

Gwen had implied her happiness was connected to her new look. She was probably right. Lucinda always felt a high after each new surgery. Even a new haircut lifted her spirits.

But no. This was more than that. This was deeper. And so she'd followed the notion to get dressed and join the ladies at church.

Lucinda was glad to see Wayne Wellington there. He hadn't seen her new look yet. She prepared herself for the thrill of new compliments.

He didn't disappoint. His face was a poster for "pleasant surprise." "Lucinda! My, my. You—"

Piper latched on to her father's arm. "Isn't it wonderful Lucinda's joining us today?"

"Uh, yes. Welcome, welcome. We're glad to have you."

Thanks a lot, Piper.

When it was time to file into the sanctuary, Lucinda tried to position herself next to Wayne, but as she slid into a pew—expecting Wayne to come in after her—she found Piper beside her. Then there was that elderly Accosta Rand woman, then Evelyn. *Then* Wayne. Great. Just great. She couldn't be any farther away from him if she'd tried.

Audra and her family slipped into the pew behind them. Greetings were exchanged, and Lucinda suddenly found Summer breathing at her ear. She turned around.

"You're here. You look pretty, Aunt Lucinda."

She felt herself blush. The organ started playing and Audra pulled Summer back to seating. Lucinda looked around at the sanctuary. It was classic, right out of *Father Knows Best*. No surprises. But in a way that was comforting. In fact, it looked a bit like the last church she'd been to.

Her memories pulled up short. How long ago had it been? She'd gone with her Grandmother Hoskins who'd died in the early eighties . . . had it truly been over twenty years?

I've been busy.

Her inner self snickered. She wasn't wrong there. She'd been terribly busy dealing with a horrible marriage, getting divorced, and moving to Florida. There, she'd gotten various nips and tucks to make herself more appealing to the rich men who seemed to populate the area, ever watchful for the next beautiful woman to put on their arms. Lucinda had often likened it to the atmosphere of an auction. *And the next item up for bid is this beautiful specimen. Notice the nice figure and the designer clothes. It should be noted that although this is a slightly used model, she has been completely updated and comes with a full warranty. Who'll start the bidding?*

People were standing. Piper held a hymnal between them. They sang a song about the beauty of the earth. How long had it been since Lucinda had read music?

When they sat down, Piper whispered, "You have a nice voice."

A woman wearing the most luscious navy suit stood at a lectern. She said a good morning and to Lucinda's surprise, everyone said "Good morning" back. Talking out loud in church?

"Today our Old Testament lesson comes from Proverbs and Isaiah. 'Charm is deceptive, and beauty does not last; but a woman who fears the Lord will be greatly praised. Reward her for all she has done. Let her deeds publicly declare her praise.'"

Lucinda felt as if she'd been slapped. She heard herself breathe. Piper looked at her. She did not look back, but kept her eyes straight ahead. Navy Woman was commenting on her fading looks! How dare she? How—

The woman continued. "Now, from Isaiah: 'People are like the grass that dies away. Their beauty fades as quickly as the beauty of flowers in a field. The grass withers, and the flowers fade beneath the breath of the Lord. And so it is with people. The grass withers, and the flowers fade, but the word of our God stands forever.'" She closed the Bible and said, "Let us pray." Everyone bowed their heads. "Father, open our hearts and minds to the wisdom and glory of Your Word. Amen."

Lucinda laughed to herself. Open her heart and mind? Were they kidding? They had just insulted her—not once, but twice! *This is why they dragged me to church. They wanted to ram down my throat the idea that looks are temporary. Don't I know it. That's why I work so desperately to keep—*

Suddenly another thought intruded. *They didn't drag you to church. You chose. You made the decision. No one made you come.*

She shivered. Or did they?

She replayed her morning: how she'd awakened in such a joyous mood, how she wasn't tired at all, how she'd suddenly found herself pulling a dress out of the closet . . .

Lucinda barely heard the offertory and blindly added a ten-dollar bill as the offering plate was passed. She could sense Piper's questions, but didn't dare look her way.

She had to figure this out. It was like every event of the past was a puzzle piece that was slowly being linked together. Spending the last of her money on one-too-many plastic surgeries. Moving to Peerbaugh Place. The disaster of her reunion. The disaster of Margaret's makeover. The revelation of her own true image in the mirror. The ladies gathering around, giving her a new look that was far better than her old one. Her feeling of elation and freshness and starting anew. Coming to church after twenty years. The verses that spoke of the passage of beauty. It was too strange. Too odd.

Too perfect.

She realized the pastor had started his sermon. " . . . our society's obsession with beauty. Transient beauty. Beauty that does not last. This is the complete opposite of what God wants us to focus on. In First Peter we read: 'Don't be concerned about the outward beauty that depends on fancy hairstyles, expensive jewelry, or beautiful clothes. You should be known for the beauty that comes from within, the unfading beauty of a gentle and quiet spirit, which is so precious to God.'"

Suddenly, instead of feeling defensive, Lucinda grabbed onto his final sentence: *The unfading beauty of a gentle and quiet spirit, which is so precious to God.* What a concept.

"God doesn't care what we look like. Getting old, aging, having our looks change and fade . . . that's all part of His plan. He *could* have rigged it so we never looked a day over twenty, couldn't He?"

There was soft laughter in the congregation. *Laughter in church?*

The pastor leaned on the lectern as if sharing a confidence. "But if our looks *didn't* fade, then we'd depend on them, we'd set our store in them, we'd fail to look beyond them—to our most important attribute: a gentle and quiet spirit. Having a fear of the Lord—a respect for Him. If our looks never faded we might not turn to Him to be our beauty. And in turn might not realize how precious we are to Him because of who we are inside."

Lucinda put her hand to her mouth, stifling a sob. Piper glanced in her direction but didn't say a thing. She just put an arm around her shoulders, giving her a gentle squeeze.

Lucinda soaked in every word. It was as if God was speaking to her through this slightly overweight man. A man who was balding, who wore bifocals, who had multiple chins above his shirt collar.

The pastor paused and smiled across his flock. "God loves you, people. He *made* you. As you are. In all your imperfections. That doesn't mean we don't have a responsibility to keep this temple of our body in good shape—" He put his hands on his ample belly and laughed. "A goal harder for some than others. But the point is, we need to keep our focus on Him, on pleasing Him by being the best person we can be, having the kindest heart, the brightest mind, and the most loving soul. 'Whatever is good and perfect comes to us from God above, who created all heaven's lights. Unlike them, He never changes or casts shifting shadows. In His goodness He chose to make us His own children by giving us His true word. And we, out of all creation, became His choice possession.' Strive for that. For Him. Let us—His choice possessions—make Him proud."

They rose to sing one final hymn. Piper kept her arm around Lucinda's shoulders. The sound of the voices blended together—in all their imperfection—reinforced everything Lucinda had heard. And with each phrase she grew stronger. By the end of the hymn she was standing tall. All tears were gone.

Piper noticed and let go. As the postlude played and people began to file out, she asked, "Are you okay?"

Lucinda was proud to say, "I'm fine. In fact, I'm perfect."

●　　●　　●

Standing around chatting in the narthex after church, the group decided not to go out to lunch. Not with Margaret at home sick. They'd go back to Peerbaugh Place.

Piper slipped her hand through her father's arm. She'd been so glad he'd sat next to Evelyn and *hadn't* sat next to Lucinda. Before church Lucinda had been so obvious in her interest, eating up her father's compliment about her new look. At one point Piper had even harbored the rude thought that she wished Lucinda *hadn't* come to church with them.

That was then. This was now. . . . Something had happened during the service. There wasn't a batted eye or a secret smile in sight. Lucinda was subdued. Not in a depressed way, but pensive. As if she was seeing life for the first time and was taking it all in. Although always confident, now the surety seemed to stem from a deeper place, as if someone had just given her the biggest compliment in her life. Some*one* indeed.

During church, as soon as Piper had recognized the stirring in Lucinda, her senses had perked up, and she'd looked at the service with the eyes of someone who knew how God could work at such times. Immediately, Piper recognized how all the verses and talk about beauty fading, and the need to look and work for an inner beauty, would strike a chord with Lucinda. She'd prayed feverishly during the rest of the service, that Lucinda's heart would be softened, that she'd hear—really *hear*—all that God was trying to tell her.

Audra was standing next to Lucinda. She leaned in her direction until shoulder met shoulder. "You're quiet."

Lucinda took in a breath, as if she'd forgotten to breathe. She smiled. "I'm just taking it all in."

Ha! Thank You, Lord! Piper slipped an arm through Lucinda's. "Shall we go, people? I'm hungry and I feel like celebrating."

"Celebrating?" Evelyn asked.

Piper looked at Lucinda, trying to ask a question with her eyes.

Lucinda smiled and nodded. "Yes. I guess a celebration is in order."

"Shall we lead the way?" Piper asked.

"Absolutely."

Piper and Lucinda left the church arm in arm, letting everyone make their own assumptions.

Piper knew they might never know the details of what had gone on that morning between Lucinda and God, but it was clear that progress *had* been made. And that was very, very good.

Praise the Lord.

•   •   •

In the car on the way home Evelyn was bursting to ask Lucinda what had happened at church, but she didn't dare. She'd seen that pensive look from people before, the shine in their eyes beneath a brow slightly furrowed from a combination of amazement and confusion. An I-can't-believe-that-just-happened look, coupled with *what* did *just happen?* Somehow, Lucinda had experienced a God moment. Evelyn knew too many questions too soon could hinder more than help. Hopefully, Lucinda would share.

She didn't. She was quiet all the way home. It was extremely frustrating. And because she wanted to hear Lucinda's story, Evelyn found herself *not* listening when the entire five-minute drive was taken up by Accosta talking about various hospital patients she'd met through her floral-delivery rounds. Evelyn let her attention be drawn to practical matters. She needed to make lunch for nine people, and check on Margaret, and—

She looked out the back window to see if Wayne's car was behind them. He was. She waved. He waved back.

Wayne was coming to lunch.

That was her own blessing.

●　　●　　●

Luckily, Evelyn had a loaf of French bread and some shaved ham and cheese. Monte Cristo's for eight, coming up.

Piper came in from checking on Margaret. "She's feeling a little better but doesn't want lunch. I talked her into some leftover pancakes. I'll get them—"

The phone rang. Evelyn answered it. It was Bobby.

"She's not feeling very well, Bobby. Can she call—?" He needed to talk to her. "Just a minute." She headed for the front hall.

"I'll bring her the phone," Audra said.

"No. I'm going to do it." For some reason Evelyn felt she *had* to do it. She carried the phone upstairs to Margaret's room. The door was ajar. Margaret was snuggled in the bed, her eyes closed.

Evelyn retreated to the hallway and spoke to Bobby. "She's sleeping right now. Can she—?"

"Evelyn? Is that Bobby?"

Evelyn told Bobby to hold on a minute, covered the receiver, and went into her room. "Why don't you call him back?" she said.

Margaret shook her head no as she sat up in bed. She reached for the phone. Evelyn had no choice but to give it to her.

"Bobby?"

Evelyn knew she could leave—should leave—but she didn't. She stood a few steps away, then busied herself by watering the African violets on Margaret's dresser. She couldn't hear Bobby's end of the conversation, but she didn't need to. The gist of it became clear when Margaret flung off the covers and started getting out of bed.

"I'm sorry too, Bobby. And I'm coming."

Evelyn spilled water on the dresser and hurried for a towel to clean it up. Margaret was going to Bobby's? No way.

"Excuse me, Evelyn."

Evelyn turned around to see that Margaret wanted into the dresser drawers. She spoke to Bobby. "I need to take a shower, but I'll hurry. I'll be there in an hour, hour and a half."

Evelyn shook her head violently, mouthing no.

"I love you too. See you soon." Margaret pushed the Off button and opened a drawer.

Evelyn pounced. "You can't go to Bobby's. You're sick." *And he's a heel.*

She pulled out a pair of jeans. "He's invited some people over from church. He needs me to make some sandwiches and—"

"But you're sick!"

Margaret put a calming hand on Evelyn's arm. "I'm fine. I had a nice sleep."

"Piper said you didn't even feel like sandwiches for lunch. She said you only thought you could get down a pancake."

Margaret got a blouse from the closet. "Now that I'm up, I'm feeling better. And a shower will help—"

"I told him you were sick. He should be coming here, caring for you, not you jumping up and going to him to . . . to make *him* food so *he* can entertain."

Margaret returned to the dresser and got out some underwear. "I need to be there for him. I want to be there for him."

"He needs to be here for you."

"He is. He's—"

Evelyn thought of something else. "What about your argument last night?"

"He said he was sorry."

"Yeah," Evelyn said, incredulous. "He said he was sorry so he could get you to come cook for him. He's being demanding. He's making unreasonable requests. Nobody—not even God—wants you to submit to that."

Margaret paused at the bathroom door. "I know you're only trying to help, but I'm going. It'll be fine. This is the man I'm going to marry. I know what I'm doing."

She shut the door between them, leaving Evelyn to mutter to herself, "Wanna bet?"

•   •   •

Needless to say, the talk at lunch was about Margaret and how she was being bowled over, duped, and taken in by this selfish Bobby person.

It was unacceptable.

As the women started to do dishes, Evelyn made a decision. She wiped her hands on a towel and threw it on the counter. "I'm sorry, people. I'm going to be a rude hostess, but there's something I have to do. Now."

"Goodness, Mom, what is it?" Russell asked.

"We all agree Margaret is on the wrong road. We all agree she's blind to what Bobby's doing to her."

"Sure," Audra said. "But what can we—?"

Evelyn grabbed her purse and her keys. "I'm going to drive to Jackson and talk to her parents. Elicit their help."

Lucinda took some plates to the dishwasher. "But maybe they like him. And maybe we're wrong about him."

Evelyn palmed her keys. "Maybe. And I am willing to be convinced. But I have to do this. I have to try to help."

Wayne took his suit coat off the back of a chair. "I'll drive."

"I think that's a good idea," Piper said.

Evelyn was too upset to be pleased for any other reason than it *would* be nice to have someone else along. "Let's go," she said.

• • •

Evelyn was glad Wayne was along for another reason. Upon getting to Jackson, when she realized she didn't even know where the Jensens lived, she knew she would have turned back if it weren't for Wayne spurring her on.

They stopped at a gas station, and Wayne looked up the address. Luckily, there weren't too many Jensens with an *e* in the book. And Evelyn thought Margaret's father's name started with an *S*. Sam, Sean . . . ? There were three *S* names. Wayne called them all and asked if they had a daughter named Margaret. The third one—Seth—was the right one. He introduced himself as a friend of Margaret's and asked if he and Evelyn could drop by.

They drove through a tree-lined neighborhood, looking for the address. "They said it has a green door," Wayne said.

Evelyn's stomach was in turmoil. "Maybe this isn't a good idea. I have no clue what I'm going to say to them."

Wayne pulled over to the curb and stopped. Evelyn frantically looked out the window. Not a green door in sight. "Where—?"

She felt his hand on her arm. "Let's stop a minute and pray, okay?"

Evelyn took a deep breath, realizing that's exactly what they needed to do. She let Wayne take her hand and was more than willing to let him lead their prayer. "We're trying to do the right thing here, Father. We care deeply for Margaret and are concerned . . . You know our concerns. Guide us as we speak to her parents. Show us the truth about the situation and show us what to do next. We ask in Jesus' name, amen."

"Amen."

Wayne looked at her and smiled tentatively. "Better?"

"Very."

He looked at the slip of paper with the address on it. "It should be in the next block."

Evelyn nodded once. "Let's do it."

•　　•　　•

Seth and Alice Jensen led Wayne and Evelyn to a couch in the living room before they sat in the two matching wing chairs facing them. The arms of the chairs were soiled, the piping frayed. A globe lamp made of spun plastic hung above the television. A spiderweb crisscrossed the bottom opening. White metal blinds hung in the window, but a twelve-inch section was badly bent—as if something had been thrown against it. A print of Gainsborough's *Blue Boy* hung on the wall next to a painting that looked to be a paint-by-number rendition of a mountain scene. A blackened brick fireplace was flanked by floor-to-ceiling bookshelves, yet not a book was present. Or a magazine—other than a *TV Guide* sitting on the table between the wing chairs.

"So you're Margaret's landlady?" Mrs. Jensen asked. Her voice had the tight breaking quality of an old woman.

Even as Evelyn answered yes and explained that she and

Margaret had moved beyond the landlady-tenant relationship to become dear friends, she suddenly realized that both of the Jensens were older than she was. They had to be in their sixties. Yet Margaret was only twenty-two.

As Evelyn talked, Seth patted the arms of his chair nervously, both feet planted flat on the floor. He kept glancing toward the television. Were they keeping him from a football game? When Alice offered them some coffee, he interrupted. "Enough chitchat. Margaret's not behind on rent or anything, is she? We told her it was dumb to move away from here after Bobby dumped her. Waste of money, if you ask me."

Evelyn saw Wayne's eyebrows rise. She hastened to answer. "Margaret is a wonderful tenant. She's a joy to have—"

"Then what's the problem?"

Oh dear. Evelyn found herself fingering the handles of her purse so she set it on the floor beside her. "I—" she looked at Wayne—"*we* are concerned about her relationship with Bobby."

Alice flipped a hand at them. "Oh that. No need to worry. They've patched everything up. The wedding's on."

"I know, but—"

Seth broke in. "And good thing too because I was none too happy about losing my deposit on the flowers and cake. You pay for a wedding you might as well have one. We were glad to hear Margaret came to her senses."

Evelyn was confused.

Wayne stepped in. "I'm sorry, but we were under the impression that Bobby was the one who called off the wedding."

Seth pushed himself straighter in the chair. "Oh, he was. Had good reason to, too. Margaret had no right acting so perfect. It's just not normal. It makes a man feel . . ." He searched for the word in his wife's face.

"Unnatural," she said.

"Yup. That's it. Unnatural. And all her talk of trying to be the kind of woman God wants her to be . . ." He shook his head as if Margaret were choosing something unsavory. "Too much God talk can turn a man off, if you know what I mean."

Wayne and Evelyn exchanged a glance. Then Wayne sat forward, ready to make a point. Evelyn was grateful for anything he had to say because she was finding it hard to put a thought together, much less voice it out loud. He took his time, leaning his arms on his knees. He prefaced his words with a smile. "We—Margaret's friends—have been very impressed by her faith. She's an amazing young woman."

"And a great teacher," Evelyn added.

Seth snickered. "Second grade. One-plus-one and 'See Jane run.' What kind of job is that? She could make more money waiting tables. Bobby's got the good job."

Alice nodded. "He sells electric stuff."

"It's called electronics, Alice." Seth pointed to a stereo on the shelves. "Sold me that entire set for cost."

"He's going to get me a new microwave too."

"You bet he is," Seth said. "A good kind of boy to have in the family. A job like his is worth something."

And teaching children isn't?

Seth sat back in his chair. "Not that *her* job matters much anyway. It's up to the man to make the money. Now if Margaret had behaved herself and been born a boy, she could have gone to work at the plant with me. I make good money there. Real good money."

Alice nodded.

Seth sat forward to make his own point. "If she was smart, she'd stop playing Miss Pris and move in with Bobby. It don't make much sense that he's in that nice apartment alone and she's living in a little podunk room in some other town." He looked at Evelyn. "Sorry. No offense."

You're not sorry and offense taken.

Evelyn found them the most offensive parents she'd ever met. There was nothing about them or their home that spoke of love or nurturing. Nothing that would explain how Margaret had come to be such a sweet, bright young woman.

Seth slapped his thighs. "Now that we have that cleared up . . ."

It took Evelyn a moment to realize they were being dismissed. Wayne stood and she followed. They shook hands and were in Wayne's car before a full minute had passed.

Evelyn took a cleansing breath and noticed Wayne doing the same. "What just happened in there?" she asked.

Wayne shook his head. "How can *they* be Margaret's parents?"

"They virtually said they wanted Margaret and Bobby to live together."

"They think her job is worthless."

"They think her values, her talk of God, is offensive."

Evelyn raked her hair with her fingers and groaned. "How did she get to be who she is—with the faith that she has—with *them* . . . ?" She looked at the house with utter distaste. "Let's go. Please, let's go."

● ● ●

They were just pulling onto the highway leading home when Wayne asked, "Are you okay?"

Evelyn realized she was puffing as though she'd run a race. Her hands were clenched, her lips pursed. She couldn't remember being so angry. Suddenly, she yelled, "I'm not okay! I hate them! I really, really hate them!"

Wayne started to say something, but she kept going. She had to. To keep it in would have been dangerous. "How dare they stifle that girl? How dare they only think of themselves and their own needs . . . talking about the deposits on the cake and flowers. Who cares? It's their daughter's happiness at stake."

"I know. They—"

"And Bobby . . . calling Margaret when she's sick—not caring that she's sick—insisting she drive to Jackson to be a hostess to him and his friends. Monopolizing all her free time, insisting on having everything his way. Eating the food he wants to eat, watching the TV programs he wants to watch, not listening to her dreams, her thoughts, her wants and desires, only thinking of how he wants to live a life even if it does mean she never becomes the woman she could become, and ends up hating him and thinking more and more about how life would be easier if he were dead. Then when he goes and dies she has to live with the guilt and—"

She gasped. How had her thoughts about Margaret and Bobby turned into a tirade about herself and Aaron?

Wayne pulled into a turnoff for an historical marker for the Oregon Trail. He shut off the car and faced her.

She couldn't look at him. She eyed the door handle. If they were in Carson Creek she'd get out and walk home. But that wasn't possible. She was a captive of her own tirade.

"That's horrible," Wayne said.

She got a tissue from her purse and used it. "I know, I know. I'm a horrible wife. Forget I said any of that. I'm just so concerned about Margaret that—"

He reached over and took her hand. "You're not horrible, Evelyn. *It's* horrible. Your situation sounds like it was horrible."

"Just forget I said any of it." She looked at him imploringly. "Please?"

"At what point did you stop talking about Margaret's situation and start talking about your own?"

The truth was too ugly. She shook her head.

"Talk to me, Evelyn. Let me help you get through this."

She blew her nose. "It won't help. He's gone."

"But maybe it will help. Aaron's been gone quite a while, so for you to still harbor this bitterness about your life . . . it can't be healthy."

Her laugh oozed bitterness, a sickening sound. "What good will it do to talk about all we *didn't* have, all we *didn't* feel? Especially to someone like you, who lost your soul mate after sharing a great marriage. You, who have no regrets, who isn't disgusted by the memory of who you were when you were together." The tears started fresh. She was glad he didn't say anything. She looked out the passenger window and let herself cry. "Why can't I remember anything good about him? Why can't I remember anything good about myself *with* him?"

"I'm sure it's not that bad."

She whipped toward him. "I wanted him to be out of my life! And he died! Don't you understand that? I'm responsible!"

Her voice rang in the car. The look on Wayne's face made her fumble for the door handle. She got the door open and tumbled out, tripping on the gravel. She fell to the ground and felt the sting of rocks against her palms. Suddenly he was at her side, on the ground himself, cradling her in his arms.

A car whizzed past and honked.

I'm making a fool of myself collided with *I don't care. Just hold me, Wayne. Make it all go away. Make the hurt go away.*

He rocked her, right there, along the side of the road, where thousands of pioneers had passed. Thousands of wives and husbands. Happy and sad. Angry and broken. Flawed and—

He whispered a soft "Shh, shh" in her ear. She dug her face into his chest, not wanting the world to see her shame, not wanting to see the world. He rocked her until her tears were spent.

He helped her to her feet and led her to a picnic table beneath a crimson pin oak, its leaves holding on far beyond when other trees had given up their bounty. She sat on the bench, facing out. He sat beside her, his arm keeping her close.

Safe. Crickets chirped. The air was cool against her hot cheeks. Her insides felt hollow, as if there was nothing left, as if it had all been scraped clean. She looked down at her bloodied hands as if they belonged to someone else. But no. They were hers. *Her* scars for *her* sin.

Wayne reached over and lifted her chin, but instead of turning it toward himself, he turned her focus toward the west. "Look, Evelyn. Look at the sky getting ready for the sunset."

The sky was an artist's palette with sweeping swaths of reds, purples, and blues. Azure puffs against white, with the globe of the sun getting ready to be cut in two by the horizon. It was moving on past today, getting ready for its journey to tomorrow when it would come up fresh and new. Cleansed. Warm. Its light so pure and intense that one dare not look at it.

"The day's nearly done," Wayne said. "Let it go."

She watched the sky. "But—"

"No. Forgive him. Forgive yourself."

"But I hated—"

"Hated. Past tense. Hate no more. Not Aaron, not your old life, not the old you. God forgives you. He forgives Aaron. He's made things fresh and clean."

Evelyn's throat tightened. "But I don't deserve to be fresh and clean. I—"

"No, you don't. Neither do I. Neither do any of us. But Jesus forgives you—whether you want Him to or not. His work was done on the cross. He's not taking it back. It's a done deal. Just accept it. Accept His love and forgiveness as a gift, as a way to look forward, to move on."

She filled her emptiness with a deep breath of cool November air. "How can I refuse?"

He laughed. "You can't."

She put her head against his shoulder, and they watched the sun disappear from today. Forever.

• • •

Evelyn looked at the ceiling. The moonlight created odd shadows across her room, casting a bluish glow to items that were ripe with color in the light.

Everything had changed.

On the side of the highway, with hands ripped by gravel, Evelyn had experienced an encounter with her Savior. It hadn't been planned. It hadn't even been sought.

How was it possible to go through a gauntlet as complicated as forgiveness without ever having a previous notion that it was even a needed step? It's not like she'd been moping around for nearly two years thinking, *If only I could forgive Aaron. If only I could forgive myself.* She'd thought things had been going well. She'd gotten the widow thing down. Life was breezing along.

And how odd that a meeting with Margaret's parents about *her* man problems had elicited such a crossroad moment in her own life. After leaving Margaret's parents she'd thought the entire excursion a waste of time. But it wasn't. And how amazing that Wayne had just happened to be at Peerbaugh Place when Evelyn had gotten the idea, and had just happened to offer to drive. Would she have had the same experience if she'd been alone in the car? And if she hadn't gone to meet the Jensens at all, how long would it have been until she'd faced the forgiveness issue? Months? Years?

She turned on her side, toward the space that had been Aaron's. Thirty-one years she'd slept next to him, thinking she knew him. And yet, in many ways, she'd learned more about him—and herself—in the months since he'd gone. Had the close proximity of day-to-day marriage made her blind to who they really were? Or was it logical that she understood their life better in hindsight?

She put a hand on the extra pillow where he used to lay his

head, stroking it as if he were still there, sleeping. "It's okay now, Aaron. We're okay."

She closed her eyes, leaving her hand on his empty pillow.

•   •   •

Lucinda looked at the ceiling. The moonlight created odd shadows across her room, casting a bluish glow to items that were ripe with color in the light.

Everything had changed.

In a hotel restroom, on a darkened Boston street, in a church pew—her pride ripped by the truth—Lucinda had experienced an encounter with Jesus. It hadn't been planned. It hadn't even been sought.

How was it possible to go through a gauntlet as complicated as pride without ever having a previous notion that it was even a needed step? It's not like she'd been moping around thinking, If only I could quit putting so much stock in my looks. *If only I could forgive myself for growing old.* She'd thought things had been going along pretty well. She'd gotten the single thing down. Life was breezing along.

And how odd that insults, church, and a makeover on Margaret had elicited such a crossroad moment in her own life. She'd expected church to be a waste of time. But it wasn't. And how amazing that she *hadn't* been able to sit next to Wayne and had sat next to Piper. Would she have had the same experience if she'd sat next to a handsome man? And if she hadn't gone to church at all how long would it have been until she'd faced the pride issue? Months? Years?

She turned on her side, toward the space that had often been occupied by various males who had meant little to her. For fifteen years she'd thought she knew what she wanted. What she needed. And yet, in many ways, she'd learned more about herself in the time she'd been alone. Had the close proximity of day-to-day flir-tations made her blind to what was really important? Or was it logical that she understood life better in hindsight?

She put a hand on the extra pillow where men used to lay their heads, stroking it as if they were still there, sleeping. "It's okay now. I'm okay."

She closed her eyes, leaving her hand on the empty pillow.

Don't forget to do good
and to share what you have with those in need,
for such sacrifices are very pleasing to God.

HEBREWS 13:16

$\mathcal{T}$essa was in a tizzy. She felt like a pinball in a machine, *boink*ing against the obstacles in her apartment, always in motion, always on the verge of falling forever into the black hole.

Today was the day of the costume party. The logistics of the event were being handled by dozens of friends and volunteers.

She wasn't worried about that.

Hundreds of tickets had been sold, and the items up for auction were ready.

She wasn't worried about that.

Her costume was pressed and assembled, her speech written. She wasn't worried about that.

But what happened tomorrow? When all the money was in her hands, when all the prayers and well-wishing of her supporters hung expectantly in the air, how would she help the women of the world? How would she do it?

She'd been so consumed with igniting the vision, with putting together the kickoff, that she hadn't had time to figure out the details of *after*.

She stopped in the middle of her living room, stomped a foot on the carpet, and clenched her fists. "Stop it!"

She forced herself to take two deep breaths. She remembered this feeling of no-going-back once before in her life—forty years earlier. She'd been eight months pregnant with Naomi and had experienced a similar moment of panic when she realized there was no going back. She *was* going to have a baby. She *was* going to go through labor and pain. There was no way out. Same with today. She was going to have a global ministry. She was going to go through labor and pain. She was going to birth something amazing and good.

But she needed to remember who had birthed the birth . . .

Tessa held on to the back of a nearby chair and got to her knees. She used to be able to put her forehead to the floor, but her muscles weren't as limber as they once were. Instead, she clasped her hands and leaned them against her forehead, bowing her head. "Father, You are the one who gave me this idea. You are the one who loves these women around the world. Thank You for bringing me this far. Be with me today as the ministry finds its feet, help me tomorrow as I start to use its hands, but most of all, be its heart. And don't let me ever lose the knowledge that this is Yours. I am Yours."

She knelt in silence a few moments to make sure there was nothing else and to see if she sensed any immediate response.

What she felt was peace. A verse came to mind and she laughed with the knowledge of its roots. She rose and gathered her Bible. She opened to 1 Chronicles, where God was talking about building the temple. She read it through once, smiled, then said it aloud, as if her voice were God's, giving her instructions: "'Be strong and courageous, and do the work. Don't be afraid or discouraged by the size of the task, for the Lord God, my God, is with you. He will not fail you or forsake you.'"

She closed the Good Book and smiled. It would be all right. God had declared it so.

•   •   •

"Move your sombrero, Mr. Husband."

Collier moved his hat from the bench of her makeup table so Mae could sit. She lined her lips in bright red and painted them in. She adjusted the braided chignon at each ear. "I should have dyed my hair black. I definitely look like a Mexican of Irish descent." She turned to look at him. To accuse him. "I still don't know why you wouldn't go the Irish route with me."

He messed with the red sash around his waist. "Although you honor your Irish-Fitzpatrick roots, I must honor my English-Ames roots. Since neither one of us was willing to step over to the other side, this Mexican attire is a good compromise." He tossed his hands in the air. "How am I supposed to tie this thing?"

She got up and did it for him, adding his wide sombrero, dipping her head beneath it for a kiss. "These hats make you work for it, don't they?"

"But I'm worth it."

She wouldn't disagree with him. She looked to their door, thinking of Starr across the hall. "Do you think she'll come?"

"She's not interested, Mae."

"She's not interested in much of anything other than work. I should have followed through with my instincts and called Ted. Surprised her."

"Upset her."

"Tough toenails. She needs a little upset in her life. She's getting way too comfortable here."

"You want to tell her to move out?"

Mae swished back and forth in her magenta skirt, liking the feel of the petticoats against her legs.

"You're not answering me."

She stopped her swaying. "I refuse to answer on the grounds that I'll sound like a mean mom."

"If you're a mean mom, then I'm a mean stepdad because I'd really like to have you all to myself again."

She moved close. "You would?"

With a little practice they got the sombrero thing down.

• • •

Evelyn stood in the doorway to Margaret's room. Margaret hadn't been there all day. She was at Bobby's. She was always at Bobby's. Unfortunately, not much had changed since they'd had a talk about how submitting to meanness was wrong. Maybe if Evelyn had shared more about her own experience with giving in to emotional cruelty . . .

Out of habit she felt the hate well up. *No. Don't bring it up again. It's forgiven. It's over. It's the past.*

Old habits were hard to break.

"Where is she?" Piper asked from her own doorway.

"Bobby's. At least I assume she's at Bobby's."

Piper tied a white apron around her full milkmaid skirt. "She's going to Tessa's bash, isn't she?"

Evelyn thought of something. She opened Margaret's closet and rifled through it. "She was going as an American Indian. Her costume is gone. That's a good sign."

Lucinda's voice came from down the hall. "This is absolutely ridiculous."

They left Margaret's room to see what she was talking about. She came toward them, walking awkwardly in wooden shoes. She stopped, lifted her skirt to her knees, and said, "I can't do it. I can't."

"You'd better wear regular shoes," Evelyn said.

"But it will ruin the outfit."

Piper laughed. "If Tessa can wear Hush Puppies with a kilt, you can wear comfortable shoes—" she held up a finger—"just a minute." She ran to her room and came out with a pair of leather clogs. "Try these."

"They're a little big, but they'll do. They look okay, don't they?"

"Crisis averted!" Piper said.

Her problem solved, Lucinda looked at Evelyn. "You look like Betsy Ross."

"I represent colonial America. Does anyone know what Tessa is wearing?"

"It's going to be hard to top the outfits she's already worn."

Evelyn glanced at Margaret's room. "I guess we'd better go. I hope Margaret meets us there."

Sans Bobby would be good.

• • •

Starr sat at the kitchen table with a huge bowl of chocolate-mint ice cream before her. She knew the sugar fix was a childish reaction, but didn't her mother know by now that the more she pushed, the more Starr dug in her heels and did the opposite? Why had her mom made that last attempt to get her to come to the costume party? *I know it will turn out to be a very surprising evening, honey.*

Now there was no way Starr could go and save face.

But maybe it was okay. It was much more fun to stay home and pout, especially when she had plenty to pout about. No one understood her. Everyone was against her. Piper disapproved of the book she was editing; her mother and Collier disapproved of her not going along with Ted's new rules for a relationship; Ted kept calling, trying to make the case for Jesus. . . . No one was on her side. No one tried to see things her way. No one cared about her opinion.

No one cared. At all.

Sure, her mom and Collier said they loved her; they were praying for her. Ted said the same thing. But if that was so, then . . .

She used the spoon to make a point to the empty chair across the table. "Why don't they just leave me alone?"

Because they love you and they're praying for you.

"But who asked them to? Who—?"

A sudden sadness came over her that even ice cream couldn't erase. What was she saying? That she didn't want their love and prayers? Did she really want to be utterly, totally alone?

"Ted . . ."

With his name came tears. She missed him so much it hurt. And though she had yet to call him, she looked forward to his calls—even if they did turn into arguments. Even if he was wrong.

She turned to look at the phone. *Call him. Make an effort. Reach out.*

Then the other voice that had been dogging her for the past two weeks interrupted. *Don't you dare! He'll hound you until you give into his Jesus. That's not love. That's coercion. That's—*

"No!"

Starr moved to the phone and dialed. Her heart pumped against the wall of her chest. She didn't let herself wonder why she was doing it. She didn't let herself think at all. Thinking too much was what got her in trouble. Sometimes wasn't it best to just act? follow your instincts?

The phone rang. And rang. Four rings in, the answering machine picked up.

Starr shouted "No!" a second time. For a different reason. "Where are you, Ted? You're always home on Friday nights."

Suddenly, Starr remembered the costume party. It was a big deal. Her mother said hundreds of people had bought tickets.

Her mother had wanted Ted to come visit.

Her mother bugged her incessantly about going to the party.

I know it will turn out to be a very surprising evening, honey.

A surprise.

One plus one equaled . . .

Starr hurried upstairs. She had a party to go to and someone to see.

●　　●　　●

Margaret came out of Bobby's bedroom wearing her Indian dress with beads braided in her hair. "How do you like my moccasins, Bobby? Mary Jo from school loaned them to—"

He looked up from the television. "You look ridiculous."

She tried not to be hurt. "It's a costume party; we're supposed to look ridiculous. Your costume is in the closet."

He flipped the channel. "I'm not going."

"But we talked about it. It's here, in Jackson. I already spent the money on the tickets and the rental of these costumes."

"I told you I'd *think* about going. I thought about it. I don't want to go."

She sank onto the chair near the couch. "Why not? It'll be fun."

"Fun for you. They're your friends."

"There're hundreds of people coming from all over. I'm sure you'll know lots of people there." *Even if you don't . . .* "Besides, it's for a good cause. All the money goes to help women around the world."

He snickered.

"There's a real need. Millions of women are persecuted in terrible ways, even killed. They're treated like chattel, as if they don't have a heart, a mind, an opinion. Even a soul."

His shrug was a knife. He stood. "I feel like Chinese food. You buy; I'll fly. You've got more money than me."

Since when?

He got his coat on and she hurried to stop him. "Come on, Bobby. Do this. It means a lot to me."

"Hey, you've already bought the tickets. They've got from you what they wanted to get from you."

"But there's an auction to earn more for the charity."

He grabbed her purse and started rummaging through it. He pulled out a ten and two ones and laughed. "You barely have money to buy dinner, much less change the world. You want sweet-and-sour chicken or moo goo gai pan?"

She thought of the ladies and their declaration that it was acceptable—even responsible—to *not* submit if the man was being ungodly. Did Bobby being a jerk count?

"Never mind. I'll surprise you." He left.

What was happening to them? Ever since Bobby had taken her back, he'd been acting strange. Rude. He seemed to take great pleasure in putting her down, as if he'd determined that her tendency to be too perfect could be addressed by cutting her down to size. It was working. She felt anything but perfect. She felt . . .

Angry!

The feeling swelled inside, bringing with it a decision: *I'm outta here.*

She stormed into the bedroom to gather his costume. She would *not* be here when he returned. She was going to the party without him. Alone. She'd made a commitment to her friends, and she was going to follow through with it—which was more than some people she knew.

She yanked his matching Indian costume out of the closet. The chief's headdress (which she'd paid an extra twenty-five dollars for) was on the shelf. As she pulled it down, a shoe box fell to the floor. Some papers scattered.

As she bent to pick them up she noticed an opened envelope addressed to her. From Fenton, Davis, and Walgren, Attorneys-at-Law.

What's this?

She sat on the bed and removed the letter. It was on fancy

letterhead. The subject heading leaped out at her: *Estate of June Dalloway, deceased (October 14).*

June's name and the word *deceased* did not go together. *Could* not go together.

Margaret pressed a hand against her chest, attempting to keep her heart from leaving her. June had been a professor in college, in elementary education. She'd taken Margaret under her wing and had encouraged her, guided her, taken extra time with her, to make sure Margaret excelled at her calling. Professor Dalloway— June—had retired before Margaret had graduated but they had stayed in touch. And October 14? She and June had shared dinner the end of September, right after Margaret and Bobby had broken up, just days before she'd moved into Peerbaugh Place.

How could she be gone?

She went back to the letter, hoping it would offer some details.

Dear Margaret Jensen,

A Notice of Petition to Administer Estate of the above-named decedent is enclosed. The purpose of the notice is to give anyone who desires to contest the will an opportunity to do so in the manner provided by law. If you do not object, it is not necessary for you to appear personally at the hearing.

The will of the decedent leaves you $75,000.00 (seventy-five thousand dollars and no cents), which will be distributed on the closing of the estate. At least three months will be required to complete the estate proceedings, as long as there are no unforeseen complications.

As soon as an inventory is completed, a copy will be sent to you. Also, when the estate is being closed, a copy of the final account will be sent to you so that you will be fully informed of all proceedings.

If you have any questions about the estate, we will be pleased to answer them.

Margaret looked across the room and saw her reflection in the dresser mirror. An Indian maiden with her mouth open. Seventy-five thousand dollars? The amount was unfathomable in its size—and didn't make sense. June had been a widow for thirty years and had lived in an extremely modest home. She had simple tastes. But perhaps that's why she'd been able to save so much. Margaret assumed the one son had received much more.

Oh, June, you didn't have to do this. And what am I going to do without you?

She cried until the tears dried up. She read and reread the letter. Then it hit her. Why hadn't she seen this letter before now? Why was it hidden away in a box in Bobby's closet? Why had he opened it in the first place?

She turned the envelope over. It had been sent to this address—which made sense because this was the place they were going to live as a couple after they were married. Margaret started having her mail sent here two months prior to their breakup. Better here than at her parents' . . .

"Why didn't Bobby show it to me? Why—?"

She looked at the date of the letter. *October 27.* It was certified. Bobby signed for it. He'd probably received it on October 29. She ran to the calendar hanging on the wall in the kitchen. *Please, no. Please, no.* Her finger pegged the Friday night square that she had decorated with sparkle stars. Margaret had stuck them on Bobby's calendar to commemorate the day he'd showed up at Peerbaugh Place and they'd gotten back together.

The date was October 29.

Her breathing became heavy. She slid her finger backward to the Sunday before, the Sunday when she'd gone out to lunch with Audra and Russell. The meal when she'd seen Bobby in the restaurant—rudely hiding behind his menu. Wanting nothing to do with her. October 24.

She looked down at the letter again. *October 27.*

It was all brazenly clear. Bobby had wanted nothing to do with her on the twenty-fourth. The letter saying she was rich was sent on the twenty-seventh. It was received—by Bobby—on the twenty-ninth. After which he'd made a sudden effort to find out where she was living. Not to tell her the sad news about June or the amazing news about the inheritance, but to snatch her back into his life so *he* could have the money.

"No wonder he talked about buying a house." She thought of something else. "When was he going to tell me?"

Obviously after they were married. After what was hers was his. This explained his suggestion to move up the wedding. He wanted to be married before the check was cut.

A noise in the hall of the apartment building broke through her thoughts. She realized he would be back any minute with the Chinese food. Should she stay and confront him?

She looked to the box of papers littering the floor. Let it speak for her.

She left him—in every sense of the word.

•   •   •

Tessa looked out the door of the community center. Snow! Of all nights. She hoped it wouldn't keep people away. *Lord, why couldn't You have held off until tomorrow?*

But apparently it wasn't holding people back that much, because there was a constant stream, most dressed in marvelous costumes. She greeted them at the door and led them to the sign-in table for their name tags and programs.

"Aunt Tessa!"

She hugged Summer and greeted Audra and Russell. They were dressed like a family in Jesus' time. Audra's business partner, Heddy Wainsworth, was with them, accompanied by her boyfriend, Steve Mannersmith. Heddy and Steve were dressed in matching mandarin coats that had accents of gold metallic thread.

"My, my," Tessa said, having to touch the fabric. "You've outdone yourself, Heddy."

"Oh, just something I whipped up."

Audra spread her simple caftan. "I feel completely underdressed. I went for quick and easy."

"As you should," Tessa said. "You have a family to take care of."

Heddy slipped her arm through Steve's. "They'll be another family in Carson Creek soon . . ."

"You're engaged?" Russell asked.

Steve nodded. "She caught me."

Heddy pulled him close. "We caught each other."

"I happen to know a great company that makes bridesmaids' dresses," Audra said.

"Will they give me a discount?"

"Absolutely."

Summer was looking intently at Tessa's costume. "What country is this one from, Aunt Tessa?"

"Actually," Audra said, "I was wondering that too."

Tessa took a step back so all could see. "My costume combines something from every continent. I'll explain it all later."

"It's very . . . unique," Heddy said.

A line was forming behind them. Tessa didn't want to be rude but . . . Russell noticed and spurred his little group on.

It was going to be a marvelous night. Tessa could feel it.

• • •

Stupid snow.

Margaret was having a hard enough time seeing to drive because of the dark and because of her tears, much less having to deal with this other type of moisture.

It was coming down in huge wet flakes. The transition time between true rain and true snow was always the most treacherous, as ice was usually added to the mix.

But she couldn't slow down. She couldn't pull off the road. All she wanted was to get home to Peerbaugh Place. By now Bobby had returned to an empty apartment. *"Meg? Where are you? Food's on."*

He would set the Chinese on the kitchen counter and wind his way through the few rooms, looking for her. He'd come into the bedroom and stop short at the sight of the box of papers on the floor. Scattered. He'd fall to his knees, searching for the one envelope that would ruin everything.

She looked at the seat beside her, at the envelope. Sorrow at her mentor's death collided with the astonishment at her monetary windfall and slammed back against Bobby's betrayal.

"I loved him!"

The *whirr* of the engine was accompanied by the *whip-whap* of the wiper blades.

Loved? Past tense? Was her love so easily discarded?

"He betrayed me!"

Maybe there was a logical explanation. Maybe he was going to surprise—

No. There were other signs the relationship was unhealthy. Ever since the day Bobby had reappeared in her life, wanting her back, he'd been different. More possessive, yet distant. As if he wanted her around in proximity, but not close. Not emotionally connected.

The snow was heavier now, and with its momentum combined with the speed of the car, it came at the windshield in a hypnotic, spinning spiral. Her headlights didn't light the road as much as they lit the swirling snow. She tried to concentrate on the centerline . . .

She started crying again, not out of anger but out of frustration.

She'd tried to be a good woman. She would have tried to be a good wife.

But shouldn't Bobby be trying too? Trying to treat her as God wanted her to be treated?

Margaret didn't say a prayer, but when her mind paused long enough, it seemed her thoughts cleared a bit. All the teaching she'd heard about the biblical husband-wife relationship came flooding through her tears. She wanted to voluntarily submit to a man who loved her. Loved her sacrificially. Yet submission didn't mean being a doormat. It didn't mean allowing him to be mean or rude or—

A thief.

He hasn't taken the money yet.

Margaret shook her head. He couldn't get the money without her, without being married to her. That's the only reason he'd come back into her life.

She was a fool. An incredible—

Headlights in her lane!

She steered to the right.

Wheels hit the uneven shoulder.

The car tilted.

It flipped over.

The snow fell.

● ● ●

Lucinda did a double take at a matador as she examined the items to be auctioned. Sixties. Gray hair. A bit rotund for such a costume. Where had she seen him before?

As if he felt her eyes on him, he turned toward her. He smiled and came close. "Lucinda Van Horn?"

The voice was familiar too. A customer at Flora and Funna?

He looked down at her legs. "Your knee all healed up?"

The reunion. The man who'd saved her on the street. "Pastor . . ."

"Enoch," he said. "What are you doing here?"

"I could ask the same about you."

"I work at the Haven's Rest Mission downtown."

It took her a moment. "But you were at the other shelter in Boston."

"We were on a mission trip there. My home base is here. You live in Jackson?"

"In Carson Creek."

"But you were at a reunion in Boston."

"I was."

He shook his head, incredulous. "How did that go?"

"The scraped knee was the highlight."

He nodded. "Would you like some punch?"

"I'd love some."

He left her to question the odds of them meeting again. What a coincidence.

Pastor Enoch returned with the punch. "I'd say God's at work here, wouldn't you? Only He could arrange for us to meet again."

"It certainly is a coincidence," she said.

He shook his head adamantly. "Sorry. No go. There's no such thing."

Before she had a chance to argue with him, he continued. "You look marvelous. Whatever you did, I approve."

She felt herself blush. "Thank you."

He was eyeing her intently. "What *did* you do?"

She laughed softly. "I let myself look my age. I let myself be old."

"Baloney. Old is a state of mind. And your age is perfectly fine with me."

She'd never heard that one before. It was quite . . . refreshing.

He took a sip of punch, studying her. "How would you like to come to the mission tomorrow noon and help us serve lunch?"

She'd never considered such a thing.

"Come on. It will be fun. I'd love to show you where I work."
How could she refuse?

•   •   •

Starr felt like a fool—for many reasons—mainly for wearing her
mother's muumuu, with sandals, under a winter coat, when it
was snowing outside. Ah, vanity. Yet when Tessa greeted her at
the door, wearing an absurd costume that belied all logic, she
knew her costume concerns were minimal.

She moved to the check-in table and got out her checkbook.
"Hi. I need to buy a ticket."

The woman eyed her. "Aren't you Mae's daughter?"

"Yes, I'm Starr—"

"Starr. Yes," said the woman, checking her list. "Yes, here
you are."

"Here I am?"

"You're paid."

She didn't like the fact her mother had assumed—

"Starr!"

Her mother ran toward her, scooping her into a hug. "I'm
so glad you came."

"Aren't we a bit overconfident?" she asked, nodding toward
the list.

"Gracious gecko, honey. It's for charity." She linked arms.
"Besides, I knew you'd come."

Collier countered. "You knew no such thing. But we're glad
you're here."

Her mother walked her through the crowd. Toward Ted? Starr's
stomach stirred. Did they have him hiding in a corner as the big surprise? The prospect of seeing him sent conflicting emotions up and
down her spine. Anticipation and dread. Joy and wistfulness.

Her mother was talking about costumes and items to be auctioned—she'd donated a few pieces of silver jewelry—but for the most part Starr wasn't listening. She was trying to gather two words to say to Ted when she saw him.

When her mom stopped the promenade, Starr knew it was time. She tried not to look too eager. She scanned the crowd.

Collier was talking. "I bought a dozen crossword books and three jigsaw puzzles, and your mother helped me put them in a basket, along with a crossword dictionary."

"We called it the Rainy Day Game Basket," Mae said.

Collier glanced toward the entry where the driving snow could be seen. "It would work for snowy days too. I hope it brings a good—" He turned to Starr. "Are you all right?"

It was then she realized Ted was not coming.

Told ya. You got yourself all worked up for nothing. Serves you right for—

"Get her some punch, Collie. That's what the girl needs."

Not really. But it would have to do.

* * *

Evelyn spotted Herb across the room. He was dressed as a cowboy. Next to him was a fiftysomething woman as a cowgirl. His date? She experienced a twinge of jealousy, but finding it absurd, shoved it away.

He looked in her direction. Evelyn looked away; then realizing how guilty it must seem, she looked back. He raised a glass of punch in her direction. She waved. The woman looked at Evelyn, then whispered something to Herb. Probably, *Who's she?*

I'm the woman who could have married your man.

Could have. But not should have.

The other man in her life came toward her, bearing two cups of punch. He was wearing a white sheet as a toga—which was fine. But the plaid shirt underneath looked a bit silly. Yet she couldn't imagine Wayne Wellington baring a shoulder in public. Not that she'd want him too. Discretion was an attribute she admired.

Piper was close at his heels with her own punch. "Here we go," Wayne said, handing Evelyn a cup.

They all took a sip. "It's not that I don't like your costume, Dad," Piper said. "Actually I'm relieved you didn't wear the sheet with the pink roses on it."

"Don't be silly. I save that one for Sundays."

They looked around the room as they talked. It was full, the buzz around the items to be auctioned intense. "It's quite a success, don't you think?" Evelyn said.

"Mmm," Piper said. "I wonder what the final head count will—"

When she stopped midsentence, Evelyn looked in the direction of her gaze. Just entering the building was Gregory Baladino. He was dressed in Italian Renaissance garb. His eyes searched the crowd—and locked on Piper.

As soon as their eyes met she let out a soft *oh* as if his look was a physical touch.

Evelyn took her arm. "Oh, Piper . . ."

"Well, well," Wayne said. "The good doctor has joined us."

Gregory walked toward them.

•   •   •

He's coming to talk to me! What am I going to say?

Hello would be good.

Wayne held out his hand. "A good evening to you, Doctor. It's nice to see you again."

Gregory shook his hand. Piper hoped he wouldn't shake hers. Somehow that act of polite greeting would be the epitome of distance. Yet a hug would probably be too much . . .

"Evelyn. You look quite colonial this evening," he said, but his eyes flitted to Piper.

Evelyn curtsied. "And you are quite the Renaissance man."

He pulled a paintbrush out of his pocket. "I'm Michelangelo."

"Excellent," Evelyn said. "I *do* have a ceiling that needs painting."

Piper was glad for the banter because she was still too discombobulated to trust—

He looked right at her. Then he took a step toward her, took both her hands, and spread them wide. "And look at you, dear Piper. You are the essence of an English countryside."

Wayne leaned forward. "Her sheep are in the back room."

She still hadn't said anything and when Gregory let go, her first impulse was to grab his hands back. She didn't want to lose him again.

He's not here for you, Piper. He's here for the charity event. Get a grip.

They all heard a high-pitched "*Hola*, people!" Mae swept toward them with Collier holding on to his sombrero with one hand and a plate of chicken wings with the other. Starr followed close behind with a look on her face that said she'd rather be anywhere than in her mother's wake.

Mae stopped short when she saw the doctor. "Gregory!"

"Hello, Mae. Collier."

Suddenly, Starr came to life. She stepped forward to shake his hand. "So you're Gregory."

He looked confused. Piper stepped in. "This is Mae's daughter, Starr. She's visiting from New York."

Starr offered a mischievous smile. "I've heard all about you, Doctor."

Piper knew her face was red. And she was still tongue-tied. All the times she'd hoped to run into him and now . . .

No need to worry. Tessa was at the microphone. "Ladies and gentlemen, it's time to start. If you'll all take your seats, we'll get this auction underway."

The crowd took seats, some at tables, some in rows of chairs. Gregory extended a hand toward a row. "After you?"

Butterfly city.

• • •

Tessa looked out over the crowd. *Thank You, Lord Jesus! Give me Your words.*

As soon as her audience quieted she began. "I want to welcome you here tonight. You may be wondering about my costume." There was soft laughter. She knew she looked ridiculous but it didn't matter. She had her reasons . . .

Tessa lifted up her pashmina shawl. "I stand before you, representing the women of the world. This costume combines all that is different into one unit just as we have come here tonight, one unit helping the world. I have sandals from Kenya, a bamboo hat from China, jewelry from Pakistan, a skirt from Sweden, and a blouse from Indonesia.

"Nearly a year ago I won the prize of a world cruise. Those of you who know me well know I thrive on anything historical, so you can guess what a blessing this was for me. But beyond seeing the buildings, the ruins, and the art, something else happened. I met amazing people." She felt herself choke up and put a hand to her chest. "It started on the ship when I met three dear ladies whom I hope will become lifelong friends. It expanded to the shore where I met a myriad of women. So different and yet so much alike. The experience was revealing. And life-changing.

"Beyond acknowledging that in the Western world we have much in the way of the material elements of life, I was struck by the fact that we are blessed with something priceless. Freedom. Freedom to learn, to worship, to follow our dreams. Freedom to think and express our thoughts. Freedom to bond. In other parts of the world this is not a given. It can even be an unknown commodity."

Tessa drew a deep breath and found her nerves had settled. She wasn't speaking for herself. She was speaking now for Him. For them. "Though governments and traditions bind women, they cannot stop individuals from using their brains, from dreaming, from sharing. They cannot contain hope. Within every woman I spoke with—in spite of her living conditions, in spite of her struggles and persecutions—there was a spark of hope and a need to bond with other women. It might have been wavering and weak, but it was there. And their example to me . . ."

Her voice broke and she had to pause to regain control. She straightened her back, not caring if a few tears had escaped. "I came home with a desire—no, a *need*—to help, to share with them what has been shared with me." She searched the audience for her dear friends and found them. She extended a hand, pointing them out one by one. "When I was staying at Peerbaugh Place I met a group of women who were diverse and annoying and—"

Mae spoke up, "Watch it, Tessie!"

Everyone laughed. "As usual, you didn't let me finish, Mae. A group of women who were diverse, annoying . . . and precious. Though we didn't always agree, we connected in a way that I believe is unique to women. We formed a Sister Circle." She remembered the friendship ring Mae had made each of them and turned it now on her finger. "We are bonded together. For life. No matter where we go our sisterhood will remain. That's what I want for the women of the world. I want them to feel the security and love of a sisterhood. That's why—after much prayer and consideration, and help from a lovely woman in Rome—I'm starting the Sister Circle Network. Through it, I—we—are going to help these women who are so strong when they could be weak, so brave when they could be cowardly, so hopeful when they could be broken. They are so much, right now, as they are. And yet they can become so much more—together, with the help of each other and our Lord."

Tessa pointed out the door of the community center. "They are out there, waiting for our help. They are there, and we are here. I have no explanation for why God has placed us here in this land of the free, in this time, with these blessings. But I know we have been told to share. 'Much is required from those to whom much is given, and much more is required from those to whom much more is given.' 'Give as freely as you have received!' That's what I want us to do tonight. Give. Freely, and with reckless abandon. For our sisters of the world who need us to be their brothers and sisters from afar. The money we earn tonight will go toward implementing a Sister Circle Network that will address the emotional, spiritual, and physical needs of our sisters."

There was applause. Tessa hadn't wanted applause and she quieted them with her hands. "So now it's time for the Sister Circle auction to begin. Let me leave you with the words of the apostle John: 'If anyone has enough money to live well and sees a brother or sister in need and refuses to help—how can God's love be in that person? Dear children, let us stop just saying we love each other; let us really show it by our actions. It is by our actions that we know we are living in the truth, so we will be confident when we stand before the Lord, even if our hearts condemn us. For God is greater than our hearts, and He knows everything.'"

She looked across the crowd, praying He would touch them. "God knows your heart better than you do. He knows what you're capable of sharing. Do it now. Love others as He has loved you."

Tessa left the stage and the auctioneer took over. She already felt drained and the evening had just begun. But so it was, sharing one's heart.

Her son-in-law, Calvin, held out a chair for her and kissed her cheek. "Bravo, Tessa. Bravo."

Her grandson, Leonard, gave her a thumbs-up. She looked to her daughter. Naomi had given her a hard time about starting such a venture at her age. But now . . . Naomi got up from her chair, knelt beside her mother, looked into her eyes, and said, "I'm so proud of you, Mom. I'm so proud to be your daughter."

As far as Tessa was concerned, the evening was complete. Praise God from whom all blessings flow. . . .

●   ●   ●

The charity event was a huge success. When it was over people gathered their coats and their purchases and headed into the night. The snow had stopped, leaving behind four inches. It was a fairyland.

Gregory held Piper's coat for her. She bemoaned the fact that their evening was over and they'd had so little time to really talk. Just a few words in between the auctioneer's gavel. And now they only had a few more moments before they would each be in separate cars, driving back—

"Would you like to go out for coffee somewhere?" Gregory asked.

She knew she was beaming but did nothing to stop it. "That would be wonderful. Let me tell Evelyn." She *did* have to restrain herself from crossing the room at a hop, skip, and jump. What had her mother called it? Bopping? Feigning calm, she moved to Evelyn's side.

Evelyn looked up from putting her punch cup on a tray of dirty dishes. "You ready to—?" Evelyn did a double take. "My goodness. Why are you grinning so?" Within seconds she was looking in Gregory's direction.

Piper filled in the blanks with a nod. "We're going out for coffee. He'll take me home."

Evelyn grabbed her arm, pulling her close. "Are you sure?"

Piper nodded. "We haven't had a chance to talk all evening. Not *really* talk."

"But are you sure? Are you up to this?"

"No, I'm not sure. But I haven't seen him in so long, not even as friends. I want to find out what's going on in his life."

Evelyn gave her a motherly look and Piper's heart pulled, knowing it was the same look her own mother would have given her. Evelyn drew her into a hug. "Be careful, Piper. I don't want you to be hurt again."

Piper pulled back. "That may not be avoidable."

Evelyn gave her a nod. Odd how sometimes a person chose struggle, chose the hard thing on the wings of hope.

Piper returned to Gregory. His smile made the risk of pain worth it.

• • •

"Where shall we go?" Gregory asked.

Piper knew of a coffeehouse in downtown Jackson and was just about to suggest it when a big gust of snow pummeled the windshield. Suddenly home was the place to be. "Would you mind if we just went to Peerbaugh Place to talk? We could go back in the sunroom. . . ."

"Sounds good to me." He headed out of town.

Piper suddenly realized she didn't know what to say. Not when she knew she still loved him but couldn't have him. Not when she didn't know how he felt about her. A thirty-minute drive, then coffee . . . if things were awkward it would seem like a lifetime. But if things went well . . .

She sent up an urgent prayer: *Lord, be with us! Give me the words You want me to say, but help me not say too much because You know how I can talk on and on . . . like now. Oh dear . . . if there's any chance . . . I know it's a long shot. It's probably not even possible.* "But

with God everything is possible." Help me not blow this . . . oh, Father,
help! I need You! Make this work. Somehow, make this work.

She took comfort in the knowledge that God would weed
through her disjointed snippets and get the point of her prayer.
He knew her heart. The actual words were for her benefit, not His.

"Did you have a good time?" she asked Gregory as they
headed toward the highway spanning Jackson and Carson Creek.

"Mission accomplished."

"Mission?"

"I came with the sole purpose of seeing you."

So much for small talk. With difficulty Piper swallowed the
lump in her throat. "You did?"

He offered her a glance and a smile. "I've missed you horribly."

Piper put a hand to her mouth. "I'm going to cry."

He didn't tell her not to. "Is that a good sign?"

She could only nod. Then she realized her emotions were taking over. There was never any question her feelings for him had
never lessened. But feelings weren't the issue. She'd broken up
with him in *spite* of her feelings. To spite her feelings. She *had* to
focus on the issue that stood between them. She had to talk to him
about Jesus. She had to ask—

"I've been going to church."

She sucked in a breath, immediately hoping it didn't sound
too much like a gasp.

"At Tessa's church."

Her mind raced. "So she knew . . . has she seen you?"

"Every week."

"But she hasn't said—"

"I asked her not to." He took a deep breath and looked
straight ahead. "I didn't want to come to you until it was right.
Until it was real. Until I was . . ." He suddenly slowed and
whipped his head to the right and back. "Oh! There's a car down
there!"

"What?"

He put on his turn signal and eased to the snowy shoulder. Cars zoomed past. "I think there's been an accident. My headlights caught a fender, a wheel—upside down." He shut off the car and reached into the backseat for his medical bag. "There's a flashlight in the glove box."

Piper got it out and handed it to Gregory.

He waited for traffic to pass, then opened his door. "Stay here!"

No way. If someone needed help . . . she looked at her Mary Jane shoes that went so well with her milkmaid costume. If only she had boots. If only she were wearing pants. *The person in the car is far colder than you'll be. Go!*

Her car door nipped a bank of snow, and she had to use extra effort to get it open. She stepped out, her feet and legs immediately bitten by the cold. Gregory was already running toward the car. His flashlight skimmed an overturned vehicle.

Piper reached back into the car, grabbed her cell phone, and dialed 911. She looked around trying to figure out a description of where they were. Everything looked so different in the dark. "There's a car in a ditch—overturned—south side of the highway, about fifteen miles outside Carson Creek coming back from Jackson."

The dispatcher asked a few questions, then hung up. Help was on its way.

Gregory scrambled down the embankment toward the car. "Hello? Help's here. I'm coming!"

Piper ran through the snow toward him, a new prayer going up with each awkward step. *Lord! Help! Lord! Help!*

Then she saw the car. The color of the car. It was blue. It looked familiar. It had a *LV2TCH* bumper sticker. Then she knew. But she didn't want to know. *No. No. No!*

"It's Margaret's car!" she screamed.

Gregory was already on his knees on the passenger side. He didn't answer her. He was speaking to someone inside through a broken window. *Which must mean she's alive. Margaret's alive!*

Gregory looked up at Piper. "Go back to the car. Pop the trunk. Blankets. And a shovel. I need to pry this door open."

Piper ran as fast as she could. *She's alive! She's alive! Thank You, Lord! Help!*

More than anything she wanted to call 911 again, make them hurry. She returned with the items, finally getting close enough to see a bit of what Gregory was seeing. Margaret's foot was against the windshield.

"Here!" Gregory said, shoving the flashlight toward her. "Hold this so I can see what I'm doing."

She did as she was told, but as he could see, so could she. Margaret was crumpled into a tiny space. There was blood. Yet she was conscious. Their eyes met. "Help's coming, Margaret. I called 911," Piper said.

Margaret's eyes closed.

Gregory worked with a fervent intensity, his words to Margaret soft and soothing. "I think your arm's broken. You have a cut on your head, but it will be okay. I don't want you to move too much, but can you use your good arm to pull the blanket . . . ? Good, good. Hold on just a bit longer. We're going to get you safe in a cozy bed and put some heated blankets on you. Doesn't that sound good?" Margaret moaned. "I know it hurts. But help is coming. I'm going to try to get your door open." He stood to use the shovel.

Margaret opened her eyes and looked at Piper. "I've been praying."

Piper nodded. "I *am* praying. You'll be fine. We're here."

Margaret closed her eyes again. "*He's* here."

A siren got louder. Piper stood to see. Coming from the direction of Carson Creek . . . "Red lights! They're here!"

But Margaret was right. *He* was there.

You must always act in the fear of the Lord,
with integrity and with undivided hearts.

2 CHRONICLES 19:9

$\mathcal{E}$velyn was just pouring Wayne a cup of decaf when she heard
the front door open.

"Evelyn!"

They ran into the entry to find Piper, hair disheveled, feet wet.

"Oh—what happened?"

Her words came out in a rush. "Margaret's car crashed in a
ditch. Gregory and I found her. She's at the hospital." She took
the stairs two at a time. "Gregory dropped me off. I have to
change."

Lucinda came out of her room in her robe. "Did I hear—?"

Evelyn told her the news as Wayne got their coats.

"I'm coming too," Lucinda said. "Give me one minute."

Evelyn had never seen Lucinda take only a minute, but hoped
tonight would be an exception. She felt her mind flitter over what
needed to be done, what could be done. "I have to call Mae, turn
the coffeepot off—"

Wayne took her hands in his. "I'll do it. Calm, Evelyn. Take
a breath."

He was right. When he returned she felt more in control. Piper burst out of her room wearing jeans and a sweater, carrying her shoes. If only Lucinda—

Evelyn heard Lucinda's door shut. "Ready!"

Wayne helped them with their coats. Out the door they went. Evelyn was happy to let Wayne drive.

The car filled with their voices, overlapping, exclaiming, wondering what to do. It was Piper who calmed them and got them on track.

"Pray, people. We need to pray."

•   •   •

Lucinda was amazed at the words being tossed around the car on the way to the hospital.

Wayne, as the driver, had his eyes wide open, yet he asked God to help Margaret, to *be* with her. Evelyn sat beside Lucinda in the backseat, her hands clasped in her lap, her head bowed, asking God to take over. Piper sat in the front seat, her elbows at her side, her palms raised, along with her face. She prayed with her eyes closed, telling God they would accept whatever He wanted, but if it fit into His plans, could Margaret be whole and healed.

His plans? Whatever *He* wanted? Lucinda didn't think it was a very good idea to give God free rein. What if He wanted Margaret to die? Surely that was unacceptable. Yet as these three friends prayed out loud, finishing each other's sentences, their words flowing between them like a constant thread being passed, Lucinda wanted what they had.

Peace.

It made no sense. How could they be peaceful when they were rushing to the hospital? And they *had* been agitated at Peerbaugh Place. Their frenzied reaction was her frenzied reaction. But once they got in the car and started the prayers, everything had changed, from the tone of their voices to their body language.

Somehow, in the span of a few minutes, they'd spanned the chasm between panic and peace.

Though Lucinda didn't feel comfortable praying aloud, she found herself nodding. *Like she said, God. Like he said.* And as she let herself be drawn into the circle of prayer, the peace found her too. She couldn't pinpoint a distinct moment when it happened, but as they turned into the parking lot of the hospital, she realized it was there. In her. With her.

He was there?

It was something to think about.

•   •   •

Evelyn was amazed at how busy the emergency room was at 12:15 a.m. Carson Creek was a small town. Not much happened here.

As they sat in the small waiting area, that supposition still held true. There were no gunshot wounds, no knifings, but there were people who looked ill or who were holding sick children.

Evelyn couldn't sit. She got up and paced, her eyes watching the area where doctors and nurses used their skills. Where was Gregory? Why hadn't he come out to talk to them?

Mae, Collier, and Starr burst in the door of the ER. "Any word?" Mae asked.

"Not yet."

"Tell us what happened."

Evelyn looked to Piper, who went through the story again. She was happy to let her do it. She'd been in this very waiting room for a car accident before. This repeat performance was not easy. *I'm sorry, Mrs. Peerbaugh, your husband is dead.*

Mae's words broke through her memories. "So only her arm was broken?" she asked.

"I don't know," Piper said. "That's what was evident at the site, but there could be internal—"

Mae's head was shaking. "Uh-uh. We'll have none of that."
She looked to the ceiling, "Father, God, You take care of our little
Margaret. We're counting on You."

"He arranged for us to find her," Piper said. "I know He did.
We were going to have coffee in Jackson. I was just about to suggest a coffeehouse when this wave of snow hit the windshield,
and I suddenly just wanted to be home. So I suggested we drive
back to Peerbaugh Place. If we hadn't . . ."

Evelyn pulled her collar close and let a shiver run its course.
"Praise God," she whispered as both an exclamation and a prayer.

Wayne suddenly popped out of his seat. "Gregory!"

They all turned in his direction. He scanned their faces, but
found Piper's eyes. He smiled even before he spoke, and Evelyn
wondered if they taught doctors that: *Give them a positive indication
as soon as possible.*

"She'll be fine," Gregory said. "There's no internal bleeding,
only some mighty bruises and contusions, and a broken arm. We
want to observe her for a few hours, but then she should be able
to go home."

There was a chorus of applause and shouts.

"Are her parents on their way?" Mae asked.

Evelyn's first reaction was not kind: *as if they'd care.*

"She hasn't asked us to call them," Gregory said. "But she has
asked for Evelyn."

"Me?" Evelyn said.

He stepped back. "Do you want to see her?"

"Of course."

Gregory led her to Margaret's room. She was in bed, her face
bandaged, her arm in a splint. She opened her eyes. She extended
her good arm. "Evelyn."

Evelyn took her hand. "How are you doing?"

"I'll live." She looked away. "Physically."

What an odd comment. "Talk to me, Margaret."

Her hand left Evelyn's and cradled her hurt arm. "I've been a fool."

"How so?"

"Bobby." She looked back, finding Evelyn's eyes. "He doesn't love me."

"Oh, I'm sure he does." *Why did I say that?*

"No, he doesn't. I found a letter that said I'd inherited seventy-five thousand dollars from a mentor of mine, an old teacher."

Evelyn remembered Margaret mentioning a woman who had been very supportive. "June?"

"Dalloway. Yes, that's her."

"She died?"

Margaret's forehead crumpled with emotion. "I didn't even know. And Bobby's known for weeks. He got a notice from a lawyer saying she passed away and I was inheriting the money."

"Why did he get it?"

"It came to me, at his apartment—it was going to be our apartment, remember? I didn't like my mail being sent to my parents' house. I felt more grown-up having it sent to Bobby's. It's dumb, I know."

"No, no. You had every reason to believe you would be living there."

"After I moved in with you I hadn't gotten around to changing it. I guess June still had the old address."

Evelyn got a tissue and dabbed Margaret's cheeks, then handed her a fresh one. "Bobby opened your mail . . ."

Margaret nodded as she blew her nose. "He shouldn't have opened it in the first place, but that's another matter. Anyway, it's the date that's significant. Bobby got the letter the same day he showed up at Peerbaugh Place wanting to make up. He didn't want me. He wanted my money."

Oh dear. Evelyn wished she could counter with something to make Margaret feel better, but she realized there *was* nothing. And more important, Evelyn shouldn't try to get the two of them back together. Bobby was wrong for Margaret, bad for her. In so many ways.

When Margaret took a breath from her diaphragm she winced and held her side. "Things haven't been right," she said. "He kept wanting more of me while he gave less. But it wasn't because he wanted *me*," she repeated. "He just wanted to keep me close so he'd be sure to get the money."

"I'm so sorry." The full picture became clear. "You found out tonight?"

"I found the letter while he was out. I ran out and was driving home." She shook her head at her own stupidity. "I was upset. Crying. Mad. I shouldn't have been driving. I lost control and flipped over." She shivered. "It was so cold. So incredibly cold."

She sought out Evelyn's hand again. "You know how people say their entire life flashes before their eyes? My *entire* life didn't flash before me, but the last few months certainly did. I've been so obsessed with trying to be perfect. My motives were good, but I was doing it all wrong. *Doing*. That was the key. Out there in the cold, I told God I'd start *being* what He wanted me to *be* instead of *doing* what I thought I should *do*." She started to cry. "Then I prayed and prayed that He'd send help." Her face brightened. "And He did. Suddenly, Gregory and Piper were there."

"Praise God."

She nodded. "Right after I moved into your place I prayed that God would help me understand about the breakup and would show me what I did wrong." She snickered. "Be careful what you pray for."

"The breakup *wasn't* wrong," Evelyn said.

"But the lesson still isn't easy to take." Margaret let her head sink more deeply into the pillows. She closed her eyes. "How could I have been so blind? All of you tried to get me to see . . ."

"That's what sisters are for. To be your eyes when you're too close to see."

Margaret nodded but did not open her eyes. A tear slipped out of the corner. Evelyn stroked her hair. *It will be okay. It will be okay.*

And it would.

* * *

It was two in the morning. Everyone went home to sleep. God willing, they could come get Margaret later in the day.

As the others headed for the parking lot, Piper lingered a moment, hoping Gregory would appear. They hadn't finished their talk. She felt horrible for even thinking such a selfish thing, but she couldn't help herself. After all these months, to be so close to spending time with him, to have him say he was going to church . . .

There, in the middle of the hospital lobby, she covered her eyes with a hand and bowed her head. *Forgive me for thinking only of myself. You must not have wanted us to talk. I need to accept that. Thank You for taking care of Margaret. Heal her broken body. And her broken spirit. Be with—*

"We'll have none of that."

She looked up to see Gregory a few feet away. "None of what?"

"Praying in the lobby."

She didn't know what to say.

"You *were* praying, weren't you?"

"Yes, yes, I was."

He nodded and looked around. "Has everyone gone?"

"They're waiting for me. We're heading home to sleep."

His face fell. "Oh."

Her insides fluttered. "Oh what?"

"I was hoping you'd still like that coffee. We could partake of the hospital cafeteria." He suddenly smiled. "They have pie. You love pie."

"I love pie." She turned to the door. "I'll go tell them I'm staying."

"I'll be here."

Three little words that meant so much.

•   •   •

As Piper cut the tip off her cherry pie she had a flash of déjà vu. "The first time I really talked to you was in this cafeteria. When Mom was first diagnosed."

"I was thinking that too," he said.

You were? Yet this time they were alone except for the cashier. There weren't many people hungry in the wee hours of the morning.

Where to begin?

In the car before finding Margaret, they'd only started to talk. She'd found out he missed her and he was going to Tessa's church and—

"So," Gregory said, poking his meringue with a fork, "where were we?"

"You missed me horribly."

His eyebrow rose. "I said *that*?"

She was suddenly fearful. "Yes . . ."

"Mmm. *Horribly* is not the most romantic choice of words, is it?"

She could breathe again. "You were trying to be romantic?"

He put his fork down and found her hand across the table. "I've tried not to love you, you know."

"You're going to make me cry again."

"If you start, I'll start. So don't, okay?"

She laughed and the tears dissipated. "I tried not to love you too." She laughed more. "How odd this must sound."

"Not odd," he said. "True. A truth. One of the things I like about us is the presence of truth. There is no pretending between us. There is no artifice."

"What you see is what you get?"

He nodded. "But because we both hold truth in such high regard, I have to be truthful now."

Piper's first impulse was to withdraw her hand, as if by not having physical contact whatever he was about to say wouldn't hurt. He must have sensed it because he let his other hand join the first in holding hers where it was. She found her voice. "What truth are you talking about?"

"I told you in the car I've started going to church."

"At Tessa's church."

"Yes."

"I think that's wonderful. Marvelous. I'm excited for you."

He opened his mouth to speak, then closed it. A moment later he found the words. "I'm not *there* yet, Piper. I haven't fully committed my life to Christ." He was quick to add, "I know He is God, I know He died for my sins, I know He rose from the dead . . ."

"You know He loves you?"

He nodded. "I know that. And I'm beginning to feel that." He sighed. "Since you've believed so long you may not realize how far removed from a loving God I've felt. All I knew was a God who condemned, who had rules . . . that is the God I'd heard about. Or if I did hear 'God loves you' it sounded hokey."

"Too good to be true?"

"And weak. It was like a child hearing 'Grammy loves you.' It's nice, but lacked . . ." He searched for the word.

"Impact?"

He smiled at her. "I love when we think alike. Yes, impact. A grandparent is supposed to love a grandchild. It's a wonderful exchange. And not to put down the importance of a grandparent's love, but it doesn't have the impact that I need. That I'm searching for."

"Are you finding that kind of love now? from Him?"

He bit his lower lip. "I'm starting to." He put his fingers on his chest. "It's like there's something happening inside. I'm feeling a depth here, as if something is filling me up."

Piper nearly cried. "Oh, Gregory, it's Him. *He's* filling you up. He's showing you what He's got to offer. He's ready to change everything. Whatever resistance you have, let it go. The Holy Spirit is knocking, Jesus has opened the door, and the Father is waiting for you to say yes."

She saw him swallow. "But yes to what?"

"Yes to Him!" *Please, Lord!* She took both his hands in hers and willed him to hear the truth in her words. "You said you've learned the basics. Here are two verses that summarize those basics. John 3:16-17: 'For God so loved the world that He gave His only Son, so that everyone who believes in Him will not perish but have eternal life. God did not send His Son into the world to condemn it, but to save it.'"

His face lit up. "They said that verse last Sunday."

"Of course they did. And God arranged for you to hear it then—and now. It's the basis of our faith. Believe that, and you are His. He doesn't want to condemn you; He wants to save you. That's why Jesus died on the cross, taking the rap for all our sins so we don't have to."

Gregory suddenly pulled his hands away from hers. He covered his face and pulled in a breath. "Oh. Oh."

Piper was out of her chair, on her knees, her arms around him. He turned, letting her in. "Say yes, Gregory. Just say yes."

He nodded, then a moment later, the word came. "Yes. I say yes."

They cried together—their present, their future, and their eternity now forever intertwined.

• • •

A tap on the bedroom door awakened Evelyn. She sprang from the bed, afraid it was bad news about Margaret.

Piper stood in the hall. But her face was not sad. It was beaming. "Can we talk?"

"Of course." Evelyn let her in and shut the door quietly. She saw the clock. It was 4:13 a.m.

She started to put on a robe but Piper said, "Get back in bed. It's cold." As Evelyn got under the covers, Piper sat at her feet. Evelyn didn't have to prompt her. As soon as they were settled she said, "Gregory accepted Jesus."

Forget the covers. Evelyn had to sit up. "When? How?"

Piper told her the wonderful details. They shared a joyful cry. "I can't believe it," Evelyn said. "Right there in the cafeteria?"

"It doesn't have to be in a church, you know."

She did know. Her yes moment had happened in the kitchen. Downstairs. With Piper. "You've brought two souls to Him, Piper. First me, and now Gregory."

Piper shook her head adamantly. "God did the bringing; I just helped close the deal."

Evelyn grinned. "So when's the wedding?"

"Hey, one step at a time. We have a lot of dating to do. We need some getting-to-know-each-other time."

"But now it's possible. You're equally yoked and God's blessing it. I know it."

Piper nodded. "I know it too."

• • •

Lucinda turned down the alley behind the Haven's Rest Mission in Jackson. Pastor Enoch had told her there was parking back here. She found a place by the Dumpster. She walked toward the back door and spotted a sign that read "No Loitering. Come Inside!" She realized her entire mind-set was going to be challenged. The very people she avoided, the very people she tried not to even think about, were welcome here. She was going to be serving them. Who'd have thought?

She opened the heavy metal door and found herself in a kitchen. Two men looked up from an industrial-size stove. "I'm looking for Pastor Enoch?"

"Out there, setting up," the tall one said.

She stood still, suddenly stagnant. It was going to take all her willpower to move farther into the building. Enoch hadn't seen her. She could turn and run. She'd never given him her phone number . . .

The swinging door opened. "Lucinda, you're here!"

Too late. "I'm here."

"Come on in; I'll show you the ropes."

He led her into the dining room, to two long tables that had been set with plates and aluminum trays to keep food hot. A line of people in various stages of dishevelment had already formed.

"Grab a spoon and dish it out," he said.

And away we go.

•　　•　　•

"Have a seat." Enoch—he'd told Lucinda to call him Enoch—motioned toward a table in the corner. "I'll be right back."

Lucinda gladly sank into a chair. She'd rarely worked so hard. The meal line had seemed endless, and more than once she'd feared they would run out of food. But somehow there'd always been more. Enoch had said something about the "loaves and the fishes" but she didn't know what he meant.

He returned with a tray of food: two bowls of chili, some bread, crackers, green salad, and two brownies. Lucinda had told herself she wouldn't eat, but now that it was set before her, she dove in.

"It's not bad," she said.

"Simple fare is often the best fare," he said. "Meat loaf day is the fav—" He looked up as a tall woman with bushy long hair came up to the table.

"Excuse me, Pastor Enoch. I don't mean to interrupt."

"No problem, Eunice. I heard you have a job interview Monday." She glanced nervously at Lucinda and he hurried to make introductions. "I'm so sorry. Where are my manners? Eunice, this is Lucinda. She's a new volunteer."

For today. We'll see about tomorrow.

Enoch patted the bench beside him. "Sit. Tell us what's on your mind."

Eunice sat and ran her thumb and forefinger along the edge of the table. "It's been a long time since I've had a good job, and this one is in a real nice office. I got a new suit at the WWW to wear but—"

Enoch explained to Lucinda. "WWW is Women's Work Wear. It's a place that takes in donations of work clothes for women trying to get back into the workplace."

"That's a good idea," Lucinda said. "Clothes are very important for first impressions."

"I know," Eunice said. "But there's a problem . . ." She touched a hand to her hair. "I've never been very good at hair stuff or makeup, and during the last couple years while I was on drugs . . . well, let's say I had other things to think about."

Lucinda felt a stirring.

"I just want to look nice, you know? I really need this job."

"I'll help you." Were those her words? Out of her mouth?

Enoch beamed. "That's a marvelous idea. Lucinda used to be a model. She knows all about looking beautiful."

Lucinda felt herself blush. "I don't know about that, but—"

"You'd help me?"

Lucinda retrieved her purse and scanned the room. "There. Let's go over there for some privacy and I'll teach you what to do."

• • •

"Oh my." Eunice stared at herself in Lucinda's hand mirror. "I look nice."

"You look very pretty," Lucinda said. And she wasn't lying. With a little taming of her hair with a hair band, some foundation, eye shadow, liner, and especially some lipstick, Eunice's features came to life.

"Me next!" said a woman holding a baby.

Another woman wearing a stocking hat, pulled it off. "Then me."

Two others nearby nodded. Lucinda hadn't planned on having a beauty class, but as soon as the other women in the dining room had seen what she was doing for Eunice, they'd gathered round.

"Now, now, ladies," Enoch said. "I'm sure Lucinda wants to go home. We don't want to overuse our volunteers, do we?"

The women looked crestfallen.

"I . . . I could come back tomorrow afternoon," Lucinda said. "I could bring all my makeup and hair things. I only had a few items in my purse."

"Then I get first dibs tomorrow," said the mother.

The women chattered and Enoch laughed. "It appears you have some takers. What time, Lucinda?"

She wouldn't be able to back out . . . "Three?"

"We'll be here." They walked away.

Eunice gave Lucinda the mirror and pulled her into a hug. "Thank you. I feel so much better about myself."

Lucinda wasn't sure how to respond to such praise. All she'd done was apply a bit of makeup. Speaking of . . . she handed Eunice the lot. "It's yours. You keep it. Use it on Monday."

You would have thought Lucinda had given her gold. Another hug was given and Lucinda was left with Pastor Enoch. "What just happened here?" she asked him.

"An act of love."

"I didn't plan—"

"But God did." He shook his head, beaming. "Will you admit that it was God who brought us together in Boston? It was God who made sure we re-met last night at the costume event. And it was God who brought Eunice over to our table today."

Lucinda could think of no arguments. "He'd do that?"

"You bet He would. He loves those ladies and He loves you. And He knows what each of you needs. That's why He brought you together."

Lucinda looked across the room at Eunice as she excitedly accepted the *ooh*s and *aah*s of her friends. "I helped, didn't I?"

"Of course you did. And I bet if you think about it, they helped you too."

She looked at Enoch.

He raised an eyebrow and nodded. "Our God is an awesome God, Lucinda."

A God she'd have to get to know better.

·   ·   ·

Starr opened the door to let Piper out. "Thanks for stopping over to give us an update on Margaret, Piper."

"No problem. Just tell your mom and Collier to come over this afternoon and say hello to her. We know Margaret needs her rest, but we also figure she needs to know she has friends who'll be here for her. Evelyn's baking a cake."

Starr looked behind her into the house. "I don't know where

Mother went off to—probably work. And Collier's out to lunch with some buddies. But I'll tell them." She smiled. "Is Gregory going to be there?" Piper had told her the entire story of their reconciliation. In spite of herself, Starr had to admit it was kind of amazing.

"He's on duty this afternoon. But I'll see him tomorrow. He's going to church with us. With me."

Starr felt a twinge of jealousy.

"You want to come along?" Piper asked.

"Three's a crowd."

"Oh, pooh. You know we always have at least one car going. There's room for one more if I have to be strapped to the luggage rack." Her voice turned serious. "We've missed having you there."

A part of Starr missed being there. "We'll see."

Piper said good-bye and headed across the street. There was a definite spring to her step.

Love did that.

Starr couldn't think about love. Yet if Gregory had come around to God, making it possible for him and Piper to be together, then maybe she . . .

Stop it. You're letting yourself be affected by a romantic moment. This is real life we're talking about with you and Ted.

She headed to the kitchen where strawberry ice cream beckoned. She looked at the clock. It was nearly two. She had just plopped her first scoopful into a bowl when she heard her mother's car in the drive. She kept the carton out, just in case her mom wanted to join her. She sat at the kitchen table, expecting her mother to come in the back door. Instead she heard two sets of footsteps . . .

The door opened. Her mother came in.

Then Ted.

She dropped her spoon.

"Hey, Starlight."

Her chair toppled as she ran to him. She wrapped her arms around his neck and felt his arms around her. Encasing her. Enveloping her. *Don't ever let me go!*

She saw her mother start to cry—then withdraw to the living room, leaving them alone.

They held on to each other as if separating would cause the end of the world. They did not kiss. This moment wasn't about kissing; it was about bonding, melding, molding.

She found herself crying and he put a hand to her head, shushing her. "It's okay. It's okay. Let's sit. I want to hear how you've been."

Reluctantly, Starr let go and moved to the table. Ted sat catty-corner from her, holding her hand. "I missed you," he said.

Her throat was tight, and she wasn't sure if it was from emotion or from the battle going on in her mind—a battle to be strong and unrelenting versus being soft and vulnerable. She put a hand to her mouth, not ready to trust what would come out.

"Your mother got me here. She picked me up at the airport. She was afraid you'd be mad."

Starr shook her head.

Ted withdrew his hand, but kept it an inch from hers. "I have to tell you I haven't changed my mind about living together. But I also haven't changed my mind about wanting to marry you when the time's right; when we've come together to a common place. I'd love to elope like Ringo and Soon-ja, but I want it to be right. In all ways." He pulled his hand to his lap and looked down. Then up. "Have you ever heard of the term *equally yoked*?"

If it hadn't been for Piper she wouldn't have. She nodded. *Why can't I speak?*

He looked relieved. "I know my new faith has been hard for you, yet I wouldn't change it for the world. I cannot go back to the way my life was before." He took a deep breath, looking over her head. "I'm so full now. Colors are brighter; there is more depth and texture; every sound is quadraphonic."

Starr smiled. "You should be a writer."

At her words she saw some of the tension leave his shoulders. "What Jesus has done for me is amazing. I used to see life through a dirty window, but now . . . it's like I've moved to the other side of the window, with nothing between. Everything's clear."

His passion moved her. "All this because of Jesus?"

"Yes!"

She rubbed her hands over her face and through her hair. *Don't you dare listen to him. He's trying to trick you. Jesus won't give you a better life than you have—*

"No!"

She only realized she'd shouted the word when she saw the shocked expression on Ted's face. He studied her. "That no is not for me, is it?"

Her breathing was heavy. How could she explain? Yet she had to try. "Ever since I went to church a few weeks ago . . . every time I start thinking of something good, start thinking that maybe, just possibly, what everyone says about God and Jesus could be true, there's this other . . ." She looked up at him. She didn't dare say she was hearing voices.

"Another voice?" he asked.

She nodded.

Her mother suddenly came into the kitchen and rushed to her side. "Oh, honey. Why didn't you tell me?"

It took her a moment to realize they weren't laughing at her. Quite the opposite. They believed her and were concerned for her. "So I did hear something?"

"It sounds like Satan was trying to keep you from God," her mother said.

She laughed nervously. "Satan isn't real."

"Oh dear, that's his biggest lie. As long as you believe that . . ."

Ted took Starr's hand. "The point is, Jesus wants you. And His voice is louder and stronger than any other. You just have to listen. You have to want to hear."

Mae took her other hand. "God loves you, Starr, and is aching to draw you right up close."

"Then we'll be the same," Ted said. "Then we can be together."

Starr didn't know what to say; she didn't know what to do. She was glad her mother and Ted didn't say anything else. She needed to listen . . .

The negative voice was gone. She didn't hear the voice of God speaking to her, but there *was* a sense of peace, of possibilities, of hope. It was a wonderful feeling. She didn't want it to leave, and knew, somehow, it *could* stay. If she let it. The choice was hers.

She looked at her mother and Ted. There was such love and hope in their eyes. Expectation. When was the last time she'd felt excited expectation about anything?

Starr took a breath. "I'd . . . I'd like to say yes."

Ted beamed. "Then say it. That's all you have to do. He'll do the rest."

Her heart was pounding. "Then . . . yes. I say yes to Jesus."

You would have thought she'd won the lottery by the commotion her mother and Ted made in that kitchen. Jumping up and down, doing a little jig together, hugging her, shouting happily. Starr let herself be drawn into the celebration—even though she wasn't sure exactly what it meant.

When they calmed down she asked, "So what now? I'm still rather oblivious as to what this all means and what's involved."

Ted pulled her close, under his arm. "Now comes the fun part. We'll learn about Him together. The two of us. It's going to be wonderful."

The funny thing was, Starr believed him. She believed every word.

● ● ●

The phone in the kitchen rang just as Lucinda walked by.

"Don't answer it!" Piper lunged toward the machine as if it were a bomb that could go off.

"Why not?"

"We're screening all calls," Tessa said. "That Bobby has called four times since I've been here."

"Does he know Margaret was hurt? in the hospital?"

Evelyn took the cake from the oven, little Summer at her heels. "No, and he's not going to know. Not yet."

"But he was her fiancé. Surely even he deserves that much."

Evelyn let the oven door bang shut. She was in a defensive mood. No man was going to hurt one of her sisters and get away with it. "He was only pretending to love her. He was an imposter. A charlatan." She suddenly looked to Audra and Piper. "Is that the right word?"

"A charlatan and a creep. The man earned many titles." Piper turned to Lucinda. "How was your time with the poor?" She smiled. "With cute Pastor Enoch?"

Russell ran a finger along the edge of the bowl of frosting. "What's this?"

Audra swatted his hand away from the icing. "I told you. Lucinda met him in Boston. He saved her from a drunk on the street."

Russell shook his head. "You probably told me, but it's hard to keep up."

"Get with the program, Son," Evelyn said, laughing.

"I need a program," he said.

Lucinda finally had a chance to answer the question. "My time at the mission was fine. Nice. Even exciting in a way."

"A soup kitchen exciting?" Audra asked.

"In a way . . . actually, I'm going back tomorrow. Chances

are I'm going to be seeing a lot more of the good pastor—and the ladies."

"Ladies?"

They heard the front door open and Mae's voice reached them. "Yoo-hoo! We have arrived, and I do mean *we*."

Lucinda waved a hand at the gathering. "I'll tell you later."

Mae came through the swinging door with Starr close behind. But then an unfamiliar man appeared. A scholarly type, smiling shyly, showing off dimples. Collier brought up the rear.

"Ta-da!" Mae said, presenting the man as if he were the prize behind Door Number One. "I present to you our darling Ted, visiting from New York, come to sweep my baby Starr right off her feet."

The man's ears turned red. "I don't know about that, but I did come hoping to bring her home with me."

"And?" Piper asked.

Starr rolled her eyes. "And—" she looked around the room— "you know, I hate to tell you ladies what happened because then you'll pounce and say I told you so and—"

Tessa crossed her arms. "This is going to be good. I know it."

"Come on, honey," Mae said. "Tell them how you opened your heart to God, said yes to Him and—"

"Yay!" Piper pulled Starr into a hug. "I've been praying for you!"

They all gathered close, like groupies trying to get a piece of a star—their Starr. Evelyn noticed Lucinda standing to the side. She looked hurt. Evelyn put her arm around her shoulder. "What's wrong, Lucinda? Aren't you happy for Starr?"

She nodded, but there were tears in her eyes.

Summer stroked her arm. "Are you okay, Aunt Lucinda?"

The group celebration died down. "Lucinda?" Piper asked.

Now that she had everyone's attention, Lucinda looked as if she wanted to bolt. Evelyn didn't want that. Whatever it was, it needed to be attended to.

"I'm sorry," Lucinda said. "I didn't mean to break up Starr's celebration. It's just that I—" she looked to the floor—"I decided today that I want to get to know God better too."

There was a moment of silence, then a new eruption of celebration. Two sisters turning to God? Was there anything better?

"Hey, hey, don't start the party without us!" Wayne came into the kitchen, holding the door for Margaret.

All attention turned to the patient, who was helped to a chair, even though it was her arm that was broken and in a sling.

Evelyn pointed to the counter. "I've made a cake to celebrate your homecoming."

"I helped," Summer said.

Margaret smiled. "I'm sure you did, little one."

The phone rang again. "Just leave it!" Evelyn said. She saw Margaret's questioning look. "It's probably Bobby. He keeps calling."

"He doesn't know about the accident," Tessa said. "We didn't think it was any of his business."

"It's for you to tell him," Piper said. "Or not."

They all looked at the phone. Then Margaret said, "Someone get it. I'll talk to him."

Before they had any time to argue, Russell had answered the phone—it was Bobby—and had given it over to Margaret.

It was odd to be in a room full of people yet have them all be silent, eavesdropping on a conversation that was surely going to be painful. Margaret must have felt it too because she took the phone into the parlor for privacy.

"I'd hate to be him," Audra said.

"I'd like a chance *with* him," Mae said. "I'd teach him to never hurt Margaret again."

Summer ran to the swinging door. "Can I go be with her?" she asked her mother.

"No, baby. Aunt Margaret needs to be alone."

Evelyn let out a sigh. "Well then. Who'll pour the spiced cider while I frost this carrot cake?"

By the time the cake was ready to cut, Margaret was back in the room. She put the phone back on its mounting.

"Well?" Tessa asked.

Evelyn expected Margaret to cry. She truly expected the next action in the room to be an offering of comforting arms and words.

But Margaret took a cleansing breath and actually smiled. "I'm free."

Mae let out a puff of air. "That's it?"

Margaret's face turned serious. "That's huge. I didn't fully realize it until I got off the phone, but I've been a prisoner to a relationship that was never healthy, to being a woman who wasn't truly me, to trying to please others at the expense of doing the right thing, to being afraid to trust God's plan instead of my own, and most recently, a prisoner to my inability to forgive Bobby and forgive myself." Her face seemed to shine from the inside out. "I'm free!"

Summer spoke for them all when she wrapped her arms around Margaret's waist. "I'm glad."

Enough said. "Who wants some cake?" Evelyn asked.

•   •   •

Evelyn knew she should be with the others. There was so much to celebrate: Ted and Starr's reunion; Starr, Gregory, and Lucinda coming closer to God, Margaret's return from the hospital.

But it was Margaret's words that spurred her away from the group and onto the porch by herself.

I'm free.

She wrapped her jacket tight around her torso and stood by the post at the top of the steps. A few leaves still danced in the air, taking their time getting to the ground. Their last hurrah. Their final burst of freedom.

Was Evelyn free? Like Margaret, how many years had she been prisoner to a relationship that was never healthy, to being a woman who wasn't truly her, to trying to please others at the expense of doing the right thing, to being afraid to trust God's plan instead of her own, and most recently, a prisoner to her inability to forgive Aaron and forgive herself?

In her own defense, Evelyn had come a long way since Aaron died. She'd grown more in the past two years than she had in the thirty-one she'd been married. And though it was a good thing, the wasted years made her sad.

She heard the door open behind her. It was Wayne.

"May I join you?"

She could think of nothing she'd like better. For Wayne was a big part of her looking forward instead of back.

He leaned against the railing, facing her. "What's wrong, Evelyn?"

The fact that this man before her, this dear man, asked her this simple question . . . she began to cry at his kind interest. It was something she'd lived without too long.

He didn't hold her, didn't draw her close. He took her hand until the tears passed.

"Sorry," she said.

"We all have regrets, Evelyn. We all have *if only*s that can eat us up."

He was amazing. "How did you know—?"

He gave her a steady look. "We *all* have regrets."

She nodded and knew it was true.

"The thing is, we can't change the past; we can only learn from it. Nothing good comes of letting our heart be divided— part sitting in the past, part here, part in the future. We need to approach life with a whole heart."

346

"I like that," she said.

"Then like this too. For God says, 'I will repay you for the years the locusts have eaten.'"

Evelyn had to smile. "I never, ever imagined locusts would come into a conversation today."

"You never know." Wayne let her hand go and pinched a leaf that had made its way onto the porch. "The years that seem bad, damaged, without worth . . . God wants us to let those go. Look forward, Evelyn. Look forward—" he looked up at her—"with me."

This time *she* took his hand. She nodded toward the celebration inside. "Shall we?"

And what a party it was. For now there was even more to celebrate. For now Evelyn was finally ready to face the future with an undivided heart.

> *Praise the Lord, I tell myself;*
> *with my whole heart, I will praise His holy name.*
>
> PSALM 103:1

A Note from the Authors

$\mathcal{D}$ear Readers,

The Peerbaugh saga continues. And the sisterhood expands. We are eager to hear about Sister Circles that have been established all over the country. And if you haven't started one—now's a good time (don't force us to sic Mae on you).

What's a Sister Circle? It's a small gathering of women. It's not intended to add another meeting to your schedule, nor be something that drains you. It's an opportunity, a chance to get together for some bonding. Meeting in a Sister Circle is a time for you and your friends to read a book, share some thoughts, and maybe indulge in comfort food, but most importantly just be together. No formal agenda, no pressures. You don't even have to clean house if you don't want to. Just call up a few friends (or we have invitations you can print up at the Sister Circle Web site at www.sistercircles.com), gather together, and share.

The key to a Sister Circle is that it can be whatever you want it to be. Perhaps it will start out as a means to discuss the Sister Circle books (questions are in the back of each book or on the Web site, but it can evolve into whatever binds you together: quilting, movies, preschoolers, cooking, traveling. . . . The key is to bond, hopefully, for life. "A triple-braided cord is not easily broken" (Ecclesiastes 4:12). So braid yourselves together, ladies!

In truth, our dream is Tessa's dream—that Sister Circles will spread throughout the world and provide women of every nationality a way to gain strength from each other. And who knows where it can lead? The world *can* be changed one woman at a time. A great activity for any Sister Circle would be to find a local charity that provides an opportunity to be personally involved in helping other people.

Until next time . . .

Nancy and Vonette

P.S. If you've had some wonderful Sister Circle experiences, we'd love to hear about them. Post them to the Sister Circle Web site (www.sistercircles.com) or write to us in care of Tyndale House Author Relations, 351 Executive Drive, Carol Stream, IL 60188. Or if you have comments about the books, feel free to e-mail a note to nancy@nancymoser.com.

About the Authors

NANCY MOSER is the best-selling author of seventeen novels including *The Good Nearby*, *Mozart's Sister*, and the Christy Award–winning *Time Lottery*. She also coauthored the Sister Circle series with Campus Crusade cofounder Vonette Bright. Nancy is a motivational speaker, and information about her Said So Sister Seminar can be found at www.nancymoser.com and www.sistercircles.com. Nancy and her husband, Mark, have three children and live in the Midwest.

VONETTE BRIGHT is cofounder of Campus Crusade for Christ along with her late husband, Dr. William R. Bright. She earned a degree in home economics from Texas Women's University and did graduate work in the field of education at the University of Southern California. Vonette taught in Los Angeles City Schools before joining Bill full-time in Campus Crusade. Bill and Vonette have two married sons and four grandchildren.

Vonette's commitment is to help others develop a heart for God. She founded the Great Commission Prayer Crusade and the National Prayer Committee, which helped to establish a National Day of Prayer in the U.S. with a permanent date on the first Thursday in May. She presently serves as chairwoman for the Bright Media Foundation and maintains an amazing schedule from her home in Orlando. Vonette's desire is to see women of faith connecting, serving, and supporting each other with such genuine love that women who do not know Christ will be drawn to them and will want to meet Him.

Scripture Verses in *An Undivided Heart*

Chapter	Topic	Verse
Chapter 1	Hope	Psalm 43:5
Chapter 2	Joy	Jeremiah 31:13
	Heart	Luke 6:45
Chapter 3	Friendship	Philemon 1:7
Chapter 4	Friendship	Philippians 4:1
Chapter 5	Advice	Proverbs 13:13
	Truth	John 8:32
Chapter 6	Love	1 Corinthians 13:13
Chapter 7	Motives	Jeremiah 17:10
	Motives	Proverbs 16:2-3
	Trials	Romans 5:3-5 (paraphrased)
Chapter 8	Seeking	1 Chronicles 28:9
	Obedience	2 Corinthians 3:18
	Truth	John 9:25
	Revelation	John 14:21
	Love	1 John 4:19
Chapter 9	Truth	Proverbs 23:23
Chapter 10	Love	1 John 3:18
	Seeking	Matthew 7:7

Discussion Questions

CHAPTER 1

1. Evelyn rejects Herb's affections when they get serious. Is she doing the right thing? Would staying with Herb be just "settling"?
2. Mae says, "It's a sister's job to read another sister. Sister sighs are almost as telling as sister moans." Do you think women are more adept at reading each other than men are? Name a time when you've read the mood of a friend.

Faith Issue

Piper gave up Gregory because of God's instructions to not be "unequally yoked" to an unbeliever. What do you think about this instruction—and Piper's sacrifice?

CHAPTER 2

1. Lucinda Van Horn lives in the past. In some ways we all hold on to some glory day in our past. What are you holding on to?
2. Evelyn believes there are different levels of love for different times of life. How does love change? Or does it?

Faith Issue

In the movie *Shadowlands*, C. S. Lewis says (in regard to grief and love), "The pain then is part of the happiness now. That's the deal." Do you believe this is what God had in mind? Why does love have to hurt?

CHAPTER 3

1. Heddy is moving out and new tenants are moving in. Yet "once a sister always a sister." Who are your lifelong friends? How do you stay in touch?
2. Evelyn feels an instant bond with Margaret and a lesser one with Lucinda. Share how you found immediate kinship with someone you met.

Faith Issue

Peerbaugh Place receives a constant supply of tenants who need this place as much as Peerbaugh Place needs them. Where have you moved that changed your life in a good way? Do you see God's hand behind the move?

CHAPTER 4

1. Lucinda grew up with money and now has none. Do you think it's tougher to be poor after having money or to have never had wealth at all?
2. Some women are expert flirters, and in truth, flirting is fun. Why? What need does it fill? When can it go wrong?

Faith Issue

God created us to need each other. Yet men and women go to great lengths to "catch" one another. In your opinion, what does God think of the mating game?

CHAPTER 5

1. Mae is fearful of "blowing it" with her daughter, of being too pushy about her faith. Have you ever gone overboard and turned someone off to God? What's the right way to do it?
2. Ted tells Starr he can no longer live with her because he's become a follower of Jesus. Do you agree with his decision? Or is this living-together issue a gray area?

Faith Issue

Tessa feels called to start a global ministry. She's taken a few months to think about it, to pray, to seek guidance. Have you ever taken an extended time to consider a point of God's direction? How did it go?

CHAPTER 6

1. Accosta Rand talks to Evelyn about seeing Jesus in Gregory's face. Have you ever seen such a thing?
2. Widower Wayne is thinking of dating again. It's been three months. What determines the right amount of time between mourning and moving on?

Faith Issue

Piper is concerned that, if given the chance, she would take matters into her own hands rather than wait for God's direction. When have you done either? What were the results?

CHAPTER 7

1. Piper challenges Starr regarding the type of work she does. Starr says if she doesn't do it, someone else will. So why should she stop?
2. Evelyn's a nice woman, yet at the concert, she is clearly using Herb to be near Wayne. Have you ever blatantly used someone? or been used yourself? What were the results?

Faith Issue

Wayne has trouble tolerating Lucinda, yet vows to be polite. Jesus tells us to love the unlovable. When have you been asked to do such a thing?

CHAPTER 8

1. Evelyn used to be nonconfrontational to a fault. Piper says arguments can be healthy. What do you think?

2. Describe the different motivations Margaret and Audra have regarding their "philosophy of order."

Faith Issue

As she attempts to be perfect like Christ, Margaret's engagement is broken. How have her good intentions gone wrong?

CHAPTER 9

1. Evelyn snoops, reading Lucinda's reunion registration form. Is snooping ever justified?
2. Wanda Wellington left a tangible legacy through her letters to her family. What do you think about writing such letters to family—even now—sharing your thoughts and feelings before it's too late?

Faith Issue

God says we shouldn't "bear false witness"—lie. Lucinda lies about herself on her registration. Is there ever a good reason to lie on such a form?

CHAPTER 10

1. Lucinda is caught in an embarrassing moment in her duckie pj's and turban. What outfit have you been caught in? How did you react?
2. Lucinda accuses Margaret of acting superior by cleaning up after her. Would the issue have been solved more satisfactorily if Margaret had confronted Lucinda head-on?

Faith Issue

When Starr goes to church, the verses and sermon seem to fit what's happening in her life. When has God provided just what you needed to hear in church?

CHAPTER 11

1. The world seems to be conspiring to get Starr to realize she's stubborn—she's getting it from all sides. Has this ever happened to you regarding one of your less admirable traits?
2. Evelyn can't seem to tell Herb the truth about her lack of feelings for him, plus she wants to hold on to him in case a relationship with Wayne doesn't work out. Name a time you've "hedged your bet." Did it work out as you hoped?

Faith Issue
Margaret and Evelyn share their disappointments regarding love. "God never wastes a hurt." How so? Give an example from your own life.

CHAPTER 12

1. Lucinda is desperate to look younger, grabbing on to every "magic serum." What miracle cures have you tried and what were the results? Is there such a thing?
2. The ladies of Peerbaugh Place feel that something isn't right about Bobby's sudden return into Margaret's life. What do you think about women's intuition?

Faith Issue
God hates gossip and warns against it because of the very situation in Peerbaugh Place: gossip hurts. When has gossip hurt you? When has *your* gossip hurt another?

CHAPTER 13

1. Lucinda is humiliated at her high school reunion. Nothing turns out as she had envisioned. Why do you think this often happens at reunions?

2. A drunk, groping man enters an elevator with you. It's just you and him. What do you do?

Faith Issue

On the night of the reunion God provided Lucinda with two men who saved her, encouraged her, and had a lasting impact on her life. Who has God sent to "save" you?

CHAPTER 14

1. Lucinda made sure LeJames received a thank-you for his good deed, and she also told someone in charge. When was the last time you did this? When *should* you have done it, but didn't?
2. Collier gets Mae to slow down and not make things worse with Starr. Do you have a tendency to forge ahead when you shouldn't? Or are you the one who helps others restrain themselves?

Faith Issue

LeJames tells Lucinda in his note: *I can't make you feel safe forever. No one can. . . . Only God can do that. With Him you'll never be alone or lonely. And He's available to you any time of day. Anywhere.*

Name a time God was with you when no one else was.

CHAPTER 15

1. Lucinda's friend and boss squelches her positive feelings about the revelation she had regarding her reunion. And Tessa's daughter does the same for Tessa's Sister Circle idea. Describe when you have been squelched. Or done the squelching.
2. Audra is exhausted yet she finds it hard to slow down or ask for help. What should she do? What have you done during such stressful times?

Faith Issue
Satan makes us doubt. But God often counters with encouragement. Share such a time.

CHAPTER 16
1. Traditionally, women have waited for men to make the first move in a relationship. Mae encourages Evelyn to make sure Wayne knows she's available. Do you agree?
2. Lucinda means well with her makeover offer, but her taste clashes with the other ladies' tastes. What is the best way to handle such a situation?

Faith Issue
Mae is faced with the joy of a grandchild, but is disappointed in how it came about. Explore a time when your love for your children collided with the need to forgive them.

CHAPTER 17
1. With her new look, Lucinda feels like a new woman. Share your makeover successes—and disasters.
2. Piper wants to nudge her dad toward Evelyn, but Evelyn says, "I don't want a man who's been nudged. I want one who turns toward me of his own free will." What do you think about helping two people find each other?

Faith Issue
God instructs women to submit to their husbands as the husbands submit to the Lord. But what's the difference between submitting and being a doormat?

CHAPTER 18
1. We're supposed to honor our father and mother, but what should you do—as in Margaret's case—when your parents don't deserve the honor?

2. Evelyn's relationship with her late husband shows that love and hate are sometimes intertwined. Have you ever experienced such a thing?

Faith Issue

At church Lucinda heard the pastor say, "If our looks never faded we might not turn to Him to be our beauty. And in turn might not realize how precious we are to Him because of who we are inside." How do we help society recognize this truth?

CHAPTER 19

1. Margaret finds the lawyer's letter about her inheritance. Betrayed by Bobby, her reaction nearly leads to her death. How else could she have reacted?
2. Piper's patience and obedience to God's ways are rewarded when Gregory becomes a Christian—and truly becomes hers. Share a time when God rewarded your obedience.

Faith Issue

Tessa has taken a huge leap of faith with her women's ministry and finds it daunting. Has God called you to do anything out of your comfort zone? What is (was) your answer?

CHAPTER 20

1. Evelyn is hurled back into the same hospital ER when Margaret is hurt, resurrecting her memories of her husband's death. Do you think such an encounter with a difficult point in your past is necessary or productive, or should it be avoided?
2. Never *ever* did Lucinda think her modeling experience would lead her to be a beauty consultant to the homeless. Has life ever tossed you a curve where you used one of your talents/ experiences in an unexpected way?

Faith Issue

After the accident, Margaret realizes, "My motives were good, but I was doing it all wrong. Doing. That was the key. Out there in the cold, I told God I'd start *being* what He wanted me to *be* instead of *doing* what I thought I should *do*." Is this a lesson you've learned yet? How?

a place to belong

$\mathcal{A}$ll she wanted was a little sun.

If all the world was indeed a stage, then Mae Ames was the director, star, and propmistress. The plan for today's scene was to portray an idyllic summer setting. A striking woman (who teased the edge of pretty when she tried), could be seen reading a book on the front lawn of a charming 1920s bungalow, bettering both her mind—and her tan.

She'd started with just a book and a lawn chair. But once she got the chair positioned in the front yard, she quickly realized the June sun was hot and she needed her sunglasses, a straw hat, sunscreen, her pink Japanese fan, a glass of raspberry tea, and four Milano cookies on a plate. Never mind. Bring the bag.

Mae was just settling in—realizing to be really comfy she should get one of the toss pillows from the couch—when she heard a familiar clearing of the throat. She didn't have to turn toward the porch. "You grunted, Mr. Husband?"

"What are you doing out here?"

She opened her paperback. "Reading a book."

"Looks like it would be easier sitting inside. Or on the porch swing."

"Easier, perhaps. But it's a proven fact that books read better when accompanied by the proper accoutrements."

"Want me to hire a neighbor kid to fan you with a palm leaf?"

She fluttered her own fan. "No need. I have it covered." She turned around to look at him. "Care to join me?"

"Nah. I'm not sure the recliner would fit through the door and I'd want—" His eyes moved to look at a car that was driving toward them.

Mae looked too. Then she popped out of her chair—or attempted to pop, as the lawn chair objected and tipped, forcing her to straddle it or put a foot through the webbing. Collier was halfway down the front walk when she finally got free of it, knocking over her tea. She tossed her hat toward the house like a Frisbee. It capped a mound of black-eyed Susans. She ran toward the car. "Ringo! Soon-ja!"

Ringo parked. Collier opened the door for their daughter-in-law, while Mae made a beeline for the backseat, where the love of her life was seated backwards. She got him free of the car seat, pulling him to her shoulder. "Ricky, baby. How's my sweet-ums?"

Ringo came around the front of the car and kissed her cheek. "I'm fine, Mom. How are you?"

"Oh. Sorry, Son. Never work with children or animals. Scene stealers, every one."

"I'll remember that."

Mae took a deep breath, filling her nostrils with the luscious smell of baby. If only they could bottle it. She turned her attention to Soon-ja. The girl's skin always did look pale against the black of her hair, but today, there was a pallor . . . "And how are you doing, Soon-ja?"

Soon-ja smiled but looked to Ringo, as if needing advice on how to answer.

And she didn't answer.

Uh-oh. Something was up.

Collier led them to the porch, where Soon-ja and Mae took seats on the swing. "What brings you to town?" he asked.

Ringo and Soon-ja exchanged that look again. "Life."

Double uh-oh. Mae held Ricky even closer. "Okay. Out with it. What's wrong?"

Ringo took a position against a column at the top of the stairs as if ready to flee. "I've lost my job."

Mae didn't quite understand. Ringo was a roadie in a rock band so the work always was seasonal. "The tour's over," Mae said. "You knew that was going to happen."

"But my next gig fell through." He looked at Soon-ja, then at his son. "And I have responsibilities now."

"And no income," Soon-ja said.

Ringo gave her a look.

She gave him one back. "It has to be said, Go-Go. Now is not the time for subtlety—or pride." She angled in the swing toward Mae. "Can we move in here?"

"Just for a little while," Ringo added.

Mae sought her husband's eyes. Poor Collie. They'd been married only eighteen months and already they'd endured one adult child coming home. Just last fall, Mae's daughter, Starr, had lived with them while she and her fiancé worked things out. Now, to have her son's family move in . . . was she pushing the limit of her darling Mr. Husband?

have you visited tyndalefiction.com *lately?*

Only there can you find:

- books hot off the press
- first chapter excerpts
- inside scoops on your favorite authors
- author interviews
- contests
- fun facts
- and much more!

Sign up for your **free** newsletter!

Visit us today at: **tyndalefiction.com**

Tyndale fiction does more than entertain.

- *It touches the heart.*
- *It stirs the soul.*
- *It changes lives.*

That's why Tyndale is so committed to being first in fiction!

TYNDALE FICTION

CP0021